HIDDEN BONDS

Compound Series Book 3

by Katy Morgan

Dedication

To the betas: Emily, Meredith, Sarah, Sophie, Shayla, and the parentals.

And to every reader who's taken a chance on this series. I hope you've enjoyed the ride as much as I have!

Prologue

"TELL ME WHY you did it."

The girl sitting across from Henry is picking at her nails, the handcuffs around her wrists shifting slightly as she moves. She's slouched in her chair at an angle only a petulant teenager could manage, and there's a bruise under her left eye. Henry doesn't have to use much imagination to figure out how it got there. Mariah hasn't exactly earned herself a reputation for being agreeable, and neither have the officers here.

After a long pause, she looks up at him, her limp, dark hair falling back from her face, and he knows exactly what sort of answer he's going to get.

"They deserved it," she says.

She has the luxury of being angry. She doesn't know what's coming; not like he does.

He was angry, too, at first. But now it's settled into a dull, desperate ache that he's learned to live with. Like his injuries from the fire didn't heal quite right. Though of course they did—the Compound Network needs him in working order because they need him to . . .

He can't stop this, and it's pointless to try.

But he has to try anyway.

Henry glances toward the two-way mirror on his right. Dr. Urashima isn't providing any commentary through Henry's earpiece at the moment, but he's definitely watching. So is Officer Garrand, standing in the far corner of the room near the door, her presence making the back of Henry's neck prickle. Or maybe that's just the scratchy collar of his regulation-issue shirt.

He leans forward, resting his own shackled hands on the table. "Mariah," he says in a low voice, "you need to give me something so I can—"

"They cuffed you, too?" Her eyes have gone straight to his wrists. "Why?"

"Stay on task, please, Mr. Mortimer," Urashima says mildly through Henry's earpiece. "Unless you'd like us to use a different approach for this interview."

Henry clenches his teeth, not taking his eyes off Mariah. Then he sits back in his uncomfortable metal chair. "Tell me what happened at the compound."

She stares at him, apparently thrown off and trying to recalibrate. After a moment, she slips her disaffected expression back into place and pokes at a jagged nail. "They wanted to do another round of experiments, so they tried to stick me with more of that serum stuff that makes our powers stop working. But they were too slow, and too much of it had worn off since the last time. So I made sure they couldn't do it again."

"You killed two officers."

She looks up at him, eyes unbearably sharp. "And I'd do it again."

"Sounds like a confession to me," says Garrand. Out of the corner of his eye, Henry sees her hand tighten on the gun at her belt as she starts to move forward.

"Wait," Henry says quickly.

Garrand pauses and tips her head to one side, like she's listening to something. Then she grimaces and moves her hand away from her gun, leaning back against the wall. Urashima must have told her to let it go for now; there's no way she'd back off just because Henry told her to.

Mariah is practically radiating electricity now—at least metaphorically. She can't actually summon a storm in here. Not with the precautions taken to protect the room from asset powers.

Well. Asset powers other than Henry's.

"You told me the compound would help me," Mariah says, her voice rising. "When you first found me, you said I had a *gift* and that you worked for a place that could teach me how to use it. Well, I *did* learn how to use it. And then I used it to hurt the people who hurt me. Who hurt all of us."

Henry swallows around a dry throat, trying not to think about how quickly she's ruining her chances. "If it was self-defense—"

"Everything is self-defense now. You have to defend yourself because no one else will. Well, except for your stupid boyfriend, but it's not like that's helping anyone. It's definitely not helping him."

Henry forgets how to breathe.

(He remembers the compound burning around them, Bastian holding him up, practically dragging him to the exit as the healing draft Laurel gave him slowly wore off and the pain cut back into Henry's head and chest and legs, and then he couldn't stand anymore, even with Bastian's help, but he couldn't pass out yet because he had to know—)

"Is Bastian—?"

"If you're unable to focus on the task at hand, Mr. Mortimer, we'll move on to other options with regard to the prisoner," Urashima says through the earpiece. His voice is irritatingly mild but firm, like he's patiently admonishing a fussy toddler instead of a formerly high-ranking compound officer. "And we'll need to seriously reconsider your ability to handle future interviews."

Henry takes a breath, digs his nails into his palms, and meets Mariah's gaze. Something like concern flickers briefly in her eyes, but it's gone before he can be sure. "This isn't the first time you've had run-ins with officers, is it?" he asks, although he already knows the answer.

Mariah smiles humorlessly. "No."

"But you never went this far. What was different this time?"

Her cold expression falters again, but she quickly gets it under control. "Nothing. Everything. Does it matter? They're dead. They can't hurt anyone else now."

Henry's eyes go to the bruise on her cheek. The way she holds her hands, like she's about to lash out . . . or do whatever it takes to get herself away from anyone who gets too close. If the cuffs would only let her.

He remembers finding her sitting in a puddle at the bottom of a ravine—a memory from another life, when he still thought he could help people, when he didn't know what the Compound Network could do. What *he* could do. He'd told her what he thought was the truth, and when that turned out to be wrong, he'd tried to *make* it true as the compound's new commanding officer. Like it was actually possible to take something as broken as a compound and make it better so that people like Mariah could have somewhere to go. Somewhere that would help them learn to use their powers.

Not somewhere that runs barrage after barrage of dangerous tests in order to gather data that benefits the Network. Not somewhere that interrogates and then discards anyone who steps out of line because powers are meaningless if they don't come with obedience.

Not somewhere like this.

A sigh in his ear. "The subject is clearly uncooperative. Please terminate the interview, Mr. Mortimer."

A jolt of fear lances through Henry's stomach. He tries to stuff it down. "We still don't know what happened. Mariah might've been justified in—"

"In killing two officers who were just doing their jobs? The subject clearly lacks remorse and is a danger to her fellow assets."

They're all a danger, Henry thinks. *That's why you're afraid of them. Of* us.

"Please terminate the interview, Mr. Mortimer," Urashima says again, a bit of steel in his voice this time. "Or I'll have Officer Garrand do it for you."

"That's not necessary," Henry says, hating how desperate he sounds. "If we could just give Mariah a little more time to—"

"You are not in charge of these proceedings. Do as I've asked. Now."

"Who are you talking to?" Mariah demands. Her shoulders have tensed, like she senses something is wrong but hasn't chosen between fight or flight yet. As if she really has a choice.

Henry turns in his chair. "Officer Garrand—"

But Garrand has her gun out and is coming around him to the other side of the table to stand next to Mariah. She doesn't look at either of them, just pauses there, unmoving. Waiting.

Mariah scrambles to sit up straight, her face blanching. "What's going on?"

"Give me your hands," Henry says quietly. His cuffs scrape against the table as he reaches out.

She doesn't look like she wants to, and he can't blame her. But she also seems keenly aware of the armed officer standing next to her. Of the way everything hinges on what she does next, even if she doesn't quite know why.

She hesitates a moment longer, then holds out her hands so he can take them in his. They're damp and a little too warm. He can feel small welts on her knuckles—not a recent injury, but one that must've hurt. What did she cut them on? And why didn't the med techs heal her properly? Have things gotten so bad at the compound that basic medical care is this slipshod?

"I didn't mean to," Mariah says in an almost-whisper. "It was only supposed to be some lightning, maybe some rain. Enough to scare them a little. But I was angry, and . . ." Her hands have started shaking.

"I know," Henry says gently.

Then he closes his eyes.

It's pathetic that he can't force himself to look at her while he does it. But he has to concentrate, and if he takes too long, Garrand will get ideas about how to use that gun of hers, now that Mariah is officially on the blacklist. He quickly focuses on the energetic shield around him, gathering up the strands of his power that are linked to it and *pushing* them out toward Mariah.

They're leaning in close enough to each other now that he can hear her tiny gasp of surprise when it hits her. But even if he couldn't, he'd know that it worked because he feels a sudden, sharp pain across his lower back, like he's had the wind knocked out of him. Then there's a split second of panic before he can breathe again, his heart racing with the absolute *wrongness* of it.

He opens his eyes to find Mariah staring at him, confused. "What did you do?" she asks, sounding a bit dazed as he drops her hands.

Henry wants to answer her, but he also wants to keep from throwing up, and he can only focus on one thing at a time.

(The smell of the compound burning, a pair of eyes slowly widening as they look at him, as their owner realizes what he's done, what he can't undo—)

"Finished?" Garrand asks.

Henry nods, still fighting against the bile in his throat.

"Let's go." Garrand takes Mariah's arm and pulls her to her feet.

Mariah is still staring at Henry and frowning. "What happened? I feel weird, like—"

"Less talking, more walking." Garrand herds Mariah toward the door, which is just opening to admit another officer. Garrand hands Mariah off, saying, "Take her to med bay and get her tested. If she's clean, process her like the others."

If she's "clean." A nice way of saying, "if we can confirm that she'll never be able to use her power again."

Henry once asked what happens to the assets he permanently negates. Of course, Urashima wouldn't give him a straight answer—just said it wasn't necessary for him to know in order for him to "do his duty."

It almost made Henry wish he were still the kind of person who could accept that bullshit as a legitimate explanation from someone in charge. As if someone in that position would only withhold information because they were trying to keep people safe.

He knows too much about how the Compound Network operates now to have any hope of making himself believe that.

"Thank you for your cooperation, Mr. Mortimer," Urashima says in Henry's ear. "We'll wait to hear from med bay, and then we'll do a debrief."

Henry carefully gets to his feet and takes a shaky breath, trying to settle his stomach. Very distinctly, so there can be no mistaking his words through the two-way mirror, he says, "*Fuck* your debrief."

Then he rips the earpiece out of his ear, unhooks the rest of the comm, and throws the whole thing against the wall, where the small, expensive pieces shatter.

He turns to find Garrand pointing her gun at him. She won't shoot to kill, of course. They can't afford to lose him. Not when he's their only way of permanently removing an asset's power. For now.

There's a crackle over the interrogation room's speaker, and then Urashima's voice comes through, still maddeningly calm. "Maybe I was too quick to call it cooperation."

It's pointless, Henry reminds himself. They all know how this is going to end.

(But there was something about watching Mariah's obstinance crumble so quickly into fear, about knowing he's taken something from her that she can never get back . . . about the mention, even so briefly, of Bastian still being out there somewhere, still acting like an idiot, still *alive*—)

"Yeah," Henry says, eyes locked on Garrand. "I guess I'm done cooperating for today."

There's a long, tense pause. Then Urashima sighs, an oddly harsh noise over the intercom. "Let's get this over with quickly, Officer Garrand. We have another interview this afternoon."

Henry doesn't even have time to raise his shackled hands in defense before Garrand slams her gun into the side of his head. Then he's on the ground without quite understanding how he got there, the pain radiating across his cheek, his teeth and the side of his mouth practically vibrating with it. Must have bitten his tongue; he tastes blood.

He should get up and fight, say something back, *do* something, but his ears are ringing, and every coherent thought slips away from him faster than he can properly think it. And none of this really matters, does it?

Five seconds—or maybe five years—later, Garrand reaches down, grabs his arm, and hauls him to his feet.

Another sigh comes over the speaker. "This will be noted in your file, Mr. Mortimer. Officer Garrand, take him to med bay if you feel it's warranted; otherwise, get him back to his room."

As Garrand drags him out, Henry feels his anger sink back down to wherever it usually lives these days. He should've kept his mouth shut. Getting clocked in the head hardly makes up for what he's already done to all the assets they've brought him.

At least they're not dead, he reminds himself, stumbling as Garrand moves them down the hall at a fast clip, her fingers digging into his arm. If he negates the assets after questioning, Urashima doesn't have them killed for infractions against the compounds. That's what he says, anyway, and that's what Henry has to believe. That's the deal. That has to be enough.

But Henry knows it isn't.

Chapter 1

Three months later

"I STILL THINK we should've come up with a secret handshake," Laurel says to Bastian as they walk down the Level 25 hallway. He can feel her practically vibrating with excitement-determination-focus, but at least she's not actively bouncing off the walls. Yet. "Secret missions are supposed to have secret handshakes, right?"

"Secret missions are supposed to be *secret*," Bastian mutters. "As in, not something you talk about out in the open."

"You don't have to take off your gloves, if that's what you're worried about," Laurel assures him, her voice a little lower now. "I just think—"

"Quiet," says the black coat behind them. It's a bit lackluster—just the right amount of lackluster, actually, which means Kwan has been practicing. Or else being able to project a convincing veneer of boredom is just part of the typical training for black coats, who have to pivot quickly from herding assets around the compound to shooting them if they step out of line.

To be fair, Bastian hasn't ever seen Kwan do the shooting part. But plenty of Kwan's security teammates have threatened to, not to mention the higher-ranking officers stationed around the compound.

Of course, it's frowned upon to needlessly injure or kill assets. But that doesn't mean it doesn't happen, particularly if said assets are being more trouble than they're worth. The only reason Bastian himself has managed to stay off the too-much-trouble list is because of who he is and what he can do.

It was far too easy for Bastian to use his power to manipulate the black coats into arranging the hallway escort duty roster so that he and Laurel would get Kwan today. That's bad news for the compound, given that assets are on low doses of negation serum all the time now and shouldn't be strong enough to use their powers outside of experiments. In fact, in most cases, anyone who shows even a hint of using their power without permission is whisked away to the lower levels of the compound for punishment. Possibly even removed from the compound entirely, depending on what they got up to while they could.

That makes things a little tricky for Bastian, whose power has remained almost entirely functional, serum or no—except for when he's covering his ass by pretending it isn't. Which means he didn't have much trouble rearranging emotions to get the black coat situation they wanted today, although he had to be careful to ensure that the use of power wouldn't register on the compound security system. Sure, he was exhausted afterward, and he got his first bad nosebleed in months, but he's not going to think about what that means.

"Our friend is awfully grumpy, isn't he?" Laurel says—mostly for the hallway security feeds, Bastian suspects. Got to keep everyone thinking this is a normal day with normal assets being normally irritating. "Maybe he got up on the wrong side of the bed this morning. Or is it the uniform? I think I'd be grumpy if I had to wear black all the time."

Kwan sighs loudly, but Bastian catches the note of amusement tucked carefully inside of his weary-annoyed-vigilant. Nothing that's likely to stand out to anyone who isn't an empath, though. And since Bastian is the only one of those around here—and the only one in existence, so far as most people know—they ought to be safe.

They turn a corner, and Bastian stops suddenly in spite of himself, distracted by a tiny jolt of fear-anger-pain so sharp and quick, he almost wonders if he imagined it.

(Don't think about how recently everything here was engulfed in flames, how these same gray corridors were lined with injured officers, terrified assets, and charred remains, how easily General Carter had everything cleaned up and rebuilt and painted over like it never happened, except for the fear that leaked into the walls and stained underneath, emotional echoes that can't be washed away, and Bastian can wear his black leather gloves as much as he wants, keep his energetic shield tight and close around him, but it won't matter; there's always some other place where—)

"Bastian." Laurel's voice has gone soft. She moves a little closer, her concerned-patient-comforting gently overtaking the sickness coming from the wall. His flinch must have been bigger than he thought.

He shakes his head slightly and forces himself to start walking again. If he stops any longer than a few seconds, Kwan might get suspicious about just how well Bastian can still use his power. Kwan isn't dumb enough not to suspect at this point, but he's very carefully not said anything about it in the five months they've worked together, which is a smart move on his part. Helping an asset get around the compound without being caught is bad enough; if the higher-ups suspected Kwan was hiding evidence of an asset in control of their power despite the serum, he'd lose more than just his security clearance.

Most of the compound floors are looking better now, leaving aside the hidden pockets of emotion still clinging to the masonry. Not all of the repairs have been finished; just enough to start housing assets again. Which also merited adding to the seriously diminished staff pool with new officers straight from Council HQ—loyal ones who are prepared to report back on any misbehavior, real or imagined.

Not that there's been much of that for quite some time. The tendency was stomped out within the first few weeks after the return to the compound, when troublesome assets began disappearing at record rates to unknown locations. There's much more shuffling of assets between compounds these days, probably because no one's entirely sure how to function in a world where a compound can be so quickly destroyed by a rampaging group of angry assets taking advantage of chaos.

Presumably, the mission is still to collect people with powers, train them, and ship them off to the city and surrounding areas on under-the-radar assignments per Compound Network agreements with various organizations. Since the fire, though, the compound seems more focused on experiments and getting rid of dissidents than anything else. Maybe this is General Carter's idea of payback for the destruction.

Bastian grew up watching people get moved around like chess pieces on the Compound Network's whim, but even he's been startled by the number of here today, gone tomorrow cases. More than a few of them were the unruly teenagers Laurel used to work with, back when they were running this place with Henry. Back when . . .

Bastian clenches his jaw and slams the metaphorical door shut on that one. He can't think about Henry. Not yet.

Laurel tenses beside him as they approach a T-shaped junction. Straight ahead, there's a door labeled as an experimentation room. "That's where Chloe was when she sensed the dead zone," Laurel says out of the corner of her mouth.

There shouldn't be anything like a dead zone in the compound. There certainly never was before. But ever since the compound was rebuilt, Bastian, Laurel, and now Chloe have felt little pockets of . . . nothing, where their powers stop working.

It would be useful to be able to ask other assets if they've noticed, but there hasn't exactly been a good time. Safe places to talk without fear of being overheard are few and far between. The three of them only get away with it with help from Kwan—and even then, only occasionally.

And anyway, it's risky to bring up any situation that involves using powers outside of sanctioned experiments. If other people are noticing the dead zones, they aren't about to admit it, and Bastian can't blame them.

He wants to ask how sure Chloe was about this one, but that's just the anxiety talking. Chloe's intel has been solid so far. Over the past few months, she's taken advantage of the opportunity to use her full tracking power during experiments to sweep the compound for more of the dead zones, as well as any new paths or hidden areas they might be able to use to talk or plan or do *something*. Anything other than live in this cloud of hushed voices and trigger-happy officers and the sense that everything is hanging by a thread. A very, very thin thread.

Kwan was actually the first one to clue Bastian in to the existence of the dead zones, explaining that he noticed something odd during security sweeps but hadn't been able to clarify what it was exactly. That said, even Kwan seems startled by the fact that they keep popping up—and then disappearing. When Bastian told him that they had a line on yet another one, Kwan got a funny look on his face (wary-hesitant-determined) and said he wanted to see it.

Naturally, it's occurred to Bastian that trusting—and worse, helping—a black coat might not be his brightest idea. But Kwan hasn't been anything other than trustworthy so far, providing excuses for Bastian, Laurel, and Chloe to exchange messages when they wouldn't have been able to otherwise. And he seems just as interested in the possibilities of the dead zones as they do.

Thus, today's mission.

Kwan clears his throat loudly. He must be getting antsy, or else he's really into playing his role.

"You'll want some eucalyptus oil for that cough," Laurel says, sounding both cheerful and menacing in the way that only she can manage. "I'd ask the plants around here where you could find some, but I'm not supposed to use my power in the hallway."

Someone else didn't get the memo about assets not using their powers in the hallway, though, because all of a sudden, a blast of wind shoots around the corner and knocks them all backward. There's a yelp, then loud noises and a jumble of fury-embarrassment-fear-dread.

"I didn't mean to!" someone yells. Someone young and afraid and about to be in a world of trouble.

Kwan grabs Bastian's arm (strained-alarmed-worried). "Stick to the plan," he says in a low voice.

Bastian shakes off his hand. "Plan's changed."

For a split second, his eyes meet Laurel's, and her frown makes him think she's going to team up with Kwan to try to restrain him. But when he makes a break toward the sound of the scuffle, she matches him step for step, Kwan following close behind.

The gangly blond teenager holding up their hands and trying to sputter their way out of an officer's wrath is, objectively speaking, the worst de-escalator Bastian has ever met. Gabe is also one of the most gifted windmovers currently at the compound, if you ignore the part where they're still subpar at containing their power when stressed. From what Bastian's heard, not even the higher end of the usual serum dosage can completely mute Gabe's power if they're having a significant emotional response to something. Which is probably why they've got a full-fledged officer as a chaperone today rather than just a black coat.

Given the way the officer is looking at Gabe, though (grim-angry-afraid), trying to explain Gabe's tendency toward anxiety-driven power outbursts probably isn't going to help much. Which means they're in serious danger of being sent away. Or worse.

Bastian isn't much of a de-escalator himself. But it's best not to waste the opportunity for a distraction, and anyway, it's not like this would be the first time he's done something stupid in a situation like this.

Better him than Gabe, anyway.

"Hey!" he yells. "Calm down. They said it wasn't on purpose."

The officer, a pinch-faced, middle-aged woman with a severe hairdo that hurts to look at, turns sharply at the sound of Bastian's voice, gaze hardening. Either his reputation precedes him, or she's just determined not to back down.

"What's the matter, Kwan?" she says, sneering over Bastian's shoulder. "Can't keep your charges restrained?"

"I could say the same about you," Kwan says. "But I won't because I'd never tell an officer how to do their job when I could be focusing on my own."

The woman snorts. "Of course, you would need to be a *real* officer for your thoughts to matter. But you're just a—"

"—very nice person who would never stand around in a hallway being rude to a coworker," Laurel says emphatically. Then she turns to the windmover with a smile that's tight but still genuine. "Hello, Gabe. How are you?"

Gabe glances between the officer and the others, shoulders still shaking slightly. "Oh, well, you know. Just getting yelled at for walking down the hall and breathing. I guess I do that wrong, too."

"You *attacked* me," the officer spits. "I could have you removed from this compound in the next ten minutes."

"Debatable," Bastian says. "You'd have to prove it wasn't accidental, which would be hard, given Gabe's record. At most, you've got a case for sending them to the med techs for more serum. And if you're concerned about *that* display, you've clearly never played air hockey with Gabe. You should see what they're like when they win."

"It's a problem," Gabe agrees quickly. "I used to always beat Bastian, so he'd know."

"I let you win," Bastian says.

Gabe grins. "No, you didn't."

The thinning of Gabe's outer layer of anxiety is nice, but Bastian can't help thinking that all the bravado in the world won't prevent Gabe from becoming another number on the list of removed assets, if this officer has her way.

The officer glares at both of them, then at Kwan. "If you aren't going to keep these assets in line, I'll do it for you," she says, hand dropping to her gun.

"Discharging a firearm in the middle of the hallway doesn't seem like a good call here," Kwan says quickly, his tone shifting to something careful and placating. He doesn't reach for his own firearm, but his voice carries enough of an edge that it's clear he means business. "I'm sure the windmover didn't mean to cause problems. All of these assets have experiments to get to, so let's just drop it."

The officer's annoyed-insulted-angry says just what she thinks of that option. She must be having a bad day—or she's one of the new recruits whose deep-seated fear of assets is going to get people killed. Or both.

Bastian does a quick scan and feels three people heading toward them (bored-tired-lazy). Probably officers or black coats, given the underlying lack of concern about their surroundings—they're not worried about what they might come up against, likely because coming up against something is less concerning if you know you can shoot it. But even if they're just overly confident med techs or something, they could still dredge up the right kind of commotion to get the focus off of Gabe and maybe even give Laurel the opportunity to finish up the reconnaissance they're supposed to be doing right now.

Kwan and the officer are still engaged in an increasingly heated back-and-forth, so Bastian turns and finds Laurel side-eyeing him in an annoyingly perceptive way. "Is it worth it to tell you not to be stupid about this?" she asks.

"Consider it part of the secret mission. You like secret missions, remember?"

(resigned-wary-nervous) "Yes. But I don't like when you—"

Bastian grabs Kwan's shoulder, turns him around mid-sentence, and punches him in the stomach.

"—do stuff like that."

Kwan doubles over with a grunt. Laurel reaches for him but gets interrupted by a loud yelp as another blast of Gabe's power goes wild, sending the officer staggering across the hall and away from them. Kwan manages to grab hold of Bastian's shirt with one hand, his overwhelming startled-annoyed-angry slapping Bastian in the face. "What the *hell*?"

"Distraction," Bastian tells him. "I'm pretty sure there are officers on the way, but I need you to—"

Having his arm nearly yanked out of its socket as he's shoved face-first against the wall makes Bastian suspect that maybe punching someone he's supposed to be conspiring with wasn't the greatest idea, even if it did get the focus off of Gabe. A moment later, Bastian's suspicion is confirmed when he feels the barrel of a gun pressing into the back of his head.

"Way to sell it," Bastian mutters, face mostly smooshed against the concrete (remnants of terror-fury-desperation that make his stomach churn).

"Shut up and let me handle this," Kwan hisses in his ear. The force of the gun against Bastian's head lessens, but only slightly.

"Report!" someone yells. Bastian can't exactly move to see, but the voice is coming from the direction of the officers he felt moving down the hall a moment ago.

"There was a bit of a ruckus, but it's contained," Kwan says quickly. "And you might want to remind your buddy over there that she's not getting paid to shoot teenagers."

Someone grabs Bastian's arm and turns him around roughly. A captain, judging by her jacket. Probably one of the newer ones, since he doesn't recognize her. There are several other officers standing warily behind her.

"These assets engaged in unauthorized use of their powers," Gabe's officer calls. She sounds winded, and Bastian can't help but wonder if Gabe did it on purpose this time.

"Unauthorized use of powers?" Bastian repeats. "I didn't *feel* at him; I hit him."

"So, you admit you attacked a black coat." The captain frowns, then lets her frown deepen as she gets a better look at Bastian's face. "You're Sebastian Lucas, aren't you? The empath. Major Tremain will want a word."

"Will I?"

Bastian groans inwardly. Causing a hallway scuffle within earshot of Major Tremain, the new commanding officer of the compound, doesn't exactly bode well for the outcome.

Tremain's mild curious-interested-thoughtful is just as confusing now as it was the first time he felt it. They're a front, of course—she'd never have made major if she weren't smarter than she seems, let alone major of a troubled compound like this one. But it's an incongruous emotional signature for someone who's just walked in on a disturbance like this.

She takes her time joining them at the hallway intersection, like coming across officers threatening to shoot assets is something she sees all the time. And maybe it is, given how the compound officers and black coats behave these days.

She turns her nondescript brown eyes on Bastian, sizing him up in a way he might call half-assed in someone with a less layered set of emotions. "Striking a black coat is a serious offense."

"Yeah? How about striking an asset?"

Tremain raises her eyebrows. "Did one of these officers hit you?"

"Not yet. But I'm sure they will after you leave, which is sort of my point. And I saw officers hit three different assets in three different hallways yesterday. Are you going to keep your people in line, or do I need to?"

Okay, so he's probably pushing it, if Laurel's alarm-concern-frustration is any indication. She and Kwan are poised in his peripheral vision, but he has no idea what they're poised *for*. Do they really think he can't handle this? Officers and black coats might be overstepping more and more boundaries every day, but they're not stupid enough to kill the only empath in this damned place. Even Tremain, whose motives he isn't sure about, doesn't seem like the kind of person who would waste a valuable resource.

So if these idiots need a punching bag, let it be him.

(It's stupid and pathetic, something he never would have dreamed of doing before he met Henry, but Henry isn't here to be the brave one, the one who knows how to make sure people don't get hurt, which means all these assets have is Bastian, and all he's good at is getting in the way, but at least that's better than—)

Tremain's face remains placid, her serene-attentive-calculating muted enough that he almost has to strain to read it. She has an exceptionally good shield. Someone trained her far better than most officers and non-assets.

The silence has just started to get awkward when she backs away. "Put him in solitary. Inform me if there are any other problems."

The assembled officers salute her, then look at each other.

As soon as Tremain is far enough away, they turn back to Bastian, and he doesn't have to read them to know what comes next.

Five months ago

BASTIAN'S EARS ARE still ringing from the last blow when the door to the solitary room screeches open. He cringes at the noise, then cringes again when the movement sends a shot of pain through his temples.

He hears the sound of work boots on the floor and tenses for another round, but nothing happens. After a moment, he manages to look up from where his cheek is pressed into the concrete, registering the wary-thoughtful-concerned as he does. It's the black coat from the hallway—the one who stood there and watched the beating but didn't join in.

"You saved that asset's life by getting in the way of those officers," the man says.

Bastian sits up carefully and leans back, equally carefully, against the wall. "So, you agree that your buddies were going to kill her." It hurts to talk with a split lip and a sore jaw, but not any more than it would hurt to stay silent. At least this way, he looks like he's capable of speech rather than just barely holding it together.

The black coat grimaces and comes the rest of the way into the room, letting the door fall shut behind him. "Not my buddies. I'm a black coat; lowest rung on the ladder, as far as the officers are concerned."

Bastian watches him cautiously—as much as is possible through the swelling of a fresh black eye, anyway. "So, what? You had to wait your turn until the others were done?"

The black coat crosses his arms over his chest. He's smaller and willowier than the officers who brought Bastian in here, but he still looks sturdy. If physical appearance is anything to go by, he didn't slack off during training just because he went into security rather than becoming a "real" officer. There's no way Bastian will be able to outmaneuver him if he decides he really does want to get in on the action.

"Not everything is about making sure you have a bad day, Lucas," the black coat says.

"Could've fooled me." Bastian isn't sure if it's the beating or the extra negation serum they pumped into his arm before leaving, but he can't quite get a read on this guy. He's too calm to be an active threat, but there's an edge of nervousness around his hesitation-worry-calculation, and somewhere in that jumble, there's also . . . hope.

Wait. What?

The black coat stares at Bastian for a few more moments, then starts toward him. When Bastian flinches involuntarily, the other man raises his hands in a placating gesture and nods toward the bed. "Okay if I sit down?"

Bastian shrugs, then tries to ignore the pain that lances through his shoulders and neck. "I'm not really in a position to say no, am I?"

The black coat frowns as he goes over and sits. After another brief, awkward silence, he says, "My name is Peter Kwan, and we've got about five minutes left for me to tell you something that could get you out of here."

"What, out of solitary?"

Kwan reaches into his jacket and takes out a small metallic object that has absolutely no business being there.

"Out of the compound," he says.

Chapter 2

LAUREL IS NOT at all excited about the prospect of leaving Bastian in the hallway with a bunch of armed officers who are looking more than a little grumpy. She doesn't get a chance to lodge a formal complaint, though, because Kwan grabs her arm and does that tiny, almost imperceptible shake of his head that usually means something along the lines of, "You should follow my lead if you don't want that thing Bastian just messed up to get any messier."

This is the real reason Laurel has decided to trust Kwan. Not because Bastian says he feels moderately trustworthy (a big concession coming from Bastian, Mr. Cranky and Distrustful), but because Kwan has racked up five months of experience heading off the potential catastrophes Bastian tends to cause inadvertently.

It's hard not to trust someone who seems so hell-bent on keeping her best friend alive, even if said best friend isn't making it easy.

Aside from that . . . well . . . there are guns in this hallway. Far too many within easy reach of people who would have no trouble using them. And then there's an anxious windmover on the other side of the hall who keeps looking at Laurel for reassurance while clearly trying to pretend they're *not* looking at Laurel for reassurance.

Will Gabe be taken away now? Made to disappear the way so many assets have?

And then there's Bastian himself, rigid and angry and also somehow resigned at the same time. He glances at her, then down the hall, then back to the captain holding him in place. That's Bastian speak for, "Get out of here and go find that dead zone." As if she shouldn't be bothered at all about leaving him to get beaten to a pulp by stupid officers with stupid *guns*.

"We'll take care of this one, Kwan," says the captain. "Get yours to her session."

"Understood."

No, it is *not* understood. Not by her. Not when people keep making her leave her friends behind.

(Like when she had to leave James behind, watching him disappear into the smoke of the burning compound, the compound he and his fellow firestarters helped burn, and she shouldn't keep thinking about it because he's probably dead for real this time, and even if he isn't, he's probably *still* not sorry for what he did, and now things are worse than ever, and she's being kept away from her plants and her sunlight and her fresh air as much as possible, and it's starting to feel just like it did nine years ago when they first brought her to the hidden compound in the forest, gray walls closing in—)

"Laurel," Kwan says. It's the quiet tone that he usually keeps hidden under the cranky black coat exterior, the way a prickly hawthorn still flowers in the spring even when it seems like it's going to be all thorns.

Secret mission, Laurel reminds herself, stuffing down her fears. One thing at a time.

Kwan herds her around the corner before she even has a chance to give Bastian a final warning look.

This hall is mostly empty at the moment, which is just as well, since they're about take a detour. The fewer people around, the better.

"Here," Kwan says after a quick glance through the glass of an experimentation room door. Laurel doesn't need any coaxing at this point—she quickly opens the door, and they hurry inside.

It looks like every other experimentation room Laurel has ever been in: empty counters on top of immaculate sets of drawers, all white, probably containing instruments Laurel doesn't want to know about; a disturbingly clean tiled floor; white walls that look like they've recently been repainted without any consideration given to how boring they are. Not all of the rooms like this are back in service, but this one probably is, given how functional it looks. Or it will be soon.

"Jammer's going. Fifteen minutes." Kwan is looking at the small metal device that he's just pulled out of his jacket pocket.

Kent told them that the jammer is functional—or as he put it, "a technological atrocity" that will probably get the job done, even if the tech is "a shadow of its former glory," according to the compound's most beleaguered security expert.

Laurel thinks he's selling himself and his work a bit short, which is actually pretty unusual for Kent. After all, he and his fellow tech expert/girlfriend Sybil have managed to keep a few jammers functioning despite, or maybe because of, their involvement with the compound's increased security measures. The one he gave Kwan, for example, muffles the use of asset powers as well as tricking the security cameras so they have a little more room to move around the compound and investigate the dead zones.

Of course, if anyone catches them with it, it's game over. And the timer means Laurel had better get on with it.

Taking a deep breath, she closes her eyes and focuses on listening intently. The unpleasant buzz of the negation serum still in her blood makes things more difficult, but she can just barely hear a snake plant mumbling to itself a few rooms over and a very long-suffering fern whining about being drooped over someone's desk. It helps that Kwan "forgot" to give her a full dose of the serum last time she was due, so she has some wiggle room to test out where her power works and where it doesn't. Except . . .

"Anything?" Kwan asks impatiently, eyes on the jammer's countdown sequence.

Laurel considers reminding him who's doing the actual work here but decides it would probably be better to focus on the mission. "I can still use my power," she tells him. "So if there *was* a dead zone on this level, it must be gone now. Or maybe—"

Laurel hears the sound of voices approaching. She shoots Kwan an alarmed glance, and then they both make a beeline for the supply closet in the back of the room, scrambling inside just as two people step into the room.

"You're saying the lower facilities are stable now?" booms a very familiar voice. Laurel can't see much through the slightly ajar door of the closet, but she can easily imagine the shiny boots and imperious shoulders of General Carter, head of the Compound Council.

"The labs on Level 49 still need some tidying," says Major Tremain at a more tolerable volume, "but yes. Access to the Fail-Safe Protocol area has been cleared, too. But in terms of working with subjects, wouldn't it be easier to use one of the refitted rooms like this one?"

General Carter makes a rumbly noise and ignores her question. "How's the security around here? Tighter than it's been in the past, I hope?"

"Kent Turner and Sybil Tassos have been convinced that assisting the new hacker team is in their best interests, if they want to prove that their past actions aren't a continuing problem."

"And you believe them?"

"They've given me no reason not to. Yet."

Laurel tries not to think about how the device Kwan has slipped back into his pocket is exactly the sort of reason Major Tremain has her eye out for.

General Carter grunts. "Then let's get started. I've arranged for Mortimer to be transferred to the nearest safe house in the city. I'll let you know when he arrives."

Laurel's heart lurches like a jewelweed pod bursting apart. *I've arranged for Mortimer to be transferred.* You can't be transferred if you're dead, right?

Which means Henry is alive.

"You'll have to focus on gathering data on the girl for now," Carter is saying. "I understand she's being kept in the children's dormitory?"

He sounds disapproving, but that doesn't seem to deter Major Tremain at all. "Pinelli has shown a tendency to separate herself from the other children without our needing to encourage it, so there haven't been any problems. It would be convenient to keep her in this compound for testing, but there are other options, too."

Well, that explains why they were never able to find her. The younger assets have been watched even more closely than the adults since the change in compound leadership, making it harder for Laurel and Bastian to keep track of them. And an unusually powerful memor like Angelica Pinelli is more closely watched than most.

Not that it would make much sense for her to be involved with the Fail-Safe Protocol. As far as they could tell from the top secret data fragments Henry received last year, the Fail-Safe Protocol seems to be an elaborate experiment designed to use Henry's power as a negator to keep assets in line by removing their powers. What would a memor like Angelica have to do with that? Being able to experience someone's memories doesn't seem particularly relevant to that goal.

General Carter grunts. "I'll let you get started, then. Make sure the documentation on all of this is secure—we have three converging experiments to keep track of, and we can't afford to leak data like we did when Valentine and Wright were arrested. We've got enough of a security issue already with the lost Fail-Safe Protocol files, thanks to Senator Nunez's aide."

"Yes, sir. I'll let you know as soon as I have updates."

As they head back into the hall, Laurel briefly considers jumping out of the closet and strangling both of them. Who talks about a little girl like she's a piece of property they can poke at just because they want to? Who talks about *anyone* like that? Maybe Tremain and Carter need a stern talking-to. Maybe someone needs to show them that they aren't the only ones who can hurt people. Maybe—

(Maybe the plants can help her come up with something, maybe there's something she can do to keep them from hurting more of her friends, from hurting anyone ever

again, maybe this concoction James has her making will help, it's only enough to make them see that they need to listen, *it's not going to hurt anyone, but maybe it should, maybe—)*

Laurel flinches against the light—and the memory—as Kwan opens the closet door and steps out. He turns back to her and frowns when he sees the look on her face. "Don't even think about it."

"Henry's alive," Laurel says numbly. "And Angelica is in trouble."

Kwan's frown gets deeper, but there's a tiny bit of sympathy in his eyes, which sort of ruins the look. "There's nothing we can do."

"They're going to take Bastian to solitary, right? He's already been there, what, twice this month? If he keeps this up—"

"They'll send him away. I know."

"So we need a new plan."

"I don't think—"

"It's okay," Laurel says, reaching out and patting his arm. "I can do the thinking."

She takes a breath and considers the pieces: Henry is alive. Angelica is in trouble. Bastian is unable to *not get into* trouble.

Laurel sighs. "Okay, here's my first thought: I'm going to need your help with this plan because I'm pretty sure Bastian won't like it."

Chapter 3

BASTIAN IS STANDING in a familiar forest full of eerily white birch trees illuminated by a faint glow that seems to come from nowhere. It's night, but there's no moon, and the stars are weirdly dim and washed out—the memory of starlight rather than the real thing. The knots in the tree trunks stare at him like large black eyes.

He's had this dream for months now, and it always goes the same way. So, while the birch skeletons are creepy, he knows that all he has to do is ignore them and follow the path until he gets to the pond.

Through the tree branches, he can just make out the storm on the horizon, always approaching but never arriving. He can hear the thunder and feel the prickling anticipation of raindrops on the back of his neck.

The holes between the birch trees slowly fill with other trees and brush as he walks, and the quiet becomes deafening. No birds, no animals, no wind in the bare branches. He probably ought to be grateful for the lack of emotions to deal with, but the silence is too unnatural to be calming.

He's not sure how long it takes to get to the pond—time doesn't have much meaning here—but he knows he's getting close because the trees thin out while the lower brush thickens. A few more steps, and he comes out into the clearing, the night sky above him reflected in an enormous blue-green pond.

A figure in white hospital scrubs is sitting next to the water, knees drawn up to her chin. From far away, she looks like a little kid rocking back and forth. As Bastian gets closer, though, the illusion is shattered: He can see the streaks of gray in her dark brown hair and the comfortable lines on her face.

"Moira," he says.

"Back to see me again, kid?" She's looking at the pond rather than at him, but she doesn't seem surprised or alarmed at his approach. Like she was expecting him. "Didn't have anything better to do?"

"Sleeping, maybe." Bastian sits down next to her. "I don't suppose you'll let me get back to it?"

"I've told you; I'm not controlling this. If you're getting sucked into my dream, that's your fault."

"Given how often it's happening, I might start thinking you enjoy seeing me."

"Don't flatter yourself." Her voice is dry, but when she finally turns to look at him, she's smiling. "Seriously. Why are you here?"

"Looking for fashion tips. Aren't you cold?"

The smile turns into a cheeky grin. "Aw, are you worried about this old lady? That's sweet. But no, I'm not cold. Or warm. Or anything. No feelings at all, right?"

He can attest to that: He's never felt anything from her. It's like the emotions are there, but they're behind a wall he can only just see through, blurry blobs that don't connect. Like she has a shield up, but it's more solid than anything he's ever felt in real life. It's weird and slightly uncomfortable to be around, but it doesn't make her seem any less vibrant or alive.

He'd chalk it up to the whole dream thing, but this doesn't feel like any other dream he's ever had. It's too real, *despite the strangeness of the scenery. And he's never heard of someone being completely emotionless during sleep. He ought to be able to feel something from her.*

Of course, Moira hasn't been much help. She doesn't know anything about who she is or where she came from, although she does know she's some kind of asset. And she's familiar with the Compound Network, even if she can't say which compound she's from.

And she knows he's an empath. She knew it right away, before he told her. There's no explanation for that, either.

They sit by the pond for a while, watching the still water, like they often do. No bugs, no ripples; just an otherworldly quietness that's both beautiful and disturbing.

"You sure it's sleeping you're doing?" Moira asks suddenly.

"What?"

She frowns at him like she's assessing something. "Doesn't feel like sleeping. More like you're unconscious. Someone beat you up, Junior?"

The pain comes back then, needles in his temples and a sharp line of fire across his stomach. The forest around him bleeds away like watercolors spreading across paper.

"Is he well enough to be moved?" a familiar voice is asking, laden with tension. It's coming from somewhere to Bastian's right.

"He's stable," says another voice, also familiar. This one sounds calmer, at least on the surface. "But that doesn't mean—"

"They'll send him away," says a third voice. Laurel. "You know they will. So we have to make sure he can—"

"Do I get a say?" Bastian mutters, blinking open his eyes. His throat feels scraped raw. He suspects he shouldn't be moving, but lying still and staring at the ceiling doesn't seem like it will get him anywhere. So he very carefully turns his head to get a better look around.

He's in a med bay recovery room, scratchy regulation sheets against his skin and the smell of antiseptic cleaner wafting up from the floor. There are several beds positioned around the room, but they're all empty except for the one Bastian is in.

Dr. Rowe—head of med bay and owner of the calmest voice in this or any other situation—hurries over to Bastian's side. "Close your eyes," she says, putting a firm but gentle hand on his arm. Bastian feels the jolt of her afraid-focused-determined through a slight haze—the officers who worked him over must have given him another dose of the serum before they dumped him here. Here being *not* solitary, which means they got in a few more kicks and punches than usual and decided to have Rowe patch him up before they lock him away, just to cover their tracks. Classy.

Bastian lets his eyelids fall closed, but not before catching a glimpse of Kwan, arms crossed, watching the proceedings. And partially blocking the most obvious security camera in the room. That's all three voices accounted for, then. "Gabe?"

There's an awkward pause. Then Laurel says, "They're fine, we think. They haven't been transferred yet, anyway. Kwan will keep an eye on it. Now, you need to lie still while we figure this out."

"Figure what out?"

"Well . . . *Gabe* isn't being transferred right away, but *you* are. That officer from the hallway, the one who was with Gabe, is going to make an official recommendation that you be moved to another facility. You know, the kind assets don't come back from."

Bastian grimaces. The safe houses that popped up to temporarily house assets after the compound fire have gone on to serve as a chain of facilities used for even shadier things. Kwan has told them stories based on rumors based on lies, to the point where no one really knows where these places are or what experiments get done there. But one thing seems clear: The compounds themselves aren't the only action sites for experiments anymore—and safe houses don't have the kind of official guardrails that compounds do.

Which explains Laurel's hazy worried-concerned-afraid, but not entirely.

"I'm the only empath on the Compound Network roster, remember?" Bastian says. "Even if Tremain did sign off on sending me away, no one would hurt me."

"Would you like me to describe what you look like right now?" Rowe asks dryly.

"This is nothing." Bastian takes a breath, then winces against the sharp pang of bruised ribs. "Okay, it's *something*. But—"

"I'll use my salves to stabilize you enough for transport," Laurel says. "And Dr. Rowe can do the rest. But you'll need to—"

Bastian's slightly muddled brain catches up. "Transport? Wait, you *want* me to get shipped out?"

(hesitation-guilt-apprehension) "Yes. It's a big part of the plan, you being shipped out. Think of it as an adventure!"

"Laurel—"

"Or an escape, I guess. Only maybe don't use that word too loudly; people don't seem to like it much these days." Laurel clears her throat and continues before he can get a word in. "See, we've all talked it over, and we think you'll have a better chance out there than in here. And it's a really good opportunity."

"For what?"

"To save Henry."

(Desperately running through the burning halls, clawing at the flaming masonry that buried Henry underneath it, carrying him out of the compound, bruised and battered, only to have Carter show up and take him away while Bastian had to just stand there—)

Bastian swallows against the lump in his throat. "We don't even know if he's . . ."

"Yes, we do. Kwan and I overheard Tremain and Carter talking about it. Carter said he's in a safe house in the city."

Bastian feels his chest tighten, and the resulting burn hurts far more than a few bruised ribs ever could.

(It's stupid, *so stupid* to hope, to think that he has any chance of finding Henry, never mind what Laurel and Kwan heard, this is exactly what the compound does, makes you think things aren't as bad as they seem, that there's a way out, just so it can ruin you all over again because you were pathetic enough to—)

"So you get it, right?" Laurel says very quietly. "You have to go. It's the best chance we've had so far, and it might be the only one we get."

It was so much easier to escape the first time. Well, maybe not *easy*—he was bleeding to death for most of it. But it was easier than now. Because now, it means leaving more people behind. People he was trying to—"We were trying to—"

"—figure out a way to get as many people out as possible. I know. But right now, all that's possible is one, so that's what we're going to start with. You understand that, don't you? It's like when a plant drops a bunch of seeds all at once. The ones that have good luck end up in fertile soil and need to go for it, even if the others aren't as lucky."

Bastian frowns. "This isn't about *luck*, Laurel."

"Isn't it? Maybe I'm getting the definition of 'luck' wrong. Or you are. Anyway, we don't have time to find a dictionary."

There's a noise, like she's grabbing something off of the bedside table. "I'm going to apply some of this salve that Dr. Rowe was holding for me, and she's going to give you some stabilizing fluids to help you heal faster, and Kwan is going to stand there and be a grouchy black coat. You should see his face right now; it's a perfect example of grouchy black coat. Oh, but don't actually look— we're supposed to be speaking soothingly to you as you fall unconscious again like a docile asset who isn't about to cause any more trouble. Can you do that? Not cause any more trouble? I mean, I know that'll be hard for you, but I think you can give it a try. I believe in you."

Bastian makes a face at her, but he doubts it does much good since he can't glare at her while he does it. A moment later, he feels the cooling sensation of the salve on his arm.

He hears some more movements, and then Rowe's voice is in his ear. "They'll expect you to be unconscious for the transport, but I don't think you'll need full sedation, do you?"

They expect him to try something en route, then. Not a bad idea, assuming he can wake up and pull it off in time. Although even if he's able to escape the transport vehicle itself, he'll still likely be stuck between the compound and the city. Is that actually any better than being stuck in the compound?

He hisses at the feeling of Laurel's salve on a different part of his arm— some injury that would probably bruise much more heavily if left to its own devices—and tries not to think about the futility of it all. Is he really supposed to just leave them all behind? For something that probably won't work?

"It won't be safe here," Bastian mumbles.

Laurel pauses (amused-sad-afraid). "It already isn't safe here. Haven't you noticed?"

There are several moments of silence as she finishes applying the salve on his arm. Then, very carefully, she asks, "Bastian?" Which doesn't sound like much of a question for something that absolutely is. Despite everything, Laurel isn't going to move forward without his say-so.

He sighs. He hates this, and he hates how little that matters. The compound is going to ship him out no matter what, despite him being an extremely rare type of asset. Maybe that's actually better for the compound in the end—if the rumors are true, they can do more to him at a safe house than they could here.

So if he doesn't have a choice about that, the only thing left to have a choice about is how it happens, and what he does about it.

"Okay," he says.

Rowe jumps into action. "I kept the dose of stabilization fluids as low as possible, but it'll still knock you out in a moment. Try to relax."

Bastian feels the fluids hit his bloodstream and grimaces as his thoughts begin to blur. He forces his eyes open and finds Laurel frowning at him, probably ready to admonish him. Ignoring that, he says, "Be careful."

She blinks, then swoops down and hugs him gently. "I promise I'll look after them. Tell Henry I said hi and that he's a jerk for making us worry."

Bastian is starting to drift, but there's one more thing to take care of. He waves his arm—not well, since the IV is in it—and manages to catch Kwan's attention. He can feel the annoyance-concern-irritation as Kwan walks over. "You're supposed to lie *still*, Lucas."

"I'm protesting," Bastian says, voice already sounding slightly garbled in his own ears. "And you're warning me to behave. Smile for the cameras."

"Lucas—"

Bastian flails for Kwan's sleeve and pulls him closer. "I don't understand why, but you're not . . . you're not trying to hurt us. So I need you to . . . look after them. Laurel and Chloe and Gabe and . . . everyone. Don't make them do everything on their own."

From the other side of the bed, where she's gone to put salve on his other arm, Laurel looks up, eyes widening. "Wait, did you just ask for *help*? Are you being *nice* and *thoughtful*? I mean, it's not necessary because we can look after ourselves, but—"

"Forget I said anything."

"Absolutely not. Ugh, I wish I'd recorded it! Do you think Kent could get it off the security feed for me? Although I guess we don't really want it on the security feed in the first place, so—"

Kwan sighs. "Fine, I get it. Now shut up, both of you."

"You're the best black coat in the entire compound," Bastian mumbles, eyes falling closed again.

"Emphasis on shutting up, Lucas."

"Consider me . . . shut up."

There might be more conversation after that, but Bastian isn't awake to hear it.

Chapter 4

LAUREL SPENDS THE rest of the day and part of the next trying to look normal instead of like she's just masterminded a plan to sneak a cranky empath out of the compound.

Not that it really counted as *sneaking*. Kwan reported this morning that Bastian was added to the completely aboveboard group of assets being moved out of the compound today, transferred to . . . wherever they're taking unruly assets this time. He's probably already left on a vehicle from the loading dock.

Laurel briefly considered reaching out using their empath link, but she quickly dismissed the idea. For one thing, he wouldn't be able to answer if he was still unconscious. And for another, that sort of unusual power use could draw Major Tremain's attention if Laurel got caught doing it. And drawing Major Tremain's attention is the last thing they need right now.

Assuming Dr. Rowe got the level of sedation right—which is to say, just slightly wrong enough—Bastian will wake up not far into the transport's route, which gives him a chance to escape and find Henry. Maybe.

Which leaves Laurel here in her garden, fretting that she might have just made things worse. Both for Bastian, given the danger he's going to be in, and for the people left behind once someone finds out what happened.

In fact, she's been so busy fretting, she hasn't been able to properly enjoy her recess: a brief stint of supervised outdoor time. She's only allowed it because a lot of what she expertly grows here can be used in the compound—assuming the weeds don't get to it first.

Weeds, it turns out, don't much care if you politely ask them to please leave your garden alone because they're choking the vegetables. That means Laurel has to pull them up until they get the hint. And *that* means she has to studiously ignore their indignant cries as she does so.

Maybe it's a good thing that the negation serum, even at low levels like she's on today, tends to drown the tinny voices out.

Anyway, this is all part of the *point*, she reminds herself as she gently but firmly removes some crabgrass. They need to explore anything unusual and make use of whatever they can. Like the chance to get Bastian out of the compound. Like taking advantage of Kwan's help to figure out what's going on with the dead zones—because weird patches of nothingness in the compound are definitely not normal. It was weird enough when Bastian, Chloe, and James encountered one in the forest last year; to have multiple dead zones showing up in the compound now, and then disappearing . . .

Laurel shakes her head and pulls up another weed, a bit more violently than necessary. Its irritated squeak sounds like it's coming from the other end of a tunnel, thanks to the serum. She sends it a genuine apology even though she's not sure if it can hear her with the serum still in her bloodstream.

She considers talking to the grumpy officer serving as her chaperone today about allowing her a fuller range of her power when she's working in the garden, but she already knows what the answer will be. And she's been called on more than once to help treat med bay patients who asked their officers the wrong questions.

"Sorry," she whispers to the crabgrass. Just in case.

"Look," says a loud voice coming from the entry to the garden, "I just need to check on the exterior security upgrades. And before you ask, yes, it has to be here. We're testing the distance, so being closer to the main building won't work."

Laurel looks up to see Kent Turner, co-head of the compound hacker team and inventor of the very unsanctioned jammer, waving his hands at Laurel's grumpy officer.

The officer glances at Laurel. "I don't think—"

Kent's hand-waving manages to come off as condescending. A neat trick, really—equal parts nervous energy and a genuine sense of superiority. "Major Tremain entrusted me and my hacker team with the security of this compound. Do you really want to keep me from taking care of that because you're worried about a plantspeaker playing in her garden?"

Okay, rude. Laurel frowns, and Kent quickly looks away from her. "This won't take long, Officer. Now can I just get on with it? I don't do well in sunlight."

The officer blocks his path for a moment longer, then sighs and steps aside. "I'll be right here, keeping an eye on things," she says sternly, arms crossed over her chest.

"Yeah, sure," Kent replies, flippancy back in place now that he's gotten what he wanted. Still, he must not be entirely calm because he comes into the garden and hurries right past Laurel's vegetable bed like he didn't see her. He only stops when he's a few trees away. Then he gets out his phone, turning toward the outer compound wall and tapping quickly as he looks up and down, like he really is checking on some sort of remote security system.

Except Laurel is pretty sure there aren't any security cameras nearby, so there isn't anything for him to be working on. She watches him for a moment, then shrugs and goes back to her weeding.

Kent makes a hissing sound.

"Most people begin a conversation with 'hello,'" Laurel says, not looking up. "Did you forget? Kind of a weird thing to forget, but I guess we all deal with stress differently."

Another hiss, this one accompanied by a hand-wave that Laurel catches out of the corner of her eye. "Come *here*."

Laurel sneaks a glance at the officer, but she's turned away slightly and is busy talking to someone on her comm. She isn't totally distracted, but she's more focused on whoever she's talking to than on them.

Laurel gets to her feet, brushing dirt off of her hands, and walks carefully over to Kent. This puts her back to the officer, which makes her neck feel uncomfortably prickly and uneasy, but it's not like she can keep looking over there without making it seem like she's doing something she shouldn't be doing. Which she isn't. Yet.

Once she's close enough, Kent clears his throat. "Sorry. It's just that I don't know how long that fake call is going to keep your friend busy."

"Oh. That's you on her comm?"

"Well, it's a computer program I designed, but yeah, basically."

"Wow!"

"Yeah. I'm pretty amazing at my job. Speaking of which, I saw the med bay security footage from yesterday. Nothing too damning, but Sybil and I agreed that it should become ex-footage before anyone else saw it. What the hell were you doing? Not that I care, you know, but I can smell a headache when I see one."

Laurel frowns. "I don't think that's how headaches work. And I'm not sure I should tell you about the med bay. Which I know nothing about, by the way."

"Oh, come on—"

"No, really." Laurel gives him a small, anxious smile and definitely doesn't think about another time and another compound where it was dangerous to tell anyone about anything. "Thanks, though. How's Sybil?"

"Busy. I'm busy, too. So busy, I definitely didn't see anything about the order to ship Lucas out of the compound that came through yesterday."

"Oh. Um. I don't know anything about that, either."

"I was also too busy to see who else was on the roster for this morning's transport."

Laurel blinks. "You were?"

"And I was definitely too busy to recognize the FSP numbers in the related documents. Or the fact that Tremain is the one who personally signed off on all of them."

"That's . . . a lot to not notice," Laurel says carefully, like she's picking her way around a clump of cranky poison ivy.

"The other asset was Angelica Pinelli, by the way." Kent finally looks Laurel in the eye. "What the hell is going on?"

Laurel swallows, but it doesn't do anything to dislodge the fear-shaped lump in her throat.

(It doesn't feel safe, but this isn't like before, and not telling him would be worse because of course he's going to notice no matter what, *has* noticed even though he's saying it like that, which means he can help, *which means he's in horrible trouble if he helps*, but—)

"Well," Laurel says, "'FSP' means it has to do with the Fail-Safe Protocol, right? And if Bastian and Angelica are together, that's a good thing. Probably. Maybe. Unless, you know, they get killed."

Kent goes pale. "And why would they get killed?"

"Well . . . Bastian was going to be sent away because he's an idiot who keeps getting into trouble, so we thought we'd, er, let it happen. Because the thing is, there's a chance he might actually be able to escape and help Henry. Who's alive, by the way. I guess it must all have something to do with the Fail-Safe Protocol and the Compound Council wanting to use our powers to control assets. We should really try to find out more about it."

"Yeah, I'll add that to my work queue. Then I'll add 'get killed' right after it." Kent has a funny, squashed look on his face that almost makes Laurel wish she were an empath so she could read it better. Afraid? Annoyed? Concerned?

"Lucas barely made it out last time, you know," he says, oddly serious. "What makes you think he won't mess things up now?"

"Nothing, really. But that has to be better than just staying here and letting bad things happen."

(Bad things like at her old compound, when she and her friends tried to collect enough information to report Major Valentine and Dr. Wright, when they thought someone else would *care*, when the officers took Vanessa away and left her in a hidden room where she was trapped until James's power went haywire, and the fire came, and—)

"Sure," Kent says. "But what do you think is going to happen when someone in charge realizes that a high-profile asset has escaped?"

"Ha! So you *do* think he can do it!"

"Yeah. And then the rest of us will pay for it."

Laurel presses her lips together and tries to ignore the sinking feeling in her stomach. He's right, of course. Freedom for Bastian—and maybe Angelica—could mean catastrophe for everyone else in retaliation.

But it's worth it. It has to be worth it. Right?

"We should stop talking," Kent says, glancing over his shoulder. "That officer is going to—"

His phone beeps loudly, and he looks back down at the screen. After a pause, his fingers go wild, the tapping and scrolling getting wilder as his frown gets deeper.

"What?" Laurel asks.

When Kent finally looks up at her, his eyes have narrowed, and his shoulders have gone tight. "You know what I just said about Lucas messing stuff up? Well, I hope this was part of your plan, because if it isn't, he's gone and done something really stupid."

Six years ago

"IT'LL BE TOO suspicious if I write it all myself," Perle says, picking at her gray sweatpants, her stringy blond hair trying to escape her ponytail. "I can teach all of you to read the code, of course, but it'll be slower since you're not codecs like me."

"It's better than doing nothing," Xavier says. His large, powerful body seems relaxed, despite the topic of conversation. "We need a secure way to keep in touch, and we need to record what we're seeing."

Laurel glances over at the officer standing near the compound entrance. He's doing a pretty good job of looking at them without looking like he's looking. Laurel considers going over and suggesting that he relax and enjoy the afternoon—and maybe let her finally set up the garden she's been dreaming of planting near the edge of the clearing—but she suspects he won't go for it. The officers at this place aren't particularly friendly, even though they get to work in a lovely forest with very nice trees. Then again, they spend most of their time underground with assets and the rest of the staff, only coming up here for supply runs and little recesses like this one.

Maybe it'd be better if Laurel just stays back and hopes for the best. It's probably best to avoid calling attention to the fact that she and her friends are planning a coup, anyway.

"Alice will use her power to help us remember what they make us forget during the experiments," Xavier is saying. "But we should write down and hide whatever we can in between sessions with her. She's part of a lot of experiments now, so we won't always have access to—"

"You sound like them."

James's face is pale, and there are dark circles under his eyes. He and Laurel haven't talked since she found him hiding in the corner of one of the training rooms a

33

few days ago, sallow-skinned and shaking. But he clearly hasn't gotten any better. She assumes this means that she's not supposed to say anything about that, which is too bad, given how he looks. Not that she's going to betray a confidence, but she knows how difficult it can be to deal with things here. Maybe if he let his friends help . . .

There's a sharpness to his movements now, an edge to every comment. He's nothing like the suave, annoying playboy he was before, and Laurel definitely does not *prefer this version. Sure, he's quieter and less obnoxiously flirty, but she no longer gets the impression that he's putting up a façade—that underneath, there's an awkward kindness that would come through if he'd just let it.*

Now he just seems angry all the time. Which is a bad thing for a firestarter to be.

"We have *to sound like them," Xavier says. "But we don't have to* be *like them. Let's not forget that."*

"Funny thing to say after treating Alice and Perle like assets rather than people."

Laurel blinks at him, startled by the venom in his voice. Perle freezes, and Xavier's eyes narrow briefly before his face evens out again. "We are *assets, James. There's a reason they call us that. But we're people, too. And if we want to get out of here and expose what's going on, we need to work together. We don't have time to—"*

"If we're worried about time, let's forget the code and do something easier." James's eyes meet Laurel's, and for a moment, she sees some of his old cheekiness. "What do you say, Laurel? Want to get some of your friends to help us?"

"That depends on what they're helping us with," Laurel tells him. "The beech trees over there are fighting off a fungal infection, so they're kind of cranky at the moment. But we could probably get the ferns to—"

"I was thinking of something a little smaller. Like getting them to help us make something we could sneak into the officers' drinks at the right time."

Laurel frowns. "Like a sleeping draft?"

"Sure. Something like that."

"Even if we found a way to knock out all of the staff, we'd still need to collect enough evidence to convince the authorities of what we're saying." Xavier taps his leg impatiently, then sighs. "But we should definitely consider every option we can think of. This is a smaller compound that isn't even supposed to exist, so that gives us more room to act. If we can raise enough of a stink about something they'd rather keep secret, that could work."

He turns to Perle. "Find ways to meet up with everyone when you can and teach them the code. You're right that we won't have the knack for it that you do, but we can learn it the slow way. James, you and Laurel look into your plant idea and figure out how we can use it. I'll make sure everyone else is on board. And let's be careful*. The compound staff will know something's up if we don't watch our backs."*

"Strictly speaking, we should probably watch each other's backs," Laurel points out. "I'm not sure how we'd watch our own backs, anyway. Unless there's some sort of asset power that gives you eyes in the back of your head."

"*You never know in a place like this, Pipsqueak.*" *Xavier gets to his feet and offers her a small smile and hand up.* "*Babysitter's coming.*"

The officer approaches them with a frown set so deeply into his face, Laurel wonders if he was born that way. "*Playtime's over.*"

As they walk back to the compound, James gently bumps into her, winking when she turns her head. "*Let's show them what happens when they piss off the wrong asset,*" *he says under his breath. His eyes are brighter than they have been in days, and the corner of his mouth is turned up slightly. There's something a little . . . feral about it, honestly. Like a vine creeping up the side of an oak and sucking all the life out of it, the damage unnoticeable until it's too late for the tree to be saved.*

But Laurel quickly swallows the thought. This version of James is so much better, so much more alive *than the scared, haunted boy he's been masquerading as for days. If there's something she can get her plants to do to keep him like this—and to help all of them escape—then of course that's what she'll do.*

No matter what.

Chapter 5

BASTIAN IS JOSTLED awake by the transport vehicle's worn-out suspension and a vague memory of Kwan's stern voice washing over him as they headed for the loading dock. There's something Bastian is supposed to remember. Something that will help him escape. Only it's hard to bring the details to mind when he was nearly passed out back then and is barely awake now.

Bastian opens his eyes very slightly and immediately wishes he hadn't. The dregs of the sedation in his system make his stomach queasy, and his head starts to pound. If this is the less intense version as concocted by Dr. Rowe, Bastian doesn't want to know what the full dose feels like.

He's strapped down to a gurney and headed who-knows-where in a vehicle that is obviously moving—not quickly, but steadily. There are two other people in here with him: med techs, probably, given their low murmurs and the familiar air of focused-intent-wary. They're comfortable around semi-comatose assets, but that doesn't mean they're not going to keep an eye out for anything unusual.

He thinks he might hear other vehicles nearby, but he can't be sure. If he used his power more overtly, how quickly would it alert the med techs, not to mention anyone else in the convoy who's paying attention?

Hello?

Bastian starts and nearly opens his eyes all the way before he catches himself. Then he's hit with the strange sensation attached to the pinprick of a voice: familiar and tremulous, like a tiny bit of water trickling through a crack in concrete. Close by, but not in the vehicle. So that confirms that there's another transport out there.

Except even if there is, there are only two people who should be able to contact him like this. And it doesn't feel like either of them.

Laurel wouldn't be stupid enough to use their empath link so soon, especially when they could easily be caught using their powers. And Quentin . . . well. Bastian can't think of a good reason for Quentin to contact him, now that Bastian has refused what he offered.

But if a link can only be formed by an empath . . . or someone like Laurel, who's been spliced with an empath's power . . .

Bastian feels another tentative, desperate poke at his mind, followed by a waterfall of fear-anger-frustration-sadness-loneliness, all tightly jumbled up into a ball of misery. It's like the emotions are inexpertly tethered to him specifically, rather than existing as the diffuse cloud he usually feels when reading someone. And it's strong enough to break through the haze of the drugs still in his system.

There's someone out there he knows—someone trying to reach him. Trying to form a link with him, even though they don't know how. Even though they shouldn't be able to.

The vehicle jerks to a halt, and the two med techs pause whatever they were doing, their confused-alert-wary sharpening. "What was that?" one of them asks.

"The captain wants us to stop for a minute," calls the driver. "Some issue with the tech. Stand by."

The second med tech sighs. "Guess we're stuck here for a bit. Are his vitals still within normal ranges?"

More shifting around as they arrange their equipment, and Bastian realizes that this is his best opportunity to see how stupid he can be. He reaches for the nearest med tech's emotions and *pushes*, just slightly.

The pain is immediate, an insistent throb at his temples. He tries to ignore it, focusing instead on braiding some curiosity-interest-concern into the med techs' emotional signatures. It helps that they've been stuck in this vehicle for a while now, so they're eager to seize any opportunity for a break in the monotony. Unfortunately, they're still the sort of people who feel like they shouldn't be incompetent at their jobs. But Bastian figures he can manipulate them just enough to feel okay about not being incompetent *somewhere else*.

"He's stable," says the closest med tech. "No significant changes. Should we go check on the captain? See what's holding us up?"

"And leave this guy alone?" says the other (incredulous-concerned-worried). "You can't just leave assets *alone*."

Bastian grimaces inwardly and *pushes* a little more, encouraging the anxiety and lessening the trepidation about leaving him here. They need to go figure out what's happening *right now* because that's much more important than an unconscious asset.

"It's all right," says the first med tech. "He's not going anywhere."

As if restraints have ever kept Bastian from getting into trouble.

It takes another few seconds of prodding, but at last they open up the back of the vehicle and hop out to see what's going on.

That just leaves the driver, but his fuzzy emotions imply that he's decided to take a quick nap. If Bastian stays quiet, he should have time to take stock and get out of here.

He knows he needs to move quickly, but he lies still for another moment on the gurney, breath shaky. This is far from the first time he's manipulated other people's emotions, but that doesn't mean it's not still . . . unpleasant. He has to be precise, pushing past the pain to make someone feel things they wouldn't necessarily feel of their own free will. It's . . .

He thinks of that scared emotional nudge in his mind—now conspicuously silent—and decides that the moral quandary can wait.

It's not quite as easy to get rid of the restraints as Bastian remembers from the compound experimentation rooms of his childhood, and the headache doesn't help. But his fingers remember the way, eventually. He wobbles as he gets to his feet, managing to grab onto the edge of a storage box to avoid face-planting on the floor. The cool metal under his fingers steadies him as he carefully extracts himself from the monitoring devices, cringing every time he thinks he hears a noise.

Now that he's standing, he remembers Kwan's last-minute instructions: Supplies in the cabinet, worth taking along if at all possible.

Bastian spends a few seconds listening and feeling out to make sure no one's coming for him, especially after removing the wires. Then he carefully opens and closes several cabinets until he finds what he's looking for: a small black duffel bag, nearly hidden in the back of one of the lower cabinets. He quickly pulls it out and unzips it to find a collection of clothes, medical supplies, and non-perishable snacks. He doesn't have time to go through everything and take inventory, but he does pull on the black hoodie to protect against the cool wind he feels coming through the slightly ajar back door. He finds a pair of gloves in the pockets, which shows a surprising amount of thoughtfulness from Kwan. Who knew a black coat would care about whether a touch-sensitive asset had to touch things during his ill-advised escape from the compound?

Bastian pulls out a pair of sneakers and puts those on, too, wondering if he ought to be impressed or concerned that Kwan knows his size.

That done, he slings the bag over his shoulder, then pauses to feel out again. The med techs from before have moved up the queue of vehicles to talk to the captain (curious-conciliatory-confused). He can feel other people in other transports (tired-anxious-annoyed), but they're busy dealing with their own issues—the tech problem seems like it might be widespread, given the cadence of their irritation. They're not paying attention to what's happening here right now, but if Bastian were to just pop out the back of this vehicle, someone would definitely notice.

A thought sneaks past his refusal to think it: There are enough people here that if he drained them like Quentin showed him at the sanctuary, he could get rid of this increasingly annoying headache and daze everyone in the area all at once so they couldn't stop him. After all, it would only be temporary, and he needs that energy more than they do right now . . .

Bastian shakes his head and tries to ignore his roiling stomach. This is *not* about Quentin's so-called cure. Bastian just needs to manipulate a few more emotions—lightly, gently—so he can figure out who that other asset is and get out of here. He can worry about stealing energy and how quickly his power is or isn't killing him later.

His mind feels chafed raw by the time he's done, but after a period of intense focus, he's fairly certain no one will feel like paying attention to him for a while. He pulls up his hood, then opens the vehicle's back door and takes a quick look around.

The convoy is stopped on the side of the road, which is empty at the moment except for the line of compound trucks and other vehicles. In the distance, Bastian can see the winding, polluted rivers leading to the city and the bridges that go across them, each with its own security checkpoints. The sky is overcast and gray, but it doesn't look like rain. Given all of that, it would be smart to make a break for it and find a place to hide while he figures out what to do next.

But Bastian has never been good at doing the smart thing.

So instead, he pinpoints the med techs inside a truck several vehicles down, set away from the others. Ignoring his protesting head, he gently pokes at their bored-curious-restless enough to make them climb out of the vehicle and move toward a group of officers, leaving the door open. Bastian hurries over and slips inside.

He was expecting to find the owner of the feeble voice that was in his head, of course, but this isn't quite what he had in mind.

The number of wires and tubes hooked up to the small body lying on the gurney seems wildly unnecessary. This must be an extremely rare asset, one the compound is very interested in observing and analyzing—and maybe hiding, since they're being sent away. Bastian never managed to completely memorize the asset roster when he was director of the asset program, but he doesn't remember anyone who might merit this kind of treatment.

It's a child, he realizes as he gets closer. A familiar one, even though her tawny skin is much more pallid than he remembers from the last time he saw it.

"Angelica," he whispers.

It doesn't make any sense. Angelica is an unusually strong memor, but memors aren't so rare that they'd require any of this. Then again, she practically disappeared off the face of the earth after the destruction of the compound.

And now she's part of this convoy, and she reached out to him through an empath link, which isn't possible. Except it obviously is because she did it. So what the hell does *that* mean?

"Angelica?" he says again, a little louder.

Her eyes flutter open, just as dark and piercing as always, although she seems to be having trouble focusing. She's probably been sedated even more than he was. "Oh. You heard me."

That's when the yelling starts.

Bastian curses and drops all of the emotional threads he was holding. The sudden lack of their weight feels like the nauseatingly abrupt release of gears in an elevator right before it plummets. He sucks in a breath and grabs onto the edge of Angelica's gurney to steady himself.

He can feel her watching him (dazed-worried-concerned), but she stays silent. He knows he ought to say something reassuring, but he's busy feeling out again, trying to determine what's going on. Everything feels increasingly jumbled, a cacophony of anger-fear-alarm-aggression that makes his vision swim. More people have arrived, but he can't tell how many. They all seem to be preoccupied with some sort of disturbance at the head of the convoy line.

Angelica lets out her own sudden jolt of fear, straining against the straps and wires holding her down.

"Wait," Bastian says, and she stops, eyes wide, expression otherwise blank. He realizes belatedly that he must have sounded sharper than he meant to—her fear develops a thin coating of hurt around it—but he's distracted by the increasing noise outside (Is that *fighting*?) and the need to figure out how to extract Angelica from all of these wires as quickly as possible.

He feels a shiver go down his spine just as he's reaching toward one of the machines, and he goes cold when he sees a shadow pull away from the wall of the truck. It materializes into a woman with warm brown skin and copper-colored hair tied back in a bun. She's wearing black, the same color as the shadow she just was, and her eyes are alert as she looks around, gaze landing on the machine.

"Let me do it," she says, stepping forward.

Bastian feels the sharp jab of Angelica's alarm-fear-dread even as he moves between her and the woman. Without meaning to, he sends Angelica a quick pulse of calm-reassuring-safe, the way he might send an emotion to Laurel over their link. And it . . . works, somehow. He feels her relax slightly.

"I'm here to help," the woman says calmly, not trying to move any closer.

"I've heard that one before," Bastian says. "Not from an umbra who hitched a ride on a compound transport vehicle, though."

"You need to get out more, then. Live a little. See the world. We can talk vacationing tips when we're out of here, maybe. And speaking of out, can you check outside and see how things are going? I can tell the time we bought with the technical failure is up, which means we're headed toward an all-out ruckus. So we need to move fast once I get your girl free."

Bastian can't sense any malicious intent from her; just a thin strand of amused-concerned-focused as she turns her mind toward Angelica's predicament. Maybe the fact that Bastian couldn't feel her immediately—likely because of her power and the sedation still in his system—won't come back to bite them in the ass. Maybe.

Luckily, he doesn't have to turn around to figure out what's going on outside. He sidesteps slightly so that the woman has more access to the gurney and the nearby machines while he feels out to the area around them. He's aware of more people than before, but they seem to be fighting each other rather than paying attention to the rest of the convoy at the moment.

"Well?" The woman is removing the last wire from Angelica's skin with the ease of someone who's done this before.

"There are more people now, but—"

"Don't worry about them; they're just here to distract the compound forces." She pauses, then frowns. "You didn't look out the door, did you?"

She doesn't know what type of asset he is, then. Probably for the best. "I don't think your distraction is going to last long, so let's get out of here."

The woman narrows her eyes, then nods and turns back to Angelica, offering a hand down. "I'm Tallis, by the way. What's your name?"

Angelica looks at her for slightly too long, obviously sizing her up. "Angelica."

She considers Tallis's hand for a moment, then takes it. But instead of using it to get off of the gurney, she holds it in hers, eyes going glassy. "You remember when he told you not to," she says, voice monotone. "He always tells you not to, but you do anyway because sometimes you can make the assets safe. You think he's not *really* angry when you do it, but—"

Tallis pulls her hand back, then lets out an embarrassed laugh and scratches her head. "Memor, huh? Maybe a little warning next time you do your memory-sucking thing?"

"Sorry," Angelica mumbles, rubbing her hands against her hospital gown.

"I'll get her; you get us a way out," Bastian says firmly.

"Lucky for you, I've already got one." Tallis tucks her ashamed-awkward-concerned under a layer of cheeky self-satisfaction. "We've got a van stashed nearby—not as luxurious as this vehicle, but I think it'll do for a quick getaway. You gonna tell me your name?"

Bastian hesitates, but there's no reason she would know either of them if they stick to first names. "Bastian."

"All right, Bastian. Ready to get out of here?"

He helps Angelica down off of the gurney and lets her lean against him while he rummages around in Kwan's bag and pulls out a sweatshirt. It'll be much too big for her, but it will also help with the shivering she's trying to hide.

"Yeah," he says when she's all set, swimming in cheap cotton. "Let's go."

He realizes a split second later that this isn't going to work; Angelica nearly topples over when she tries to move.

"Here." He throws the bag at Tallis, who easily catches it—her reflexes are good, even for an umbra. Then he turns back to Angelica. "I'll carry you."

Angelica eyes him appraisingly. "You don't look strong enough."

"And you don't look strong enough to walk."

Angelica sniffs. "I can walk." She shakes off his arm, goes one wobbly step, and nearly collapses again.

Bastian sighs and crouches down. "Get on my back."

She does as she's told this time, arms going around his neck as she clings to him. Bastian hasn't ever given someone a piggyback ride—not exactly on his list of duties as either an interrogator for the compound or as director of the asset program—but he figures he's doing all right when Angelica doesn't immediately slip off. She's warm and a little heavy, but he doesn't think he'll drop her.

And he decides not to pay attention to the way her afraid-anxious-distress subsides as soon as they're touching.

Tallis is looking at both of them when he turns around, the hint of a smile in her eyes and at the corners of her mouth. "Okay?"

"Okay," Bastian says.

Tallis opens the door to the vehicle, and then they're out the back and running.

Bastian can feel the moment when the tide turns, and the distraction fails. There's a single shout, and then the noise coming from the front of the convoy starts to shift. Then more shouting and footfalls and a few shots in their direction—hopefully tranqs rather than bullets—that go wide.

Tallis breaks into a sprint, and Bastian grits his teeth and follows, gravel and grass pushing against the thin soles of his secondhand shoes. They head for a small patch of trees through which he can just barely make out the hubcaps of what had better be a very, very fast van.

He hears more shots and hunches down, which is pointless, of course. He can't exactly protect Angelica from them if she's on his back, and unless Tallis has a *lot* of friends, the compound forces vastly outnumber them. And the sparse patches of brush here and there aren't enough cover to ensure that they'll make it to the van in one piece.

This situation requires much more than just a distraction.

Bastian skids to a stop and sets Angelica down. "Go with Tallis."

He can feel her eyes on him, but he doesn't have time to argue. He turns back toward the officers, takes a deep breath, and *pushes*.

The best bet would be to focus a single emotion into one powerful attack, the way he used his anger that time in the forest against John Doe. But he can't risk it falling back on Angelica or Tallis, and he doesn't have time to strategize. So he goes with something more subtle and more likely to cause confusion. He has to convince the officers that they feel like halting their charge, and he has to make sure whatever he does doesn't hit anyone else, and he has to work past the vestiges of the sedation in his system, and he has to *not mess this up*.

He hears Tallis yell something at him, but he ignores her and focuses on the *push* instead. He can feel it hit some of the officers, who slow down and pause their firing. But then they shake their heads and get right back to running, hands going to comms, calling more people over. More people who are probably also armed.

Bastian grimaces and, without thinking, shoves more energy into the *push*: fear, anger, frustration, his desperate need to protect people it's laughable to think he could ever protect. The guilt of leaving Laurel behind. The shame of needing Kwan's and Dr. Rowe's help.

It's the move from the sanctuary *and* the move from the forest, and he's not sure exactly how he's doing it. But it's forceful and jarring, both to him and to them, scooping out all of his emotions and throwing them like a bomb at the people he wants to stop. To hurt. To *stay down*.

And they do. One by one, every officer approaching them across the field drops to the ground, like they can't remember how to stand upright.

He's vaguely aware of Tallis's eyes on his back and, to his surprise, Angelica's hand in his. The first makes him wary, but the second feels . . . strange. He gets the sense that if Angelica weren't there, he'd be on the ground, too. Possibly permanently.

Bastian turns to find Tallis still staring at him. "What the hell was that?" she asks.

"Made us an exit," Bastian says, swiping with his free hand at the blood he suddenly feels dripping from his nose. "I don't think they're going to stay like that for long, and they've got friends coming, so let's go."

She looks at him silently for another quick moment before self-preservation wins out, and she starts running again. Bastian gets Angelica settled on his back and follows.

The van Tallis leads them to is a beat-up clunker, which doesn't exactly bode well. It's easy enough to clamber into, though, and it starts quietly when Tallis turns the key.

"Going to leave your friends behind?" Bastian asks as she takes off, the momentum jostling both him and Angelica where they're huddled in the back.

"We'll meet them at the safe point before the city," Tallis says (concerned-resigned-hopeful). She's obviously worried about the assets she came with but focused on the mission.

"Wait, we're going to the *city*?" Bastian repeats. "Where there are more people?"

Tallis grins at them through the rearview mirror. "You'd be surprised how easy it is to hide from compound thugs there. We can—hey, you all right?"

"Fine," Bastian says, although he's suddenly dizzy, and he's not sure that holding his sleeve against his bleeding nose is helping much. "You try to take out compound transports often?"

Tallis laughs. "It's kinda what I do. A hobby, I guess."

"Dangerous hobby."

"You're not the first one to tell me that. It worked out for you, though, didn't it?"

"Not yet." Although he can't feel anyone following them. Then again, in his current state, he's not sure how useful or accurate his power is.

Tallis is silent for a while, focusing on the road—or rather, the dirt track they've veered onto in order to avoid the area where the compound forces will be looking for them. "You going to tell me what that was back there? I mean, thanks, but it looked like it hurt."

She wasn't too put off by Angelica's power—more startled than anything—so it might be all right to tell her more. Only Bastian isn't sure how she'll react to having an empath on board. There's only supposed to be one of those, and if she knows that, she may be less inclined to finish this escape, given all the trouble it will cause her. Especially if she knows who he is.

Henry would say she's owed an explanation. Bastian may have helped with the escape, but it was mostly down to Tallis and whoever is working with her. Without their distraction, there's no telling if Bastian and Angelica could have made it out of that vehicle, let alone away from the convoy. Henry would say—

"You've done this rescuing thing before?" Bastian asks.

"Sure. Why?"

Bastian presses his lips together, then says, "Because I know someone else who could use some rescuing."

Chapter 6

One month later

THE LEVEL 14 med bay storage rooms are so cold that Laurel's fingers are starting to feel thick and slow as she inventories the herbs.

She supposes she shouldn't complain, though. She's lucky that she still gets to do chores around the compound instead of being shuffled between experiments and otherwise locked in her room. At least this situation implies that they value her exceptional organizational skills.

Laurel frowns at a misplaced sachet of lavender. If she's honest, it doesn't make sense that she hasn't been locked up for good. After all, Major Tremain has access to her file, which must have lots of top secret information about Laurel's previous compound and what happened there.

But despite all that—and despite Bastian's escape from the convoy a month ago, which anyone with half a brain would assume Laurel knew something about—everything is just . . . carrying on. Laurel gets her daily injections of the negation serum, participates in experiments, and works in the med bay or her garden. Rinse and repeat.

While other assets get sent away for the littlest infractions.

Laurel shoves a box of willow bark tea between a container of verbena and another filled with yarrow. Maybe it's only a matter of time before it's her turn to become a target. Maybe she should be taking advantage of the reprieve to find more dead zones and collect more information and figure out how to get more assets out of the compound instead of pretending she cares about alphabetizing.

She's about to ask the black coat babysitting her to take her to the next storage room when the door opens, and a familiar figure walks through.

"I'll take it from here," Kwan says to the black coat, who shrugs and leaves without a word.

Laurel raises her eyebrows. "Wow, I guess they don't teach manners in black coat school. Should I take it personally that he was so eager to get away from me?"

"Let's go to the next storage room," Kwan says. He stands back to let her go first, visibly impatient. This is the most excited Laurel has ever seen him be about chores.

The second storage room is right next door to the first, and it houses more equipment than herbs. Laurel passes refrigerators full of blood samples and tries not to feel sick to her stomach, thinking about what they might be used for.

After a moment, she realizes that something weird *is* happening in her stomach, although it doesn't seem to be refrigerator-related. She stops partway down a row of shelves, turns, and walks back to Kwan. Before she can say anything, though, he opens his jacket a little to show her the jammer in his interior pocket. "Dead zone?"

They'd need Bastian to be sure, since his is the only power that works reliably even in dead zones. Laurel has had too much negation serum today to be able to check with her own power—it wouldn't work whether or not a dead zone was blocking it. But it does *feel* like a dead zone in the way that dead zones tend to make her head buzz and her stomach tighten.

"How did you know?" she asks Kwan.

"That girl you sometimes get intel from—the tracker—said she found it during her last experiment. Wanted me to run it by you."

Laurel grins. "Chloe's gotten quite sneaky, hasn't she? I'm glad I've been such a good influence. Or possibly a bad one. How did you contact her?"

"I was her assigned escort a few days ago. Took me a while to arrange security duty on Level 14, so I couldn't get in touch with you about it until now."

"Hmm. Well, I've got too much negation serum in my system to know for sure if it's that or a dead zone, but . . ."

The thing about dead zones is that they feel *wrong*, like some basic law of nature has stopped working in a very specific location. Her temples are filled with the static of . . . not just a lack of growing things, but the idea that there never *were* growing things anywhere nearby. Just a creepy-crawly emptiness. Like nothing was allowed to exist here from the start.

Bastian once described dead zones as areas where emotions aren't allowed to settle. Laurel isn't an empath, of course, but she thinks maybe she feels a similar unpleasant nothingness.

Ah, says a voice. *I see you found it.*

Laurel starts and turns back to Kwan, but he isn't looking at her like he's just spoken and is expecting a response. Which means either she's hearing things, or . . .

It would probably be best if you found us some privacy.

"What is it?" Kwan asks.

"I'm going to try on the other side of these shelves," Laurel says in her best I'm-definitely-not-up-to-anything voice. "See if I can get anything different over there. Be right back!"

She can't go too far—best not to risk going outside the range of Kwan's jammer—but she can get a little distance for the sake of the voice in her head. "Who are you?" she hisses.

She can feel the gentle amusement in response, which she shouldn't be able to do unless—

I know you're familiar with empath links, and we don't have time for more explanation at the moment. I just needed to see if it would work.

If it would *work*? Laurel has been trying for nearly a month to contact Bastian through their link, resulting in a whole lot of nothing. Now this random voice comes in like it knows things and just—

"Introductions are important," Laurel says, her tone sharp. "Jumping into someone's head without one is pretty rude."

The voice is still amused, but also harried and . . . concerned? Laurel isn't as good at reading emotions as an empath, and the link feels tenuous. Not at all like the one she has with Bastian. That one is strong and comforting; this is something else.

I can help you, says the voice. *But you'll need to find a safer place for us to talk properly.*

"I don't understand how we're talking at *all*, never mind properly," Laurel says, frowning. "This is a dead zone—or at least, I think it is. So I shouldn't be able to use my power at all."

You can't use your natural *power. Just the one you were . . . gifted with through the splicing experiments. The one you know is strong enough to work past the serum and whatever other safeguards the compound thinks it has.*

And all at once, Laurel forgets to be concerned about getting caught because this is so much more important. "But . . . if you can do this—I mean, I know you weren't part of the splicing experiment because they're all—so you must be—"

My name is Quentin, says the voice. *I think we have a friend in common.*

Quentin. The healer and only other living empath, who offered to help Bastian keep his power from killing him. The one who offered Bastian a "cure" he refuses to use or talk about.

Speaking of friends, I'd advise you not to bring your black coat friend next time we talk, Quentin says.

"You think I should lie to him even though he's helping me? And how do you even know—?"

Not everyone who offers to help has your best interests at heart.

"But you do."

His amusement gets a little spiky around the edges—exasperation or annoyance, maybe, but he's still mostly amused. *I hope we'll be able to talk longer next time so you can form your own opinion on that. For now, I'll just point out that, unlike your friend, I don't have to answer to a major presiding over a compound teetering on implosion. I can help people who deserve to be helped, without reservation.*

It's true that Kwan is still a black coat. If Tremain asked him point-blank whether he's been helping assets, he would have to admit it, right? But someone outside of the compound, someone without mixed loyalties . . . well, they might be helpful in a way no one else could be.

If they were telling the truth.

I hope you'll let me help you, Laurel. It's so important to accept help when it's offered.

"Laurel?" Kwan calls. "Anything?"

Laurel squeezes her eyes shut and reaches for the voice again, but it's gone, leaving just an echo of concern and hope. And she's not entirely sure what to make of that.

Chapter 7

HENRY ISN'T SURE he's awake at first. His eyes must be open—he can see the dim lights around the room begin to brighten per the instructions coded into their timers—but everything is still washed out by the vagueness of his half-consciousness.

They can't always keep him drugged to this level, of course, since they still need him to use his power on command, and that's harder to do if he can't think straight. But Dr. Urashima has him drugged every night, ever since Henry stopped being able to sleep.

But he isn't sleeping now. Probably.

Henry forces himself to sit up slowly, the room spinning a little as he does it. He can hear voices outside of the room: at least two people. The words are muddled, partly from the drugs in his system and partly because the room is mostly soundproof. He learned that early on, when they stopped responding to his yelling and pounding on the door. Probably just as well; at some point, one of the officers guarding him was going to forget that they're not allowed to kill him, and things might've gotten ugly.

He takes a breath and tries to move to the end of the bed, closer to the door. It hurts; one of his wrists is cuffed to the bed frame, and the movement slides the metal against his bruised skin. He flinches but pulls a little more, earning himself another inch. At least the pain is waking him up.

The muffled noise outside rises, then cuts off abruptly. There's a pause, and then the door opens, light from the hallway pouring in and forcing Henry to shield his eyes with his free hand. After a few moments, he risks squinting at the person in the doorway.

Not an officer. Not Urashima or any of the med techs.

Just someone who absolutely, positively can't be there.

Bastian strides into the room like it's totally normal for him to waltz into the heart of a high-security safe house. He's wearing the same sort of dark green jacket as Henry's usual guards, although it looks like he just grabbed it off of someone and threw it on haphazardly. His face is partially obscured by a hood—definitely not part of the uniform, so he must be wearing a hooded sweatshirt or something underneath.

Without pausing for more than a quick glance around the room, Bastian hurries over to where Henry is sitting on the bed, still staring at him like an idiot. Wordlessly, he crouches down and reaches for Henry's wrist. Henry flinches away without meaning to, and Bastian's eyes finally meet his.

Up close, he looks like shit: even paler than Henry remembers, though it's hard to tell for sure with the hood. He's got a fading bruise under his right eye—some earlier tussle?—and his dark hair has gone a bit long around the edges. Henry wonders stupidly if it would still feel as soft as it used to if he ran his fingers through it.

"Bastian," Henry says. He can't quite manage anything else.

Bastian smiles, small and a bit strained, but not so far off from the smile Henry still tries to dream about. "Hi."

A tinny, indistinct noise comes from somewhere extremely close by, and Henry starts. Bastian seems to be expecting it, though. He turns away slightly, raising a hand to his ear. "I know," he says, voice sharp. "I can handle it. Get our exit ready."

He's wearing a comm, Henry realizes. Which means someone else is in on this, too.

Bastian turns back to Henry and holds out a small key that looks an awful lot like the ones Henry's guards use to secure his handcuffs. Low tech to avoid any possible interaction with the powers of the assets who pass through here. "This rescue comes with a timer," Bastian says, "so we have to move."

Henry opens his mouth to ask, then decides against it—too many questions and not enough time for answers. Instead, he takes the key and unlocks the cuff, breathing in sharply as the metal scrapes against his tender skin. When he tosses the key aside and looks up, he catches the edge of Bastian's frown being quickly tucked away.

They both get to their feet, Henry with a slight wobble. Bastian steadies him with one hand, then uses the other to press something into his palm: a gun.

Henry stares at it, then at Bastian. He decides to risk a question after all, mostly because he's already started asking it. "This is standard issue, like the ones the guards have. How did you—?"

"I convinced the very nice man in the hallway to give it to me just now. Let's get out of here before he asks for it back."

Henry takes the gun and follows Bastian to the door. Just before the threshold, he stops and grabs Bastian's arm. "Wait. There are guards. And cameras."

"Not anymore."

Henry doesn't like the sound of that, but Bastian doesn't seem inclined to make a conversation of it. In fact, he's much more focused on placing one gloved hand on the wall to the right of the door and pausing there for a moment. When he tips his head to one side and frowns, Henry realizes that he's using his power. Without thinking, Henry checks his negation field and pulls it back.

If Bastian notices, he doesn't say anything. He removes his hand from the wall and glances at Henry, who nods once. Then he opens the door.

The hallway is empty and silent—two things it never is, in Henry's experience. Just like in his room, the lights are set back into the walls and ceiling, only these are at full blast, buzzing slightly and giving off a harsh glow. They make it impossible to guess what time of day it is, but regardless, there ought to be guards on duty.

There are probably Compound Network safe houses that are actually *houses*, but this one is a small office building, meant to fit inconspicuously into the city's business district. A quick and easy transfer hub to get assets from one side of the city to the other without fuss. The size of the building means it doesn't warrant the number of officers a compound has, but even so, there should be enough security here for at least a small a contingent to be on them in seconds.

And yet . . . nothing.

They hurry down the hallway, which Henry is getting a good look at for the first time since they brought him here a month ago from Council HQ. It really does look like an office building: They pass white boards, insipid workplace motivational posters, and doors that seem to lead to meeting rooms.

Henry still doesn't know why they wanted him here rather than sequestered away at Council HQ, but if it's somehow made it easier for Bastian to find him, Henry isn't complaining.

The idea that Bastian was looking at all, that he's willing to take such a huge risk, that they might not make it out of here no matter who or what Bastian has in place . . . It's terrifying. Henry can't decide whether he wants to yell at him or kiss him, but he can't do either at the moment.

Bastian leads them down the hall and into an open area filled with empty cubicles. Henry hasn't been in this part of the building before, and he can't tell if it's meant to be part of the office cover or if they really do push papers around here. He can't detect anything out of the ordinary aside from the eerie silence, but his hand tightens on the gun anyway. "Where is everyone?" he asks in a low voice.

"Must be lunchtime," Bastian says dryly. Then he stumbles, grabbing onto the side of a cubicle with a choked-off noise.

Henry frowns and reaches for him. "Are you—?"

"Keep moving. Time limit, remember?"

They pass through the open area and into another hallway. This one looks a little more like the deceptively bland, antiseptic-scented corridors from the Council HQ facility where he was kept before. Empty white walls, unlabeled doors on either side, bright lights glaring down from the ceilings, cameras everywhere.

Henry eyes them warily. "You're sure you have these covered?"

"Probably."

"*Probably?*" Henry stops dead.

"Not my problem. *Keep moving.*"

"How the hell are the cameras not your problem?"

From somewhere not far off, there's the sound of approaching footsteps—not running, so no one's raised the alarm yet. But the footsteps are too quick for someone just taking a stroll. And more importantly, they're getting closer.

Bastian curses, opens the nearest door, and shoves Henry through into what looks like an experimental recovery room. Henry immediately scans for any signs of life, but there's nothing. Just empty gurneys and shelving units in a room that's maybe half the size of what its equivalent would be in a compound. Things aren't exactly covered in cobwebs, but it's obvious that this room hasn't been used in quite some time, if ever.

He turns back to the door and finds Bastian leaning his forehead against it, shoulders taut. Henry moves closer, but Bastian flinches back with enough force to knock his hood further away from his face. Enough that Henry can see that his nose is bleeding.

"Are you all right?" Henry asks, which is a stupid question, since Bastian clearly isn't.

"Fine," Bastian says, because of course he does. "Just give me a minute."

The footsteps get closer and more purposeful—someone is walking quickly toward them. Another set joins the first, and now there are voices. Nothing they're saying is distinct enough for Henry to gauge just how much trouble they're in, so he cranes his neck to peek through the square of glass in the door.

"Stay back," Bastian snaps, holding part of his hood to his nose to staunch the bleeding. Still facing the door, he presses his free hand against it and squeezes his eyes shut.

Henry frowns and takes one more quick look out into the hallway, catching a glimpse of two officers heading their way before he has to duck out of sight.

"You heard something around here?" one of the officers asks, his voice muffled by the door. "Which room?"

"Not sure," says the other officer. "I thought . . ."

The footsteps stop on the other side of the door. Henry's gaze darts around, calculating. Trying to hide under a gurney won't do them much good, and there isn't any other furniture. The cabinets don't look big enough, even if they happen to be empty.

He raises the gun.

"You know," says the uncertain officer, her voice even more hesitant than before, "we have that handoff at ten . . . Maybe we should go check on it. I'm sure nothing's going on here."

"Yeah," says the other, his voice also sounding dazed now. "Let's go do that. I'm a little nervous about it, honestly." Slowly, their footsteps begin to move away.

Bastian straightens and pushes himself away from the door, but the movement somehow throws him off balance, and his legs give out. Without thinking, Henry grabs him with one arm around the waist before he can hit the floor. "Whoa! What—?"

"Four more on this floor," Bastian mumbles. "S'okay; they're not exactly dedicated employees. I can keep them disinterested long enough for us to . . ."

Bastian trails off, breath shaky as he leans heavily on Henry's arm.

Henry frowns, then frowns some more when the pieces fall into place. "How many people are in this building right now?"

"A lot." Bastian's voice is low, and he's hiding his face against Henry's chest. "More than we planned. Doesn't matter. We should—"

"How many are you using your power on right now?"

Bastian lets out a small sigh. "All of them. Everyone except you."

Henry's skin prickles with . . . not fear, exactly. He knows from the John Doe murder case that empaths can manipulate other people's feelings, even get them to do things they wouldn't normally do. Bastian said once that that's how things worked when he was an interrogator for the compound—that he could convince subjects they felt like confessing, although he didn't realize what was going on at the time. But that was one-on-one; this is one on . . . how many? Fifty? A hundred? The building isn't large, but it's usually full of officers. If Bastian has been convincing them all to feel like looking the other way this entire time, it's no wonder he gave himself a nosebleed.

Except, in that brief moment after they escaped the burning compound last year, Bastian told Henry that he found the cure. That the healer he, Chloe, and James went after had been able to help. So why would he still be reacting to his own power like this?

"Okay," Henry says, forcing himself to table that concern for now. "Where's the best exit, and how long do we have before someone decides to visit this part of the building again?"

Bastian tenses against Henry's shoulder, and Henry fights the urge to pull him closer and tell him to *stop*. It doesn't take long, though; a moment later, Bastian is straightening up and moving away, leaving a cold, empty space at Henry's side. "I don't think I can hold them off for longer than ten or fifteen minutes," he says.

Henry nods. "Exit?" He wasn't exactly coherent when they first brought him here, and he hasn't seen much of anything other than his room, a few hallways, the interrogation area, and occasionally, the showers.

"Down a few floors to the south side. There's someone who can cover us once we're there, but we'll have to make it out first."

"Let's do it, then."

***

Henry hasn't thought about escape for a very long time, but when he did, he didn't quite envision it like this.

Bastian walks quickly, not exactly avoiding cameras but not lingering, either. His eyes are narrowed, frown firmly in place, obviously trying to ignore his earlier weakness. Henry almost admires it: Stick to the plan, everything else be damned, because there's a job to do.

He's not sure how he feels about being the job, though.

When Bastian opens the door to the first stairwell, Henry pauses and lets out a noise that might, in another life, be a laugh.

Bastian turns back to him. "What?"

"Nothing, it's just—want me to carry you down for old time's sake?"

Bastian blinks, then rolls his eyes. Neither gesture does much to hide the hint of a smile sneaking into the corners of his mouth. "No, but you can invite me to dinner, if you want."

"Standing invitation, assuming we get out of here alive."

"Well," says a voice from just inside the stairwell. "Aren't you adorable?"

Startled, Henry raises his gun—mostly on instinct, though; he's too tired and shaky to shoot with any accuracy. There isn't really anything to shoot, anyway; just a clump of shadows that slowly resolves into a woman standing on the first step. She's dressed all in black, copper hair tied back in a bun, and her presence doesn't seem to surprise Bastian much.

"Why didn't you just call?" he asks, tapping his earpiece.

"I was busy popping back in to disable some more security cameras, so I figured I might as well meet and greet in person." She grins at Henry. "Hey there. I'm Tallis. You're Henry, right?"

"Yeah," Henry says, feeling a little bewildered. Where did Bastian pick up an umbra, and how did he convince her to help him break into a compound safe

54

house? He isn't exactly the kind of person who makes friends easily—especially friends willing to march into this kind of danger.

"If we don't die, I'm sure it'll be nice to meet you," Tallis says. Then she turns back to Bastian. "You heard me tell you that there are way more officers inside here than we planned for?"

"I said it was—"

"Well, they're outside as well. As far as I can tell, it's break time at the moment, but that doesn't mean they won't call all their friends over if they see assets sneaking out of the building."

Bastian grimaces, then blots his still-bleeding nose. "I'll use my power on them, too. Enough to clear us a path to the van."

Henry looks at Tallis. "Other options?"

Tallis shrugs. "Run?"

"Seriously?"

"No. Well, yes, because we'll have to. But I can cause enough of a distraction out front so that you two can get to the van, especially if I have my people bring it closer. There may be more resistance than we anticipated, but it's not like we didn't prepare at all."

"Let's keep moving," Bastian says, voice sharp. Henry can hear the jagged edges of fatigue around it.

"You got it," Tallis says, melting back into the shadows.

Henry bites back his questions and settles for following Bastian down the stairs.

By the time they make it to the back exit of the first floor, Bastian is wheezing. "There are . . . still a lot of them outside." He takes a shallow breath and reaches out toward the wall near the exit door. "I can—"

Henry grabs his hand. "Stop. We'll figure something else out. Tallis mentioned a distraction, right?"

Bastian stares at the place where their hands are touching, like it doesn't quite register that they're existing in proximity to each other after seven months. Or maybe that's just Henry's interpretation. Either way, Bastian seems unable to look anywhere else for a moment. Then he shakes his head and says, "The longer she jumps around in and out of shadow form, the more likely she'll get shot by someone who gets lucky. We need to . . . get out of here *now*."

He meets Henry's eyes, and in that moment, Henry sees pain—not the kind that has anything to do with empath powers and bloody noses. "We looked—*I* looked for you for a long time," Bastian says quietly. "I'm not going to—I won't leave you here."

Henry's first, stupid thought is: *You should. I don't deserve this, after what I've done.*

His next, less stupid thought is: *There aren't enough rounds left in this gun to get us past whatever's out there.*

"Okay," Henry says carefully, past the lump in his throat. Mission first; breakdown later. "Just . . . get them to look away for a bit. We'll run when it's safe, and then you *let go*. Please."

He releases Bastian's hand and steps back.

Bastian clearly wants to protest, but instead, he closes his eyes. Henry checks that his negation field is pulled back as far as it can be, so Bastian won't have to waste energy working through it.

After a moment, Bastian opens his eyes and nods. Henry carefully opens the door.

The area behind the building is littered with sedans and vans, all situated to make this look like a typical office parking lot with the usual comings and goings. Unlike a typical office parking lot, though, this one has groups of officers on the far side. Tallis seems to have been right about them: They're milling around on break rather than paying close attention to their surroundings. Not that it would take much to arouse their interest.

As Henry and Bastian crouch low in the doorway, waiting for the right moment to run, an officer in the closest group responds to something on their radio and orders their group around to the other side of the building. From this distance, they all look more annoyed than concerned, so whatever distraction Tallis has cooked up must not be something dire. But—

"It's not enough," Bastian mutters, jerking his head toward the left side of the parking lot. There are still a fair number of officers checking vehicles in that area, which effectively cuts off access to anything beyond.

"I suppose you're going to tell me that the van's that way?" Henry asks.

Bastian nods once, obviously still focusing on his emotional suggestions. His face looks pinched, like he's struggling to hold on.

That ends a moment later with a sudden, earsplitting alarm that blasts from the building behind them.

Bastian curses and grabs Henry's arm. They quickly dive behind the nearest car as the officers start shouting.

They're sluggish with their weapons, probably thanks to the last vestiges of Bastian's power. But more voices rise by the second, and shots ring out with increasing frequency as they close in. Bastian won't be able to hold them back now, especially with the building alarm going at the same time. Henry could probably try to get off a few shots, but one weapon is no match for the incoming crowd. Henry's heart is in his throat, the alarm pulsing under his skin, sounding louder and louder the longer it goes on—

(Like the fire alarms in the compound as it came down around his ears, hotter and hotter on his back and face and arms, one more thing he couldn't save—)

He suddenly realizes that the air is getting thick and dry, filled with pinpricks of something that whip his face and sting his cheeks. In seconds, it's nearly impossible to see more than a few inches in any direction as a blanket of sand swallows the parking lot.

The scattered sound of gunfire comes to a confused stop.

"Idiots," a voice growls, grabbing Henry by the arm so suddenly, he drops the gun. Before he can struggle free to pick it up, he's being dragged away in quick, powerful movements that show no concern for if—or when—the officers might start shooting again.

"What the *hell* did I tell you, Lucas?" his captor says sharply, not slowing down at all. Henry realizes he and Bastian are being herded in the direction of the parking lot exit, where the van is supposed to be.

"That you'd be happy to help but felt shy about offering?" Bastian wheezes. He's bent partially over, coughing around the words. There's sand sticking to his eyelashes.

"I *said* you were *not* to put any of my people in danger just so you could rescue your stupid boyfriend. What part of 'we don't get involved' don't you understand?"

Henry turns and finally gets a decent look at their rescuer: a tall man dressed in black, with dark skin and graceful movements. There's something familiar about him that Henry can't quite place.

Apparently feeling Henry's gaze, the man turns and gives him a quick once-over. "You look like crap, Mortimer."

"Thanks." Henry frowns. "Have we met?"

The man smiles—a flash of white teeth that shows no sign of warmth—and releases both of them. "It's cute that you don't have to remember. Keep moving and let me finish this."

"I don't—"

But the man is raising his hands, and the wind is picking up, moving the sand more quickly and widely. Bastian reaches over and pulls Henry back, positioning the collar of his pilfered jacket over his nose and mouth at the same time. Henry doesn't have similar gear, but he covers his face with his free arm as the density of the sand increases, then makes a beeline for the officers on the far side of the parking lot. There's a good cloud built up now; no way they'll be seen, if they escape quickly.

This guy must be a sandmaker, then. And his face is familiar because . . . oh.

"I thought I told you to *move!*" the man says, whirling around to glare at them.

He doesn't have to tell them twice.

Chapter 8

ALEX BARRETT WASN'T exactly pleased when Tallis brought Bastian and Angelica in a month ago, and he's clearly even less pleased about Henry. That was sort of the whole point of keeping him in the dark—Bastian has noticed that he's much more permissive once renegade assets are already at his rundown hotel hideout. Harder to turn them away when they're standing right in front of him. Besides, most of the assets who come through here only use it as a temporary stopover before disappearing into the city and beyond.

All in all, Barrett seems remarkably willing to put up with Tallis's tendency to bring stray assets home. Or he was, until now.

"They won't ignore that he's escaped, you know. Especially if the rumors are true." Barrett is standing with his arms crossed over his chest, and his irritated-concerned-calculating beats steadily against Bastian's already frayed shield.

"What rumors?" Bastian asks innocently. He rubs his temples, even though he knows it won't help. What he really needs is to ask Irene for more painkillers, but she's (rightly) busy looking after Henry in the makeshift clinic they're standing in front of. It's really just a battered hotel room like all the rest, except this one is stocked with first aid supplies and a few other odds and ends meant to help patch up anyone who comes through needing it.

Barrett frowns. "Don't play dumb. He's not just any asset, is he? That's why they had him locked up there."

"They've locked up plenty of people in plenty of places. That doesn't mean—"

"Not many assets get that level of special treatment. They were real keen on shooting at us, remember? You think we spent all day hiding out in the city afterward just for fun? If they'd followed us back here, it would've been a complete shitshow. And you had Tallis go in and—"

"He didn't 'have Tallis' do anything," Tallis says firmly. "I made my choice, Al. Lucas has done his part to keep the compound forces off our backs since he got here. It's not unreasonable for him to ask for a favor."

"Some favor," Barrett mutters. Then he shakes his head. "Look, I'm not interested in being up in anyone's business. But this place is supposed to make it easier for assets to escape the Compound Network. You're a big enough security risk on your own, Lucas. The girl makes it worse. And Mortimer potentially makes *worse* worse."

"So, what? You want us out of here?" It would be a completely reasonable, if frustrating, command. Bastian has known from the moment he first arrived that he has to stay on Barrett's good side for as long as possible. He figured that would get him as far as Henry's rescue, but probably not much further.

After a long pause, Barrett sighs. "So long as you don't bring compound forces down on us, I'll allow it. But the minute you mess things up for anyone here . . ."

Tallis tips her head to one side, listening to her comm. "New group of assets just arrived."

Even as tired and battered as he's feeling, Bastian still picks up on the approaching emotional signatures. First, there are two assets, a little younger than Bastian, giving off mostly weary-tense-afraid. They look up as they get closer, shoulders going rigid despite the reassurances of the older man showing them to their room. He gives Tallis a brief nod in greeting.

Then there's the third guy in their group, a dark-haired man with pale skin and a charismatic, double-edged grin. The grin gets a bit wider when he sees Bastian, though it's at odds with his disdainful-wary-calculating. And something else: an underlying anger that's threatening to break through and consume everything around it.

Just what you want from a firestarter.

"Hey," James says, pausing while the others go ahead. "Didn't expect to see you here."

"Didn't expect to see *you* at all," Bastian replies, trying to decide how much it would hurt to do a deeper read. "I guess this answers the question of whether or not you're dead."

"You two know each other?" Tallis asks. She sounds like she can't decide if that's a good thing or a bad thing, and honestly, Bastian feels about the same. Laurel will be glad to know James survived the compound fire, of course, but Bastian isn't so sure. Either way, answering Tallis with the truth—that this is the guy who burned down two compounds—might cause more of a hallway disruption than anyone can handle at the moment.

James smiles at Tallis. "Something like that." He sounds friendly enough, but Bastian can't get a handle on his real emotional state. He's never been able to read James well, in part because James has been sucked dry of his emotional energy at least once by a psychotic, practically immortal empath, and it seems to have messed up his brain chemistry. That said, he doesn't feel dangerous at the moment—he just has the usual air of slight instability that sets Bastian's teeth on edge.

Of course, if Bastian brings that up, he'll sound paranoid. Or else Tallis and Barrett will take him at his word and demand a *lot* more information, which could cause trouble, too. And the last thing Henry needs at the moment is more trouble.

Tallis looks between them. "Is this going to be a problem?"

"Nope," Bastian and James say in unison.

Barrett grunts and pushes away from the wall he was leaning against. "Let's get everyone else set for the night, Tallis. I think we could all use some rest."

"Isn't this where your healer is?" James nods toward the clinic door. "Think I'll wait a bit, if that's all right."

Tallis frowns. "Are you hurt?"

"Nothing serious; just a few scrapes. But I figure the healer will have the best stash of bandages."

Tallis glances at Bastian, but he doesn't give her anything in return for it, so she shrugs and moves down the hall with Barrett.

"How did you get here?" Bastian demands as soon as they're gone.

"Wandered around for a bit after—you know. Some of Tallis's group picked me up just outside the city. Quite a coincidence, isn't it?"

Bastian doesn't like the way James is looking at him, like Bastian is a curiosity, a weak specimen to observe and judge and find lacking. "Do I need to be concerned about the possibility of you burning this place down?" Bastian asks.

A shadow of an expression flits across James's face, too fast to read. Then he breaks into a languid grin. "I can say with one hundred percent confidence that that's not going to be a problem. Congrats on getting out, by the way. How many people did you leave behind?"

Bastian ignores the dig. "Have you told Laurel that you're still alive?"

"How would I have been able to do that?"

"The same way you escaped a burning compound? The same way you got so close to the city without being caught?"

"What, luck?"

"All right, let's try another one: Why are you here?"

James laughs. "Still doing the interrogator thing? I don't see how that's going to help without a compound to back you up. Unless that's part of the deal. A super special asset escaping once is one thing, but twice, especially after everything you've done to mess that place up? Sounds suspicious."

"An asset who's died twice and not had it stick could be considered suspicious, too. Incidentally, are you still working for Quentin?"

James smirks and waves toward the clinic door. "Your boyfriend is in there, isn't he? Have you told Barrett's people what he could do to them?"

There is absolutely no way James could know that. Which means the working-for-Quentin thing is a definite possibility. Although how *Quentin* would know . . .

James leans forward. "You don't have any ties to these people, do you? And you've done enough damage to assets everywhere with your little stint as an asset program director. So, I'll tell you what, Lucas: You stay out of my way, and I'll stay out of yours."

The hell of it is, it's not a bad deal at the moment. At least, it's not a deal Bastian can afford to pass up. Not when Henry needs the time and resources to recover, and Angelica needs the safety of a group of powerful assets who know how to lie low. Until Barrett gets annoyed enough to kick them out, this is their best shot at staying safe and cared for in the city. And Barrett is a lot more likely to get annoyed a lot more quickly if Bastian picks a fight with a new arrival who hasn't done anything wrong. Yet.

Apparently unconcerned with Bastian's stony silence, James steps back and eyes the still-closed door to Irene's clinic. "You know what? I think I'll check in with the healer later. See you."

He gives a little wave, sticks his hands in his pockets, and wanders off down the hall.

Chapter 9

"MARIGOLDS LIKE TO think of themselves as pretty tough," Laurel says to Dr. Rowe. "That's because they *are* pretty tough, and they won't let you forget it. But if you want to get that area on the south side of the compound grounds growing again, they might be willing to help out."

Dr. Rowe flicks a glance over Laurel's shoulder before nodding. "That makes sense. Do you think we have any seeds left in our supply? I'm told our inventory software is doing an update right now, so we can't check."

"I can take her to storage," says a familiar voice. Normally, Laurel would be quite impressed that its owner is volunteering for something, given that black coats generally aren't great volunteers. But then, Kwan knew what he was getting into.

It hasn't escaped her notice that Kwan has been . . . *around* a little more since Bastian left. Apparently, he's taking his promise to look after everyone quite seriously.

Laurel would like to pretend it's unnecessary, but she'd have to pretend quite a lot if she wanted to convince herself that it doesn't help to have a black coat on her side. She suspects that Kwan's attention is the only thing keeping her safe from cranky officers in the halls who are more eager than ever to punish assets for any perceived infraction. It's been a concerningly long time since she's seen Gabe, and more assets than she'd like to count have been disappearing. No one official is saying why, but there are whispers about experiments on the lower levels that General Carter himself sanctioned. And given what Laurel and Kwan overheard in the Level 25 experimentation room, that sounds entirely plausible.

Anyway, Laurel's lucky that Kwan was one of the black coats assigned to oversee the cafeteria earlier today—so lucky, in fact, that she suspects it had nothing to do with luck. Either way, it made it possible to conspire without looking like they were conspiring. Although someone really *should* conspire to get them better lunch options. If they'd just let her explain things to the lettuce before they picked it . . .

"Why do you want to go back to the storage room?" Kwan asked her. "Med bay can't be out of supplies already."

"Well, for one thing, the herb catalog needs updating. Also, the . . . situation from before hasn't changed, has it? Which means we should find out as much as we can." She stopped herself from being too specific, just in case one of the cafeteria staff decided to listen in.

Kwan hesitated, although there wasn't anything to hesitate about because Laurel was obviously right. Even if she wasn't being one hundred percent honest with her answer. She *did* want to find out more about the dead zones. But more specifically, she wanted to finish an interrupted conversation.

"All right," Kwan said, sighing. "I'll meet you down there after your session with Dr. Rowe."

Laurel grinned and patted his arm. "You're the best black coat in the whole compound."

"So I'm told."

And he might be told again, now that he's shown up as promised, at just the right time to herd her out of med bay and over to the second storage room.

Because she's looking for it—and maybe because her negation serum level is a little lower, given that she's close to the end of one dose and the beginning of another—she can feel the increasing pressure of the dead zone as she gets closer. She's struck again by the uncomfortable sense that her natural connection to the surrounding plants has been cut with aggressive gardening shears, leaving a barren area that just feels *off*. To be entering a place where even the possibility of speaking to a plant is gone—wiped away like it never existed—makes her skin crawl.

Who is making these dead zones, and why?

Kwan closes the storage room door carefully behind them. "Okay, now what?"

"Now, I need to try something," Laurel says in her most cheerful, trustworthy voice. "I'll just take the jammer, and you can be the lookout. It'll be an adventure!"

Kwan narrows his eyes. "I'm not the adventurous type."

"Okay, *you* can be the fuddy-duddy, and *I* can have an adventure." When he continues to look unimpressed—and disinclined to hand over the jammer—Laurel sighs and adds, "I want to keep trying my power in different parts of the dead zone. It probably won't work, but I don't want anyone to know if it does. And I should check on those marigold seeds, too."

"You don't actually need it," Kwan says.

"Need what?"

"The jammer."

"Well, I don't want any of this, er, very-not-at-all-bad thing I'm about to do to get caught on the security cameras because I'm very shy, so—"

"The cameras don't work in dead zones."

"Oh. Wait, *what*? You're just telling me this *now*? After all the excellent sneaking around we've been doing?"

Kwan sighs and runs a hand through his hair. "I only found out today when I talked to Turner and Tassos in hacker HQ during our security meeting. They must have just figured it out. Which means they've been helping with the investigation, even though we told them not to."

That does sound like Kent and Sybil. It also sounds like something worth a serious chewing out. But Laurel doesn't have time to plan the details of said chewing right now, because Kwan is pulling the jammer out of his pocket and tossing it to her. "We should still be careful."

Laurel looks down at the screen and sees that the timer is already going. "But you just said—"

"Insurance. You have fifteen minutes to do whatever it is you want to do in here. Then I'm going to ask you about it, and you're going to fill me in."

Laurel doesn't much like his tone, but she also doesn't much like the pinprick of guilt she's feeling for keeping him in the dark. All he's done is try to help, despite being in a dangerous position himself. If Major Tremain finds out what he's doing . . .

(Unless she already knows, and this is some elaborate plot to catch them trying to escape or use their powers when they shouldn't be able to, and maybe she's just being stupid because her friends at her old compound always said not to trust officers or black coats or med techs because they only cared about using assets until they dried up and stop being useful, and then—)

Laurel nods. Then she spins on her heel and hurries into the depths of the stacks, jammer held tightly in her hand.

She's not entirely sure why she wants to be alone when she tries to contact Quentin. Maybe because she doesn't want eyes on her while she uses a power that isn't really hers to use. Or maybe it's just the general icky feeling she gets when she thinks about how *very firm* Bastian was when he said he didn't want to talk about Quentin. The healer who supposedly healed him.

Except Bastian didn't *act* like he was healed. Not for long. And it makes no sense that he'd be so negative toward someone who supposedly saved his life. Well, it's Bastian, so maybe he *would* be negative toward someone who supposedly saved his life. It still seems off, though, even for someone whose default setting is "prickly hawthorn who would like you to go away now or else."

Anyway, this is supposed to be an information-gathering adventure, isn't it? Better get on with information gathering.

Laurel takes a deep breath and lets it out slowly. Then she pushes past as much of the remaining negation as she can and reaches out to the plant in Dr. Rowe's office. It isn't pleased about helping her strengthen the signal, but it doesn't protest a little hug. Once that's done, she closes her eyes and focuses on the echo of the empath link left in her brain. "Um . . . hello?"

There's nothing at first, and Laurel isn't sure if that's because she's no good at this or if Quentin is just busy on another line or something.

With Bastian, it's sometimes a bit awkward—she suspects reaching into someone's mind always is—but it generally feels more comfortable, like she's just knocking on a friend's door and asking to come in for a bit.

(She wishes she were doing that now, wishes she'd had any sort of response from Bastian through their link since she started trying again in moments when it felt safe, but he's not answering, and it doesn't *have* to mean anything, but what if it does, what if—?)

This link feels different. Ill-fitting and out of place, like she's inserted herself somewhere she isn't welcome. Her instinct is to back off, but she doesn't have that luxury right now. Not if she wants to figure out who this guy is and why he contacted her.

She's just started considering what the empath link equivalent of a poke in the ribs might be when she realizes there's a presence on the other end of the line after all. *Well*, Quentin says. *That was faster than I expected. Hello, Laurel.*

She feels an odd edge to it, like he's pleased and surprised but also . . . mocking. Like he didn't expect her to be able to pull it off. Well, he doesn't really know her, does he? Rookie mistake to assume she can't get things done.

"I don't have a lot of time," she says briskly, "so let's get to it. You said you could help. Prove it."

Would you like to get out of the compound?

Laurel frowns. "Is that a trick question? Because if it is, it's very tricky, so I can only give you an honest answer. Is that what you want?"

She feels a gentle amusement through the link, along with . . . something else. *Honesty is always what I want.*

Maybe it's just because they aren't face to face, but it feels like Quentin's words never quite mean what they're supposed to mean. Bastian might not have gone into detail, but Laurel knows this guy upset him in some way. Not at all what you'd expect a healer to do, really. Which means Laurel needs to be on her guard even if it turns out that he *can* help.

"Yes," she says, desperation seeping through despite her best efforts to hold it back. "I'd like to get out of *any* compound, honestly. Unless maybe it's one Henry's running. But he's not running any of them right now, and he didn't really get to run this one properly even when people told him to. So, the honest answer is yes, I'd like to get out of here."

She can feel enough confusion on the line to know that he didn't quite get all of that, but then, most people can't keep up with Laurel, so that's nothing new. *I see. In that case, I think we can work together.*

"How?"

I have some friends coming your way, and I'd like you to help them.

"I have very stringent guidelines on friends," Laurel says.

They're friends of James's, too.

Laurel's pulse quickens. She knew there was a connection between this healer and James, but . . . "Not a good endorsement."

Oh, Quentin says, and his voice is suddenly flooded with concern and sympathy. *You don't know, do you? James is alive. He would be coming, too.*

Laurel's heart is running a marathon. Of course she's glad James is alive—assuming Quentin isn't lying—but also . . . well, can he really still be considered a friend, after trying to burn down this compound and kill everyone in it? After his actions led to even harsher crackdowns and more assets disappearing than ever?

(Xavier always said they should do whatever it took, but Xavier is dead, the rest of them are all dead, even the officer Laurel had only intended to put to sleep, but the tincture she and the plants made at James's request was much stronger than she meant it to be, and she was actually poisoning that woman—a horrible woman, but still—and none of it mattered in the end because they all still—)

I've asked James to do me a favor, Quentin says. *Not unlike I'm asking you. Because I know you can both make difficult decisions for the good of everyone.*

"Like the one James made that led to lots of people suffering and dying?" Laurel asks, her chest feeling hot and tight.

Ah. Genuine sadness and grief come through. *What you've suffered—what we all have suffered—it never should have happened. I hate that it has. But I think we've all seen that working within the system isn't going to solve anything. In fact, it just leads to more suffering. Don't you think?*

It's a dig at Henry's attempt to turn the compound around, and Laurel wants to call out the rudeness, except . . . well, Quentin is right, isn't he? Because as much as Henry was trying to help—and as much as she and Bastian were trying to help him help—it didn't work, did it? Because here they all are.

Take some time to think about it, Quentin says. *Talking should be safe in the dead zones, but—*

"How do you know about the dead zones?" Laurel demands.

The quiet amusement is back. *I know a lot about the compounds. Didn't Bastian tell you?*

"No," Laurel says, and for the briefest moment, she's annoyed with herself for not prying. "He didn't want to talk about you, so we didn't. Which means I don't know if I can trust you."

Hmm. I'm sorry he wasn't ready to share what he learned from me. I suppose it takes longer for some people to accept help when it's offered.

"That's a lot of nice words that don't actually explain why I should trust you. I mean, I'm impressed, but not really swayed. In case you couldn't tell through the link."

His amusement grows an outer shell of . . . annoyance? Long-suffering indulgence? Maybe some concern and a desire to placate? Laurel *really* isn't good at the nuances of this empath link thing. Maybe it's easier when you're an emotionally constipated empath, despite the irony. Or maybe Quentin is just good at presenting a confusing, carefully curated set of emotions through the link.

I was at your compound a very, very long time ago, Quentin says. *I barely escaped. Before I did, I learned a lot about what the Compound Network is planning. The experiments with the negation serum. The attempts to make an artificial empath. It was mostly theory in my day, but now they're acting. Which means we need to act, too.*

Laurel considers. Chloe hasn't been very open about her trip with Bastian and James to find Quentin, either. But she did say that they were pretty sure Quentin created the dead zone they found in the forest in order to protect his sanctuary for escaped assets.

I believe in doing whatever it takes to keep assets safe, Quentin says. *I protect the people who come to me for help. And if we work together, I'll be able to protect the people who need my help but can't make it to the sanctuary. Will you help me, Laurel?*

When she doesn't answer right away, he sends her the equivalent of an understanding nod. *Think about it. Let's speak again soon, and in the meantime, please be careful.*

"Wait—"

But she can feel that he's already left her mind.

Chapter 10

BASTIAN LOSES TRACK of how long he stands there in the hallway after James leaves, trying to distract himself by rebuilding and refortifying his shield. Focusing on that means he can mostly ignore the exhaustion-pain-fear lingering in this part of the hotel. Injured assets pass through fairly frequently, and while Irene's enhanced healing skills can patch people up quickly, the emotions that settle here are stronger than those in other parts of the hotel.

Bastian is a little surprised he's still on his feet, and not just because of the botched rescue and his overuse of his power. He, Henry, Tallis, Barrett, and the other assets on Tallis's team spent most of the day wandering through the city, trying to make sure none of the officers from the safe house or any other compound force were following them. Tallis took care of the security footage from the safe house before they made a break for it, and Barrett's sand screen got them out before their identities could be tracked. But that doesn't change the fact that they just broke a very top secret asset out of a very top secret location. Barrett has every right to be concerned about what that will mean for the hotel, which is the best-kept secret for assets moving through the city. Bastian is very aware of how he might've jeopardized that today.

He's also very aware that he'd do it again in a heartbeat if it meant getting Henry out of there.

The door to Irene's room opens, and Bastian straightens up and turns toward her. She brushes back wisps of reddish-brown hair and gets right down to business. "I've healed his injuries—they were all fairly minor. He's extremely dehydrated, and he probably hasn't been eating enough. But physically, he's stable."

Bastian can practically feel the weight of her hesitation. "And?"

"He's . . . not well," Irene says, lowering her voice. "But whatever's left is something I can't heal."

Bastian goes cold. The bruises on Henry's wrists (How long was he cuffed to that bed?), the way he shrank back when Bastian got close, the dull and incessant undercurrent of anxiety-fear-loathing throughout the escape . . . it makes Bastian's skin crawl, remembering the *wrongness* of it. He wants to find whoever did this and—

"He was obviously deeply affected by what happened," Irene continues. "I think you should get him to talk about it, when he's ready. Or find him someone he can talk to. Or both."

She smiles apologetically. "I can only heal the physical, and sometimes not even that, depending on the injury. Especially with the limited supplies here. But I've done the best I can. Right now, I think you can help him more than I can."

Bastian is about to explain that leaving someone's mental health in his care is a horrible idea, but there's suddenly a spike of uneasiness-fear-panic in a familiar signature coming from the room. Without thinking, Bastian shoves past Irene and into the clinic.

Henry is sitting in a ratty but clean armchair that might have been an ugly green before time washed it out to a dull gray. He's clearly used the en suite bathroom to clean up, and someone's given him a mismatched t-shirt and jeans to replace the regulation nightmare he had on before. His hands are clean of scrapes and resting carefully on the armrests. There's an IV next to him, the tube snaking into his right arm—for the dehydration, Bastian assumes.

He doesn't *seem* like he's in distress. If anything, he looks a lot better than he did earlier. But he's also been trained to function under extreme pressure. The compound expects nothing less of its officers, and he was one of their best.

Henry looks up when Bastian enters, giving off another tiny jolt of panic that hits Bastian squarely in the chest despite his newly reinforced shield.

"What's wrong?" Henry asks. He sounds calm enough, maybe a little tired. Completely unaware of how ludicrous it is for *him* to be asking that right now, when he's the one who's been through . . . whatever he's been through.

Bastian glances around the room, though he doesn't really need to. It's empty, other than them—and Irene, who brushes past Bastian, eyebrows raised. Even if there were someone else in the room, it wouldn't matter. Bastian knows Henry's emotional signature almost as well as his own.

"Are you all right?" Bastian asks. It's a stupid thing to say, but he can't shake the feeling that something is off.

Henry's smile doesn't reach his eyes. "All things considered? Yeah, I'm great."

Bastian turns questioningly to Irene, who shrugs. "I'd like to keep him on fluids for a little longer, but—"

There. A slight tension in Henry's arm when she mentions the IV. A brief clench of his jaw, so fast Bastian might have imagined it. But he *didn't.* He can feel panic in the slight muscle shifts Henry tries to hide. Bastian might have missed it with someone whose emotional signature wasn't so familiar. Henry isn't negating so much as carefully subduing any emotional response to what's happening around him. Why?

"Is he stable enough to go now?" Bastian asks. He doesn't miss the flicker of relief-hope-embarrassment that gets from Henry.

Irene looks at her patient appraisingly. "Yes, if I speed up the fluids a bit."

Bastian isn't sure what she means by that, until she gently touches Henry's arm, and the IV fluids start to drain faster.

"It's okay," Henry says, his voice a little strained. "You don't have to—"

"Done?" Bastian asks.

Irene nods and steps back to carefully remove the needle. "Get some rest, both of you. And Henry, come see me tomorrow, all right? Just a quick check-in to make sure everything took."

"Sure. And thanks." His tone is pleasant and even, but he stumbles slightly when he gets to his feet. It's so quick, Bastian doesn't even have time to react. Still, Henry makes it to the door without any trouble.

The lights in the hallway buzz and flicker—they're coming to the end of the generators' power for the day. Keeping the hotel running, even at a bare-bones level, while staying off the city power grid isn't easy. Barrett has a system in place that involves using the power of assets coming through, along with a complicated network of supply caches and hidden meetups. All designed to keep assets moving through the city without being caught.

"What was that about, with Irene?" Henry asks. "And where are we going?"

Bastian ignores those questions for now in favor of a more important one: "How do you know Barrett?"

Henry pauses, then lets out a sound that's part rueful laugh, part exhausted sigh. "The guy who saved our asses? My team brought him in to the compound, back when I was a retrieval officer."

Bastian doesn't remember seeing Barrett on the asset roster during his time as head of the asset program, but then, Bastian was never great at staying on top of paperwork. "Huh. I guess that explains why he's not your number one fan."

The hotel isn't using key cards anymore—a waste of electricity, according to Tallis—so once they get there, Bastian only has to turn the handle and push open the door of his room. Henry follows, catching the door and letting it close gently behind them.

The ugly maroon curtains are drawn; official best practice at the hotel is to cover all windows in case of overly curious passersby. The rest of the room is made up of dust, thin carpet, a ragged armchair, and a bed. The bathroom is serviceable, but it depends on the day and which assets, if any, are keeping the plumbing going.

Bastian tries the switch for the overhead light, and it comes on with a reluctant buzz, casting the room in a hazy, plastic glow. The generators aren't completely done, then.

"Okay," Henry says, crossing his arms over his chest. "Are you going to tell me what that was about at Irene's?"

"Why didn't you tell her not to do the IV?"

Henry gives him a perplexed look. "I'm not a doctor. I don't know what calls to make about medical treatment."

"You know *you*. She would have stopped if you asked her to." Bastian has a sudden thought. "She offered, didn't she? And you said it was fine."

"Because it *was* fine."

"Was it? You didn't feel like it was."

"Don't tell me what I—" Henry stops. "You read me."

Shit. The accusatory tone squeezes tight around Bastian's chest. "I didn't mean—Look, I'm not trying to tell you what you're feeling, except . . . Okay, I guess I am, but not like—" Ugh. Might as well give him a shovel so he can keep digging himself a nice, big hole. Why is he so *bad* at this, especially when he needs *not* to be?

Bastian clears his throat and tries again. "I just . . . I could tell you were upset. *Really* upset. And you were sitting there like there was nothing you could do about it. And I didn't want . . ."

Henry's mouth forms a tight, thin line. His shield has an added layer of negation around it now, like he's shoring up for battle.

Bastian doesn't know how to explain that he doesn't have to fight alone anymore.

"Forget it," he says instead. "Let's just get some rest, okay? It's been a long day."

"You're right," Henry says very quietly, not looking at him. "I was upset, but—it doesn't feel like it used to. Nothing feels quite like it used to. It was okay when we were escaping because I had to focus on that, but when she brought out the IV, it reminded me of the way they . . . If I have the time to think too much, I can't . . ."

He goes silent for long enough that Bastian risks reaching out and touching his arm. "It's okay. We don't have to talk about it right n—"

His gloves do absolutely nothing to prevent the sudden slap in the face of Henry's negation. It comes out of nowhere, so much stronger than anything Bastian has ever felt from him. A blaring white noise that makes it impossible for Bastian to think about anything else. He isn't sure he ever needed to know what a bug feels like when it hits a windshield, but he's pretty sure it's something like this.

Henry blinks rapidly several times, and then the negation is gone, sucked away so quickly, Bastian loses his balance and stumbles away from it. Henry, on the other hand, looks horrified (horrified-startled-embarrassed—no, not embarrassed; ashamed). "Shit, sorry, I—"

Bastian shakes his head and wills his heartbeat to calm down. "No, don't worry about it. I shouldn't have pushed. What *was* that?"

"I don't . . ." Henry swallows and looks anywhere but at Bastian. "I don't know. Sometimes when they made me—I couldn't always control it. If it got too bad, they'd make sure I was drugged. Because I was only supposed to hurt people when they wanted me to."

"Henry," Bastian says quietly.

"They—they figured out that I could do it. Negate people. Take their power away permanently. So they brought me to Council HQ and had me do it to whoever they told me to, or else they'd—" He clamps his mouth shut for a moment, like he's trying to stem the tide of words, but the tide gets the better of him. "I *took* something from those assets, some intrinsic part of who they are, and then—I don't know if they survived or if they're dead or—"

His hands are shaking, and Bastian can't prevent himself from flinching at the burst of anxious-panicked-frustrated-tense-ashamed. The last one is so bad, it makes Bastian queasy. He can't imagine what it's doing to Henry.

(He should have been faster, he should have found a way to get to Henry sooner, he should have put together a better escape, just like he should know what to say now that will help instead of making everything worse—)

Bastian goes over and sits on the bed, leaving plenty of space beside him. "Come sit down?"

Henry's shoulders are stiff, his hands clenched into fists, and the shaking is all over now, despite the way he's clearly fighting to hide it. Bastian desperately tries to remember Dr. Rowe's instructions for dealing with panic attacks. "Breathe," he says, keeping it more of a gentle suggestion than an order. "Slow breaths. And maybe come sit down?"

Henry stands by the door for another few moments, eyes boring holes into the cheap carpet. Then he comes over to the bed and sits down.

"It's okay," Bastian says, even though this seems like the exact opposite of okay. "Just keep breathing, nice and slow."

Henry makes a choked noise. "I can't—"

"Yes, you can. I'll do it with you, all right?"

They sit on the bed in silence for long enough that the overhead light begins to dim, the generator losing power for the night. The buzzing fades, and after a while, the only light is what comes through the slight gap in the curtains, a faint wash of watery yellow from a streetlight in the parking lot. The dimness actually seems to help a little: Henry focuses on taking one shuddering breath after another, and Bastian silently breathes with him.

He wants to know what the hell is going on, but he also thinks he knows, more or less. He's had panic attacks of his own over the years, thanks to the compound experiments. He doesn't know exactly what Henry has been through, although he can gather enough. It's laughable to think that Bastian could be there for Henry the way Henry has been for him. But . . .

"Keep breathing," Bastian says quietly, resting his hand, palm up, between them. Just in case.

Henry doesn't look at him, but he clearly sees the movement out of the corner of his eye. He shifts his weight slightly in Bastian's direction. "I don't think I can negate enough right now, or—or I might negate too much. I don't want to hurt you."

"You won't," Bastian assures him. "But it's fine either way."

He has a sudden memory of watching a compound staff member say the same thing to Angelica. Wondering if that's what it might look like to treat assets with respect and kindness. To offer help without expecting anything in return.

Henry stares at Bastian's hand for a moment. Then he carefully puts his on top of it.

"Keep breathing," Bastian says again, lacing their fingers together.

They sit next to each other in the semidarkness for a long time, doing just that.

Chapter 11

HENRY KNOWS HE looks like shit. Bags under his eyes, old bruises near his temples, a healing cut near his left eyebrow that he doesn't remember getting during the escape. Irene probably would've preferred that he stay longer in the clinic, but he was having trouble sitting still, even before Bastian came in. And given the complete meltdown he had as soon as they got back to the room . . . maybe it's just as well that he left before things got worse.

He grimaces at himself in the dirty mirror and wonders how long he's had this much gray in his hair.

Henry's brain doesn't seem to care that he's safe for the first time in months. That Bastian is asleep in the next room, where even the dark can't hide the fact that he's there and breathing and close enough that Henry can check as often as he needs to in order to reassure himself that this isn't a dream.

He wants to be lying next to Bastian on that uncomfortably soft bed, drifting off to the sound of his occasional mumbles, looking forward to waking up with Bastian curled up against him like a standoffish cat—one that always succumbs to the opportunity for warmth, even when it pretends it's not interested.

But instead, here he is, staring at himself in a dingy bathroom mirror, too wired to sleep.

He refuses to let his eyes linger on his haggard reflection. Instead, he takes a chance on the faucet. Miraculously, the plumbing cooperates, and he splashes cold water on his face.

He turns off the tap with one hand and uses the other to reach for a towel—only to find that there isn't one hanging next to the sink. This suddenly seems like the worst thing that could ever happen, and his throat tightens. Even as part of his brain tells him to stop overreacting, his hands start to shake.

"Here."

Bastian is standing next to him, passing a towel into his hand. His voice is neutral, and he doesn't touch Henry. Not standing too close, but also not going anywhere. Somehow, that makes it both better and worse.

Henry takes his time wiping the water off of his face so he won't have to say anything. When he finally sets the towel down, he carefully keeps his eyes off of the mirror.

"Sleep?" Bastian asks.

Henry realizes he has no idea what time it is. "I don't . . . no. I think I need to walk around a bit."

Bastian nods. "Keeping to the lobby and the hallways would be safest, but if you need to go outside—"

"You'd better show me."

Bastian hesitates, then asks, "Are you sure? I thought you might want to be alone."

Henry doesn't know what his emotions are doing right now, but somewhere in there is probably the desire to have as few people as possible see him like this. It's muddled underneath so much other shit, though, that he can't keep it all straight. It must be putting Bastian on edge. It's certainly putting *him* on edge.

But he was alone for more than half a year in that horrible place, and now—

"I want"—to forget what happened, to fix everything, to make it stop hurting, to not be so pathetic—"to go for a walk. With you. At whatever time of night it is right now. Preferably without anyone trying to kill us."

Bastian gives him a small smile. The real one: slightly awkward but also much gentler than you'd expect if you didn't know him. For the first time in ages, something in Henry's chest relaxes ever so slightly.

"Okay," Bastian says.

***

They err on the side of caution and stay inside, wandering the dimly lit halls and occasionally talking in hushed voices. The silences might be awkward with anyone else, but they feel soothing with Bastian.

"This hotel has ten floors," Bastian tells him, "but the generators can't handle that much electricity for long, and there usually aren't that many assets staying here all at one time, anyway. So, Barrett tends to only keep the main floor and maybe two or three others going. Plus a bit of light in the main hallways so people don't bump into things if they move around at night."

Henry notices a figure standing near the emergency exit at the end of the hall. "And by 'people,' you mean the guards at the doors?"

"Yeah, well. Everyone's a bit punchy since the nearest compound burned down, and new management took over. And the Compound Network has become more active in the city, looking for ways to track down wayward assets. So."

Henry wants to ask about the compound and how on earth Bastian escaped. And . . . "You haven't said anything about Laurel."

There's a visible stumble in Bastian's step, almost hidden in the low light, but not quite. "I had to leave her behind."

Henry's stomach drops. "I'm sorry."

"She was fine when I . . . left. I told her I didn't want to go without her, but a chance came up unexpectedly, and it was the only way to—" He eyes Henry. "Are you sure you want to talk about this right now?"

No. Yes. "Only if you want to."

Bastian sticks his hands in his pockets. "She overheard about the safe house, and we weren't sure when—or if—you'd be transferred away from it. Plus, I sort of, er, got into a bit of trouble and needed a quick exit. There wasn't really time to talk her out of doing it like this. You know how she is."

So, it's his fault. Again.

"It's not your fault," Bastian says.

Henry smiles wanly. "You said you weren't a mind reader."

"And I said you're easy to read, even without powers."

Bastian looks at the ugly paisley carpet as they walk in the direction of the main floor lobby. "Anyway, I don't know if you noticed, but we *did* manage to save you. So, Laurel was right about taking the chance."

He grimaces, then adds, "Don't tell her I said that."

Henry lets out a short laugh. At least Bastian is talking as if Laurel is alive and well, and they might meet up again at some point. Oddly optimistic of him, actually.

"Did I thank you for that?" Henry asks. "For saving me?"

Bastian shrugs. "Guess we're even now."

"Oh, are we keeping tally? Because strictly speaking, you've saved my ass twice since we met, and I've only saved yours once."

"Huh. I guess we'd better get into another life-and-death situation so you can save me and make it even. Although that sounds stupid, even to me."

Henry swallows the comment that nearly makes it past his filter: *You looked awful at the safe house, and you haven't said anything about it. Where does* that *stand on your stupidity scale?*

Instead, because he'd rather keep seeing the hint of amusement in Bastian's eyes, he says, "Let's avoid stupid and think of some other way I can pay you back."

The corner of Bastian's mouth twitches upward into something that's almost a smirk. "Let me know if you come up with any ideas."

Henry considers sharing a few but loses that train of thought when Bastian pauses just outside the lobby. "You should know something else. Angelica is here, too."

Henry stares at him. "You broke a *child* out of the compound?"

"I broke a child out of a compound transport convoy, and not on purpose. I mean, it *was* on purpose, but I didn't know she was going to be there. And it wasn't just me; Tallis helped."

There's such a petulant tone in his voice, like a little kid caught red-handed, that Henry almost laughs again. Here they are, standing in a run-down hotel with peeling wallpaper and dirty carpet, and there's nowhere else Henry would rather be.

Henry suddenly hears the loud click of a door opening behind them, but before he can fully turn around, something smacks into his legs: A small, thin girl with tawny skin and a long, dark braid has attached herself to him.

"Hello, Angelica," Henry says over his own surprise and the sound of a door falling shut—probably the one Angelica scurried through to reach them. He pats her head gently. "What are you doing up so late?"

"I heard Bastian being happy." Angelica looks around Henry's legs. "Is it time for cereal yet?"

"It's the middle of the night, and you're supposed to be asleep in Tallis's room," Bastian says sternly.

"Does that mean no cereal?"

"What do you mean, you heard Bastian?" Henry asks, mostly to stave off a loud hallway argument at whatever o'clock it is.

"His feelings are usually quiet, but then they weren't, and then I heard you talking, so it made sense." She peers over at Bastian with her dark eyes, stubbornly focused on the agenda. "Cereal tomorrow?"

"If you go back to bed without waking up Tallis," Bastian says, jerking his chin toward the hallway they just came from as if to shoo her away.

"Get some sleep," Henry adds.

Angelica looks up at him, then frowns, her hands tightening around him. "You remember when you couldn't sleep," she says, voice going monotone. "They got angry and brought out the needles because you couldn't, and they wanted you to because—"

"*Angelica*," Henry says, sharper than he meant to.

Her eyes clear, and she shakes her head and backs away. "Sorry, I know I'm not supposed to do it. I didn't mean to."

"It's . . . it's okay," Henry says, willing his clamoring heartbeat to slow down. "I just didn't want you to remember something scary."

"I remember lots of scary stuff," Angelica scoffs, "but it doesn't bother me because I'm very brave."

Considering that she's already weathered an escape from a burning compound—and now, apparently, a transport convoy—Henry is inclined to agree.

"Go on," Bastian says, voice gentler now, but still firm.

Angelica looks at him for a long moment. When Bastian looks back and says nothing, she finally sighs and nods. "Okay. Good night."

She turns on her heel and hurries back down the hall a few doors until she finds what is apparently the correct one. She opens it carefully and slips inside, making sure it closes quietly this time.

"Something's different about her," Henry says.

Bastian shakes his head. "She did something on that convoy that she shouldn't have been able to do."

"Which is?"

"She formed an empath link with me. That's how I realized she was there."

Henry knows Angelica is an exceptionally powerful memor—he reviewed her file back when he was leading the compound, and he's seen her read memories even before tonight. But memors and empaths have completely different powers, so there's no reason to think . . . unless . . . "Splicing? Like Laurel?"

Bastian shrugs. "I don't see how. There were only twenty-one assets involved in that experiment, and there's no record of her being one of them. There wasn't much record of her at all, from what I remember."

"So . . . empath link?"

"It's like a mental phone call, but you can feel emotions through it, too. And the connection stays open even when it's not in use, although it's stronger when both people are actively trying to communicate. Helps if you don't hate the other person, too."

Henry's mouth twitches. "So, if Angelica can feel your emotions even when you're not actively trying to communicate, she must not hate you."

"Don't know why," Bastian mutters.

"Oh, I don't know. Maybe because you saved her from that convoy? Or because you're the one who originally found her and looked after her? Or because you can bond over how horrible you both are at doing what you're told?"

Bastian makes a face. "Are you ready to go back to the room and get some sleep?"

Henry smothers a smile—and the uneasy feeling that he doesn't deserve one.

(Because while he's here giving the man he loves a hard time, other assets are suffering, and people like General Carter and his senator cronies are doing whatever they want, and the assets Henry hurt are—)

"Henry?"

He shakes himself inwardly. "Yeah, sorry. Let's go back."

They walk back to their room slowly, not making any attempt at conversation. After a moment, because Bastian has maneuvered himself into just the right position, Henry takes his hand, and the tension in Henry's chest slowly subsides. For now.

Chapter 12

"I DON'T THINK it's a good idea," Chloe says. Her hands are covered in dirt from the afternoon's planting, especially her fingertips, because Laurel has taught her how to use just the right amount of finesse when spacing the pepper plants. It's not really necessary, of course—Laurel could probably convince the peppers to grow straight even if they complained about having to share space—but it's better to have non-cranky peppers from the start. Especially once the stakes go in. Just because Laurel hasn't ever seen a pepper decide to use its stake as a weapon, doesn't mean it *couldn't*.

"Well," Laurel says, carefully setting another plant into its spot, "it's probably not a *good* idea, no. But do you think it'd work?"

Chloe frowns at the ground, hands stilled on either side of the plant she just put in, her face mostly hidden behind a curtain of dishwater blond hair. "I mean, I guess it *could* work." She lowers her voice even more. "Do you really think James is coming back? And if he is, do you really want to find a way to let him in?"

Laurel glances over at their black coat babysitter for the day: a very tired-looking, middle-aged man with thinning hair and a penchant for spacing out. Laurel suspects they have Kwan to thank for the assignment.

She had to tell Kwan *something* after her talk with Quentin. Not a lot; just that her power (she didn't specify which one) does seem to work sometimes in the dead zones, even with the serum, and she wants to keep exploring the possibilities.

And speaking of possibilities she wants to explore . . . "I don't *really* know if he's coming. I mean, not for sure. But if he *is*, we should have a plan, right?"

"He might be coming to hurt people," Chloe points out. Her voice is slightly tremulous but also firm, like a bamboo plant—delicate from far away, but tough up close.

"Yes," Laurel admits. Because she has to. He helped burn down the compound, after all. "But I don't think he'd be coming alone. And if his group can help, we have to at least consider it, don't we?"

Chloe gently picks up another plant from their box and sets it into another hole. "I'm not sure there *is* a safe path into the compound right now. There are too many people going in and out, and their routes always change. And even if we found a way, what if we got caught?"

It's a completely rational and understandable argument, but that doesn't make Laurel feel any more like accepting it. She'd be stupid not to, though, especially since she just saw yet another asset being dragged off to solitary on her way out here. She didn't recognize the man, and she has no idea what his power is, but she's pretty sure he didn't deserve the split lip and broken fingers.

Getting caught trying to sneak an outside asset into the compound would probably net them an equally bad punishment. Or a worse one.

"I suppose you're right," she says to Chloe with a sigh. "We can't afford to do anything except make sure these peppers get planted, I guess. Can you go do the row over there, now that we're done being conspiratorial?"

Chloe gives Laurel an inscrutable look, then gets to her feet, brushing the dirt off of her hands, and goes to work on the other side.

Laurel sighs again, then makes a face at the pepper she just planted. "You don't have to look at me like that. It's just . . ."

She hasn't forgiven James, and she's not sure what she would say to him if she saw him again. But he was (is?) her friend, and if he comes here like Quentin suggested he might, he'll be walking into a much more dangerous situation than what he's probably expecting. If she doesn't do anything to warn him . . .

"Hurry up," says a sharp voice. The black coat is staring down at her, arms crossed over his chest. He looks much less vague and bored now, which sends little pinpricks of fear over Laurel's skin. Did he hear something after all?

"The peppers don't like to be hurried," Laurel explains. "You may not know that if you don't have a lot of pepper friends, but—"

"And I don't like an asset who can't stay on schedule," the black coat says. "Your next experiment is in half an hour. Finish up here so we can get going."

Laurel glances at Chloe, who is watching them with growing alarm. Keeping her shoulders that close to her ears doesn't look comfortable, so Laurel gives her a small, reassuring smile. Then she turns back to the black coat with a broader, far less genuine one. "Okay. But if the peppers get grumpy, that's on you."

The blow comes out of nowhere, sharp and metallic against the side of her head, and suddenly her face is in the dirt, right next to the pepper she was planting. Pain reverberates through her skull, nearly drowning out the mental yelp from the pepper plant. From somewhere far away, Chloe gasps.

The black coat crouches down as Laurel struggles to sit up, one hand clamped over her burning ear. "Don't forget how replaceable you are," he says, voice low and menacing. "Plantspeakers are easy enough to come by. We're not supposed to kill you, but that doesn't mean we have to let you talk back. Keep your mouth shut, show some respect, and follow the schedule."

Laurel's eyes sting—almost as much as the side of her head—as she watches him holster his gun and just stand there, like he doesn't trust her to finish her job without supervision.

(And he shouldn't trust her because even though she doesn't have full control over her power right now, she could still try to ask any plant in this entire garden, the garden *she* built, to help her—the bushes could attack him with their thorns, or the trees could bash his head in with their biggest branches, or—)

"Laurel?" Chloe is leaning over the row, her voice saturated with fear. "Are you okay? Should I get a med tech?"

"Keep working," the black coat says, making Chloe flinch.

Laurel takes a deep breath and checks her hand: no blood, just that pulsing pain and tenderness. He only hit her hard enough to startle. And bruise, probably.

"Let's finish these rows," Laurel says. "Just to keep rude people happy."

She puts her hands back into the dirt and hears the nearest pepper's roots relaying a calming message of solidarity, apparently alerted by her distress and sudden movements. She sends back a careful thank-you with a small flick of her fingers that she hopes the black coat can't see. Not that he'd understand it if he did.

Laurel doesn't know if James or Quentin are the answer to this problem, but one thing's for sure: She can't let things keep going as they have been. It's time for another secret mission, even if she has to do it alone.

She just wishes she had someone to exchange a secret handshake with.

Chapter 13

THERE'S A KNOCK on their door at a time that feels far too early for door-knocking. Not that it matters much; Henry and Bastian are already awake.

Henry did manage to get a few snatches of sleep last night, especially after Bastian curled up against his chest, breathing steadily enough that Henry was able to drift off to the rhythm of it.

By now, though, he's been awake for about an hour, quietly pacing and daydreaming about coffee. He'd like to think he hasn't kept Bastian awake, but he's not sure. When Henry woke up, Bastian was sitting silently in the ratty armchair, occasionally rubbing his temples.

When they hear the knock, they both look at the door, then at each other. Bastian sighs and goes over to open it.

"Cereal," Angelica says without preamble.

"Good morning to you, too. Does Tallis know you're here?"

"She says it's your job to get me cereal."

"Did she actually say that, or are you just saying she did so I'll get you cereal?"

"She said the supplies are almost gone, so I should get some soon, and then she said you would get me some because she was going back to sleep, and then I asked you the secret way, and you didn't say no, so I came over because I'm supposed to be sleeping here anyway, only you told me to stay with Tallis for a while because—"

She glances at Henry, expression suddenly a little abashed. "Oh. I'm not supposed to say anything. But your memories are really loud. Bastian thought they might be, so he told me to go stay with Tallis."

Henry isn't sure what surprises him more: the sheer number of words coming out of her mouth, or the fact that Bastian anticipated Henry's emotional state and tried to protect both him and Angelica. It's *thoughtful*. Henry wants to tease him about it, but he's having trouble getting the words out around the lump in his throat.

"It's good cereal," Angelica says solemnly. "Maybe Henry wants some."

"Henry definitely wants some," Henry manages, mostly because he knows it'll get a withering look from Bastian (which it does), but also because breakfast might come with coffee. His brain feels mushy and untethered—withdrawal from whatever drugs they were dosing him with to make him sleep, maybe. Anyway, it'd be good to get a better sense of the layout of the hotel and its supplies, now that the light is better.

Either way, Henry is too antsy to stay cooped up in this room anymore.

"You promised," Angelica says to Bastian, turning her large brown eyes on him in a truly killer move.

Bastian makes a face and admits defeat. "Yeah, all right. But you should probably eat something healthier than just sugar."

"Okay," Angelica says in a tone that implies she's not going to take that into consideration for even a moment.

Bastian rolls his eyes and holds open the door for Henry. Angelica steps back to let them out, bouncing a little on her toes but otherwise silent, now that her objective has been achieved.

"The secret way to ask you about cereal is the link?" Henry asks in a low voice as he moves into the hallway.

"Yes." Bastian closes the door carefully, and they start walking toward the lobby. "It's also the way to pester me with questions throughout the day."

"You can't just . . . hang up?"

"Not really. I mean, she's not constantly eavesdropping or anything, but she's *there*. Like when you know someone's in the apartment down the hall and could come knock on your door whenever they want."

"He doesn't really mind," Angelica says. "He's mean, but not *that* mean."

Henry grins. "She's got your number."

"Shut up," Bastian mutters without much heat.

"Wait," Henry says suddenly. "Didn't you say you have one of these links with Laurel, too? Have you tried it lately?"

Bastian frowns. "We weren't sure if compound security could pick up on that kind of power use, so we haven't tried in a while. I've been waiting for her to get in touch when it's safe, but nothing so far. I guess that means it's still not safe."

He sounds fairly flippant about it, but Henry detects more concern in his voice than he's letting on. Not that there's anything they can do about it at the moment.

The lights in the hallway are back up, steadier and brighter than they were last night. A few people pass by, but no one is talking above a murmur, and everyone keeps their distance. Henry wonders if that's generally how it goes here or if they've pegged Bastian and Angelica as assets who are best left alone. It seems unlikely that it has to do with him—he doubts that anyone knows he's a practically mythological negator who could remove the powers of everyone here against their will.

Not that he *would*. But he *could*, and that makes him a horrible risk to all of these people—not just because of what he can do, but because of who might come after him. If he were stronger, he'd leave right away, but . . .

"They'll have put out breakfast in a little place right off the lobby," Bastian says. "There."

It isn't terribly impressive: just an open area where guests probably used to get cardboard-flavored toast and burned coffee. Now it consists of a few tables and chairs and some odds and ends on the counter, including granola bars, some past-its-prime fruit, and Angelica's coveted cereal. Not a lot of options, but Henry is impressed that Barrett's group has managed to put even this much together. There's even a small refrigerator off to one side, rattling like it's in the midst of a heated argument with the wiring. Hopefully not *too* heated, if it's meant to keep its contents at a safe temperature.

Henry is about to go to the counter to help Angelica with the cereal when he notices a man sitting in a far corner table, surrounded by a small, attentive audience. The man says something that makes everyone laugh, then looks up, his eyes meeting Henry's.

(Everything around them is on fire, and Henry is sagging against the wall, feeling sick to his stomach, watching James try to use his power over and over until he turns his widening eyes to Henry and—)

"Shit," Bastian says under his breath. "I was going to warn you—"

James grins and waves them over, which attracts the attention of several other assets he's sitting with. Especially when neither Henry nor Bastian make any effort to follow up on the offer.

"Cereal," says a pointed voice at Henry's elbow. He turns to find that Angelica has already filled two bowls—for a definition of "filled" that's really closer to "so full, the fluorescent circles are threatening to spill over the sides." She's also chewing on one, and the colorful blob of sugar at the corner of her mouth implies that it's not her first.

The panic that was rising in Henry's chest abruptly dissolves into a short laugh. "I guess that answers the question of whether we need to ration."

"This one is yours," Angelica says, holding out one of the bowls. "Bastian doesn't get any because he's mean."

"Fair," Bastian says. He glances at James's table, then back at Henry, frown deepening. "Listen, Henry, I—"

"Fancy meeting you here."

James has come over, leaving his entourage, who are still watching curiously from the other side of the room but don't seem inclined to follow him.

"I'm glad you're all right, James," Henry says after an awkward pause.

"Are you?"

"Not really."

James laughs. "At least you're honest. Would it help if I promise not to burn this place down?"

"You can still—?" Something in Henry's chest squirms, and he can't decide whether he wants to know the answer to that choked-off question. Surely James can't actually use his power anymore. Surely this is just posturing. But if he isn't an asset anymore, why is he here? And who has he told about what happened to him?

"You know, Major—oh, sorry, you're not a major anymore, are you?" James taps his chin. "What should I call you, then? Are we on a first-name basis now? Last name? Pet names?"

"Get to the point," Bastian snaps.

"I just don't want anything bad to happen to the people here," James says a bit too loudly, eyes fixed on Henry. "We've all been through enough, you know? Time to let bygones be bygones. Come together and support each other. That's the point of this place, right?"

It sounds like the sort of thing Henry believed in, once upon a time. That disparate people could come together and change things for the better, no matter what was in their past. That setting aside differences and working together mattered.

Great in theory, but untenable in practice. James has blood on his hands, and so does Henry. And they're both lying about it.

If Henry has learned anything in the last several years, it's that coming together only works if everyone genuinely starts on the same page. Otherwise, it's just more of the same shit that gets people killed. And since no one ever genuinely wants the same thing, what's the point of pretending that they do?

"I'm not here to hurt anyone," Henry says. "Can we say the same about you?"

James looks affronted. "Of course we can! *I'd* never hurt anyone. Especially now. Right, Henry?"

Henry tries to ignore Bastian's eyes on him—and the way his own breath goes shallow. He wonders which of them is more of a danger to these people at the moment.

"If you're willing to hit pause on the pissing match, I need Mortimer."

Barrett has entered the breakfast area. He's wearing a black windbreaker and is clearly on a mission. Henry isn't sure what that has to do with him, but he's grateful for the interruption.

"Sure," James says easily. "We were just having a friendly chat, but we can catch up later."

His eyes linger on Henry for a moment, lips curled into a smirk. Then he turns and goes back to his friends in the corner.

"I need your help with a supply run," Barrett says. "Let's go."

Bastian frowns. "Henry just got here. I can—"

"You look like shit, Lucas. Get breakfast with your girl and then go see what Irene can do to make you look less pathetic."

Henry almost forgot about Angelica, who's been standing there, silently eating cereal and watching the proceedings with large, thoughtful eyes. She notices Henry looking at her and holds out the second cereal bowl again. "Take it with you," she says, and waits until he does.

Bastian is still frowning, which just makes the gauntness of his face more apparent. He's the one who needs the cereal—and a nap. Several naps.

"Don't worry about it," Henry says. "I'll go with Barrett and come find you when I get back."

Bastian hesitates, then nods, shoulders slumping. He really *does* look exhausted, and in a way that sugary cereal probably isn't going to help. Without thinking, Henry touches his arm, lowering his shield slightly, hoping Bastian can feel some of the reassurance and comfort he's trying to project. Henry can't do what an empath can do with emotions, of course, but since Bastian seems able to feel him remarkably well, maybe . . .

Bastian meets his eyes for a moment, leaning ever so slightly into Henry's touch. Then he breaks away abruptly and says to Angelica, "Let's go sit down."

Henry turns back to Barrett, whose face is stoic except for a slight quirk at the corner of his mouth. "Come with me," Barrett says.

***

It's a rainy day in the city, the misty kind that makes everything unpleasantly damp, and Henry almost wishes he had an umbrella. Of course, any *real* denizen of the city wouldn't dream of using one, but the appeal of the drenched rat look is pretty fleeting, in Henry's opinion.

The rain doesn't seem to bother Barrett much. He makes his way through the crowds with practiced ease, unobtrusively avoiding both puddles and slow walkers. He doesn't even bother to look back and make sure Henry is following. Henry knows he doesn't have the option of falling behind, though—not so much because he doesn't know the city after years of work with the compound, but because Barrett is using odd little side streets and alleys Henry has never heard of.

Henry isn't sure why Barrett wanted him rather than Tallis or someone else more familiar with supply runs. When he asked, Barrett just grunted and said that "everyone works." Not an unreasonable trade-off for a safe stop in the city, really.

"Here," Barrett says, leading them to the side of a run-down deli. The cracked brick wall has a slew of incomprehensible graffiti sprayed all over it: whites and reds and greens, letters and numbers and odd designs that don't add up to anything Henry can parse. Barrett seems to understand it, though. He frowns thoughtfully, like he's reading an important message.

"Clothing drop at 7th and 12th," he mutters. "Lots of officers spotted around the area, but we might be able to get there right when the shift changes, and they're not paying attention."

He starts walking again, giving Henry an appraising look at the same time. "You're keeping up all right. Guess you haven't forgotten how to move just because you haven't been in the field for a while."

Henry grimaces, thinking back to when he met Barrett in said field. "Yeah, about that—"

"Markers," Barrett interrupts, scanning the walls as they pass. "Assets in the city share supplies as we can, but we have to move 'em regularly to avoid raids by Compound Network operatives or city police working with them. So, we use the markers to leave notes about what to find and where. Sometimes we leave other messages, too. A codec would have an easier time with the codes, and a tracker would find the right caches faster, but the rest of us can get along all right with the basics."

"Is all the graffiti in the city markers now?" Henry hasn't ever noticed it before, but of course now he won't be able to unsee it, even if he can't interpret it.

"No. Some of it is just regular graffiti. But a lot more is markers these days because there are a lot more assets in the city trying to find each other and not get found themselves." Barrett gives him a jagged grin. "Not quite what the compounds were expecting when they started cracking down on us, is it?"

Henry isn't sure if this is a net positive or negative in terms of the potential fallout from the Compound Network's chaos. On the one hand, groups like Barrett and Tallis's mean more options for assets who have somehow managed to escape the compounds or avoid them altogether—both of which have been nearly unthinkable for most of Henry's career.

On the other hand, more assets trying to exist outside of the Network potentially means more conflict between different groups who might put survival above playing nice with each other. And maybe even above keeping bystanders out of the line of fire.

"That James guy seems like an asshole," Barrett says conversationally.

Henry chokes on a laugh. "You have no idea."

"And I don't care to." Barrett glances sideways at Henry as they continue down the street. "Everyone comes through that hotel with baggage, Mortimer. Myself included. As long as it doesn't endanger everyone else, I'm not going to judge."

Henry hesitates. "You . . . know where I was. Where Bastian found me. When I first brought you to the compound, it seemed like you knew about what I can do, too. You think that doesn't endanger anyone?"

"I think it means you shouldn't settle in for a long stay." Barrett jerks his head, indicating that they should turn down another street. "But you don't strike me as a reckless guy. You were hiding your power to protect your team back then, right? You didn't want them to know."

Henry barely knew about it himself at that point, but he'd uncovered enough to realize that a power like his could be used to hurt other people, including his team.

A raindrop falls from Henry's hair and onto his eyelashes. He wipes it away. "Yeah."

Barrett nods. "I'm not going to have anything to do with the compounds ever again. Maybe it was better when you were in charge of yours, but I'd already been transferred by then, so it didn't do me any good. Tried a few non-compound options once I escaped my convoy, and those were all shit, too. Any place that sets up rules that only some people have to follow is never going to work. Doesn't matter who's running it."

Barrett stuffs his hands into the pockets of his windbreaker. "Tallis is the one with a mission. Or maybe she's an adrenaline junkie with a savior complex. Me, I just want to do my own thing. But we work well together, and even I can see that assets aren't going to survive if we can't do that. And I'd like to survive, wouldn't you?"

There have been times over the last year when Henry wasn't so sure. But now . . . "Yeah. I think so."

"Then make yourself useful. Don't mess around or get anyone else hurt, and you'll be fine. And get ready to carry the heaviest stuff we find. New guy toll."

Henry smiles faintly. "Deal."

Seven months ago

THE FIRST ASSET they bring him is an old man who looks like he's well into his seventies. His thinning gray hair has been brushed back carefully, and he's wearing a tidy, nondescript collared shirt and dark slacks. The fact that his hands are shackled in front of him is a disturbing incongruence.

Officer Garrand shoves him into a chair across from Henry, but her manhandling doesn't seem to bother him. He smiles a little nervously at Henry, like they're both guests at a party where the host has just done something awkward, and they're making a silent pact to pretend not to notice.

"We'll start with AP49726," Dr. Urashima says over the loudspeaker.

Henry's never met an asset this age before, though he's heard there are a few stashed away in various parts of the Network. Most assets manifest when they're very young, though. And they don't tend to make it to retirement—not the way the compounds work them. Those who do are mostly assigned menial tasks until their bodies finally give out. For this guy to have made it this far in life, he must be in very good health, and he must have an extremely innocuous power.

When no one says anything else, Henry clears his throat and says to the man, "What's your name?"

"Irrelevant," Urashima says before the old man can respond. "Please proceed, Mr. Mortimer."

Henry blinks, then looks over at Garrand, who is standing behind the other man's chair. "Proceed with what?"

She doesn't reply, but Urashima does. "With the demonstration."

"Of?" Then it hits him. "You want me to—? Why? He can't possibly be a threat!"

"It's unwise to underestimate an asset, no matter what they look like," Urashima admonishes. "But you're correct: AP49726 won't be a danger to you."

"Then why—?"

"It's all right," the old man says, giving Henry a small smile that doesn't reach his eyes. "They weren't planning on me manifesting last week, but it means I have an opportunity to be useful. Now I can show those little punks in accounting just how much I'm out of their league." His smile becomes a bit cheeky, and he even winks.

Henry isn't an empath, so he can't really tell what this guy is feeling. But he can see evidence of it: shaky hands and hunched shoulders at odds with the smile and bravado. He's genuinely proud—and genuinely terrified.

"Mr. Mortimer?" Urashima says.

Henry thinks quickly. "He's an unusually late manifestation. Don't you want to study that?"

"Please leave the science to the professionals. You have a job to do."

Someone must have decided that this is a more important experiment. What will happen if Henry negates him? And what will happen if he can't?

"You seem nervous," the man says with what sounds like genuine concern. "Don't worry. I've been working at Council HQ for a long time. Whatever they've asked you to do, I'm sure you're up for it. They only employ the best in the Compound Network. Takes one to know one."

Henry half expects him to take some butterscotch candies out of his pocket and force them into Henry's hands, like Henry is a little kid meeting his grandparents' friend for the first time. Despite his growing dread, Henry can't help but smile back. "I hope they're giving you a good pension after this."

"Don't be silly! No one gets pensions anymore. But I suppose they will *make me retire, anyway." The man lowers his voice to a stage whisper. "No one's said what 'this' is, though."*

Something about the combination of amusement and discomfort on the man's face steels Henry's resolve. "No."

The man blinks. "Sorry?"

Henry looks up at Garrand. "No. I won't do it."

The sound of Urashima's sigh over the speaker seems to pause everything around it for a long moment. "Think carefully about what you're saying, Mr. Mortimer."

Warning bells go off in the back of Henry's mind, but he can't possibly be expected to just—"No."

Another labored sigh. Then: "Garrand?"

It's so quick, it doesn't seem real.

Henry breathes in.

Garrand draws her gun and shoots the man in the back of the head. He collapses forward onto the table with a loud thud.

Henry curses on the exhale, his heart racing even as the other man's stops.

"I hope you can now understand the consequences of your actions, Mr. Mortimer," Urashima says. "Every asset you negate per our instructions will live. Any you don't will die. Are we clear?"

Henry swallows, watching the blood pool on the table and drip onto the floor as he tries to remember how to breathe. "Yeah," he says. "We're clear."

"Good. Bring in the next subject, Garrand."

Chapter 14

BASTIAN KNOWS SOMETHING is horribly wrong as soon as he opens his eyes. He went to sleep with a splitting headache, and now he's . . . fine. Better than fine, actually. Like he slept soundly for a week rather than in the broken bits and pieces he's gotten used to. He feels *good*. The scratchy sheets aren't irritating his skin. The lumpy mattress isn't digging into his back. The hum of the lights in the hall doesn't sound quite so much like droning mosquitos just outside the door.

He feels *good*, so something is *wrong*.

He rolls over and immediately realizes what it is.

Henry is lying still next to him—too still for sleep, especially for someone who tends to move a lot at night. He's breathing shallowly, his eyes staring at the ceiling but clearly not seeing anything. His hands are positioned stiffly at his sides, almost like someone else put them there.

Bastian can't breathe.

(The dead look in Tom's eyes, the stiff way he lay on the floor, the unconcerned expression on Quentin's face, the feeling of Tom's energy suffusing Bastian's skin, taking away his pain so much better than anything they'd tried at the compound—and then the shock, like a bucket of ice water thrown over his head, because Bastian knew he'd taken something he wasn't supposed to take, even if it was freely given, and—)

"Henry." His voice barely makes it out of his mouth. "*Henry.*"

(How could he have done this in his sleep, it makes no sense, he would never—)

Bastian shoots upright and grabs Henry's shoulder, shaking him hard, unable to stop saying his name. "Henry—*Henry*—" Desperation is choking him.

It's useless; of course it is. When he did this to Tom, it didn't help then, either.

Bastian realizes with growing dread that he never actually found out if Tom recovered—all he has are Quentin's reassurances, which mean fuck all at the moment.

Henry is breathing, but he's terrifyingly still otherwise. Bastian chokes down his fear and feels out, but that just makes it worse. Henry isn't experiencing any emotions at all, just a numb nothing-nothing-nothing.

Exactly like Tom. Like Quentin. Like James when he first got to the compound. Just an empty void. Nothing like the way Henry's negation feels, soothing and calm and quiet.

He's hollow, and Bastian did this to him.

Bastian is vaguely aware that he's babbling, still shaking Henry even as part of his brain screams at him to *stop* because it's obviously not working, and he shouldn't even be *touching* Henry right now.

Should he get Irene? Would she even know what to do? This isn't a normal injury, the kind a piece of gauze and a bit of enhanced healing can fix. Maybe nothing can fix this.

His voice keeps going, desperate and pained and beyond his control: "Please, please, please, I don't want it, take it back, *take it back*—"

Something shifts—a tug in his chest, a breath forced from his lungs. He's dizzy, even though he hasn't moved except to shake uncontrollably. His stomach lurches in protest, and then . . .

Henry blinks and makes a small noise, then turns his head slowly. "Bastian?"

Bastian jerks his hand away, scrambling out of bed. It's the opposite of what he wants to do, but his skin is crawling, and his heart is still racing. He doesn't trust himself to touch Henry again. Maybe not ever.

Henry sits up carefully. "What happened?"

"I don't—I don't know." Bastian glances at the door. "I think I should go."

"I think you should stay and talk to me," Henry says firmly. Then he sees Bastian's face and softens. "Please?"

Bastian pauses, everything in him screaming to get *out*. But he forces himself back over to the bed and sits down. Maybe he doesn't deserve an out. Henry should know what he did.

It's strange, though. Bastian definitely took Henry's energy—he can still feel it under his skin, erasing the simmering pain and making him feel almost normal. But Henry seems fine now, and he got there much faster than Quentin's victims did.

Looking at Henry now, it's almost as if nothing happened.

Except something *did*, and it fills Bastian with disgust. He promised himself that he'd never do it again, that he'd never give Quentin the satisfaction, but somehow he did anyway—and in his sleep. How is he supposed to stop his brain from doing whatever it wants while he's asleep? How can he possibly trust himself not to—?

"Are you okay?" Bastian asks in a low voice.

"Yeah. Better than you look." Henry reaches out to touch him, but Bastian shrinks away. Henry's concern-hurt-confusion is clear, but he doesn't try to touch Bastian again.

"I . . . did something to you." Bastian nearly chokes on the words, but Henry deserves to know. "I didn't mean to, but I—You're sure you're all right?"

Henry looks even more perplexed, but he nods. "Yeah. I felt weird there for a bit, but I'm fine now. Whatever you did doesn't seem to have hurt me. Do you have any idea what it was?"

"Yes." Bastian takes a shuddering breath. "The healer—Quentin—that's his solution. If I want to stay alive, I have to take energy from people, like he does from his followers."

Bastian can see the exact moment when Henry realizes what happened. His eyes go wide, and he makes a tiny, almost unnoticeable movement away.

Bastian notices.

All that stupid poetry, all those stupid songs about hearts breaking, but this doesn't feel like any of that. It's just a single sharp pinprick of knowing that he's destroyed the trust of one of the most important people in his life, and he may never get it back.

Henry says carefully, "That's what you just—?"

"Not on purpose! But maybe that's worse."

He's too fidgety to keep sitting on the bed. Without looking at Henry, he gets to his feet and walks to the window, pulling back the curtain a tiny bit, just for something to do. The streetlights are illuminating little puddles of asphalt in the empty parking lot. Otherwise, it's still dark outside, the suffocating dark of late night.

The silence stretches out. Then Henry says, "Have you done it before? On purpose, I mean?"

Bastian swallows. "Once."

"And?"

(Tom's eyes slowly going dead the longer Bastian touched him; the pain receding quickly enough to give Bastin whiplash; the way his head cleared but his throat closed up, like the shame of it was physically manifesting in his body, choking him, and he knew he needed to pull his hand away, but he couldn't—)

"It worked," Bastian says. "For a while."

"The person you did it to—were they all right afterward?"

"I left Quentin's sanctuary before I could see for myself, but he said the people he does it to always recover. Like James—he got his feelings back in the end, but it took a while."

"And Quentin said it was the only way?"

It's a stupid question; just stalling for time. "Yes."

"Then . . . you'll have to keep doing it, won't you?"

"Only if I want to stay alive."

There's another long pause, and then, almost so quietly that Bastian can't hear it, Henry says, "You can't help anyone if you're dead."

Bastian turns sharply and stares at him. "You think I should—?"

"It's practical." Henry has shifted so that he's sitting up, legs over the side of the bed, hands clasped tightly in his lap. He's looking at the floor rather than at Bastian. Then he raises his head, meets Bastian's eyes, and says, "You can—"

"No."

Henry smiles slightly, a shadow of the exasperated one that always makes Bastian want to smirk back. And kiss him. "You don't know what I was going to say."

"You were going to offer, even after what I just did. I can't—no."

"You said it doesn't hurt the other person."

"That's what *Quentin* said, but he's a psychopath. Just because he *said* they were fine, doesn't mean they actually were. Especially after he kept taking energy from them." Bastian shudders. "What I did, it felt like—he looked—I don't think he'll remember it, but I will. I'll always know that I did that to someone. And now to you."

Henry looks at him silently for a moment, like he's steeling himself for battle. "For what it's worth, I'm willing."

"I'm not."

It's like the arguments they used to have about Henry permanently negating Bastian's power. Henry's desperation-determination-fear is much louder now. Like he really does believe that Bastian is turning down the last possible option.

And maybe he is.

(Why does Henry *care* like this, how can he be so willing to go this far for someone like Bastian when his own hurt is still right there on the surface, when there are other people who deserve his help so much more—?)

"I can't do that to you," Bastian says. "Not again. I can't do it to anyone. Because—because it feels disgusting, and I'm not going to do something just because an asshole like Quentin says I have to."

Henry looks at him a moment longer, then lets out a short, humorless laugh and rubs his eyes. "Okay. I mean, not okay, but I get it."

When he doesn't say anything else, Bastian frowns. "Really? That's it? You're not going to keep trying to change my mind?"

Henry smiles a little wanly. "I've told you, this is your call. Just because I *want* you to do something doesn't mean I'm going to try to *make* you. Especially when it's something like this."

The look on his face isn't defeat—not exactly. And the cloud of feelings around him is a strange, potent mixture of resignation-concern-love. But mostly the last one.

Bastian knows he shouldn't be surprised after all this time, but he stands there anyway, perplexed. So many years of Major Valentine and Dr. Wright telling him to suck it up, do what he was told, stop complaining. That nothing he did would matter. That they knew best. And now, here's a man who grew up in that same system, who's just been through hell and barely made it out—a man Bastian *hurt*—and he's just going to . . . let Bastian decide. Trust that Bastian knows what's best for himself, instead of trying to change the outcome based on what *he* wants.

Henry clears his throat and gets to his feet. "Can I ask you a favor, though?"

Anything, Bastian thinks but doesn't say. "Yeah?"

"Can you come here for a second?"

Bastian almost takes a step backward. "I—"

"It's okay if you'd rather not right now," Henry says quickly. "But just so we're clear, I know you won't hurt me."

Bastian stands there awkwardly, wanting to both run away from and toward him at the same time. In the end, he finds himself putting one foot in front of the other until he's only inches away from Henry.

Carefully and slowly, Henry reaches out and touches his cheek. Bastian shudders and leans in, resting his forehead against Henry's shoulder (because Bastian is weak and stupid and almost forgot what it feels like to touch someone he feels safe with), and Henry gently pulls him closer. Like it's the easiest thing in the world to hug someone who's prickly and awkward and can't figure out how to say "I love you" in a way that will fix this.

Chapter 15

"I WOULDN'T TELL yarrow that it's *smelly*," Laurel says to the med tech sitting across from her and taking notes on a tablet. "There's no need to be rude. But it does have a . . . scent. So if you want to use some for an infusion, you should probably ask it to tone down the smelly stuff."

The med tech looks confused. "Without telling it that it's smelly."

"Exactly. You could try telling it how nice its flowers are instead. Plants like flattery, especially when it's true."

"Except we can't talk to plants here."

"Well, you *can*. But they probably won't understand you as well as they would a plantspeaker like me. I see your point. The yarrow might still appreciate the effort, though."

The med tech raises an eyebrow, which is a neat skill even though it conveys a level of disdain that Laurel doesn't appreciate. After all, she was *asked* to come down to med bay and consult, and she's been doing it ever since she first came to this compound. Surely the people here ought to understand and appreciate her insights by now?

She knows she should be patient, but that's not exactly easy these days, not with how little she's been sleeping. Some nights, she's not sure she sleeps at all. The comment from the officer in her garden keeps playing itself over and over in her head: *Don't forget how replaceable you are.*

If asked, Laurel would say she knows exactly how replaceable she is—not at all. If anything, the current state of the herb and medicine catalog implies that the compound would run a whole lot better if there were at least five more extremely competent, extremely necessary Laurels.

But when she wakes up at odd hours, feeling like she's missed something important, like the world has moved on without her . . . well. It's a little hard to feel irreplaceable. Much easier to feel tired and strangely squishy, like she's moving in slow motion while everything around her is fast and dangerous and loud.

She's been completely useless at trying to have important data-gathering adventures on her own, too. She hasn't seen any helpful paths or lines of communication that might benefit James (or keep him away, if needed). She hasn't been able to contact Bastian through the empath link, either; just more static on the line.

Maybe she *is* replaceable. Maybe she's—

"Come with me," someone says, putting a hand on her shoulder and jolting her out of her sleep-deprived stupor.

Laurel starts and, after a moment, realizes that the hand belongs to Kwan, who is looking even more serious than usual. No, not serious; those eyes are positively *grim*.

"We're in the middle of a session," the med tech says disapprovingly.

Kwan ignores him, hand tightening on Laurel's shoulder. "Now."

The swooping feeling in Laurel's stomach might have knocked her over if she weren't already sitting. Kwan can be short-tempered, but not like this. Right now he's like a blackberry bush stretching out its brambles to make absolutely sure that anyone nearby stays away from it.

The med tech coughs uncomfortably and looks down at his tablet.

Laurel glances across the med bay at Dr. Rowe, who has just finished a conversation with another staff member. She can't have heard what Kwan said, and it's not like she could prevent him from taking Laurel even if she wanted to, but her forehead does look a little scrunched up. She meets Laurel's gaze briefly, then turns her back to check in with someone else.

Laurel is on her own, then.

She stands, puts on her most polite smile, and studiously refuses to think about why she might need to be worried. "Okay. Where are we going?"

"Major Tremain's office."

Laurel follows him out of the room and down the hall on autopilot. It's not until they hit the elevator that her brain snaps to attention and actually registers what he said. "Wait. *Major Tremain's office?*"

Kwan's mouth is set in a firm line. He doesn't respond.

Their elevator stops at Level 4, where two very familiar people get on: Kent, hair askew and bags under his eyes; and Sybil, fingers clutching her shoulder bag so tightly, her knuckles are white.

"Hello," Laurel says, trying to ignore the way her voice comes out a bit wobbly rather than cheerful. It's not like there's a definite *reason* to be nervous, right? Even if everyone else is?

They get out on Level 1, and Kwan leads them down a side hall. He eventually stops in front of the appropriately labeled room and knocks. A voice tells them to come in.

Major Tremain's office is a small, minimalistic room with a desk, a few chairs, and cabinets on two out of four walls. They look identical to the cabinets used in the experimentation rooms, which is a bit creepy. Does Major Tremain keep secret documents and needles and vials in hers, too?

One thing the office does *not* have is plants. Laurel supposes most plants wouldn't want to be around Major Tremain anyway, but still. The borderline microscopic window could let in enough light to support an easygoing spider plant. And maybe having a good plant friend would make the major less stand-offish and more willing to address the fact that her compound is a horrible place that tortures and kills people.

Then again, even the best plant probably couldn't do that.

The major glances up from her desk as they enter, and Laurel is struck once again by how unassuming she looks. Major Valentine was all ice-blue eyes and stiff shoulders, but Major Tremain looks . . . well, normal, at least by comparison. Maybe her posture is a little too good for the average person, but her passive face and innocuous brown eyes are so mundane, they make Laurel feel paranoid. Not as paranoid as Bastian gets about it, but paranoid enough.

"Sit," Tremain says, waving a hand before looking back down at whatever she has open on her tablet. Laurel hesitantly takes one of the three available chairs. Kent and Sybil take the two to Laurel's left, Sybil setting her bag down next to her. That leaves Kwan without a place to sit, but he seems content to stand by the door, almost like he's guarding it.

Major Tremain finally looks up again and smiles a tiny, polite smile that's barely a smile at all. "You haven't been to my office before, have you, Laurel?"

That seems like the sort of thing Tremain really ought to know already, but Laurel decides to help her out anyway. "No. It's . . . very nice. Utilitarian. Major-y."

"You're quite sure you've never been here before?"

Laurel is uncomfortably reminded of Senator Donnigan's interrogation of her in front of the task force—the one that ultimately removed Henry from office. The one that included making her watch footage of the destruction of her original compound while Donnigan claimed she'd lied to everyone.

Tremain doesn't seem as likely to recommend that Laurel be locked up forever. But she does sound like someone who knows a kid is lying and is waiting for them to trip over themselves.

"Yes," Laurel says firmly. "I've never been here before."

Tremain nods to Sybil, whose shoulders tense briefly, her lips pressing together. Then, without looking at Laurel, she reaches down and pulls a tablet out of her bag. After tapping on it briefly, she sets it down on the desk.

Laurel leans forward and sees a video playing. It looks like something from the security feed—grainy and indistinct, maybe taken at night, given the low lighting. It shows Laurel right outside this door, tipping her head back and forth as if assessing it.

"That's not me," Laurel says immediately. Stupidly. Because while it *can't* be her, it sure does *look* like her, and who's going to believe there's a difference?

Case in point: Tremain's tone is suspiciously neutral when she says, "Oh? How about the other ones?"

"What other ones?" Laurel asks.

Still looking grim, Sybil flips through several clips, all of which show Laurel in various areas of the compound at night, looking at doors and even trying to get through a few of them.

"You were clever to find times when these areas weren't too crowded," Tremain says. "Not as clever about avoiding security cameras. Or thinking no one would notice that you were out and about after hours."

"I didn't—" Laurel clears her throat. "I'm impressed with how much this person looks like me, but it *isn't* me. Is there some new kind of asset who can look like other people?"

"You said you registered her ID at these locations?" Tremain says to Kent.

Kent glances at Laurel, then quickly away. "Yeah. I mean, yes, ma'am. Her ID has pinged our system multiple times over the past week. When it became obvious that it wasn't an error, we immediately reported it to you."

That doesn't sound at all like Kent and Sybil—no way they'd take that long to figure out a security issue. They must have been trying to help by hiding it, like when they deleted the med bay footage of Bastian's escape plan and let Kwan know about the lack of security around dead zones.

"I'm pretty sure I'd remember being stupid enough to try this," Laurel says. "But I don't remember because I *didn't*. And even if I had, I wouldn't have done it like this."

"Really?" Major Tremain sounds both curious and a little condescending. "How would you have done it?"

With the jammer, Laurel doesn't say. "Well. Some way that wouldn't get me caught, I suppose. But that's just theoretical because I wouldn't have done it at all. I *didn't* do it at all."

Tremain looks at her with those unassuming eyes for an awkwardly long amount of time. Then she transfers her gaze back down to her own tablet. "Your file is interesting. Serious allegations from the compound liaison committee last year—some concerning the mishandling of leadership at this compound, others tied to the destruction of your previous one. And then there are the links between you and the assets who set this compound on fire last year."

Laurel does her best to sit still in her uncomfortable chair and say nothing. This is the sort of thing powerful people like to say to prove they know things. Any response just makes them puff up and yell some more. And anyway, Laurel knows what she did—and didn't—do, and so does Tremain. So it's all a bit silly.

It *does* make her wonder, though. Laurel has been under plenty of scrutiny based on everything Tremain just said, but she hasn't been locked up or chained to an experimentation bed on a secret lower level of the compound. Why wait to bring her to the office now? And why wait to accuse her with the footage?

"You also have a connection with Sebastian Lucas, the empath who's been causing a lot of trouble for the Network," Tremain continues, scrolling through her data. "Were you involved in his escape last month?"

Laurel is startled by the matter-of-fact accusation. Most compound leaders would try to meander around it and get Laurel to incriminate herself by accident, not ask outright.

"I have no idea what you're talking about," Laurel says. She feels a little bad about not being honest, but then, Tremain seems to believe lies about *her*, so the truth clearly isn't much of a factor here.

"We could be wrong," Kent pipes up. "I mean, we're not, but we *could* be. Uh. The footage could've been tampered with or something. Maybe it's not Laurel. Maybe . . ." He falls silent when Sybil puts her hand on his arm.

Major Tremain lets the silence linger for a bit. Then she leans back in her chair and asks, "Do you think I'm stupid?"

There's another very long pause. Then Kent says, "Um . . . no? That's the right answer, isn't it?"

"Major, we gave you the information you asked for," Sybil says, polite but firm. "I understand that it's potentially incriminating, but nothing was stolen or damaged, so—"

"Do you really think there's anything happening in this compound that I don't know about?"

Laurel considers this for a moment, mostly so she can ignore the increasing feeling of being cornered. "Well, surely there's *something*. I mean, it's a large compound, and there are a lot of people here doing a lot of things, so—"

Major Tremain's eyes have gone so cold, she almost—*almost*—looks like Major Valentine. Do they teach cold eyes in major training?

"Let me be clear," Tremain says. "I'm aware that the three of you have been engaging in security breaches since I took control of this compound. I've allowed it because it dovetailed with my plans. Now, however, I'm concerned about the consequences of your sloppiness, showing up on multiple security cameras near top secret areas. This compound is being closely watched by Carter and his goons, and I won't allow you to ruin everything just because you're incompetent."

Laurel blinks. "Are you—?"

"Five minutes," Kwan says.

Laurel turns slightly in her seat and sees Kwan holding a jammer in his hand, checking the timer. Out in the open. Where Tremain can see it. Where Tremain seems *unsurprised* to see it.

"Are we certain that the footage hasn't been tampered with?" Tremain asks.

Kent is busy gaping at her, so Sybil responds. "Not completely, but we didn't see any indication of that."

Tremain turns to Laurel. "And you claim you weren't in any of those locations at any of those times?"

"I don't *claim*," Laurel says stiffly. "I *know*."

Tremain pauses, then waves at Sybil. "Delete the videos—off the servers, off the cameras, off of wherever else it might show up. You have permission to destroy hardware if needed. And make sure no one else has seen it. I know you quarantined the data right away, but we can't take chances. Send any suspicious hackers to me immediately."

Kent and Sybil's matching expressions make it clear they're not about to throw any of their coworkers under the bus, but Tremain is busy looking over Laurel's shoulder. "Kwan, take Laurel to the Level 15 jail block."

"What? Why?" The stupid questions are out of her stupid mouth before she registers how stupid they are. When has a compound officer ever needed a legitimate reason to do whatever they want to an asset?

"Kwan will escort you," Tremain says, "and you'll stay there until further notice. If it's too difficult for you to follow orders, I'll assume I was wrong when I chose to disagree with the liaison committee's suggestion that you be permanently removed from this compound after last year's hearing."

Laurel swallows. "Um, when you say 'permanently removed,' I don't suppose you mean 'allowed to leave and live whatever life I want outside of the Compound Network,' do you?"

"I do not."

"Right, okay. Just checking."

"Four minutes," Kwan mutters.

"Why didn't you, though?" Laurel asks, because the answer is more important than her impending nervous breakdown. "Why didn't you lock me up from the start?"

For a moment, she doesn't think Tremain is going to answer. Then: "For the same reason I'm having Kwan use the jammer. I have things I need to do here. As long as you don't get in the way of those plans, you'll be fine."

She laces her fingers together and turns sharp eyes on Kent and Sybil. "Remove that information immediately, and let me know when it's done. Best to come back in person; I don't want any possibility of interception."

Kent sniffs. "As if we couldn't come up with a fully secure line in less than—"

"Yes, ma'am," Sybil says. "We'll take care of it."

"Good. Kwan?"

"Yes, ma'am."

Kwan ushers everyone out of the office and back into the hall. Laurel catches a glimpse of Tremain scanning her tablet again before the door closes.

Kent turns on Kwan. "Did you tell the major about the jammers?" he hisses. "Do you have any idea what she's going to do to us?"

"Maybe she'll send you to Level 15 with me," Laurel suggests. "We could all hang out with Prison Officer Templeton. She's very nice for a prison officer. Or at least, she was when Henry and I got locked up last year."

"Tremain isn't going to do anything, apparently," Sybil says, putting her tablet back into her bag. "She must've known for ages, and she didn't mention it until now. If we were going to get in trouble for it, we already would have."

"Just do as she says," Kwan tells them. "And stop talking about this—the jammer is almost out of juice."

"I wish I'd never given it to you," Kent mutters.

"You didn't; I confiscated it. And you're lucky it was me rather than someone else."

"All that beautiful work, and who knows what she'll make us do with it now?" Kent laments. "You heard her! She was talking about *destroying hardware!*"

"I'll help you protect the hardware," Sybil says reassuringly, looping her arm through his. "Come on."

Kwan waits for Laurel to follow them to the elevators, but she clears her throat instead. "The major must trust you a lot."

"I work security. It's in the job description to be trustworthy."

"Is it? I'd like to see the official job description. I have questions. Especially since I don't think either you or Major Tremain are what you say you are."

Kwan makes a face. "What *you and I* are is wasting time instead of getting you to the jail block like the major ordered. So let's go."

He's just the right amount of grouchy and dismissive, like he always is. Laurel gets the distinct impression that he's cultivated it for a specific reason, the way a burr has cultivated its hooks for a specific reason.

She's not going to let it go, of course. Just like a burr, she knows when to stick.

For now, though, she follows him to the elevator bay.

Chapter 16

THE STORM IS still on the horizon, thunder occasionally rumbling, though the rain doesn't get any closer. All Bastian ever sees in this dream is the gloom of the clouds and the occasional flash of lightning between the tree branches. Close enough to know that the storm is there, but not close enough that he needs to prepare for it to hit.

He walks to the pond just like always, his feet leading the way without him consciously deciding to go. The birch tree eyes stare at him as he passes, and he tries to ignore the shiver they send down his spine.

Moira, still dressed in immaculate white scrubs, is waiting for him. She turns away from the pond when he sits down, her expression going through an odd little journey: amusement, then confusion, then concern. It's strange, watching someone feel in real time the things he usually only senses through his power. Except his power doesn't work here.

"Something good happen?" she tries.

He thinks of Henry's hand in his as they walked down the hotel hallway. The way it felt to lie next to him in bed and watch his breathing slowly even out as he finally fell asleep.

The horrible, dull expression on his face when—

"I don't know," Bastian says.

Moira raises her eyebrows. "Kind of a weird thing to not know, isn't it?"

"Not really." His voice sounds sharper than he meant it to. "Why do you ask?"

"You've entered my domain feeling all . . . squishy." She wiggles her fingers. "I can't feel it like you do, obviously. It's more like hints. You usually barge in here with a certain atmosphere around you, but now it's different. Lighter, but held down somehow. You gonna tell me what's going on, or do I have to guess?"

There's absolutely no reason to tell her anything, of course. But there's something strange about the way she asks—like she wants to tease him relentlessly, but she's also worried.

It would be so much easier if he could just read her. Figure out what she's really feeling so he can decide what's safe to say and what isn't.

But even if he knew that, it wouldn't matter because he doesn't know how to explain it. The desperation, the irrational need to keep Henry close, while also knowing it would be safer if Bastian stayed away from him because . . .

"There's someone I—someone I care about," Bastian hears himself say. "He was in trouble, but I helped him out of it. Only then I did something that might be even worse."

He can feel her eyes on him—not calculating or judging; just considering. Even so, he probably should've kept his mouth shut. She could be manipulating him, trying to get him to admit to something. And how stupid would he be for letting her?

"Want some advice?" she asks. Then she laughs at whatever she sees on his face. "Okay, forget advice. How about I share a thought with you?"

Bastian shrugs. "Not like I can go anywhere."

"Your incredible enthusiasm for my wisdom is noted." Moira pulls her legs up and wraps her arms around them. "So, the way I see it, there aren't a lot of people we form really tight bonds with, you know? People we'd drop everything for. People we'd protect with our lives. If you've found someone you feel that way about, that's a powerful feeling."

"Or a significant weakness," Bastian mutters.

"Sure. It can be both. That's what makes it powerful." She gives him a small smile, and there's something surprisingly wistful about it. "All I'm saying is, that bond is important. That feeling *is important. If you're worried that you've done something to damage it, you should sort that out rather than running from it."*

She grins and pokes him in the arm. "Especially if it makes you feel all cute and bubbly underneath."

Bastian feels his face go hot for absolutely no reason. "It's not that simple."

"Oh? Why not?"

"He's . . . been through a lot. I might just make things worse."

"Or you might make things better. Or something in between. So?"

"So, I don't want . . . that. To make things worse."

"You were listening just now when I mentioned other options, right?"

Bastian grimaces. "This is different. It's . . ."

Stupid, is what it is. He shouldn't be blabbing all this nonsense to someone who might not even be real.

But it doesn't feel *stupid. Awkward and uncomfortable, yes. But only in the way regrown skin feels a bit uncomfortable when you're recovering from a wound. Sure,*

Moira is looking at him thoughtfully, but not like she's collecting and cataloging data she intends to use against him later. She's not Major Valentine.

But then . . . who is she?

Bastian leans back on his hands and stares up at the dark sky. "I . . . don't think I'm the right person to do this."

"Do what? Be there for someone you care about?"

"Yeah. That."

Moira laughs. "You know that's not something you need a resume for, don't you?"

"Some skill might help."

"Maybe skill is overrated." Moira shrugs. "Life is short and all that. Best to spend it with the people you care about."

"I wouldn't know." Bastian frowns. "Shouldn't you be doing that? What do you do when you're awake?"

"I wouldn't know," she repeats back at him. "I'm never awake."

"Wait, not ever?"

"Nope. It's just me and this forest and that damned storm that never hits. That's how it's been for as long as I can remember. Well, except for you, of course. You're new."

That can't be much of a life, existing in a place that feels like the embodiment of a sharp intake of breath before a catastrophe, with only him for occasional company.

"Don't feel bad for me, Junior," Moira says, patting him on the arm. "It is what it is. I don't have anywhere else to be. Not like you do."

He wakes with a start and finds himself curled up at an awkward angle in one of the oversized hotel lobby chairs. He's sore and groggy and . . . not as cold as he could be because someone has covered him with a blanket. It's gray and mostly devoid of its fuzz after years of use, and it looks suspiciously like the one from the room he and Henry are sharing.

He sees a movement to his left and half expects it to be Henry, caught red-handed as a blanket-bringer. Except the movement is actually two small legs kicking back and forth against the base of a beige couch.

"I like her," Angelica says.

Bastian sits up, groaning at the stiffness of his muscles. He grabs the blanket before it can fall to the floor. "Who? And is it even worth it to remind you that you're supposed to stay with an adult rather than wandering around the hotel on your own?"

"The lady in your dream. I like her."

Bastian freezes. "What?"

"I wish I could talk to her," Angelica says, still kicking her feet against the couch. "I tried, but nothing happened. Maybe because it's not my dream. Is it yours?"

"No," Bastian says slowly. "But how do you—?"

"You remember her." Angelica's voice goes monotone. "You remember her pain. It was—"

Bastian shoves the blanket aside and scrambles over to Angelica, grabbing her hand just as her face starts to scrunch up with the memory. Touching her could make it worse, of course—memors' power is enhanced by touch—but he's not sure how else to get her attention quickly. "*Angelica.*"

She blinks, and her eyes clear.

Bastian lets go of her hand, a flicker of guilt passing through him as he kneels on the carpet in front of her. "Sorry, you were—I thought you might remember something bad."

Angelica frowns. "It's okay if *you* remember something bad, but not me?"

"Not—not if it's *my* bad thing."

He wants to ask her what the bad thing was, in spite of that, because he doesn't know what she was about to remember for him. But he suspects it was bad.

Her silent stare and curious-thoughtful-confused pokes at his mind. "What?" he asks.

"James didn't care," she says. Not a memory; a statement. "You and Henry did, but James didn't care if remembering something hurt me. He just wanted to know."

"That's because James is a jerk. Wait, when was this?"

"Before he remembered things. In the forest with Laurel and Chloe. He knew it would hurt me, but he didn't care. Or he cared about remembering more."

I don't think I'm the right person, Bastian told Moira, and he's not the right person to do this, either. But there isn't anyone else, so . . . "You remember when I was teaching you about shielding?"

"I remember you weren't very good at teaching."

Bastian rolls his eyes. "I said shielding was about setting a boundary. Figuring out where you stop, and the rest of the world begins. So you can decide what you want to let in and what you want to keep out. Remember?"

Angelica nods.

"Using your power is like that, too. You can use it to help other people if you want, but they can't just *expect* you to, especially if it hurts. Well, I guess they *can* expect you to, but that's their problem, and you don't have to do anything about it. You get to decide."

Angelica is silent for a long time before saying, "That's not what it's like in the compound."

"No," Bastian says grimly. "It isn't."

She presses her lips together, still looking intently at him. Then she says, "I can help you. I think. But I don't know how yet. I've never dreamed someone else's dream before. Or talked with feelings. Or any of that."

"Yeah. It's new for me, too." And it makes no sense. It's like she's copied part of his power, but there's also a part of it that seems completely unrelated to any asset power he's aware of. And none of it is something a memor should be able to do.

"Henry brought the blanket," Angelica tells him. "I saw him go back to your room after that. Then I came here and dreamed your dream. Or her dream, I guess. Now I'm going to go get cereal."

She hops down from the couch and hurries over to the breakfast nook before he can stop her. Bastian wonders if it's safe to be giving her free rein over cereal acquisition, but he spots Tallis and Barrett heading in as well. That's probably enough adult supervision to head off disaster. He'll just check on Henry and meet them there.

He isn't sure he believes what Moira said about skill not being necessary, but he might at least be able to make sure both Henry and Angelica get breakfast.

Chapter 17

HENRY FINDS IT when he's searching the closet for a relatively clean shirt: a dented metal tin tucked into the duffel bag Bastian brought from the compound convoy. Henry pauses, staring like an idiot as his hand hovers over the partially hidden lid. He tries to convince himself that he must be wrong about how familiar it looks—because surely that's the only logical explanation here.

But it's hard to keep up the act when it looks exactly like the metal tin he found attached to the underside of the desk chair in Sybil's room, just before the compound fire. That tin had a USB drive in it. An entirely *unauthorized* USB drive containing all the fragments of the Fail-Safe Protocol files—fragments sent to Henry by a dead woman in an effort to take down the Compound Network.

A USB drive that now sits accusatorially in this tin.

What the hell is it doing in Bastian's bag?

Henry doesn't have the equipment to check the contents of the drive— hardware seems pretty limited in this run-down hotel, and that's probably for the best, at least for now. These documents got Senator Nunez's aide killed, which makes them dangerous.

Something bubbles up in his chest, something he quickly tries to squash down. It wouldn't matter, he tells himself. He can't fix any of this. Trying to find out what's on this drive will just get more people killed. And even if it doesn't, no one will be willing to do anything. He should know that by now.

Henry starts at the sound of the door clicking open. Without thinking, he shoves the USB drive back into the bag.

Bastian pokes his head in, then pauses. "Oh. You're awake."

It's the sort of obvious comment he wouldn't normally bother with, which must mean he's still nervous about yesterday. Henry half expects him to back out of the room to avoid even breathing in Henry's direction. Like being in his presence might lead to another incident.

(It's a constant itch of shame and frustration, the way Bastian alternates between coddling Henry and having so little faith in himself that he'd rather they be apart, especially when Henry wants the opposite, wants to be together as much as possible before—)

"There's breakfast," Bastian says. "Maybe cereal, if Angelica hasn't eaten it all yet. And, uh, thanks for this."

He holds up the blanket Henry brought down to him earlier.

Henry stands there briefly, idiotically, silently, before taking the blanket back. "Of course," he says, folding it quickly and tossing it back on the bed. *I wish you'd stayed here so we could share it*, he doesn't say.

"Breakfast?" Bastian asks after another awkward pause.

Henry gives him a small smile. "Yeah. That cereal was pretty good."

"That cereal tastes like sugar-covered cardboard."

"So you've tried it!"

"Under duress."

"You're saying a little girl forced you to eat breakfast?"

"Shut up."

Bastian holds the door so Henry can follow him into the hall. Once there, he seems to forget about keeping his distance. Like his default setting is not to worry about it. He even moves a little closer as they walk toward the lobby.

It's enough to make Henry feel . . . hopeful. Despite his best efforts to avoid hopeful.

The breakfast room is sparsely populated this early in the morning, and the offerings are sparse, too. Henry and Barrett didn't find much food at the drops they went to the other day—mostly canned stuff hidden in a restaurant alley, and that area had clearly already been picked over. Otherwise, it was primarily batteries and medical supplies rather than breakfast material. So, this morning, it's stale granola bars and some fruit that's just this side of edible. Henry wonders what happens if—when—that runs out.

"A big group just left," Tallis is saying to Barrett in a low voice. They're sitting across from each other at one of the few tables in the room. "We'll be all right on supplies for now, Al. But—"

"No more of your pickups for a while," Barrett says. There's a mug of something in front of him, but given the lack of steam rising from it, it's probably just water.

Tallis frowns. "We can't—"

"People have to fend for themselves," Barrett interrupts. "Helping where we can is all good and well, but we're not a big operation. If you keep bringing people in—"

"We have to look out for each other," Tallis snaps. "The compounds certainly won't."

"Yeah, what about the compounds?" a loud voice asks.

James is sitting nearby with a few younger assets, leaning his chair back against the wall. There are several wrappers on the table in front of him. His eyes are on Barrett, and there's a hint of a smile on his face.

Barrett turns in his chair. "What about them?"

"We're not going to be able to hide from the compounds forever," James points out. "So what are we going to do about that?"

"Nothing. We stay away from the compounds."

James snorts. "That's not going to work."

"I didn't ask for your opinion," Barrett says, expression hardening.

There are some murmurs from James's crew. Nearby, Angelica is sitting on the floor, silently watching. Irene and another few assets are nearby, also keeping an eye on the proceedings. In fact, everyone in the room seems to be watching. James has his audience, which was likely the plan to begin with.

James holds up his hands placatingly. "I can respect the whole live-and-let-live thing, I really can. But I'd be lying if I said I'm not concerned about the assets who come through here. This is a nice temporary solution, but it doesn't solve the larger problem."

"We're not trying to solve the larger problem," Barrett says, eyes narrowing. "We're just trying to survive."

"Yeah, and how's that going to go when the larger problem shows up?"

Henry frowns. It's weird to find himself agreeing with James on something. Barrett's solution is only as good as his access to supplies, and even that only holds if the other assets manage to avoid getting caught or leaking information.

Barrett glares at James. "If you want a revolt, you're in the wrong place."

James grins, and Henry can't help but think of fire and smoke and the compound burning down with people trapped inside. "Nah, I don't have the energy for something like that. I'm just saying, it'll be hard for you to throw your weight around once everyone here gets rounded up."

"Are you threatening—?"

"No! No, of course not! Just expressing concern, like I said. And wondering if you shouldn't consider bringing on some additional allies."

"What's that supposed to mean?"

"Well, strength in numbers, right? Even if you don't want an outright fight against the Compound Network, it might help to have more people on your side." James drops his chair down and leans forward. "I know someone who could help. Someone who could—"

"No."

Henry starts and turns to Bastian, who seems just as surprised as everyone else to realize he's spoken.

"If you want to stay out of things with the compounds, you need to lie low," Bastian continues quickly. "Bringing more people into the mix will just make things harder."

James's gaze turns appraising. There's something else in his expression, too—something Henry doesn't like. "That's interesting."

"What's interesting?" Bastian asks.

James ignores him and turns back to Barrett. "Look, I'm just offering an alternative to skulking around in the city, waiting for the Network to come for you. The end goal is survival, right? I think there are better ways to do that."

Bastian opens his mouth, but Henry puts a hand on his arm. "James might have a good idea. Let's hear him out." He keeps his tone calm and steady, like he's trying to diffuse the tension between two officers on his team. Back when that used to be a thing he did. Back when he thought that mattered.

Now, it's about collecting evidence. If James is doing what Henry suspects he's doing, it's best to let him get to the offer. To see clearly what they're up against.

James looks surprised by Henry's support, but he presses on while he still has the floor. "I know a guy. Someone who's good at looking after people. He's got a place in the forest where assets can be safe from the compounds for longer periods of time. If anyone here is tired of having to pack up whenever compound officers get too close, his sanctuary might be a better fit."

And there it is. *Sanctuary.* The place Bastian and James went looking for a healer. The healer whose "cure" for Bastian was to take energy from other assets in order to stay alive.

Bastian may have decided against it, but James . . . Well, James wouldn't need energy himself, would he? He's not an asset anymore, and even if he were, firestarters don't have the same self-destructive aspect to their power that empaths do.

So this is about Quentin.

Something hot and angry tightens Henry's chest. James *could* be planning to tell them what the tradeoff is. He *could* be doing this out of a genuine desire to help, to get them somewhere a powerful asset can protect them. It's a mutually beneficial partnership: protection in return for letting someone suck you dry of your emotions. Assuming you survive both the person doing the sucking and any compound forces who might come after you.

But if James was willing to burn down a compound and potentially kill everyone in it, only an idiot would assume he has anything other than his personal interests at heart here.

It's survival, Henry reminds himself. Everyone does what they have to in order to survive. Henry ought to know that better than anyone after the last seven months. He, of all people, doesn't have a leg to stand on. Especially since he was prepared to support Bastian in doing exactly what Quentin is doing.

But . . . Bastian was upfront about what he did and what it cost. He didn't try to trick or coerce anyone into it—even when Henry was willing. He's prepared to die to prevent anyone being hurt just so he can live, and while Henry desperately hates what that choice means, he can also respect it.

Manipulating others into becoming temporary sacrifices for Quentin is understandable, if the only goal is survival. But it's a pretty shitty way of treating people.

"The sanctuary isn't going to do anyone much good if they're caught trying to get there," Bastian is saying.

Barrett grunts at him. "You know this place, Lucas?"

Bastian hesitates, then says, "Yeah. I don't recommend it. For starters, it's really close to the compound I came from, and they're on high alert these days. Also, I can't say I'm a fan of the guy who runs it."

"This option won't work for everyone," James says easily, "but people deserve to make their own choices, don't they? Anyway, I'm not sure we should give much weight to Lucas's opinion. He's not exactly a people person. And isn't he the one who brought you two of the compound's most wanted? If anyone's looking out for the safety of the people here, it's definitely *not* him."

The murmurs from the other assets make Henry's skin crawl. He knows the beginning of chaos when he sees it. But it's not like James doesn't have a point. And if he and Bastian try to head this off now, it'll bring up the question of how *they* know what they know—and how much more trouble they might bring the assets here.

"You haven't said why we should trust *you*," Tallis points out. Her voice is strong, though not particularly loud; just enough to gather attention without making it seem like she's reaching for it. James should take notes.

Instead, he just grins. "You shouldn't. You shouldn't trust anyone, really. Any of us could have baggage that might endanger everyone else. The best we can do is go into things with our eyes open. Can you honestly say that that's what everyone here is doing?"

"We're all safe for now," Barrett says. "But only if we can trust each other not to cause trouble. Are you going to cause trouble, James?"

"Nope." James smiles broadly. "No trouble at all."

He gets to his feet, sticks his hands in his pockets, and saunters out of the room. His entourage waits a beat or two, then follows him.

"He's recruiting for Quentin," Bastian says in a low voice.

"Yeah, I got that," Henry agrees. "But—"

"You two, stay in today," Barrett says. He and Tallis have come by on their way out, both looking more than a little disquieted by James's speech.

"What happened to 'live and let live'?" Bastian asks. Because this is definitely the best time to pick a fight.

"There have been more compound forces around than usual lately," Barrett says, not rising to the bait. "So do us all a favor and keep the stupidity to a minimum. No leaving the hotel until things calm down, and we can figure out just how safe we really are here."

"Best behavior," Bastian says. "Got it. Might want to make sure James has got it, too."

"Oh, I will." Barrett gives Henry a quick nod. Then he and Tallis leave.

"I need to talk to you," Henry says to Bastian as soon as they're gone.

***

When they get back to their room, Henry makes a beeline for the closet and grabs the duffel bag. He carries it to the bed and upends it, spilling clothes, toiletries, and first aid supplies all over the comforter.

Henry digs through the pile until he finds the tin. With Bastian's eyes on him, he opens it and takes out the USB drive. "I'm pretty sure this is a backup of the Fail-Safe Protocol files that Kent and Sybil put together at the compound. The ones Emily Tezuka sent to us before she was killed."

Bastian stares at the drive, and then at Henry. "What's it doing in the bag?"

"You tell me. Where did this bag come from?"

"A black coat who was helping me and Laurel. He put together the supplies before Angelica and I escaped." Bastian takes the drive from Henry and peers at it, as if that might somehow confirm what's on it. "You're sure it's the same one?"

Henry sits on the bed and runs a hand through his hair. "No. But I'm *mostly* sure."

"And you want to know what's on it."

He *doesn't*—not after the reminder from James that any actions they take could get people killed. But doing nothing could get people killed, too.

"I'd feel better if we could check it," Henry admits. "And also worse, because if it's what I think it is, we'd be doing more than just endangering the people here a little."

"We'd be endangering them a lot." Bastian sits down next to him and hands over the drive. "We could destroy it, if you think that'd be better."

Henry stares at the bit of metal and plastic and tries to talk some sense into himself. What's the likelihood that these files will do anything other than get people hurt—or worse? What's the likelihood that someone in power can actually use them to help?

What's the likelihood that something horrible will happen if they sit here and do nothing, knowing there was something they *could've* done?

Henry closes his hand around the drive and looks at Bastian. "No. I think we should figure out what's on it. But I should be the one to—"

"I know who we can go to for help."

Henry hesitates. "I'm not sure we should be getting someone else in trouble."

"What about someone who can handle a bit of trouble and might actually be in a position to do something with this information?"

That damned pinprick of hope again. "How much is this going to piss off Barrett?"

"Probably a lot."

"But you think it can save lives?"

Bastian eyes the drive in Henry's hand. "Yeah. If it's you doing it."

It's dangerous—the hope, the documents, the idea that Bastian still thinks Henry is capable of doing something like this. Of helping people. But Henry can't stomach the alternative.

"Well, then," he says. "I guess we'd better do it."

Chapter 18

"THIS IS A stupid idea," Bastian says as they wait at the 3rd and 20th crosswalk.

"It's *your* stupid idea," Henry reminds him. Which is true, and therefore annoying.

"Yeah, well. The part where we make her go somewhere and then follow her until she notices and shoots us? Maybe not the strongest part of the plan," Bastian admits. "Aren't *you* supposed to be the responsible one who pays attention to that sort of detail?"

"We can't exactly drop in on her at the Hall, and we can't call or email; all of that would get traced right back to us. So that leaves—uh—stalking, I guess."

They've completely disregarded Barrett's orders about going out, but they're still doing their best to stay covert—or at least to avoid drawing attention from anyone tied to city security. They took an extremely circuitous route to the government district, all on foot, since trying to find transportation would be begging for trouble.

The city hasn't resorted to Wanted posters for assets or anything, but its partnership with the Compound Network is more active than ever. And that includes sharing intel on high-priority assets. If they get caught on security footage or spotted by law enforcement, this outing is going to end fast.

"You're sure Officer Michaels is working today?" Henry asks.

"I'm sure she's working with the liaison committee, which means she's stationed at the Hall unless someone's making a visit to the compound." That's what Kwan told him a while back, anyway. Bastian suspects Michaels got stuck with this duty so she'd be under supervision, but also not underfoot—Tremain probably couldn't afford to keep someone with close ties to both Henry and

Bastian as her right-hand woman. An assistant to the compound's command-ing officer would have access to a lot of sensitive information she might be inclined to pass along. But Michaels is extremely competent and has a lot of history with the Compound Network, so Tremain couldn't get rid of her en-tirely without raising eyebrows. Thus, the transfer to the Hall.

"Are you okay with the crowd?" Henry asks in a low voice. "If not, we can find another way to—"

"It's fine."

It's *not* fine—not exactly—but Bastian isn't about to ask Henry to negate. Not when they're out in the open like this, and not when he's spent the last seven months being forced to do it against his will. Besides, thanks to the energy he took from Henry, Bastian's pain isn't too bad. He can suck it up and deal with the bombardment of emotions from morning commuters for one day.

The light turns green, and they join the foot traffic heading toward the Hall. Mostly office drones this time of day, along with a few tourists in brightly col-ored t-shirts who stop in odd places and block everyone else, then apologize profusely when they're shoved aside by tired government workers dragging themselves to the Hall or nearby offices.

The Hall grounds are still immaculate. They're designed to intimidate, with ostentatious greenery and marble pillars everywhere. The topiary looks even more intense than Bastian remembers. What *is* it with this city's landscapers and their aggression toward bushes?

"Anything?" Henry murmurs.

"Not yet. Hang on."

Once they've found a location with enough traffic to hide them from the nearest security cameras, Bastian closes his eyes and carefully feels out. He flinches against the wave of bored-tired-determined-interested-smug-calculating that goes along with the collection of politicians, aides, and tourists congregated here on a workday morning. Nothing stands out right away in terms of an emotional signature that might belong to an unflappable liaison committee support staff member.

"Looks like security is more on top of things than normal today," Henry says suddenly.

Bastian opens his eyes and follows Henry's gaze. A small group of officers has gathered by the Hall entrance, as well as at one of the side doors. It might not seem unusual except that they're trying really hard to make sure it doesn't look unusual. And their tense-concerned-focused isn't exactly subtle.

"Doesn't matter," Bastian says. "We're not trying to get in."

"Sure, but how nice are they going to be about letting people out?"

"She could just use one of the other exits."

"They're covering them all, and they're spread out over the grounds, too."

Bastian frowns and takes another look. Henry is right: There are little pockets of extra security everywhere. "Visiting dignitary?"

"Maybe. Seems odd that they'd try to hide how prepared they are if that's the case, though."

Bastian doesn't feel the cluster of fawning-plotting-manipulative that he'd expect from an event like that, anyway. Still, the stationing of security is indicative of *something*. And it means it'll be harder to find Michaels and convince her to come out where they can talk to her.

"Let's focus on Michaels for now," he says. Then he turns away from the crowd and directs his attention to the Hall, pushing a little harder to get past all the noise.

The sheer *weight* of all of the emotions slams against his shield like a typhoon trying to push water through a dike. He was expecting a strong reaction, but not *this* strong. Just how many people are there at the Hall today?

(Excited-fearful-anxious-stressed-harried, so many people feeling so much all together, the pressure of each individual and the pressure of everyone all at once, like wading through an ocean of riptides while trying to find one tiny fish, and he's hyper aware of absolutely everything, burning him hot and cold—)

"Bastian." Henry is touching his arm with just his fingertips. "Okay?"

Bastian half expects to find that his nose is bleeding, but it isn't. His head is pounding, and his stomach is unsettled, but it's nowhere near as bad as he'd usually expect from this kind of exertion. Whatever he took from Henry isn't solving the problem, but it's making it less intense.

Bastian swallows the guilt and moves away, enough so that Henry isn't touching him anymore. Just in case. "It's fine. I've got it."

Henry presses his lips together but doesn't say anything else.

Bastian takes a moment to shore up his shield, then feels out again. Henry's concerned-patient-uneasy hits first, though it's dimmed by his usual resting level of negation. Bastian brushes past it and focuses on the Hall. Nothing seems familiar, except—wait. That might be Senator Nunez's baseline annoyed-strained-determined. Reassuring how some things never change. And a few offices down . . .

"She's on the third floor," Bastian says. "Find us a good place to chat, and I'll convince her that she feels like going there."

Henry looks around for a moment, then says, "Café down the street. It's too early for lunch, but she might decide to get coffee there instead of in the atrium."

Bastian squashes down the discomfort of manipulating the emotions of a friend—Why should that be worse than all the times he's done it to strangers?—and gently pokes Michaels's thoughtful-placid-curious into a desire to get out of the Hall for a bit.

She exits the building not long after, stopping to talk briefly with one of the security guards before continuing down the steps.

"She ought to be motivated enough now," Bastian says. "Let's go."

The sidewalks are a little less busy now that the morning is wearing on. The café they head to isn't terribly busy, either. They're able to sit at one of the outdoor tables without attracting attention, although the people behind the counter do seem alert enough to eventually notice non-customers taking up valuable table real estate. They'll have to get Michaels to order her usual macchiato.

While Bastian monitors for any sudden changes in the feelings of the people around them, he also sneaks glances at Henry. The tense set of his shoulders and the forcibly calm exterior make sense, given where they are and what they're doing, but they also make Bastian uneasy. He remembers the thin shell of functionality Henry was wearing during and after the rescue from the safe house: mission over mental breakdown for as long as possible. So of course he'll keep a cool head while they're out in public, but . . .

But it's a nice, cool day with only a few clouds in the sky, and the murmur of the café patrons around them is ambiance rather than irritation, and if Bastian and Henry were two completely different people in the city right now . . .

"I'd buy you coffee, but I don't have any money," Bastian says suddenly.

Henry blinks, turning away from what was clearly another scan for security cameras. "Sorry?"

"That's what you're supposed to do when you're out with your . . . whatever. Right?" Bastian averts his eyes, pretending to observe the crowd.

Henry's surprised-amused-teasing is hard to miss even without looking directly at him. "Are you saying we should make this a date?"

"Well, it's better than eating an energy bar in a tree while we're on the run from the compound, at least."

Bastian tries to imagine what it would be like to go on a real date. To go someplace nice for dinner without having to worry about a strategically vital Compound Council meeting the next day. To walk in the city without wondering if nearby security cameras might be sending data to the compound. To not be worried that Bastian's power is going to go haywire at any moment and throttle him with a headache or a bloody nose. To just relax and spend time with someone he—

Henry's amusement shifts to slight regret before evening out to something sterner. "Here she comes."

Since he's facing away from the street, Bastian can't look directly without being too obvious. But he manages to catch a glimpse of Michaels' approaching figure with a subtle tilt of his head. Rather than the compound uniform he's used to seeing her in, she's wearing a very simple but well-tailored black suit. Along with her short, dark hair, it's a little severe, but she wears it well.

He can tell from her alarm-surprise-confusion that she spots them almost immediately. None of it registers on her face, though—she strides right past their table and into the café. A few minutes later, she comes back out with a drink and sits down.

"Should I question whether I actually wanted this macchiato?" she asks.

Bastian grimaces. "You always want a macchiato. I just . . . convinced you that you felt like getting one right now from this café. Uh. Sorry about that. But we needed to talk to you."

"I see." Michaels takes a sip. "I'm pleased you're both alive. Information about your current whereabouts hasn't been easy to come by."

"You've been looking for us?" Henry asks (startled-concerned-impressed).

"Not openly. Discretion seemed particularly important in this case. Especially for you, sir," she says, eyes on Henry. "I hadn't heard anything in quite some time."

Michaels has never been one for emotional flourishes, but Bastian doesn't need to read her to know she's genuinely pleased to see Henry alive and well.

Henry seems struck by it, too, but he recovers quickly. "You heard something at some point, though? You were getting reports?"

"Not exactly. I work primarily with Senator Nunez now, and you might remember that she's on the compound liaison committee, coordinating compound and city interests. You might also remember that she's on a subcommittee that's very . . . interested in collecting certain kinds of information."

The subcommittee involved with the Fail-Safe Protocol. Carter's front for collecting and hoarding information about it, according to what Nunez told Bastian and Henry not long before they lost control of the compound. Nunez made it sound like Carter basically uses the subcommittee to do whatever he wants—including getting aides like Emily Tezuka murdered if he doesn't like where their research is going.

A gaggle of emotions is getting louder as it comes toward them, the cheerful-excited-curious, like a flurry of pebbles knocking relentlessly against Bastian's shield. He can't see anyone on the sidewalk yet, but he notices a big tour bus slowly passing by, apparently looking for a place to park.

"We shouldn't talk long," Bastian says quickly, already splitting his attention between their conversation and the emotions of the current customers, gently redirecting them as needed. Henry, Bastian, and Michaels aren't particularly obtrusive, but with this many people coming into a public space, Bastian needs to be aware of everyone and everything in order to prevent anyone from noticing the handoff.

The part of Bastian that's paying attention to Henry does *not* like how perceptive his frown is. "You don't have to—"

"Let's just finish up before someone decides they want this table," Bastian tells him.

Henry hesitates, then turns to Michaels. "We have some information that needs vetting, but we don't have the resources. We were hoping you could help."

"Of course," Michaels says immediately.

"If it's what we think it is, it's extremely dangerous," Henry continues. "You'll need to make sure no one knows you have it."

"That won't be a problem."

Bastian suspects it *will* be a problem, but not one Michaels can't handle. Of course, that's leaving aside the question of whether she should *have* to.

Even if they really, really need her to.

Henry gets the USB drive out of his pocket and slides it over to Michaels. "We think these are the files that got one of Senator Nunez's aides killed. The Compound Council doesn't know we have them, and we'd like to keep it that way."

"Understood." Michaels takes the drive and swiftly tucks it into her suit pocket.

The transaction takes seconds, and as far as Bastian can tell, it doesn't cause any sort of emotional blip anywhere around them. Not a guarantee that no one saw it, but a pretty good indication that no one cared or is likely to remember if asked.

Bastian grimaces. Monitoring this many people is making him lightheaded. Not as bad as at the safe house, but bad enough.

"How long do you think it will take to confirm what's on there?" Henry asks.

"I'll need time to establish a secure location for the process. End of the week?"

"We'll find you at the Hall," Bastian says. His voice only sounds a little bit strained.

Michaels looks at him a little too intuitively, then nods. "All right."

"Thank you, Michaels," Henry says with a careful smile. "And sorry for getting you involved with this."

"I appreciate your concern, sir, but it's unnecessary." She hesitates, then adds, "If you could indulge me for a bit longer . . . ?"

Bastian mentally grits his teeth. "Go on."

"There's a guest at the Hall today. I'm told it's someone from the Compound Council, although I don't know who it is or why they're here."

"Why, Michaels, have you been *spying*?" Bastian asks, smiling in spite of himself.

"The acquisition of useful information is an important part of my job," Michaels says in a tone that isn't entirely innocent. "In this case, I mention it because the security around this visitor's identity and schedule are even tighter than normal for a Council member."

"You think it's someone who outranks Carter?" Henry says thoughtfully.

"There isn't anyone more highly ranked on the Council than General Carter. At least, not officially."

Bastian frowns. "But unofficially . . ."

"Maybe we shouldn't have asked you for that favor," Henry says with a burst of shame-concern-unease. "With that sort of guest in town, it's—"

"Please don't worry about it. I mention our guest only because it seems to be causing some anxiety for the liaison committee. There might be a link between that visit and the files we're investigating. The committee seems equally concerned about both."

"It's not worth endangering yourself any more than you already are," Henry says firmly. "If there's a connection, we can look into it once we're sure about those files."

"Yes, sir." Michaels gets to her feet. "I'd better get back. Please take care of yourselves."

Bastian doesn't have time to tease her about this uncharacteristically emotional response because he's distracted by the arrival of the tourists, a large group of retirees that includes several dogs and apparently intends to squeeze its entirety into the café. Even without the sharp slap of their emotions, the noise alone would have Bastian's teeth on edge.

Henry leans in. "She's gone. You don't have to—"

"Can't let anyone notice us," Bastian says, breathing in sharply and trying to focus. He makes the mistake of standing up too quickly and teeters briefly before Henry grabs his arm to steady him. Bastian feels him put up a very small negation field—just enough to block out some of the noise without completely negating Bastian's power.

Bastian ought to find the contact jarring while he's trying to focus, but there's something reassuring about it. He doesn't have to do this alone.

"Let's get out of here," Henry says quietly.

***

They spend the rest of the morning and into the afternoon making their way back to the hotel by a careful, circuitous route. It's not a guarantee that they won't be followed, but it's at least some insurance against it. Plus, it leads them past a cache outside of a sandwich shop that provides them with some barely palatable granola bars. Bastian suspects robbing the store would be a better way to find something edible for lunch, but Henry probably wouldn't go for it, and Bastian isn't really up for the effort himself, honestly. Never mind the ethics.

He maintains a low level of power throughout the trip, gently nudging the emotions of anyone around them who shows too much interest. Might be overkill, but it's not like he can't tell that Henry is also keeping an eye out for tails while trying not to look like he's keeping an eye out for tails.

Bastian's headache stays manageable, although the dizziness still hits him sporadically, maybe because his focus is so broad. He's not sure if it's okay to be glad for the excuse to keep a hand on Henry's arm to steady himself.

When they finally get closer to the hotel, Bastian feels a strong jolt of angry-worried-alert coming from the lobby.

"Trouble?" Henry asks.

"Get ready to be grounded," Bastian mutters.

They go in through one of the less conspicuous side entrances, not that it does them much good. Barrett is waiting for them as soon as they're inside, arms crossed, face stony. "This is you staying put? Where the hell have you been?"

"Didn't realize you'd miss us this much," Bastian remarks.

"Don't be cute, Lucas. I told you there were more compound officers around, and you should stay in. What made you think it was a good idea to ignore my warning?"

"It was important," Henry says quickly, "and we were careful."

"You sure about that?"

James is standing farther down the hallway, leaning against the wall, hands in his pockets. Bastian's head is feeling a little fuzzy after using his power so much today, but there's something . . .

"What are you talking about?" Henry asks with an edge to his voice.

(The smug-amused-triumphant coming from James, standing there calmly and planning the perfect reveal, and Bastian can feel something else approaching, something bigger and more complicated, the focus and determination of a large group of people, people on a mission, and if he hadn't been so distracted by finding Michaels and going unnoticed on the street, he might've realized that—)

"Al!"

Tallis hurries toward them, slipping around James and lowering her voice. It does nothing to hide her alarm-anxiety-fear. "Compound forces spotted on this block. I don't think it's just recon; they're heading here on purpose."

"A raid," Barrett says grimly.

"Wonder how that happened?" James says a little too loudly.

Bastian quickly goes back to the side door they just came through, Henry close on his heels. Very carefully, making sure he's at an unobservable angle, Bastian looks out through the glass and into the parking lot.

It's a stupid move, of course—he already knows what's happening, more or less. The visual confirmation just makes it worse: Vehicles entering the lot, uniformed people spilling out. Armed, uniformed people who are looking at the hotel with clear intent and emotional signatures that mean business.

"Shit," Bastian says.

Chapter 19

PRISON OFFICER TEMPLETON is very bad at her job, and Laurel can't help but be grateful for it.

"Thought you could use a friend," she says cheerfully when she brings lunch to Laurel's cell. The sandwich on the tray looks limp and unappealing, but the spiky succulent next to it is sturdy and stoic in a comforting way. Laurel can just make out its long-suffering sigh as Templeton jostles it in the process of opening the cell door.

Laurel hops to her feet and goes over to take the tray, just barely refraining from a sigh of her own. "Thank you."

Templeton gives her a wry look. "I'm not sure that sandwich is worthy of thanks, but it'll get you through till dinner, at least."

"Well," Laurel says carefully, "I don't think it's really the sandwich's fault. If the cafeteria had listened to what I told them about growing produce properly, maybe the lettuce wouldn't have given up on life so completely."

Is this what it's going to be like from here on out, then? Stuck in a cell, talking about lunch while nothing changes? Watching everything she, Henry, and Bastian tried to rebuild get torn down by a major who doesn't seem to care about who she hurts, so long as it gets her closer to some big, secret goal?

Maybe the lack of sunlight is making her overreact.

Templeton tips her head to one side as she closes the cell door. "Ah, there's someone coming in. I'll be back for that tray in a little bit. You can keep the plant, of course."

She turns the key, then hurries down the hall to deal with a noise Laurel didn't even hear.

Laurel allows herself the sigh she was holding back and sets the tray down, lifting the succulent to eye level. "Hello," she says. "I'm sorry you're trapped down here with me now, although I do appreciate the company. But don't worry; I'll have Templeton take you out to somewhere with more light when she gets back."

The succulent isn't impressed, which makes Laurel frown. "Well, that's not really fair. She probably just doesn't know what level of light you prefer. I'm sure she didn't *mean* to imply that you're okay with indirect sunlight, although even if you were, it's not like that's a bad thing."

Laurel stops, then blinks. "Wait. We're talking. We shouldn't be able to— the serum—"

But if she thinks about it carefully—gets really quiet and *listens*—she can hear all sorts of things: the succulent doing the plant equivalent of an eye roll; the wheezing potted plant in Dr. Rowe's office one level up; the rhododendrons just outside the compound gossiping about something she can't quite make out.

Her power isn't at full strength, but it's much closer than it should be, given the serum level she's usually on. Which means . . . Templeton must have gotten the dose wrong this morning, and it's wearing off much too quickly. Except dosages are determined by the med techs based on experimental factors. So one of *them* must have gotten it wrong when they sent instructions to Templeton. But they never get important things like that wrong. And if it was intentional, she would be under much stricter supervision, like when she goes to her garden. But—

"Laurel."

Laurel starts and looks over at the cell door. Standing just outside are two people she was definitely not expecting to stop by for a visit: a very stern black coat and a very anxious tracker.

Laurel lowers the succulent and gives Kwan and Chloe a confused smile. "Hello. Strange place for a stroll. Unless you're going to throw Chloe in here, but that wouldn't be very—"

Kwan unlocks her cell with what looks like the key Templeton just used to close it. "We're in a hurry," he says. "Let's go."

"Go? Go where?"

Kwan doesn't answer; just holds the door open silently. Laurel follows the direction, less because she responds well to enigmatic orders and more because she's concerned about the level of tension in Chloe's face, which is high, even for her.

"Okay?" Laurel asks under her breath as Kwan leads them down the block.

Chloe nods once, quickly, and Laurel wonders if she and Kwan have developed some sort of secret language of anxious/irritated body language that they'll expect Laurel to learn.

They come out into the jail block entryway, where Templeton is sitting at her desk with a mountain of paperwork. She looks up and gives a different sort of nod—polite and efficient—but adds some vocals, too: "Please have the prisoner back by the end of the day, Kwan."

"Understood." Kwan sets the key he just used down on Templeton's desk between two stacks of paper.

Laurel sets the succulent down next to it. "Please make sure this plant gets full sunlight," she says, trying to match Kwan's tone. Immediately deciding it isn't for her, she adds in a much softer voice, "Thank you, though."

Templeton gives her a small smile, then goes back to her papers.

Kwan herds Laurel and Chloe out of the jail block, down the hall, and into an elevator heading for Level 1. Laurel remembers this move quite well and braces herself for another meeting with Tremain, but Kwan takes them on a different route to the other side of the floor and then out of the building.

He doesn't stop until they're at the far end of Laurel's garden. They've been moving too quickly for Laurel to properly soak up all of the plant conversations in the area, but now that they've slowed down, maybe she can collect some good gossip.

"Are you listening?" Kwan snaps.

Laurel blinks and refocuses. "Sorry. Were you going to explain why we're taking a walk? Not that I'm complaining. Templeton has a nice jail block, I suppose, but natural sunlight is really more—"

"There's a retrieval mission that went into the city today," Kwan interrupts. "The major needs your help."

"Well, I'm not going to help with *that*," Laurel says immediately. "Wait. Why would she think I *could* help with that?"

"Officially, she doesn't. Unofficially, you two have the best chance of getting into the city before the outcome of that mission leads to too much trouble."

Laurel and Chloe exchange glances. "The major . . . wants us to interfere with a retrieval?" Chloe asks hesitantly.

"It's too late to interfere. By the time you get to the city, it will already have happened. But you might be able to minimize the fallout." Kwan hesitates, then adds, "We think Mortimer and Lucas are with the group that was targeted."

Laurel feels the blood drain from her face. "That's even more reason for us *not* to help."

"The retrieval wasn't ordered by Major Tremain," Kwan says. "Our team is leading it, but the mission came from General Carter and Senator Donnigan's liaison committee. They went over Major Tremain's head to get it done, which is why we're only hearing about it now. And it's not just assets who are being retrieved; there's other information involved. Something Major Tremain doesn't want Carter and Donnigan to have."

"So she wants us to get it for her? And maybe just happen to bring Henry and Bastian back at the same time? Forget it."

"She doesn't want you to bring them in."

Laurel stares at him. "Um. She doesn't?"

"They need to stay out there and keep the information safe, especially if Carter's trying to get it. Your powers can get you to them before anyone else."

"Why don't you just send another team?"

"Two unassuming assets will have a better chance of getting closer—especially if no one knows they're assets. And Lucas and Mortimer are more likely to trust you than a compound team."

Laurel narrows her eyes. "What's the information, and why does Major Tremain want it kept away from Carter?"

"We don't really have time for—"

"Right, so you should just tell me so we can get on with it."

Kwan lets out an annoyed sigh and runs a hand through his hair. "I gave Lucas something before he left. According to Major Tremain, it could be the key to accomplishing her goal with the compound. I don't know anything else except that she wants you two to confirm that he still has it and keep it away from anyone affiliated with General Carter."

Kwan turns to Chloe. "I can't get you onto the retrieval transport since it's already left. But your power might help you catch up. I'll give you some IDs and a cover story that will get you into the city and keep security off your backs, at least for a while."

"I—I think we can do that." Chloe looks at Laurel, expression a combination of terror and determination that makes something in Laurel's throat tighten. "Laurel? We can do that, can't we?"

"You need to promise they'll be safe," Laurel says to Kwan. "From Tremain, I mean. From you, maybe, since you seem to be a bit sneaky yourself. We can maybe keep Carter from getting that information, but the boys are stupid, and they've been through enough. If someone tried to make things harder for them . . . well. Do you know how many poisons can be made from the plants around here?"

(It's too fast, too much like when the fire started in her compound, and all their careful plans went out the door, and they had to act *now*, and suddenly keeping everyone safe was so much less important than lashing out and taking down whoever you could, hurting whoever you could, and—)

"I can't promise they'll be safe," Kwan says, but there's that thread of gentleness in the otherwise stern tone. "Not entirely, anyway. For what it's worth, I'll do what I can from here to make sure this mission doesn't endanger them—or you. But I can't control what goes on out there. Carter could pull the rug out from under us whenever he wants, and Tremain would have to go along with it, at least outwardly."

Kwan takes a breath. "So, if you get caught, she'll disavow everything. It can't come back on her."

Laurel frowns. "But it can come back on *us*?"

"Obviously, it'd be better if it didn't, but—"

"Yeah, better for *her*."

"We should probably go, right?" Chloe asks.

Laurel eyes Kwan warily. He's been a good ally, but he'll always be loyal to Tremain first, won't he? "Are you doing this for yourself or for Major Tremain?"

"Both. And neither. What's happening in the Compound Network is bigger than any one person. It's—" He shakes his head. "The most important thing now is to get you off the grounds as quickly as possible. So let's go."

Quentin might be right that Laurel should question Kwan's loyalties, but there's another side of that argument: Kwan has been loyal to assets, too. He's helped them investigate the dead zones for months, and he helped Bastian escape. Whatever's going on with him and Tremain, it doesn't change the fact that they've had the chances they've had so far in large part because Kwan had their backs. If he's saying Laurel and Chloe need to leave now . . . Well, at the very least, it's an opportunity to find Bastian and Henry.

Laurel looks at Kwan for a moment longer, then nods. "Okay."

The sunlight is warm on her face, the grass is gently murmuring at her feet, and Laurel wonders if she's off to save her friends or completely ruin everything.

Chapter 20

"THIS IS YOUR fault," James hisses as he and Bastian peek around a dusty set of hotel curtains. And the hell of it is, he's probably right.

Bastian should have known better than to suggest their trip to the Hall. He should've known better than to bring Henry and Angelica here in the first place. Just because Tallis likes to play hero, doesn't mean he should've taken her up on her offer of a safe place to stay. Or asked for her help at all.

Better to go it alone. Better to keep to himself. He knew that once, but he's become so much more of an idiot since then. And now . . .

Barrett and Tallis have gathered up the assets, waiting for a good moment to make a run for it. The officers haven't come in with guns blazing—they probably need to confirm the presence of assets first to avoid paperwork with the city government—but that will only take a few more minutes.

They must've gotten a tip, but Bastian can't figure out how. He and Henry were careful, and no one else has left the hotel today, as far as Bastian could tell from eavesdropping on Barrett questioning everyone. And if they were lying, Bastian would know. Just like the good old days of interrogating.

It's possible that someone staying at the hotel was spotted earlier by an asset working for the Compound Network—there are some assets out there who have been pressed into service—and the consequences are only catching up with them now. But someone would have had to be extremely careless about using their power in a trackable way, which is exactly what everyone here avoids.

"It's fine if *you* want to be stupid," James continues, "but some of us—"

"Shut up." Bastian closes his eyes and feels out carefully, just enough to brush past a few minds and get a count. The cloud of anxious-excited-determined is more annoying than painful at the moment, so he doesn't have much trouble making out a group of fifteen officers in the parking lot, trying and failing to be inconspicuous. There are about thirty more dispersed around nearby sidewalks and across the street, so three or four retrieval teams, probably. Maybe more, farther out. Seems like overkill, but the hotel is fairly large, and they probably don't know exactly how many assets are here right now. Or that most of the hotel is empty.

They'll need to be careful, but with good timing and a decent distraction—and assuming there aren't additional officers on the way—it *might* be possible to get out of here.

Bastian opens his eyes. "Henry?"

"They're new." Henry is standing one window over, looking carefully around the curtain at a few officers checking their gear nearby. "Still got the first-time jitters. Definitely compound officers, but I don't see their leader yet. And the fact that they still haven't barged in here means they're waiting on intel or a higher-up's blessing. Either way, we don't have much more time."

Bastian feels out again, just within the hotel to see where everyone is. Ten other assets in the lobby, huddled together under a blanket of restless-anxious-fearful, ready to run as soon as someone gives the word. Barrett and Tallis in the hall, their tense-worried-focused engulfing them as they try to get everyone together. Irene and Angelica hurrying to the lobby from Irene's clinic, probably loaded down with whatever medical supplies they could carry. A few other assets in other parts of the hotel, packing their things amidst a flurry of fear.

It's not a large group, but it's big enough that one person's stupidity could ruin it for everyone. Assuming Bastian's stupidity hasn't already done that.

Bastian turns his attention back to the officers outside. He could convince the nearest ones that they feel like going somewhere else. But a mission is going to come with objectives, and someone will notice if a group of retrieval teams comes back having completely forgotten the reason they went out into the field in the first place.

Maybe he ought to try anyway. If he can get the nuances right, he might be able to make them feel not only like they're ready to go, but like there's no reason to come back to this specific location. Getting the feelings right would be tricky, of course, and there's no guarantee that those feelings would last for longer than a few minutes. But it's better than nothing. If he can just ignore the tension headache that's starting to pound at his temples . . .

"Are you thinking about doing something stupid?"

Bastian opens his eyes and finds Henry standing next to him, having taken James's place. Much better setup, aside from the part where James is now standing in the corner, talking quietly with a few assets, all of them shooting Bastian wary glances. Like kids gossiping in the lunchroom, rather than adults who need to focus on getting out of here.

"No more stupid than usual," Bastian tells Henry. "But if I screw up, you may need to shoot people. Too bad we didn't keep the gun from the safe house."

Henry frowns and opens his mouth, probably to say something disapproving, but Bastian's attention snags on the lines that crease his face, the dark valleys under his eyes, the way his shoulders are rigid, but the rest of his body seems calm. Bastian suddenly, violently misses the crinkle-around-the-eyes thing Henry does when he smiles. Should've had the guts to look at him properly at the café, when he was making that face instead of this one.

"Bastian?" Henry's negation field goes up, but just barely. The concern-wariness-confusion is clear enough.

"Don't worry," Bastian says. "I'll take care of it."

It's like escaping Quentin's sanctuary or the safe house where he found Henry: lots of people to sift through, but they've got too much on their minds to notice a little tweak of intent around their emotions. Tense becomes relaxed. Anticipating becomes accomplished. This task is done, so let's move onto the next one—but gently, subtly. No coercion here. It has to be a genuine feeling that this mission would be better served by going somewhere else.

It's fewer people than he had to deal with, say, on the transport convoy with Angelica, but it's more careful manipulation than he's had to do before. There's more at stake. More nuance required.

And then it suddenly *hurts*.

He opens his eyes and grabs onto the curtain to keep from falling over as his throat closes and his head explodes in pain. Henry reaches for his arm, but Bastian jerks away unsteadily. He doesn't have the strength to work through Henry's negation, and—

(And what's the point of what he did to Henry, what Bastian took from him without meaning to, if it's barely lasted any time at all, if he can't tell anymore if he wants to touch Henry because he pretty much always does or because he wants to steal energy from him, and Bastian is too weak to know the difference—?)

"They're backing off," Henry murmurs. He's still close, but not too close. "It's okay. You can—"

Barrett strides into the lobby, Tallis on his heels. Every head turns as he stops in front of Bastian, arms crossed over his chest. "We're moving," he says after a long pause.

"That's it?" James is glaring at them. "They brought the compound forces down on us, and you're just going to ignore it? We should at least dump the deadweight, especially if it'll keep those officers off our backs."

"They'll come after us no matter what, if they see us," Bastian says, struggling to keep his voice steady. "But if you're offering to be the diversion while the rest of us escape, I'm fine with that."

James raises his eyebrows. "I don't think *I'm* the problem. I'm not the reason Barrett's little hangout is ruined. I'm not the one putting everyone in danger just by being here. I'm not the one who could hurt everyone in the building just because I felt like it."

"I wouldn't—"

"I wasn't talking about you." James's eyes go to Henry.

"*Really* not the time," Tallis says firmly.

"Isn't it? Shouldn't we make sure we can trust the people we're escaping with? Otherwise, how do we know that one of us isn't a spy or something? I mean, unless you *want* to make things easier for the compound."

Barrett grimaces. "None of you three idiots are my favorite person at the moment, but that doesn't mean I'm going to throw you to the wolves. Yet."

Bastian's head is still pounding, but his vision is clearing enough that he notices Irene, Angelica, and the last group of assets hurrying into the lobby. Angelica gives off a flicker of concern-fear-nervousness as she hurries over, though her face stays as neutral as ever.

Bastian tries to refocus. "Barrett and Tallis are right; we need to go. I've distracted their officers a little, but I can't—"

"The back way. *Now.*" Barrett turns on his heel and walks out of the lobby, stopping to help someone with their bag along the way.

In fact, everyone seems to be helping someone else, to Bastian's surprise. Even James's entourage are counting heads and making sure everyone has their belongings.

"Time to go?" Angelica asks.

"Yeah," Bastian tells her. "Stay close."

They hurry toward the back entrance. It's a predictable escape route, but before they reach it, Tallis and a few others break off and head down a side hall toward a different exit. Looks like she's going to run a distraction similar to what she did with the transport convoy.

"We'll head for the trees on the other side of the parking lot," Barrett says. "Tallis will buy us some time, but we need to move *fast*. Whatever you hear, whatever you see, you keep going. Got it?"

The mumbles from the assembled assets don't sound particularly enthusiastic. But as soon as Barrett opens the door, they're off.

And almost immediately, Bastian realizes something is wrong.

The pounding in his head becomes a strange sort of buzz that gets increasingly louder as they reach the center of the parking lot. He feels Henry tense beside him a split second before the shouting starts, and a group of compound officers appears from around the corner, sprinting toward them.

"*Go!*" Barrett yells, shoving several assets forward. The wind around him starts to kick up a swirl of sand—but then it stops abruptly, and then sand falls to the ground in a clump. He stares down at it, startled, while the assets around him falter—some heading for the trees, others hesitating.

Bastian feels a sharper buzzing on the back of his neck before a sudden explosion of fear-anger-confusion drops him to his knees with a gasp. The pain is excruciating for two horrible seconds, and then it's just . . . gone.

And he can't feel anything.

Henry is kneeling next to him. "Bastian—"

"Something's wrong," Bastian says through gritted teeth. "Take Angelica and—"

But he can see out of the corner of his eye that she's on the ground as well, holding her head and rocking back and forth, making small whimpering noises. In fact, there are assets all over the concrete in various stages of confusion and pain. Which he can't feel at *all*.

Bastian grabs for Henry's sleeve. "I can't use my—Can you—?"

Henry opens his mouth, then shoots to his feet. He quickly steps in front of Bastian and Angelica, his back to them. Bastian blinks his watering eyes until he can just make out the approaching officers.

"They told me it wouldn't affect you," says a familiar female voice. "I didn't believe it, but I suppose I should have. You really are one of them now, aren't you?"

"Smith," Henry says to his former second-in-command.

Chapter 21

HENRY WANTS TO look around the parking lot, see who made it to the trees and who didn't, but he doesn't have the luxury of looking anywhere other than at Smith. Her weapon is a standard-issue tranq gun, though it's not quite the same size or shape as the ones he remembers from the field. An upgrade, maybe, to go along with whatever they just used against Bastian and the others. Henry felt a pulse go through him, but unlike everyone else, he wasn't knocked off his feet, and it doesn't seem to have affected his power. Maybe because it's not really possible to negate a negator.

Henry supposes he should just be glad that the tranq gun implies that Smith and her team aren't here to kill anyone. She wasn't shy about expressing her opinions about assets when she served on his retrieval team, and she kept it up once they were both promoted. Whatever her status is now, though, she doesn't seem to be shooting to kill. Of course, dying isn't the worst possible fate for an asset.

(It's his fault they're trapped here, his fault for thinking the USB drive could change anything, that getting it to Michaels was something they could do safely, and now these assets are going to be sucked right back into the system they were trying to escape, all because some part of him can't stop trying to *help*, even though he knows it only makes things worse—)

Henry takes a shaky breath and gives Smith a careful once-over. She looks tired and tense, despite her immaculate uniform and stern eyebrows. He remembers what she was like on field missions: argumentative and easily irritated, sure. But he doesn't remember her shoulders looking so tight or her eyes so sharp, like her glare might cut someone in half.

That "someone" being him, at the moment.

"You'll be coming with us, and so will anyone else here who wants to survive," Smith says. "My officers are going to cuff you, so—"

"What did you do to us?" Bastian demands. Henry can't decide if he's glad to hear Bastian's voice sounding steadier or if he's dreading the incoming argument. Bastian and Smith didn't get along when they were working together, and they don't seem likely to reconcile now.

"Shut up and do as you're told," Smith says. "Assuming that's something you're capable of."

Bastian laughs humorlessly and gets to his feet, only wobbling a little. "Smith, in all the time we worked together, when did I ever give you the impression that I gave a shit about doing what other people tell me to do?"

Smith shrugs. "Your choice."

Henry barely has time to register the movement before she raises her gun and fires. On instinct, he shifts his weight and shoves Bastian out of the way, but he knows it was the wrong call almost immediately when he hears a small yelp behind him.

Tranqs, he reminds himself, but he can't stop the rush of fear and anger that chokes him at the sight of Angelica, curled up on her side, eyes fluttering closed, the dart sticking out of her neck.

"She was already on the ground," Henry snaps at Smith. "Why the hell did you shoot?"

"She was getting up," Smith says evenly. "I needed to protect my team."

The way she shot Mariah in the ravine during that retrieval. When it wasn't necessary, but she'd seemed genuinely concerned for her coworkers' safety. Only this time, she's using some sort of stronger negation serum. Twice the punishment, if Smith decides it's necessary. And it *is* punishment: Bastian and the others seemed like they were in pain. Not like the serum Henry used to use, which just knocked assets out, slowly and gently.

Several officers move toward them, guns raised but not quite in regulation position—the newbies Henry noted earlier. Even though they're the ones carrying weapons, they stumble to a halt when they get a good look at the glare Bastian is sending their way. He's kneeling beside Angelica, a wounded but protective animal about to strike.

"Captain," says an officer standing closer to Smith, his voice low but not low enough. "There's a problem in the—"

"Not now," Smith says. She nods to the officers nearest to Henry, Bastian, and Angelica. "Cuff them and bring them. They can't hurt you."

"That's cute." And before Henry can stop him, Bastian stands up, turns on his heel, and punches the nearest officer in the face.

This goes about as well as can be expected. The officer doubles over, and Bastian—cursing and cradling his hand because he's an idiot who should know better but apparently doesn't—takes the opportunity to knock him down. And then over-corrects and goes down with him.

Another officer raises her gun. Before she can properly take aim, Henry grabs it away from her, shoving her back and putting himself between Bastian, Angelica, and the rest of the compound team. Not that it'll matter; they're vastly outnumbered and likely to be taken out in the next ten seconds, once these officers get over their hesitation. "Bastian, what the *hell*?"

"Distraction," Bastian says, struggling to his feet and away from the prone officer. "I need to—"

An odd feeling cuts through Henry's stomach, like an electrical jolt. Then everything around them goes quiet and still.

The officers have gone slack-jawed, staring at nothing, and the assets have stopped in their tracks. It's like someone hit a giant pause button. No collapsing to the ground like before; just a complete cessation of movement all at once.

Except for Henry.

Bastian comes out of it first, maybe a second or two later, breathing heavily. His eyes dart around like he's expecting to see someone.

"Am I interrupting?" calls a pleasant voice.

There's a man standing at the edge of the trees, hands loosely clasped behind his back, like he's just out for a walk. His shaggy salt-and-pepper hair is a little long and ragged, and his t-shirt and pants are dull gray but clean. If he's had any trouble with the compound forces, he's definitely not showing it.

Henry feels Bastian tense next to him. "Quentin."

The man doesn't acknowledge them—probably couldn't hear Bastian from that far away—but Henry thinks he might glance over. Hard to tell, especially since he's busy taking a sweeping look at the whole scene now.

"Well, don't mind me." Quentin waves a hand.

In reaction to his movement, the scene unpauses. Everything explodes—assets scramble to their feet, yelling and running toward the trees; officers shout, raising their guns. The noise is sudden and deafening, like a video snapping from mute to full volume.

Then there's the sting of sand in Henry's face. He uses his free hand to cover his nose and mouth, scanning around him, but he quickly loses his sense of direction.

From out of nowhere, Bastian grabs his arm. "This way!"

Henry squints and looks down at the ground, but all he can see is sand. "Angelica?"

Still holding onto Henry's arm, Bastian twists one way and then the other. Like Henry, he's covering most of his nose and mouth with a sleeve, but Henry can still see his eyes go from confused to hard. "She's right—Wait—"

The chaos is getting wilder, with officers making use of their tranqs despite the low visibility while assets use whatever means they have to escape. Henry feels the shiver of a bolt of electricity passing nearby—an electrocutor's handiwork, probably—while Barrett's sand continues to provide cover. Whatever the officers used on them initially was apparently only worth one shot. Now it's tranqs or nothing.

"*Move*, idiots!" Barrett yells as he races by.

"They must have taken her," Bastian says, still looking around desperately. "She was so close, but they—"

Henry swallows the sour taste of guilt. "We have to go."

"Not until—"

"Bastian. We can't find her in this. *Go*."

Bastian clenches his jaw, then nods.

They run, Henry using the tranq gun as a bludgeon, knocking officers aside as they race toward the relative safety of the trees on the other side of the parking lot. But the compound forces seem to have caught onto their escape route. Barrett's sand, combined with a windmover's strategic gusts, is clearing a path for some, but Henry and Bastian run right into a cluster of officers blocking the way for several assets.

Bastian skids to a stop. "Negate around them."

Henry opens his mouth to protest, but there's no time. He realizes what Bastian is about to do a split second before he does it, and he scrambles to throw up a rushed negation barrier around the assets.

Despite the negation field, Henry still stumbles when Bastian unleashes the attack. The compound officers crumple to the ground, dropping their weapons, faces stuck somewhere between dazed and pained. If Henry weren't protecting himself and the other assets, they'd all be on the ground as well, mentally sliced through with the same emotional attack Bastian used years ago to subdue a fake empath in the forest.

What Bastian seems to have forgotten about that attack is that it knocks the shit out of him, too. The agonized noise he makes as he doubles over is almost as bad as the ones the officers just made, and it sends a jolt of fear through Henry's chest.

He grits his teeth, tosses the tranq gun away so his hands are free, and grabs onto Bastian's arm, helping him stand. "Go!" he says to the others, and then they all move, Bastian leaning heavily on Henry.

Barrett, Tallis, James, and most of the other assets are waiting further into the trees. Henry almost yells at them for stopping, but then he notices the shimmering border encircling the group. Two assets are holding it in place, arms outstretched toward each other, faces focused. Henry has a vague memory of seeing them in the hotel: The man with thinning brown hair is an illusior, capable of bending light; and the woman wearing the gold bangles is a sonus, capable of bending sound. Whatever protection their combined barrier offers won't last long, but it might keep the group hidden from the compound forces coming after them. Assuming they keep moving.

"Well," Quentin says. "That went better than expected."

"If that was *better*, what the hell were you expecting?" Bastian's tone is sharp, but his voice wobbles with pain, and he isn't even trying to stand without Henry's help.

"Some resistance, of course. That's why I brought help when I saw what was going on." Quentin gestures to a small group behind him who seem to be hanging onto his every word. There are maybe ten of them, dressed in similarly drab clothes.

"You just happened to be in the area?" Bastian asks. Wheezes, more like.

"We've been coming to the city periodically to look for assets who might need help. I was expecting James to meet us, but not quite like this! I'm just glad everyone is all right."

"Not everyone." Henry scans the group without much hope but asks anyway: "Has anyone seen Angelica?"

"What, you couldn't protect a little kid from that disorganized bunch of losers?" James is leaning against a nearby tree, clearly trying to look nonchalant but struggling to catch his breath from the escape.

Quentin holds up his hands placatingly. "Let's not argue. Everything turned out all right in the end, didn't it? Now, I think we should get moving."

"You're not in charge here," Barrett snaps with a surprising amount of venom. Bastian clearly isn't the only one who doesn't like this guy.

Quentin shoots Barrett a sympathetic look. "I offered to help you before, Alex, but you turned me down. After this fiasco, maybe it's time for you to consider some outside assistance."

Barrett grimaces but falls silent.

Bastian, on the other hand, pipes up. "We can't just run away. Angelica is—"

"We need to get everyone clear first," Henry says quietly. "Then we can circle back and figure out who took her and where." Not that Bastian looks like he's in any shape to do that at the moment.

"The trees and the border will give us a little cover until we reach the park," Tallis says. "We should split up there—smaller groups will be harder to track. I'll scout ahead." Without waiting for a response, she dissolves into the shadows.

The group moves quickly and quietly, the illusior and sonus maintaining the barrier as they go. They're noticeably struggling—even if they were the most well-trained assets, their powers aren't built for endurance. But working together seems to help. Quentin, James, and their group stay closest to the nexus of the barrier, while Henry, Bastian, and the others are a little closer to the edge.

The assets from the hotel murmur to each other, sneaking peeks at Quentin, who offers them reassuring smiles that don't reach his eyes.

"So," Bastian says to Barrett. "When were you at Quentin's sanctuary?"

Henry looks over and realizes that Barrett is walking next to them, moving silently as he keeps narrowed eyes on the back of Quentin's head. "What makes you think I was there?" he asks.

"You're trying to glare the guy's head off. It's pretty noticeable."

Barrett sighs. "I don't fault a guy for doing what he needs to in order to survive, but from what I can tell, most of the energy Quentin uses isn't his."

"Is that why you left?"

Barrett hesitates, then says, "Yeah. I ran into him after I escaped a transport convoy. Thought he could help me. But then I realized we have a different definition of 'help.'"

"So, you formed your own rival gang."

"I didn't ask people to stick around," Barrett says a little sharply. "I warned them against it. Too many of us in one place isn't safe—for reasons you just saw. But Tallis is right: When no one else is looking out for you, you have to look out for each other."

"Not just for yourself?"

"Maybe that would've been easier." Barrett looks over at Henry and gives him a small, long-suffering smile. "You always want to be a hero, Mortimer? Or did it just happen?"

Henry thinks of the derision in James's voice just now when he pointed out how easily they let Angelica be taken. The many, many assets he's hurt, now lost in the Compound Network, without their powers, because of him. Except the dead ones, of course.

"I'm not a hero," Henry says.

Barrett shrugs. "Maybe. But you tried to change the compound when you were in charge, didn't you?"

"Not that it mattered," Henry says. "We all saw how much it didn't."

Henry's heart is pounding, and his chest feels tight. He tells himself to keep it together just a little longer, but he's not sure he can. All his talk about focusing on escape and dealing with Angelica later—but now that it's quieter, every step he takes echoes with recrimination. That little girl is in danger because he lost his shit during a crisis. Even though he trained for years to *not do that*. And now she's probably heading back to a place where she'll be locked up, experimented on, and possibly killed.

"If you knew about Quentin, why didn't you say anything when James brought it up?" Bastian asks.

"Because everyone should have a choice," Barrett says. "I'm not going to take that away, like the compounds do. Maybe some people are willing to indenture themselves to a guy like Quentin in order to get the safety he offers. Who am I to say that's wrong for someone else? Like I said, we're all just trying to survive. Besides, it's not like James named names."

"You think this was James's idea?" Henry asks quietly. "If he knew Quentin was coming . . ."

"He could have tipped off the compound officers," Bastian says. "Made it look like it was our fault, so people would be more inclined to go with Quentin."

"It *could* have been your fault. Or his. Or anyone's. We were on borrowed time at the hotel, anyway." Barrett's face is grim—just the sort of grim Henry is familiar with: the kind that happens when someone realizes they made a bad call. Or maybe that there was never a good call to begin with.

The group ahead of them slows. Henry can see the trees thinning out as they hit the edge of the park. The compound forces must have coordinated with the city police to close it—the picnic tables and playground areas are empty, and there aren't any guests on any of the nearby paths. In fact, it looks so empty, it must be filled with compound forces lying in wait.

Except something isn't quite right. Bastian's frown deepens the more he looks around, and it doesn't seem to be due to pain.

"I suggest we split up here," Quentin says. "I've made the compound officers in the park feel like looking elsewhere for a while, so we should all be relatively safe as long as we don't linger."

Henry looks at Bastian, whose lips are pressed together in a thin line. It would be a struggle for Bastian to maintain that level of focus with his own power, but Quentin doesn't even look winded.

Barrett clears his throat. "Use the city markers to find supplies if you need to. We can leave messages about where to meet up after this blows over. In the meantime, best of luck, wherever you're headed."

"Quentin got us out of this mess," James says a little too loudly. "I'm going with him."

And there's the next step in the recruitment plan: Most of the assets who were with Barrett and Tallis at the hotel have shuffled toward Quentin and James.

Quentin looks surprised in the way people look surprised when they predicted everything that's happening. "Oh! Well, of course I'll offer whatever help I can to anyone who wants to come with me."

"Tell them first," Bastian says sharply. "Tell them what they're agreeing to if they go with you."

For the first time since his appearance, Quentin looks directly at Bastian, his expression unreadable—like a parent weighing how best to put an unruly child in their place. Once upon a time, Henry's parents used to use that look on him.

"They're agreeing to let me help them," Quentin says after a long, awkward pause. "Just because you and Alex refused, doesn't mean others have to."

"They can't make an informed choice without hearing all the facts," Henry says firmly.

Quentin turns that disapproving look on him for a moment, then sighs. "This is hardly the time—"

"This is exactly the time," Bastian says. "If there's a price, they deserve to know about it now rather than waiting until it's convenient for you."

"Did you all forget about the compound forces that are closing in?" James demands. "Let's save the details for later."

"Not much of a choice, then, is it? Just 'my way, or the compound takes you'?" Bastian smirks. "Remind me again how you're such a selfless person who only wants to help?"

Quentin sighs again, then turns to give the other assets a small smile. "I'll help you escape the compound forces, but once we're safe, I may need to ask you for a favor. You can refuse and go on your way at that point if you'd prefer. I'm sorry I can't be more specific right now, but we really do need to keep moving."

Bastian's face says he's not going to take that for an answer, but the shadows near him shift, and Tallis appears, out of breath. "Coast is mostly clear, but the officers aren't too far away. We need to get going."

"So long, then," Quentin says. "I hope we'll see each other again soon." It sounds pleasant, but Henry hears the threat—especially given how Quentin's gaze lingers on Bastian.

There's a small cough, and the illusior says, "I'm sorry, but we can't—the barrier—"

"Go ahead and drop it," Barrett says. "We'll be gone before it fades."

True to his word, everyone begins to split off. The largest group divides between Quentin and James, heading for one of the playgrounds, moving quickly and sticking to the shadows. Barrett and Tallis collect a smaller group, then turn to Henry and Bastian.

"You should come with us," Tallis says. "You don't look like you can—"

"We're fine for now," Bastian says, although his face has gone pale and sweaty. "A big group will draw attention. Leave a message at one of the markers we've used before, and we'll catch up with you later."

Tallis narrows her eyes, then nods reluctantly.

"Thank you," Henry says, for more things than he can quite articulate.

Tallis smiles at him. "Don't die, or I'm gonna think all my efforts were wasted."

Barrett gives them a quick nod as well, and then their group hurries off.

"Okay," Henry says, turning back to Bastian. "We should—"

But there's no time for should because, without warning, Bastian crumples to the ground.

Chapter 22

LAUREL SIGHS AND scans the smelly river and its steep, muddy bank, which Chloe has just informed her is likely going to be their only way into the city.

"There are too many cars," Chloe says, voice gone vague as she focuses on her power. "We should be okay to use Mr. Kwan's IDs as pedestrians on the bridge, but after that, we'd better get off the road. The path near the end of the bridge will be the clearest."

It's early evening, the commuter rush for those heading home to the city, which means a swarm of vehicles like bees returning to the hive. The crowd might actually work in their favor: Everyone just wants to get home, so the security check could be less thorough than usual.

Laurel knows she should be focused on their dangerous, important mission, but she keeps getting distracted by her ability to *feel* and *hear* again, more fully than she has in ages. The willows near the water are coughing, soaking up moisture through their roots, weary but content. The waving grass is whispering to the cattails interspersed within its long, greenish-yellow leaves. And the blackberry bushes they passed just now had lots of interesting gossip about the dandelions trying to worm their way into the roadside clique.

Laurel knew she missed her connection to living things, but she hadn't realized just how *much*.

"Laurel?" Chloe has come out of her tracking daze.

"Yes, sorry. Mucky path it is! Let's go tell that security checkpoint officer what's what."

"Um. I think we should maybe try not to stand out?"

"Yes, that's a good 'what' to tell them."

They move closer to the bridge and get in the pedestrian line behind two people pushing bicycles.

"I heard there was another raid this afternoon," the man says as he rummages around in his pouch for his ID.

"There are always raids," the woman says dismissively. "I just hope they caught them. Honestly, it was better when those people were just urban myths. Now that we know they're actually running loose in the city . . ."

"They're usually scooped up pretty quickly, though." The man pulls out his ID and zips his pouch shut. "I'm sure they'll get the rest of this bunch in no time. They were just squatting in an abandoned hotel—can you believe it? Like they were waiting to get caught."

The woman sniffs. "Good. They should all be rounded up and thrown in jail before they hurt someone."

"Excuse me," Laurel says politely, although she's tempted to ask the ivy crawling up the side of the bridge to wrap around those bike tires and puncture them. "Can you tell us more about the raid?"

The man and woman turn to her, obviously startled to have their conversation interrupted by a random stranger. "That's all I know, really," the man says. "I just heard about it in the office on my way out."

"Do you know where it happened? You said there was a hotel?"

"You seem awfully interested in eavesdropping on other people's conversations," the woman says. Her mouth looks pinched, which was not a thing Laurel thought mouths could do.

"Next," the officer calls, and the man and woman turn around and step forward.

Laurel exchanges glances with the ivy but decides not to push it.

When it's finally their turn, Laurel puts on her most polite smile and hands the guard their fake IDs. "Hello! How are you?"

The officer doesn't respond, eyes on his tablet as he looks up their information in the database. According to Kwan, it should tell the nice officer that they're students returning from a field trip to collect water and soil samples for a project on water quality. Honestly, the mud on their shoes ought to be cover enough, but people in uniforms do seem to like their stuffy protocol.

The officer looks up from his tablet and frowns. "Let me see the bag."

Chloe carefully hands him the bag they've been taking turns carrying since they left the compound. Another parting gift from Kwan, filled with water testing gear, clothes, towels, snacks, and probably a bit of dust from the road. Chloe found them quite a few shortcuts—the trip would've taken much longer on foot otherwise—but most of those shortcuts were dirty and off the beaten path.

Well. Off the beaten path for anyone who isn't a tracker.

The officer rummages through the bag with a sour look on his face. "This is a lot of stuff for a day trip."

Chloe is busy vibrating with nervousness, and she did take the last bag-carrying duty, so Laurel steps up. "Yes, well, we really want to get a good grade on this project. And have you *seen* the river lately? Or smelled it? You probably smell it every day, even from all the way up here. Anyway, the water acidity level is completely unacceptable. The willows end up having to do most of the filtration work, and I bet no one even asked them if they minded. You can see in the readings we took—"

"Yeah, all right, I get it." The officer closes the bag and tosses it back to Chloe, who barely manages to catch it. He returns the IDs to Laurel with just as little care. "Go on, and make sure you get back to your dorm before curfew."

"Thank you!" Laurel says cheerfully. She just manages to keep herself from sticking her tongue out at him as soon as his back is turned.

"Do you think the raid those people were talking about is the one Mr. Kwan mentioned?" Chloe asks as they walk toward the city.

"Probably," Laurel says grimly. "Unless there are even more asset raids than we've been led to believe. Either way, we'll have to get more information as soon as we can. And maybe find a place to change so we don't have to wander around all covered in dirt."

Information gathering would be much easier if her empath link with Bastian was working, but still no luck. Now that the negation serum is mostly out of her system, she ought to have a clearer connection, but she can't feel anything at all. And it makes no sense.

Well, since she can't just ask Bastian where he is, they'll have to get information the old-fashioned way: collecting rumors (hopefully from less odious rumormongers) and pounding the pavement.

As soon as they get to the end of the bridge, Chloe leads them off to the right and onto the muddy riverbank. Then they trudge in the muck for a bit until they hit an access trail that winds back up to a broken chain-link fence and into the city from a different, less observable angle. The vines that once grew into the fence are long dead, but the thorns poke at their clothes as they struggle through.

At the top of the hill, they come out into a parking lot surrounded by feeble brown grass and a few oaks. There are only two structures nearby: an empty wading fountain and a battered public restroom.

"Let's clean up," Laurel says, pointing to the restroom. "Then I can ask those trees where we should go to look for someone."

They wash off in the restroom sinks and change clothes, silently agreeing to keep the bag and its contents from touching the questionable floor.

When Laurel comes out, Chloe is staring at a mark on the wall of the restroom building. To Laurel, it looks like a complicated design made with bright yellow spray paint. But Chloe seems to think it's something else. Unless she's just really fond of abstract art.

"What is it?" Laurel asks.

Chloe starts, like she forgot anyone else was there. "Something's funny about this graffiti."

Laurel takes a closer look, tipping her head one way, then the other. "Well, if it's supposed to be a squirrel, it's a lopsided one."

"No, I think . . . it's a marker. Like on a trail. Something to show you the way. I can't quite read it, though." She glances at Laurel, then flushes and quickly looks away. "But maybe I'm wrong. I've never seen anything like it before, so . . ."

"Where do you think it wants us to go?" Laurel asks. "Maybe we should follow it. Worst that can happen is that we get horribly lost in the city and are never heard from again, right?"

"Um. That sounds—"

"*Or* we could have an adventure and find something interesting. That's one of the fun things about being a tracker, isn't it? Finding interesting things on paths no one else can see?"

Chloe blinks, then smiles, slightly bemused. "I guess I never thought of it as fun."

"Well, it can't *all* be doom and gloom. It's a good power; there has to be something good about it." Laurel nods firmly. "Anyway, I'll let you and your graffiti choose the direction. But first, I think I should go talk to the oaks and see if they know anything about that raid. Between all of us, I'm sure we'll find Bastian and Henry in no time!"

***

Over the next several hours, Laurel comes to realize that she might not know the right definition of the phrase "no time." They hop from one marker to the next per Chloe's instructions, which takes them to block after block of the city without finding anything other than what Laurel has heard to expect: huge, modern buildings; loud, busy streets; and severely manicured greenery. Just looking at all of it makes Laurel feel like she's being strangled.

Whenever they dip into more residential areas, there's at least one oddly open space with nothing but burned grass or the ruins of a building. Places where the city hasn't bothered to rebuild after some catastrophe, maybe because they'd rather spend their money on shiny downtown office buildings.

In one of the abandoned grassy patches, hidden behind a collapsed community center with shattered windows, they find a small box filled with fruit snacks and first aid supplies.

"Oh!" Chloe says as Laurel takes a few things and stuffs them into their bag. "They're like . . . caches. The markers lead to them."

She points to the wall, where a yellow mark has been placed right above the box. It's not obvious from far away, but up close like this, it seems to be pointing to the box.

"It's like a treasure hunt!" Laurel says, grinning despite her exhaustion. "Not as good as a secret passage, but pretty close."

They pause for a quick break, and Laurel scans the area for any trees or bushes to talk to. The mushrooms are busy relaying information through their networks, but Laurel makes a note to ask them about Bastian and Henry when they're done—mushrooms are always good for making connections. The grass is preoccupied with an ant infestation, and the nearby maple is a bit snooty when Laurel asks about groups of assets moving through the city. Laurel is about to get snooty right back when she notices Chloe approaching. "Laurel, there's—"

Laurel turns toward the sidewalk—and it's like the wind gets knocked out of her. There are a couple of young people in well-worn clothes standing there, staring. And at their center, a slow smile spreading across his face . . .

"Hello, Laurel," James says.

Chapter 23

"SERIOUSLY, JUNIOR. WHAT gives?"

Bastian opens his eyes and sees an enormous, dark void above him. A split second later, he realizes he's lying on his back, staring up at the sky of Moira's dreamscape. He has no idea how he got here . . . and there's something different about it, too.

"Hey, are you listening?"

The thunder and lightning. They're closer. The storm is closer than it's ever been.

"Do I need to explain what a dream is?" Moira asks. "You're supposed to dream when you're asleep. *Not when you're passed out. Again. I mean, I'm flattered by the attention, but this can't be healthy."*

Bastian blinks several times, then turns his head. Moira is sitting next to him, frowning. They're by the pond, enormous and dark and eerily still.

He sits up—or tries to. A wave of nausea and pain threatens to knock him flat. He bites down on a curse and goes still, waiting for the feeling to pass, before trying again—this time more successfully.

"I'd offer you painkillers, but this place doesn't seem to come with a drugstore," Moira says. Her tone is flippant, but she looks concerned. "You okay?"

"Not really." Bastian holds his head, although the pain does seem to be diminishing. Then he registers what she said. "This is your dream, isn't it? Shouldn't it have whatever you want it to have?"

"In theory, sure. In practice, there are some things I don't have control over. The storm. The creation of drugstores. You." She smiles. "One of those three ain't bad. Though I'm questioning why you feel the need to knock yourself senseless just so you can come say hello."

"I wasn't—"

Henry. The raid.

"I have to go back," Bastian says, dragging himself to his feet. "I have to—"

"You know I can't do anything about that," Moira says. Half irritation, half regret, none of it through the clarity of his power, which he still can't use here. "Why don't you tell me what happened?"

"What good will that do if you can't—?"

"Humor me, Junior. Maybe we can figure this out together."

Bastian takes a few breaths, then sits down again. His head is still throbbing. "We were in the city, and there was a raid on the place where we were staying. Compound forces came for the assets. We escaped, but—"

He swallows the shame. "I let someone get taken. Because I was too stupid to keep her safe. And then . . ."

(*The feeling of Quentin dropping the threads of emotion he was carrying, the weight crashing down on Bastian when he tried to pick them up because if he didn't, they'd be noticed, and all Quentin cared about was getting his own people safe, but it was too much because Bastian was too weak, and—*)

"And now, Henry is alone out there on his own because I'm *here*, and I need to be *there*."

He expects Moira to tell him he's being childish, that whining isn't going to solve anything. To mock him the way Valentine used to whenever he let his emotions get the better of him.

"Okay," Moira says instead. "We'll just have to get you back, then."

Bastian frowns at her. "How?"

"By doing something wildly clever and different." Moira shrugs. "I dunno. We'll try things until something sticks."

"What do you mean, try things?"

"You've spent your whole life using your power the way other people told you to, right? Whatever the compounds said. So . . . what if you did something different?"

It's like he told Henry once: that as painful and frustrating as being an empath is, it makes a difference if it's his choice. If he's using his power the way *he* wants to.

"Okay," he says slowly, trying to ignore the swell of anxiety.

"Let's start easy." Moira crosses her legs. "Shielding."

"Shielding isn't an asset power. Anyone can do it."

"Yeah, that's why I said *easy*, Junior. Try to keep up." She turns toward him and holds her hands out, palms facing him.

He frowns. "You . . . want to do it together?"

"Something different, remember?"

Shielding in the real world isn't a team activity. But this is Moira's dream, which means she sets the rules, more or less. If she can help him create something he can't create on his own, then maybe . . .

He squeezes his eyes shut and tries to focus on the boundary between where the space that's his ends and the rest of the world begins, just like he taught Angelica. To his surprise, he can feel his shield there, faintly, like an echo of an afterthought. A reflection of the real thing, backwards and slightly off somehow.

No, not off. Stronger. There's something protecting its edges, flickering in and out but mostly there: a support, like scaffolding around a building in repair. It's faint, but he can definitely feel it.

He opens his eyes to find Moira grinning at him. "Not bad, right? Not sure why I can't do everything in this dream, but I can do whatever that is, at least. Now let's try—"

There's a boom of thunder, louder than he's ever heard it here. A fork of lightning lights up the sky, then fades. Another loud boom.

Moira looks at the sky as well, mouth turned downward in a deep frown. She slowly lowers her hands.

"The storm's never actually hit, right?" Bastian asks.

She shakes her head. "This is the first time I've seen it like this."

The wind whips through the grass around them, stirring up choppy waves on the previously still pond, making it even more unsettling.

The next thunder/lightning combo is close enough that they both shoot to their feet. Bastian grabs Moira's arm—or maybe she grabs his first—and by unspoken agreement, they break into a run, away from the pool and back toward the creepy birches. They don't get very far, though, because the next bolt of lightning brings down a tree right in front of them. They both fall onto the grass, rolling away from the danger. The smell of ozone fills Bastian's nostrils.

Bastian drags himself up a second later, slightly dazed but unharmed. Moira landed not far away, but she's holding her head. "Hey!" he yells over the wind. "Are you all right?"

She doesn't have time to respond before the thunder sounds again, and there's a brilliant flash of light. A loud crack *follows, splitting another tree not far from them. Moira yells—no, screams—along with it.*

It's her dream, right? If anything in here is in pain, does that mean she feels it, too?

"Hey!" Bastian yells again. "Let's do the shield!"

She doesn't respond, so he stumbles over to her and crouches down, trying to ignore everything else. "Shield, dammit!"

She unfurls herself, meets his gaze, and carefully sits up. Then she closes her eyes and, to his surprise, grabs his hand. He thinks it's to steady herself at first, but then he realizes it's to steady them.

He can feel the shield between them getting stronger, his base structure and her outer one, feeding off of each other in a way he doesn't quite understand.

"Ah. Here you are."

Bastian starts at the sound of the familiar voice, and the joint shield starts to crack. He turns to see someone who can't possibly be there.

"Hello, Bastian," Quentin says, smiling down at them. The wind calms slightly at the sound of his voice. Almost like—

"What the hell are you doing here?" Bastian demands. "Dreaming instead of looking after the people you just said you'd help?"

"Aren't you more interested in how *I got here?" Quentin asks. "I could tell you, if you'd like. It's actually quite similar to how you did it."*

"So . . . by accident?"

Quentin raises his eyebrows. "Is that what you think brought you here? Accident?"

Moira makes an angry, guttural noise, and Bastian feels something push *against his part of the shield. Quentin grunts and stumbles back a bit.*

"Well, that's . . . interesting," he says.

"Get out," *Moira mumbles at him, shoulders tense with fury. Not that it'll be enough to get rid of Quentin; she can barely stay sitting upright, and when Quentin looks her way, she shrinks back.*

"Not a very hospitable hostess, are you?"

Moira raises her head and squints at him. "I didn't invite you, asshole. Leave, or I'll make you."

Quentin's eyes practically glitter. "But you did *invite someone else, didn't you? Even if unconsciously, you felt the way we're connected."*

"Worst pickup line ever," Moira spits. "You're not my type."

"Strictly speaking, I am. All empaths are. That's the theory, anyway."

"Don't you have some new followers to brainwash?" Bastian demands. "Or help, if you're in the mood? Or maybe you're just going to doze in the city, wherever you are, and leave them to fend for themselves."

"I'm always in the mood to help." Quentin gives Moira a small smile. "That's why I'm here. And I apologize for the way I came in. If Moira had let me through the barrier more quickly, I wouldn't have had to—"

"She told you to leave." Bastian gets to his feet, wobbling along the way but probably unlikely *to fall over again. "I think you should get on that."*

"Not until she lets me help. Moira—"

"She doesn't want you to—"

"Oh, shut up!" Moira groans and stands slowly, brushing dirt and grass off of her pants. "I didn't invite either *of you, and if I'd known this was going to end in a testosterone-fueled pissing match, I'd have found a way to keep you* both *out. As it is, Junior's slightly less annoying at the moment. And I only have enough in me to try to eject one of you."*

She jabs a finger at Quentin. "Take your damned storm and go."

"Wait," Bastian says. "Quentin is causing the storm?"

"The storm is my entryway," Quentin explains. "I didn't mean for it to be so dramatic, but it's not my dream, is it? Moira creates the imagery for whatever energy enters her dream. It probably says something interesting psychologically that she sees you as yourself, minus your power, and me as a storm."

A storm that's always been on the horizon, always threatening but never quite getting through until now. "You've been trying to get in for a long time," Bastian says slowly. "Why?"

"To help." Quentin smiles again at Moira. "I really do *want to help, you know. Helping people is—"*

"—what you claim to do before you leech them dry," Bastian snaps. "Is that what you're planning to do to Moira?"

Quentin gives him a long, silent look that makes his skin crawl. "Have you ever heard of a dreamseer?" he asks at last.

Bastian sees Moira stiffen beside him, but she stays silent, so he answers, "No. But I can guess what it is."

"Can you?" Quentin waves a hand. "A dreamseer can create an entire world just like this, night after night, with extraordinary detail. The energy they enclose in it is far more powerful than anything you or I could do with emotions. Emotions contain the energy of engagement and existence. Memories contain the energy of the past. But dreams . . . dreams contain the energy of imagination and possibility. Practically infinite."

Energy. Like a battery. A bigger, better battery than any other asset in existence could provide.

Shit.

"You're trapped here, aren't you, Moira?" Quentin gives her a sympathetic look. "I know what it feels like to be trapped. To be hunted for your power. If you let me, I can show you the way out."

"If she pays a toll, right?" Bastian says. "If she lets you take some of that energy you obviously want."

"You haven't considered it?" Quentin asks, sounding genuinely surprised. "Her energy would allow you to live for a long time. Several lifetimes, probably."

"So? What's so great about that?"

"What's so great about dying young? Is that more virtuous somehow? What will your loved ones think? What will Henry think?"

"All right, boys. It's time the walking battery got in a word." Moira glares at them both, then turns her full fury on Quentin. "You seem a bit dim, so I'll repeat myself: I don't want you here. I don't want your input on my situation, and I don't want you giving Junior a hard time. Take your storm and shove off. Last chance."

It would be more convincing if Bastian didn't know that she's never displayed the ability to do what she's talking about doing. But she seems angry enough to give it a shot. And since this is her world, maybe she can pull it off.

Still, the look on Quentin's face isn't reassuring.

Bastian clears his throat. "Moira—"

"Shut up, kid. I'll deal with you once this creep is gone." She puts her hands on her hips, and even though she's covered in grass and dirt, she's still intimidating. "Well?"

The longer Quentin stares silently at her, the darker the sky gets around them. The wind starts to pick up again, and Bastian feels cold raindrops on his head.

"I'm sorry you feel that way," Quentin says at last. "But I suppose I'm not surprised. Sometimes the people who need the most help are the ones who don't realize it."

He gives Bastian a small smile. "I guess this is goodbye for now, Bastian, but I'm sure we'll see each other again soon."

It takes Bastian half a second to realize what's happening—half a second he doesn't have. Then the connection between his shield and Moira's is ripped apart with a jarring snap, *and everything goes black.*

Chapter 24

JAMES IS SMILING at her, cheeky and amused and *alive*, and Laurel can't remember how to breathe. "Aren't you going to tell me how glad you are to see me?" he asks.

"Not until I know if I am," she replies unsteadily.

It's only a little bit of a lie. She *does* know if she's glad to see him (mostly yes). But she has no intention of admitting that anytime soon. Mostly because she's pretty sure it's something to be ashamed of.

Of course, Quentin told her James is alive, so it's not like she didn't know. But hearing the disembodied voice of a stranger in her head is different than seeing the clear evidence in front of her.

The last time she saw him, they were standing in a burning compound— burning because he arranged to have it burned, fanned the flames literally and metaphorically so that people would die. People like the black coat they found him standing over.

(And then the ceiling caved in, and she screamed, and the smoke got caught in her throat and stung her eyes, and all she could think was, One more friend I couldn't save—*)*

Except she didn't need to save him, did she? Because here he is, smiling at her like nothing happened. And is that what they're supposed to do now? Pretend like nothing happened?

The silence is getting awkward, especially with everyone poised like they're part of a standoff, waiting for someone to either pull a weapon or tell a joke to lighten the mood.

James's smile falters, and he clears his throat. "Uh. Well. We should probably talk." He turns to the people with him. "Go ahead. We can all meet up at the next cache."

One woman nods warily, and the group heads off quickly down the sidewalk. James turns back to Laurel. "Right. So. Where to start?"

Laurel looks over at Chloe, who is the embodiment of reluctant-but-willing-to-go-along-with-things-for-now. "Let's sit under that maple, and you can tell us why we should trust you."

"What, our long history isn't enough to go on?"

"No."

Laurel turns her back on him and marches over to the tree, sitting down with a huff underneath its branches. From here, she can see everything happening in three directions, which seems like the advantageous sort of position Henry would approve of. Plus, she's pretty sure the maple would come to her defense if she really needed it to, snooty nature or no.

Chloe sits down silently next to Laurel, and James sits across from them. "Okay, so, it's like this. There are assets all over the city now. No one can stay in the same place for long, so we help each other out with those markers and caches. Take what you need, leave what you can. I've even filled a few myself—this one, for example. That's how I knew to come here while we were in the neighborhood. Didn't expect to see you, but I can't say I'm disappointed about it." He smiles—the small, genuine one that makes something in Laurel's chest ache.

"We heard about raids," she says. "We're looking for information about one in particular. If you can help us find out more about it, that would go a long way toward making you seem trustworthy."

"What do you want to know?"

Despite having just asked, Laurel isn't sure it's a great idea to tell James too much about their mission. On the other hand, he seems to have some connections in the city—more than she and Chloe do, anyway. It's like when you find a really old system of firs in the forest: Even if one of them is obnoxious, it might be worth talking to it anyway, just to get access to the trees it's connected to.

(Of course, James isn't obnoxious so much as dangerous, and it hurts to look at him, to see that smirk and remember what it was like at their old compound, the way he drew people to him and made them laugh, the way he made *her* laugh—and then the way he got angry and sullen and ready to hurt anyone who—)

"Bastian and Henry are supposed to be in the city somewhere," Laurel says. "They might've been involved in that hotel raid. Do you know anything?"

James presses his lips together, then shakes his head. "No, sorry. I haven't heard anything. I mean, good on them for getting out of the compound—and good on you two—but . . . The city is big, Laurel. It's not that easy to find people. Especially people who are trying to lie low."

Laurel debates whether to believe this. But when she speaks, what comes out is something different, something she didn't mean to say at all: "I talked to Quentin. He said—he said you're going back to the compound."

"How did you—?" James cuts himself off. Then he leans back onto his hands and makes a face. "You know I hate the compounds, but . . . the chance to actually help the assets I was trying to help before? To put an end to everything they've done to us?"

There's an edge to his smile—and a sadness that's at odds with it. It's the same way he looked back at their compound, just before . . . everything. Angry and scared and hurt and desperate.

"Yeah," he says. "We're going back. Not yet, but soon."

Laurel gets to her feet abruptly, heart in her throat. "I won't let you," she says loudly. "I'll—"

"Quiet!" James hisses, looking around quickly, like he thinks the neighborhood is filled with spies. And who knows; maybe he's right.

"Listen," he says. "Quentin can answer your questions. Will you come with me to meet him? Just to hear what he has to say. Then you can leave, if you want. I won't ask you to stay."

"I—"

"He might've heard more about that raid. He's been in different parts of the city than I have. We usually split into smaller groups when we come here, and then we meet up before we head back to the sanctuary. I know where the check-in is, and I can take you, if you want."

Something in James's eyes becomes almost pleading. "Say you'll give it a chance, Laurel. For old time's sake."

(James in the empty experimentation room where she found him, uncharacteristically scared and shaken after the last experiment, begging her not to tell the others, warning her that the experiments are only going to get worse—)

"Laurel." Chloe waits for Laurel to turn, but she must see something in Laurel's face that Laurel didn't mean to put there because even though she looks concerned, she doesn't say anything else.

Quentin does seem to know things. If he can help them find Bastian and Henry . . . Well, she has to try, doesn't she? And if the group is plotting to hurt more people, she needs all the information she can get in order to stop them.

"Okay," she says. "We're in. I mean, *I'm* in. Chloe?"

Chloe looks less than enthusiastic, but she nods. "Yeah. Me, too."

Chapter 25

SOMEONE IS CALLING Bastian's name, shallow and terrified-anxious-desperate, pinpricks of emotion that dig under his skin. And there's something digging into his back as well: the sharp edges of sticks and leaves and the knotting bump of tree roots. Because he's not in Moira's dream anymore; he's . . .

"Bastian."

The voice is so afraid, Bastian thinks, but the thought skitters away like bubbles of air under water. Is he drowning? That doesn't make any sense. But the voice seems far away, like someone calling to him from the shore while he keeps getting dragged under.

"We can't stay here. You need to—"

It should have been simple. Quentin made it look simple, keeping the compound officers away. But when he stopped, and Bastian scrambled to pick up the pieces, it made something inside him break, and now he's . . . bleeding. From the nose. Like he used to all the time.

"Bastian!" The voice is closer, sterner, still terrified but trying harder to hide it now. "Hey, listen to me. There are officers in the park. We need to move *now*, so I need you to *get up*."

Bastian pries open his eyes and blinks slowly. The pressure at his temples intensifies, but so does his sluggish relief when he realizes Henry is crouched next to him, one hand holding Bastian's in a crushing grip.

Henry lets out a shaky breath when he sees Bastian's eyes focus on him. "Hey. I thought we talked about how you're not allowed to collapse on me."

Bastian feels a little more anchored in the proper place and time, but everything is still oddly fuzzy. "I'm a rebel," he says, and his voice sounds thick and far away and disconnected from him.

Henry looks over his shoulder, then back at Bastian. "We need to move before those officers find us. Can you stand up?"

His voice is gentler, now that he has Bastian's attention, but there's still steel underneath. Like he's going to figure out how to deal with this or die trying. That last part is concerning and not at all acceptable.

Bastian tries to sit up, then curses and falls back again, nearly smacking his head against a tree root before Henry can get an arm around him. Bastian's vision swims, and he keeps up the string of swearing in his head. It's not the worst pain he's ever felt, but it's bad—head, neck, shoulders, chest—and he can't seem to hold focus for long. He wants to curl up and go to sleep, preferably with Henry holding him, but even in his addled state, he knows that's a horrible idea.

"You were holding them back, too, weren't you?" Henry asks quietly. "Quentin said he would distract the compound teams, but then he left, and you—"

Bastian feels out briefly, just to see if he can tell where they are, but—

"*Stop.*" Henry's negation field collects around him, gentle but firm, keeping him from feeling anything other than the nothing-nothing-nothing. Bastian might be able to work past it, but he's so *tired*, and everything aches, and he'd much rather stop the fight. He manages to raise himself up enough that he can slump against Henry's side. This is nice. This is enough. This is—

"Bastian." Henry is holding him carefully, the negation field close but not overbearing. "I think you should—Are you listening? I think you need to . . . do what you did before, in the hotel."

Bastian tenses. "I won't—I can't—"

"I know you don't want to, and I know it's shitty of me to ask, but you can't even *stand*. And I don't think we can just hide out here. If you need to—"

"No."

"Even just a little bit—"

"No." Bastian takes a breath. "You can go. I'll meet you somewhere."

Henry frowns. "Is that before or after you get caught and shipped back to the compound?"

"I'm very good at hiding. I can—"

"Who's going to save Angelica if you let them take you?"

Low blow. "I'm not good at saving people."

"You saved me."

If Bastian was drifting before, he's damn well focused now. Henry has stopped eyeing the surrounding area for signs of the officers and is looking directly at Bastian, jaw clenched, arms around him, close but careful, like he's cradling something precious that he couldn't stand to break.

"One more save would make us even, right?" Henry takes a shaky breath. "I can't—I'm so sorry to ask, but I can't do this without you."

Bastian doesn't have to use his power to see the fear and anxiety and shame, just like Henry displayed that first night in the hotel: quickened breath, tense muscles, sweat on his pale face. Trying to hold it together, just like he always does.

(*I can't do this without you*, the same words Henry said when Bastian ended up in the compound med bay last year, and Bastian still doesn't quite understand how Henry could possibly think that, but maybe that's just because it's really Bastian who needs—)

They both go still at the sound of officers shouting to each other out on the green. They're heading toward the trees, apparently unconcerned about being loud at this point. They must have the whole area surrounded.

Without thinking, Bastian clutches Henry's shirt more tightly. "It could knock you out. Are you expecting me to carry you out of here?"

"No." Henry gives him a small smile. "Although I'd like to see you try."

"I don't—I don't even know if I *can*," Bastian says. His voice sounds vague and untethered again, and his head *hurts*.

"It's okay."

"I don't want to hurt you."

"I know."

"I—"

"Bastian." Henry's voice is even softer, although the anxiety is still there in every syllable. "Remember that time in the forest, when you helped me practice my power? You couldn't hurt me then, and you won't now. We'll figure it out together. And I'll stop you if it's too much."

The voices of the officers are getting closer.

Bastian looks at Henry, blinking to keep him in focus.

(And he thinks of the bruises on Henry's wrists at the safe house, like he'd never stopped fighting, even if he thinks he did, because trying every option, even the impossible ones, is just part of who Henry is, and maybe it's different if someone offers—not like Quentin's followers, but like Moira in the dream, the possibility of doing something *different*, the way Henry is offering to do it *together*—)

Bastian swallows. Then he reaches his shaky right hand up to touch Henry's cheek, his eyes falling closed again.

It's different than the way he touches someone to do a read. That feels like getting slapped in the face with someone's emotions.

This is . . . tentative. Like knocking on a door and listening for an answer without trying to rush the response.

There's nothing at first. Then the careful, gentle feel of Henry pulling back his negation field a bit, making it softer. Enough to protect himself, but not enough to keep Bastian out entirely.

Like he's inviting Bastian in.

It wraps around him, a combination of a shield and a border of negation that supports him rather than pushing him back. Bastian is safe here, in a way that's so unfamiliar it almost hurts.

He's not going to *take* energy; he's going to *share* it.

He feels the tug in his chest like he did in the hotel room, but it's brief. Something comes in, something goes out, like a wave.

And then the pain fades.

There's a part of him that wants to keep going, to suck all of the energy into himself and then go looking for more, like nothing will ever make him feel full. But the steady pulse of Henry's negation overshadows it, and his roiling stomach calms down.

He opens his eyes and blinks several times, and things seem clearer. Sharper and more real. He can feel Henry's heartbeat against his ear and the rough, dirty material of his shirt, which Bastian is still clutching with one hand. He can hear the wind in the tree branches and see the silver-gray strands in Henry's hair.

He can sense that Henry is nervous, but unharmed. Not hollow, like before.

And he can hear the sound of an officer only a few feet away.

"Did anyone sweep this area yet?"

Mumbles through the officer's comm in response. Bastian doesn't wait to hear more. Quickly and carefully, he reaches out to the officer and prods at his bored-listless-tired until he hears a corresponding sigh. "All right, never mind. I think we're good here."

The officer moves away.

There are others in the park, of course—Bastian knows he and Henry shouldn't linger—but none of them are close enough to be a danger yet. And none will be, now that Bastian can convince them not to be.

Very, very carefully, he gets to his feet with Henry's help, then offers him a small smile. "We're even on the saving thing now."

"Yeah? I think that was more of a joint effort, really." Henry doesn't let go of his hand, even though they're both standing now.

"You okay?" Bastian asks. Some pathetic part of him needs to hear it.

"Yeah," Henry says, squeezing his hand. "I feel good, actually. Except for the part where we really do need to get out of here."

"Agreed."

Now there's just the question of where the hell they can go.

Chapter 26

LAUREL SUPPOSES IT'S good that the city planners included so many parks, although this one feels a bit iffy. The entrance includes a nice stone archway, but the minimal number of streetlamps is concerning, especially since it's starting to get dark. And the firs are silent as Laurel, James, and Chloe walk by. Not even a hello, and barely a sense of sentience. They've retreated so far into themselves, Laurel isn't sure she'd be able to have a conversation even if it weren't coming up on tree bedtime.

They follow the main path for several minutes without coming across any-one, which makes Laurel even more uneasy. The park isn't closed yet, so why is it so deserted? On the other hand, a deserted park means less chance of being reported if they use their powers out in the open.

James abruptly leads them onto the grass, down a little hill, and into a denser patch of trees. Nearby, a flicker of light reveals itself to be a fire in a trash can with a small group of people standing around it. They glance over as the three approach, going stiff. They look about as friendly as the trees.

"Glad you found us," says a man, stepping forward from the shadows to shake James's hand. He looks exhausted, like he's just been through some sort of ordeal, but his smile is genuine and apologetic. His slightly ragged hair falls to his stubbly chin, and his clothing is on the threadbare side of things.

And his voice is familiar.

"You must be Laurel," he says, turning his smile on her. "And of course, Chloe and I have already met."

Chloe mumbles something, eyes fixed on the ground. She's clutching their shared bag so tightly, her knuckles have gone white.

Laurel gets between Chloe and the man, just in case. She keeps her tone pleasant but prepared to get *un*pleasant if necessary. A flytrap ready to devour any fly that gets too close. "Quentin?"

Something in Quentin's face shifts—and then shifts again before she can catch it. Like a ripple on a pond. "Yes, that's right. It's nice to finally meet you."

He turns back to James. "I'm sorry I couldn't catch up with you earlier. We've had to be more careful since the raid this morning, and I had something else to take care of. But now—"

"Raid?" Laurel asks carefully and with just the right amount of concern.

Quentin gives her a tired smile. "Compound forces have been very active today. Luckily, most of us made it here in the end. It just took longer than expected."

That's not much of an explanation, let alone one that confirms whether or not Bastian and Henry were there. And Laurel doesn't like the "*most* of us" part. She doesn't have time for a follow-up question, though, because James is already responding. "It's all right. We found a way to pass the time."

"Yes, you did." Quentin smiles at Laurel and Chloe again. "I'm glad you're here, but it's getting dark, and we're all exhausted. Security in the park isn't too strict right now, so this should be a safe place to spend the night. Get some rest, and we can talk in the morning. I have people on guard who can let us know if we need to move before then."

Laurel glances around. There are more assets here than she saw at first, hidden in shadows near bushes and trees. They're all hunkering down, taking blankets out of various bags and eating nuts and granola and other shelf-stable stuff like what Laurel and Chloe have in their own bag. The trees are similarly busy, soaking up nutrients from the soil and murmuring unintelligibly. Laurel wants to ask if they've noticed anything strange or dangerous about this group, but it seems rude to ask when everyone's just settling in. And besides, she doesn't see anything to be worried about—at least not right now.

Does this count as safety in numbers? Or are they just asking for compound forces to come after them?

"I suppose we can rest here for a while," Laurel says at last, taking the bag from Chloe. "But I expect some answers first thing in the morning."

"Of course," Quentin says. His face and his voice seem to be doing two different things, but he also doesn't seem to be an immediate threat. If anything, he looks like he needs some sleep just as much as anyone else here. Whatever he's been up to lately has clearly drained him.

"Laurel," Chloe says in a low voice as they trudge over to an open spruce. "Are you sure we should be staying here?"

"Nope!" Laurel says, setting the bag down and sitting beside it. "But— well—we should try to figure out what's going on, right? Quentin and James know what's happening in the city, and they're right here where we can spy on them and maybe even prevent them from going to the compound and hurting people."

She doesn't add what she knows is a horrible argument: that she can't bear to leave James just yet, even if she knows she can't really trust him. That she's hoping Quentin can explain why she can't contact Bastian but *could* contact *him*, even in the compound. That the idea of being alone in the city is terrifying, especially with compound forces all around, and Laurel doesn't want to be without a copse of trees right now. Even standoffish ones like these.

"Don't worry," she says to Chloe's concerned face. "We'll leave tomorrow. For now, why don't you get some sleep? I'll keep watch."

Chloe hesitates a moment longer, then sits down next to Laurel. She takes a blanket out of the bag, curls up under it, and is dozing almost immediately.

Laurel smiles, then sighs and pulls her legs up so she can wrap her arms around them.

And then she waits.

***

Noisy, says the spruce sometime later, startling Laurel awake even though she definitely wasn't sleeping even a little bit. Its voice is groggy and annoyed, soft enough that Laurel almost misses it. Like someone gossiping so quietly, it's hard to know whether you were supposed to overhear it or not.

There isn't anything obviously noisy nearby. It's mostly dark now, and everyone is either sleeping or speaking very softly. The other trees in the area are quiet, too, and although the grass is snoring, it's not terribly loud.

"Bit fussy?" Laurel asks the spruce, more out of amusement than anything else. When it does the tree equivalent of sniffing in reply, she reaches out and pats a branch. "Sorry. It probably *is* noisier than usual, having all these people around at this time of day."

The spruce recoils, letting out a note of leafy distress, and Laurel snatches her hand back. "Sorry! I didn't mean to—"

Noisy, the spruce says again, still sluggish with sleep but also afraid.

"Can you tell me what's wrong?" Laurel asks. "Maybe I can fix it. Or at least I can listen."

The tree seems hesitant and confused—maybe it just realized that it's talking to a human. Sometimes it takes a few hundred years before a tree understands how to hold a conversation. And Laurel isn't sure how many conversation partners an urban spruce gets to practice with.

Bad, the spruce says at last, slow and concerned and echoing in her head. *Danger.*

(And she thinks of the stagnant air on the night her first compound burned, the smell of smoke and the heat coming from under her door, and the only reason she got out in time was because of the small voices of the plants around her, warning of *bad* and *danger*—)

"Laurel?" Chloe sits up, rubbing her eyes. "Is something wrong?"

"Nope!" Laurel says quickly. "I'm just going to take a look around. This nice spruce will look out for you. Or you can look out for it. Or both. Anyway, I won't be long." She gets to her feet.

Danger, the spruce says plaintively. She pauses, listening hard in every direction its roots are stretching, but she still can't tell what it's referring to. There's a light flickering in another copse of trees off to her right—a small campfire, maybe?—so she decides to start there.

Bad, the spruce warns one last time.

Laurel wiggles the fingers on her right hand in a fan-like motion. *It's okay. I'll be right back.*

The spruce clearly doesn't believe her, but it doesn't say anything else.

Thanks to the ineffective park lights, it gets even darker as she makes her way to the trees. Once she's closer, she can make out several low voices.

"What about Laurel?" James asks.

"I see no problem with her joining us if you can convince her," Quentin says. "You need to be certain, though. Her loyalty has to be to you and the mission, and nothing else."

"I'll take care of it," James says. His voice is calm, confident, and a little amused—just like always. Laurel doesn't understand what they're talking about, but she does understand the ache in her chest from hearing James sound so much like himself. Which is a bit silly—who else would he sound like?

"James," Quentin says, his voice softer and oddly ragged. "You need to be careful. We can't afford to—"

"Quentin?" Someone approaches from the far side of the copse. Laurel creeps closer so she can see between the thick trunks. Of course, spying is bad, but she has the suspicion that she shouldn't interrupt.

"Ella. Thank you for coming."

James and Quentin are blocking her view, and the visibility isn't great even with the campfire, but Laurel can see that a girl has joined them. She's maybe thirteen or fourteen, her pale blond hair held back in a messy ponytail. Her shirt and pants are covered in dirt and patched-up holes. She's only said one quavering word, and Laurel is already on high alert. Is this what the spruce meant about danger?

"They said I could stay if . . ." The girl swallows, then straightens her shoulders. "They said you needed help."

"Yes." Quentin smiles at her. "Thank you for coming."

The girl bites her lip, then says very carefully, "What do you need help with?"

James snorts. "He's not going to hurt you, all right? You don't have to act like—"

"Ella has every right to be worried, James," Quentin says mildly. "You were, too, the first time."

"But he's right," Quentin continues. "I won't hurt you. I just need your help to heal myself. Do you think you can do that?"

Laurel feels the blood drain from her face.

(This needle won't hurt, we just want to run a test, it's only so we can understand, you'll be perfectly fine when you wake up, this experiment is so important, there's no need to struggle so much—)

"Okay," Ella says.

She and Quentin sit down across from each other, cross-legged, and he murmurs a few things that Laurel doesn't catch. She isn't sure she *wants* to catch them, although maybe she should. Maybe she should barge in right now and stop this. They said they weren't going to hurt her, but there's something . . .

James crouches down next to Ella as Quentin closes his eyes and touches her arm.

After a moment, Ella begins to sway, but Quentin and James stay perfectly still and silent. It's creepy, like watching a disturbing video with the sound off. Laurel can't move or look away, even though she senses the *wrongness* of it.

Then Ella topples over, dead weight in James's arms.

Something in Laurel's chest breaks open in fear and anger, and she's on her feet just as Quentin opens his eyes and looks directly at her.

"Well," he says. "This is unfortunate."

Chapter 27

PIGEONS SCATTER AS Henry and Bastian approach the crumbling building. Henry can see the overcast sky through the breaks in the beams, and partially dried mud covers every surface that isn't wood or concrete.

They've been skirting the edges of the city all day, trying to find a safe place to hole up for the night. After walking for what felt like an eternity, they've ended up here: a rundown building that might've once been a school. Now it's a wreck that's probably on some long-forgotten demolition schedule.

If Henry ever needed evidence that the city's infrastructure is a mess, he's gotten plenty of it on this trip. But on the plus side, long-overdue beautification projects have created a decent number of places for assets to hide.

"No one nearby," Bastian says under his breath. He's stayed close since they did whatever-it-was in the park, but he doesn't seem to be in pain anymore, and he's far more alert than he was when he woke up.

Henry tries not to think about how he looked before that.

The weird thing is, Henry's been feeling good since then, too. Still anxious and terrified of what comes next, but not bone-crushingly tired the way he'd expect to be after everything they've been through. He thought Bastian was taking energy, and he did, but he also left something behind. An extra reserve of *something* that's left Henry feeling oddly rejuvenated.

Of course, the minute his thoughts stray to Angelica, or Barrett's hotel, or the danger he's helped put them all in, he feels *less* rejuvenated.

"We should get out of the open," he says.

The walls of the abandoned school are made of reddish brick cut through with ivy and other plants Henry can't identify. They form a kind of secondary structure, loosely holding together the walls and parts of the ceiling. From the inside, everything seems a little more intact, although it still looks like the entire place was burned out.

(The smoke, the unnatural flames all over the compound, people yelling and screaming and dying, and no matter how many people he went back in to save, it didn't matter because they still took compound leadership away from him, like he was never meant to have it in the first place, never meant to do anything other than be a weapon they could use to hurt everyone he was trying to help—)

"Henry." Bastian touches his arm. "Let's go a little further in and find a good place to rest."

Rest for what? Henry wants to ask but doesn't. Feeling useless and angry isn't going to help anything.

Around the corner, the hallway floor has the memory of being linoleum, and there are rows of dented metal on the walls—lockers, probably. The roof here is whole except for one large opening that shows the sky fading into night.

"I think I preferred the hotel," Bastian says, looking around. "The wallpaper was ugly, but at least there was enough wall for it."

He sits down very carefully and leans his back against what wall there is.

Henry lets out a halfhearted laugh, then glances in the direction they came. "I should check the perimeter. Make sure—"

"It's okay. I can tell there's no one around." Bastian looks at him for a moment, then adds carefully, "But—I mean, if you want to . . ."

Henry forces himself to shake his head and sit down next to Bastian like he isn't an anxious mess. "No, it's fine. If you're sure. It doesn't hurt to use your power?"

"No. I feel better than I have in a long time, honestly. I'm just not sure how long it'll last."

They sit in silence for a while, and Henry tries to focus on the warmth of Bastian's body next to him rather than his sore muscles or muddy shoes or the sneaking suspicion he'll break apart if he stops moving.

"So, what do you want to do now?" Bastian asks.

"Find Michaels, once it's safe," Henry says. Not because he feels anything like conviction about it, but because it's the next logical step. "We have to confirm what's on that USB drive. See if it's a good bargaining chip and decide who will give us what we need for it."

"And what do we need?"

Henry shrugs. "Something unifying that will get the Compound Network off our backs and also keep assets from turning on each other and making things worse. Although I suppose it's pointless to try to stop the inevitable."

After a long pause, Bastian says, "That . . . wasn't the inspiring speech I was expecting."

"What kind of speech would you prefer?" Henry's voice is suddenly sharp. "The one where I tell you we'll definitely find Angelica safe and sound, even though we have no idea where she is? The one where I tell you we'll magically be able to bring all the assets together so we can join forces and work together to save the day?"

"No, I just meant—"

"Because I don't know if any of that is possible now, or if it ever was. There's no proof that anything we do matters even a little bit. If anything, there's plenty of evidence that it doesn't. And even if it somehow *did*, there's no guarantee that we could do anything but get a whole lot of people hurt or killed. So what's the point?"

Because that's the real problem, isn't it? Henry could find the right words to say, maybe keep it together long enough to say them . . . and then what? They've endangered Michaels; they've endangered Barrett and Tallis and their group; they've lost Angelica. The mission is clear—rescue the people who need rescuing, protect the people who need protecting—but what's the point if the Compound Network is just going to make them keep doing it over and over?

Bastian clears his throat. "Maybe there doesn't need to be a point. Maybe it's just who you are. Someone who wants to help other people."

Henry laughs humorlessly. "Then I should try being someone else, since I'm clearly not excelling at that."

"Helping people isn't the same as never hurting them. It's more like . . . you try not to hurt them, but when you do, that just means you have to keep trying."

"And when you get tired of trying?"

Bastian falls silent and stares at his beat-up sneakers. Then he looks away.

"All those months . . . I thought you were probably dead." His voice sounds unstable, raw, desperate enough to be startling. "So, I thought—I thought, if I couldn't be with you, at least I could do something, *anything*, that might help someone else. The stupid sort of stuff you always do. But it's not as easy as you make it look. I can't *care* the way you do. And even if I could, the compound would just beat it out of me like it does everyone else. Except you."

Henry frowns. "That's not—"

"All the shit they put you through—put all of us through—what's the point of fighting it? If it makes someone like you give up, what chance does anyone else have?"

Henry thinks of all the people who treated him like an idealistic idiot with no common sense: Major Valentine, who hid what she knew about his power because it suited her; Major Alexis, who mentored him and then betrayed him when he refused to be a good pawn; everyone in training who let him know that it was laughable to believe in what the Compound Network claimed it stood for. All the people who told him he needed to be "realistic" rather than stand up and work hard toward a better way of doing things.

Henry clenches his fists. "You can't put all of that on me. Not when—I mean, I hurt people, too. It's not fair to—"

"Yeah, you're right. It's not fair. You shouldn't have to be some beacon of . . . whatever. But you . . ." Bastian scratches his head awkwardly. "You make people—you make *me*—feel like it matters. Like it's possible to change things. And even if those changes don't stick, it still matters that we tried."

He makes a face. "Look, if someone had asked me before I met you whether I thought things could ever get better at the compound, I would've said absolutely not, and it would be stupid to think otherwise."

"Says the guy who escaped when it was supposed to be impossible," Henry says, smiling faintly. "Who tried to find something better."

"Or who was just trying to run away."

Very early on, Henry fell into the trap of seeing Bastian as selfish, someone who didn't give a damn about anything other than protecting himself. But now, watching him struggle for words—after nearly dying because he was so desperate not to hurt Henry—it's hard to see how he ever could have thought that.

"Maybe it *is* hopeless," Bastian says, eyes on a patch of mud across the hall. "Maybe nothing we do matters. But if we don't try to do it anyway, they win. And I'm *so fucking tired* of them winning. Aren't you?"

Henry thinks of Mariah's dazed, horrified expression as Officer Garrand led her away. The sound of Dr. Urashima's voice in his earpiece, reminding him that he was only useful as long as his power was useful. The careful way General Carter and Senator Donnigan and Major Alexis worked together to destroy the compound he led without ever really giving him a chance.

"Yeah," Henry says, nearly collapsing under the weight of the word. "I'm tired of it, too."

Bastian turns to look at him. "Then tell me what we should do, and I'll prove to you that we can do it. That *you* can do it. Only—maybe without any more speeches. I already feel like an idiot."

Henry smiles in spite of himself. "What you should do is kiss me."

Bastian blinks. "Oh. Uh . . . are you sure? I mean, this place isn't really . . ." He waves a hand at the hole in the ceiling and the brown grass poking through the cracks in the flooring.

"What, you don't like the ambiance? The mud everywhere? The fact that the walls might finish collapsing any second and—?"

Bastian rolls his eyes, leans over, and kisses him.

It's not exactly passionate, and it's over before it's really begun. But when Bastian pulls back, just far enough to touch Henry's cheek and rest their foreheads together, Henry thinks that maybe not *everything* that came out of the compound is awful, after all.

"I don't know if I can do this," Henry says quietly. "What you think I'm capable of, I mean. But I want to. I think I'll always want to."

"That's enough," Bastian says, brushing a thumb over Henry's cheekbone. "It's enough that you want to. We can fake the rest."

Henry snorts. "That's it? Fake it till you make it?"

"Fake it till we convince Michaels to do everything for us." Bastian makes a face. "Whatever. Let's just figure out a way to kick their asses, once and for all."

"I can get behind that." Henry considers, then adds, "Might need a little more incentive, though."

"Yeah? What kind of incentive?"

It's obviously not a real question because he doesn't seem at all surprised when Henry kisses him again. And then Bastian's arms are around Henry's neck, and he's smiling against his mouth, and Henry remembers, with a sharpness that's both pain and relief, what it's like to be this close to someone he—

"I love you," he says, and they might be the three most important words he's said in more than seven months.

Bastian blinks, looking briefly startled before his face relaxes into the genuine but slightly awkward smile that might be Henry's favorite. Like he's as out of practice hearing it as Henry is saying it.

"I think you're going to love me a lot less," Bastian says, "when I remind you that we have to lie low for a few days before we can meet up with Michaels, and our accommodations probably aren't going to get any better than this."

"Not ideal," Henry admits, brushing back a strand of Bastian's hair. "But I'll probably still love you, even if we have to temporarily live in squalor."

"And if we're on the run and living in squalor forever?"

"There's no one I'd rather be on the run and living in squalor with."

Bastian gets an odd look on his face, but before Henry can ask, he shifts position so he can rest his head on Henry's shoulder. "Me, too," he says softly.

"Which part? Being on the run, living in squalor, or—?"

"All of it. Any part where I'm with you."

And while Henry is still more of a bundle of nerves than a whole person at the moment, that seems far less important than the fact that Bastian is beside him, warm and alive and determined to find a way to do this together.

Chapter 28

"WHAT DID YOU do to her?" Laurel demands.

"Please keep your voice down," Quentin says, getting slowly to his feet. "We don't want to wake the others."

"You mean you don't want them to know what you just did. Which is what, exactly?"

When he doesn't answer, Laurel hurries over to Ella. James is holding her upright, and she seems to be breathing. It's almost like she's sleeping.

Then she opens her eyes, and Laurel's skin crawls.

Ella's expression is blank and dull, and she's looking at Laurel without actually looking at her. Looking *through* her. Sitting there like a doll, waiting for someone to activate her by telling her what to do. Which Quentin does.

"Thank you, Ella," he says, brushing dirt off of his pants. Whatever fatigue he was experiencing seems to have evaporated. "You can go get some rest now."

Ella nods, then gets to her feet and walks out of the circle of trees and back toward the other assets. Laurel starts after her to make sure she doesn't run into anything in the dark, but James gets in her way.

"Move," Laurel says sharply. So of course he doesn't.

"I'm surprised Bastian didn't explain how this works," Quentin says. His voice is mild and infuriating, and the words make no sense. "Empaths require infusions of emotional energy in order to survive. Asset energy is best. It doesn't hurt them, but—"

"She looked—" Laurel shudders. She tries to imagine Bastian doing this, but it doesn't compute. He's rude, of course, but not . . . whatever someone would have to be to do this.

(But people do what they have to do to survive, like her friends hurt and killed and destroyed as their compound was burning down, like she did when she poisoned that officer, even if she didn't mean to—)

"Ella will be fine," Quentin reassures her. "The process is quick, and her emotions will return soon."

"Emotions? You took her *emotions?*"

Laurel suddenly remembers how Bastian described James when James first came to the compound: Emotionless. Gutted. Empty, somehow. Like someone had stolen something from inside him.

Because someone had.

Laurel glares at James—less because she's mad and more because she can feel the prickling fear on the back of her neck. "You did this, too."

James shrugs. "It's not that big of a deal. Like he said, it doesn't hurt, and—"

"Did you agree?"

"Of course."

"Ella didn't."

"Yes, she did. You heard, didn't you?"

"But you—it sounded like this was the only way you'd let her stay. The only way she'd be safe. And she didn't know what was going to happen. She didn't know she'd be like *that* afterward, did she?"

"You're a plantspeaker, Laurel," Quentin says. "Surely you understand the concept of symbiosis. In order for the community to survive, compromises must be made."

"Symbiosis doesn't mean the relationship is good for everyone. Parasites live in symbiosis with their hosts—until they kill their hosts. Ask a witchweed if you need an example."

"But the parasite does its best to keep the host alive, doesn't it? After all, it needs the host to live."

Laurel feels her face flush. "Is that how you see these people? Like food?"

"If plants do it, why isn't it okay for assets? Isn't this all just part of nature?"

There's genuine curiosity in Quentin's eyes—but also condescension. Like Laurel is an unruly weed that needs to start being useful again or else get ripped up and thrown away.

"You could ask," Laurel says, annoyed that her voice sounds so shaky and uncertain. "You could tell her what to expect and let her decide. You could be honest instead of lying to get your way."

"Perhaps. But sometimes people aren't capable of making the best decisions for themselves. They need someone to—"

"You sound like them," Laurel snaps. "The compound officers. The med techs. The people you escaped from. You were smart enough to escape to the forest fifty years ago, to set up your sanctuary, but you're just as bad as them.

You haven't learned *anything*. I can't believe the forest didn't chew you up and spit you out."

She realizes a bit belatedly that the trees around them are shaking their branches ominously, leaning in ever so slightly, responding to the anger in her voice. Even these trees, who seem more interested in keeping to themselves, have picked up on her tone. They're preparing to lash out at whoever she wants to hurt, the same way the spruce tried to warn her earlier. Even here in the middle of the city, there's an ecosystem of living things looking out for each other.

Laurel takes a shaky breath and flicks her fingers slightly. *It's okay. Don't attack.*

"There are very few options for someone like me," Quentin says quietly. He doesn't seem to have noticed the trees, or he's pretending he didn't. "Bastian told you that this is the only way, didn't he? Or maybe he didn't because he didn't want to worry you. But it's true: If an empath doesn't take energy, they'll die. Luckily, the process doesn't cause any permanent harm. And if I live longer, I can help more people."

"You mean you can find more people to feed off and lie to. What . . . what did you lie to *me* about?"

Quentin considers her silently for a moment, then says, "I needed someone on the inside of the compound to be my eyes and ears. To look for information for me. You were suited to the task."

"I didn't—" She stops. The headaches, the missed sleep, the footage of her on the security cameras in places she never went . . . "What did you do to me?"

Quentin smiles faintly. Sadly. Genuinely? "I asked for your help, Laurel. And I removed all the distractions so that you could do what I asked."

"Distractions?" A sudden thought occurs. "Like my link with Bastian?"

"Maintaining multiple empath links is difficult even for a full empath. I couldn't risk not being able to communicate with you, so . . . I suppose you might say I put the other line on mute. And because of that—because of people like you and Ella and James, who rose to the occasion, we can work together to—"

"No, we can't."

If he had *truly* asked, then *maybe*. But he manipulated her—took away her ability to contact Bastian, to think for herself, and now—

Laurel turns on her heel and marches out of the circle of trees and back toward the spruce. She looks around for any sign of Ella, but there's nothing. And anyway, what could Laurel do to help her? This isn't something a tincture or herbal remedy could fix.

"Laurel!" James calls. He's followed her and isn't making any effort to stay quiet. "Wait!"

She does *not* wait. She also makes a sharp motion with her right hand, keeping it close to her body but making it clear to all of the plants in the vicinity: *Keep him back.*

James stumbles over something, letting out a loud, "*Oof.*" Laurel reaches a streetlight and turns to see him getting to his feet, having just taken a nosedive over a bumpy root.

"Where are you going?" James asks, swatting at a bit of dirt on his nose. In another life, Laurel might have found it cute.

"I'm going to get Chloe, and then we're going to go find Bastian and Henry."

"Didn't you hear what Quentin said? We're stronger together. We should—"

"*He's* stronger together. I'm not convinced that him being strong helps anyone else, though."

"It helped me."

"Did it?" Laurel puts her hands on her hips. "Why do you think he healed you? Out of the goodness of his heart? Or did you just make a really convenient battery? A firestarter spliced with empath blood—what sort of energy could he get out of you?"

"There wasn't anyone else," James says. "You think I should've crawled out of that hellhole and died rather than doing whatever I could to live?"

Yes, says some horrible, shameful part of her. *If you'd died, I could have kept my memories of you rather than finding out how little you actually care about anyone else.*

Laurel takes a shaky breath, then gives him a small, strained smile. "I'm going to leave now. I know you won't ask me to stay because you said you wouldn't. Please tell Quentin it was nice of him to host us. I mean, it wasn't, but tell him that anyway because it would be rude not to."

She makes a small gesture with her left hand to let the area plants know they can hold off unless James acts out. Over James's shoulder, she can just barely make out Quentin still standing in the circle of trees, a dark, unmoving shadow in the low light. Laurel can't be sure whether he'll be a problem, but she doesn't think so. Not right now.

Because Laurel isn't a threat to him, is she? He's already gotten what he wanted from her, and he probably expects James to take care of things now. Either convince her to stay, or . . .

"So instead of staying here to help, you're going to look for *them*," James says. It sounds petulant, like he's a little kid who can't stand not being the center of attention. How could she ever have found that charming?

"*They* didn't burn down a compound. *Two* compounds."

"The first one wasn't my fault. And the second one . . ." James looks away, mouth twisted into a tight frown. "I did what I had to do. If I hadn't, things would've gotten worse."

"Things *did* get worse, but you weren't around to see it, were you? Because you killed all those people, and then you just *left*."

"I'm not the only one who killed people," James says, voice sharp and hard. And Laurel can't really argue the point. He may have encouraged the other assets to bring the compound down, but it was their choice to use their powers like they did.

And it's not like *she's* entirely pristine here, either. She can still see the green-faced officer lying on the ground, the one she dreams about all the time, the one she accidentally—or maybe on purpose—killed with her plants at the old compound. She can't exactly give James a hard time for doing something she's done herself.

It would be so much easier if she could hate him. If she could hate Quentin, too. But then she'd have to hate herself and Bastian and Henry and all the other assets who have had to make difficult decisions. And that would be a lot of people to hate.

"Oh. I didn't mean—I wasn't talking about you, Laurel." James reaches out toward her, but she flinches back.

"Who *were* you talking about, then?" she asks, rubbing her arm and narrowing her eyes at him.

"Do you know what Mortimer has been getting up to for the last seven months?" James's face has gone hard again.

"No. And I don't see how you could know, either."

"Quentin has connections. He tries to keep track of everything that's happening in the Compound Network so he can keep assets safe. There were loads of rumors about a culling happening at Council HQ—assets going in and never coming out. Only a few *did* come out eventually, and they'd all lost their powers."

Laurel stares at him. "You think Henry had something to do with it?"

"He's a negator. It makes sense."

"He wouldn't—he'd never hurt someone like that."

"You have no idea what he'd do," James snaps. "Or what it'd feel like, losing a part of yourself. Feeling it ripped out of you all of a sudden and knowing you'll never get it back. Even if he didn't kill those assets himself, he hurt them. Might've been kinder to kill them, honestly."

"That's—he's not like that. He would never—"

"He *would*, and that's my point. We do what we think is necessary. Sometimes people have to die so other people can live. Sometimes taking the moral high ground is stupid because there are other things that matter more. Quentin understands that. The assets from the sanctuary understand that. Stop acting like you don't."

She *does* understand that. Just like she understands that he expects her to accept him as the authority on the subject. "So, you're saying . . . what? That Henry—?"

James steps closer, eyes both sad and furious. She wants to move back again, but she stands her ground. "All that shit about protecting assets, but he's not above stealing from them, is he? How is that any better than what Quentin does? At least Quentin gives back. Mortimer just *takes*."

Laurel stares at him for a moment, and then it suddenly becomes clear: Henry must have permanently negated him. Henry only ever talked about it as a theory, one he read about in a book about negators. Not something he could actually do. But if he *could* . . .

. . . then James isn't an asset anymore.

It must have been self-defense. Henry wouldn't just *do* that, even to someone he doesn't like. If he came across James in the burning compound after seeing everyone hurt and dying, he must've thought there was only one way to end it.

Because his back was against the wall. Because this is what happens when an asset can't think of any other option. Henry would never hurt someone if he could avoid it, but if all the other options had been removed . . .

"I'm sorry for what he took from you," Laurel says quietly. "I'm sure he didn't want to, and he probably feels really awful about it."

She takes a breath and tries to ignore her roiling stomach. "Do *you* feel awful about it? What you did at the compound?"

"No," James says, eyes locked on hers. No hesitation. "I did what I had to do."

That makes it both easier and harder, somehow.

Laurel nods. Before her throat can close up, she says, "Okay. Then I'm going to need you to never speak to me again."

He looks startled and, of course, he ignores her order and opens his mouth. "Laurel—"

"It's a simple request," Laurel says, standing up straight, a poplar facing off against a nasty gale. "Please don't speak to me ever again. Don't ask me to work with you and Quentin; don't ask me to listen to you brag about the next compound you try to take down; don't remind me of how much I owe you from before. That was before, and this is now. Now I have two stupid friends to find and protect—friends who try to do the right thing and not hurt people, and who own up to their mistakes. I don't know why those weren't always prerequisites for me when it comes to friendship, but they are now. So that counts you out."

James starts to say something again, but he's interrupted by the sound of quickly approaching footsteps.

"Laurel," Chloe says, clutching their bag, "I overheard some—oh." She tenses at the sight of James.

"Never mind him," Laurel says briskly. "We're leaving. Well, *I'm* leaving, and I'd be happy to leave with you, especially since it's not safe here. But you were saying . . . ?"

"Um." Chloe flicks another glance at James, then says in a low voice, "The other assets, some of them were at the raid at the hotel earlier today. They said James was there. And so were Bastian and Henry. And a little girl who got caught by the compound officers."

"Oh," Laurel says frostily. "A raid where Bastian and Henry were? Like the one James said he knew nothing about?"

James frowns. "I was only—"

"Nope. We're done here."

"Quentin won't let—"

Laurel turns before she's gotten very far. "It would be very unfortunate if Quentin were to keep us from going. There are a *lot* of trees with pine cones around here. And roots. And there are parasitic plants that would have no problem hurting you if it helped them or their hosts. Sounds familiar, doesn't it?"

Laurel sets off again, Chloe at her heels. From the shadows, various assets look up as they pass, then quickly away, obviously not wanting to cause trouble.

Under her breath, Laurel says, "Just to be clear, I have no idea what we're going to do now."

"That's okay," Chloe replies, eyes surprisingly bright. "I think I know how we can find Bastian and Henry."

Chapter 29

THEY GET TO the Hall even earlier this time. Henry leaves the empathic scanning to Bastian, but he takes on the more mundane scanning himself: security camera locations, guard rotations, where people are most frequently coming in or going out. All the stuff they kept an eye on last time, only now in triplicate.

So, he notices right away when Michaels approaches them. Or rather, walks right past them, muttering, "Back exit. Ten minutes." Her voice is so soft, Henry isn't sure he actually heard it at first.

"Didn't even have to buy her coffee this time," Bastian says as she moves on.

"We didn't buy her coffee last time, either," Henry points out. "Do you think she's still keeping a tab? Because the number of macchiatos I owe her by now must be astronomical."

"She deserves every one of them."

"Yes, she absolutely does."

They meander carefully toward the back of the Hall, narrowly avoiding what looks like a third-shift security guard on her way out. She's unlikely to be keeping a close watch for assets after eight hours on duty, but Henry makes sure to keep a few people between them, just in case.

The back of the Hall is less busy this early in the day, but Henry notes two more security guards and four cameras nearby. Bastian doesn't seem concerned: When Henry turns to give him the count, Bastian just sighs and starts walking toward the parking lot. "Head for that black car."

Henry gets it a second later as a large tour bus chugs past them, eager faces at the windows. The bus comes briefly between them and the Hall, providing a straight shot to the car with less chance of being seen.

Said car, it turns out, contains Michaels in the front and, to Henry's surprise, Senator Nunez in the back.

Nunez is wearing her usual severe navy suit. Her dark eyes are keen and observant, and her mouth is turned slightly downward. She was clearly expecting them.

"This seems familiar," Bastian says cheerfully, getting in and scooting over to make room for Henry. "Didn't realize you had so much fun the last time we did this that you'd want to do it again, Senator."

Nunez's frown deepens. "Michaels said we should compare notes about the . . . item you brought us."

"Is it okay to talk about it here?" Henry asks quickly. They're at a fairly safe distance from Hall security, but someone could still get photos or a recording if they were very dedicated.

"I've taken precautions with this vehicle," Nunez says, her tone implying that he's very stupid for asking. "We should keep it short, though."

"The USB drive contained what you thought it did," Michaels informs them. "And a few other things."

"What other things?" Bastian asks.

"Things related to a particularly pervasive rumor," Nunez says, tapping one perfectly manicured nail against her thigh. "General Carter has alluded to it in several meetings without being terribly specific, but . . ."

"But?" Bastian prompts after a moment. "Didn't you say we're on the clock?"

"The Compound Council has an information repository called the 'vault,'" Nunez continues. "From what I can gather, it houses historical data, research findings—things they don't want anyone else to know about. Very few people have access, and even within the Network itself, the vault is made to sound like a rumor unless you're high up in the organization."

Henry hasn't ever heard of anything like this, including when he was running the compound. But then, he was probably never in a position to. If it even really exists. He sneaks a glance at Bastian, who looks just as disbelieving, before he says, "How do we know it's *not* just a rumor?"

"Because we have evidence now, thanks to this drive. The Fail-Safe Protocol documents have an extra bit of code embedded in them—notes that suggest a vault like the rumors describe. There's also a numbering system that lines up with references from documents Carter shared with the liaison committee. And some documents I never saw until now." Nunez frowns. "Emily was doing additional research behind my back. It's probably part of why she was killed."

"There wasn't anything like that on the files she sent us at the compound," Henry says. "Our hackers would've seen it."

"She did something to them before she died, didn't she?"

Bastian says it like it's a completely normal thing to suggest, even though it makes no sense to Henry. Sure, cyberreaders like Emily can interact with computer code in a way others can't, but he's never heard of one sneaking in code that could stay hidden for months and randomly pop up later.

Nunez raises her eyebrows. "It could be that your hackers missed it."

"No, it couldn't."

Henry can't quite bite back a smile at Bastian's obvious pride. He might give Kent and Sybil a hard time, but he knows they're good enough at their jobs that they'd never let something like this get past them—unless they were literally unable to see it in the first place.

"Officer Michaels was able to connect me with someone in the city who's familiar with cyberreaders and was willing to speak off the record," Nunez says. "Apparently, it's not unheard of for a cyberreader to speak code into existence without realizing they're doing it, particularly if they're untrained. Emily didn't know what she could do, and she was the kind of person who soaked up everything around her. She wanted to keep those files safe, and she wanted to make sure they constituted a good enough case against Carter and whoever he's working with. If she overheard something and inserted it into the code, either consciously or unconsciously, it might be our best chance of proving what Carter has been doing."

"No one will care," Henry says, trying to ignore the frustration simmering in his stomach. "The Compound Network probably greenlit the whole thing to begin with—the Fail-Safe Protocol, the splicing and empath experiments, whatever else is going on at the compounds these days. And if we bring this to anyone, they'll just say it's suspicious that the data has only shown up now."

"We may have a solution for that." Nunez laces her fingers together. "There seems to be someone else on the Council, some sort of higher-up, who doesn't agree with Carter's agenda. Carter has been unusually anxious in meetings lately, desperate to move forward with the Fail-Safe Protocol. Something to secure his reputation and position. Almost as if he feels threatened that someone else is going to take it."

"We think this person was at the Hall earlier this week," Michaels says. "You may have noticed the increased security. None of that was officially on the books, as far as I can tell from my research. And whoever it was, they didn't meet with anyone other than General Carter and Senator Donnigan. No one has any details about it, except that the meeting apparently took place in a top secret part of the Hall with extremely restricted access."

Bastian raises his eyebrows. "You got someone talking about things they shouldn't be talking about?"

"I am, as you know, extremely congenial. But I also have documented evidence."

Michaels offers Henry a tablet. There's a paused security video on it: two people, one in a Compound Network uniform and one in a suit, standing in front of a wall. The picture is too grainy to pick out details, but they seem to be having an animated discussion. After a moment, one of them reaches out to touch a small rectangular plate on the wall, and it slides open to reveal a long hallway lit with pale blue lights—the same kind used on the compound's lower levels.

The figures go in, and the wall closes behind them.

"This particular footage is from level 1," Michaels says, "but not any part of level 1 I've ever seen. No one I spoke with was familiar with it, either. Of course, the digital files ought to have some sort of identification number, but there wasn't anything in the security database beyond the general level 1 notation."

"Is there any way to enhance this?" Henry asks. Something about the operation of the panel seems familiar.

"No. But there was one other camera recording from a different angle."

She takes the tablet back, swipes a few times, and hands it over again.

He can't make out much about the figure farthest from the camera, except that they're slightly smaller than their companion. The other person, though, is easier to see from this angle: larger and more willing to take up space, dressed in a uniform with four stars. A general. And even though it's blurry, the face is familiar.

General Carter.

He reaches out and touches the panel with what looks like an ID, but narrower than the usual kind.

(Henry remembers cutting his finger multiple times so he'd bleed onto the plaques that opened the doors on Level 49, the ones that led to the rooms where Carter and Valentine drugged him and took his blood for the Fail-Safe Protocol, the experiment that was supposed to let them control all of the assets, hiding his ability as a negator except when they could use him to—)

"You don't have any idea where this might be on level 1?" Henry demands.

"There are a few areas in the Hall with restricted access," Nunez says. "They were used much less frequently before the compound burned down—mostly for discussions that might impact security. Now, they seem to be used more often, primarily for meetings with Compound Network visitors. And whatever we're seeing here."

"They just left this footage lying around?" Bastian asks. "So much for security."

"Actually, this footage was very difficult to get," Michaels says. "Luckily, I'm very good at poker, and the security team hadn't deleted it yet. I may also have ensured that they had less to bet with than they thought, which made it easier to win."

Bastian stares at her. "You stole their wallets and won this footage off the Hall security team in a poker game?"

"I'm *very* good at poker."

Henry turns to Nunez. "Whatever you're paying her, double it."

"Don't think I haven't already." Nunez's mouth twitches upward into something that's almost a smile. Then it flattens out again. "We can't be *sure* they're entering the vault, but it does seem likely, especially since they did their best to hide evidence of their visit. I don't think we'll get anything else out of security, though; they're too concerned about getting fired for losing the data."

"Why would this vault be in the Hall, anyway?" Henry asks. "Isn't that the compound basically putting their most important valuables in someone else's house?"

Bastian frowns. "Not exactly. No one would think to look for it here, right? But because of the liaison committee, Council members would still have easy access."

"Even if you're right, and this *is* the vault, it won't necessarily help," Henry warns Nunez. "We could find all the evidence in the world, and Carter would just figure out a way to bury it."

"Not if the Council replaces him," Nunez says. "That's how it's done, isn't it? New leadership, new lackeys. You just need to figure out what's in there and how you can use it. Play your cards right, and you could upend the whole system. Especially if there's someone waiting in the wings to take Carter down."

"Except we tried that, and Carter still won." Henry's voice comes out harsher than he intended it to, and he can feel Bastian's eyes on him.

He *wants* to believe what Bastian said at the old school. *Wants* to believe that whatever action they take here is better than doing nothing. But how many times are they going to try and fail? How many times are they going to make things worse in their attempts to make things better?

Then again, what's the alternative? Become a complacent part of the system like Major Alexis? Or someone who manipulates it to get whatever they want, everyone else be damned, like General Carter or Senator Donnigan?

"Carter is desperate," Nunez says. "He'll be cutting corners right now, which means it's the perfect time to look into this vault and the new player, whoever they are. Put that together with what's on the USB drive, and I may be able to do something on my end to make the case to the right people that Carter should be removed from office."

"Did you develop an altruistic streak, Senator?" Bastian asks. "Or is this still about putting you in a good position?"

Henry is about to caution Bastian against antagonizing an ally, but Nunez just gives them both a glare. "I do what's best for my constituents, as I've told you before. The longer Carter and Donnigan let the Compound Network run things here, the less the Hall will do to actually run the city. It's not as exciting, maybe, but we need to be talking about infrastructure and economics, not shady deals with covert organizations."

She locks gazes with Henry, her eyes even sharper than normal, which is to say, sharp enough to slice through skin. "Michaels tells me you were missing for seven months. I won't ask what happened, but I will ask you this: Was there anything that you experienced during that time that makes you think the Compound Network's power *shouldn't* be minimized as soon as possible?"

(Mariah's confused and betrayed eyes; the old man bleeding out on the interrogation table; the countless number of times he was locked in that room, screaming until his throat was raw, knowing he'd still do whatever they told him to do the next day because there weren't any other options—)

"No," he says, mouth dry, unable to keep his voice steady. "They—we need to do whatever we can. Whatever it takes."

Even if it's hopeless. Because hope doesn't enter into it. They owe it to all the assets, to everyone who's been affected, to do whatever they can, whether or not it works.

"There's a lecture at the Hall tonight," Nunez says. "Minimal staff will be present, and everyone will be focused on the atrium and east wing. There will still be security, but Michaels can help you with that. I'll be at the event and doing what I can to keep eyes off of the rest of the building so you can investigate."

Bastian raises his eyebrows. "You want us to find the vault *tonight*?"

"I want you to make use of a good opportunity to investigate. We're unlikely to get this lucky again anytime soon."

"Please arrive at the back door promptly at eight," Michaels says. "I'll make sure security there is lax and give you as much information as I'm able to gather by then."

Henry hesitates, then says, "It's probably not safe for you to hang onto the USB drive."

"Not a problem, sir. I'll make sure it's secure until we need it."

Henry takes a breath. "Bastian?"

"I'm good if you are."

Henry doesn't really know what those words mean in this context. But Bastian's eyes are clear and calm, and he's sitting close enough that his hand is almost brushing Henry's. And maybe it was always going to come down to this: the two of them and the few allies they managed to keep, for better or worse, just trying to do the best they can.

"Okay," Henry says. "We'll see you tonight."

Chapter 30

"IT'S NOT STEALING if the guy in front of us *accidentally* drops his wallet on the ground, and I *accidentally* pick it up," Bastian says.

"It is if you make him feel like dropping it in the first place." Henry gives Bastian a moderately disapproving side-eye. "You seriously can't think of anything better to do until tonight?"

Bastian stuffs his hands in his pockets and kicks a pebble into the street. "I can't think of a better way to buy you lunch," he mutters.

They've been walking around the city all morning, trying not to stay too long in any one location. The buzz of the city's usual emotional discord isn't bothering Bastian as much as it probably ought to be, but he can feel the drain as he tries to keep his shield locked in place while also staying aware of the emotions of the people around them. They can't afford to be noticed right now—even more than they couldn't afford it before.

But no matter how much Bastian tries to focus on the task at hand, his mind keeps wandering to other things. Moira's dream and Quentin's invasion. Where the other assets from the hotel ended up. How he can get Henry something to eat before they stroll into enemy territory this evening.

It's obviously pathetic to be focusing on lunch right now, but . . . well. Bastian is a little pathetic where Henry is concerned. He was clearly agitated in Nunez's car (agitated-concerned-hopeless underneath a reflexive negation barrier), and Bastian can't help but want to do something. Anything.

Pathetic.

Henry's mouth twitches upward. "Well, as fun as it would be to watch you get yelled at in the street and maybe arrested, I'd rather find another one of those supply drops Barrett and Tallis used. They've gotten us through the past few days, and they're supposed to be all over the city, right? If we luck out, we might find one with some food, and—"

Bastian stops in the middle of the sidewalk without meaning to. There's something familiar approaching: a determined-cautious-intent that suddenly grows a spiky outer layer of surprise, then relief. He has maybe half a second to start turning around before a bundle of nervous, grateful energy throws itself into his arms and nearly knocks him over.

"Laurel?"

He barely has time to process or figure out what to do with his hands before she pulls away, turns to Henry, and bursts into tears while repeating the flinging action. Henry is quicker to deal with it, steadying her in his arms while also giving Bastian a slightly alarmed look.

"Er," says a small voice. "Hello."

Bastian looks over and sees Chloe standing awkwardly on the sidewalk behind them. She looks muddy and exhausted, but her embarrassed-relieved-grateful is almost as familiar and comforting as Laurel's.

Laurel backs away from Henry, eyes still wet and bright. "Sorry. This is the definition of making a scene, isn't it? It's just—we've been asking the trees and following the markers for days, and we weren't sure if—"

She clears her throat. "Thanks for, you know, not being dead."

There's a rawness in her voice, like something sharp and painful is scratching against her throat, and Bastian suddenly, desperately needs to know why she's so upset. "What happened?"

"Well, it's a little weird that you forgot, but we thought Henry might be dead, and then you—"

"No, I mean—"

"Um, sorry to interrupt, but we should probably get off the sidewalk," Chloe says. "I can find us a path to somewhere safer, if you want."

"Yeah," Henry says. He sounds a little dazed but, like always, ready to focus on the mission. "Let's do that."

***

"I wasn't sure at first if it was safe to use the empath link," Laurel says. "Then I kept trying, but it didn't work."

Bastian frowns. "We've used it over long distances before. Why would it be a problem now?"

"I think Quentin blocked it somehow. So he could—he said it was to 're-move distractions.'" Her mouth settles into a grim line.

They're sitting together on the green attached to one of the city's art museums. At this time of day, there are more trees than people, but the few other groups lounging around keep theirs from sticking out. Chloe found them a drop point with a few sweatshirts and energy bars, so at least they've been able to switch out dirty clothing and eat something. The weather is cool but not cold. It's almost pleasant, all things considered.

Although the topic of conversation . . . not so much.

"He always wants to be in charge of everything," Bastian says. "He must have sent James to the hotel to stir things up and get more assets on his side. And using you at the compound . . . that sounds like the way he used James to find information. But what was he looking for?"

He can feel the way she emotionally flinches away from the mention of James, even if she's calm on the surface. He wants to ask but knows that anything he says would be woefully inadequate. The fact that she met with James and Quentin and didn't try to bring either of them along implies that she doesn't think they were *worth* bringing along. Quentin makes sense, given how he used her. But James . . . well, Bastian may never have been his number one fan, but he is—was—Laurel's friend. Her only remaining link to her life at her first compound. If she's decided to sever that tie . . .

Laurel shakes her head. "I don't know what Quentin is looking for. But I *do* know that the major is doing more than she lets on. And Kwan knows about it—or at least, he knows about *some* of it. Maybe that's what Quentin wants to know, too."

"We need a bargaining chip," Henry says thoughtfully. "The USB drive might help, but it's not enough. We need something that will give us enough leverage so that the Council can't afford to ignore us. Something that will put us in charge of the conversation ahead of anyone else."

"The vault," Bastian says.

"But we don't know what's in it."

"No, but we will after tonight."

"Assuming we can actually find it and get in."

"What's the dress code for breaking into a secret vault?" Laurel asks, looking down at her secondhand sweatshirt. It's faded orange, and the sleeves come down over her wrists. "This doesn't seem dressy enough, somehow."

Bastian frowns. "It's going to be dangerous. I don't think you should—"

"I'll be very useful and careful and helpful. Do you know how many plants there are in and around the Hall? Plants are excellent backup when you're planning to do something nefarious. Even the well-behaved ones like a little nefariousness."

"Laurel—"

Her face darkens. "I appreciate your concern, but I am *not* in the mood for someone to tell me what I can and can't do right now. I have just as much reason to want to kick Carter's ass as anyone else here, so I'm going."

"Me, too." Chloe's jaw is set in the same way it was when she and Bastian came back to the burning compound, and she made the decision to guide them through the fire, despite Bastian's misgivings. It was stupid and brave, and he's never stopped being grateful for it.

Henry and Bastian look at each other, and then Henry nods. "You're right. We all have good reasons to go tonight. And if we go together, we can watch out for each other."

Laurel thrusts her hand out, stopping it briefly in front of each of them, an expectant look on her face. When no one responds, she wiggles her fingers. "Secret handshake!"

Bastian rolls his eyes. "That's—"

She grabs his hand and shakes it once, hard enough to nearly knock him off balance.

"Needs more choreography," Henry suggests, completely deadpan.

"You're right," Laurel says. "Luckily, I have fifteen possible additions, and we have plenty of time to go through all of them before we have to go to the Hall."

Bastian is about to protest, but then he sees the smile tugging at the corner of Henry's mouth and the way he's *almost* doing the crinkle-around-the-eyes thing. Feels the tiny, gentle wave of amused-grateful-happy coming off of him.

And Bastian decides that maybe a handshake concession isn't too high a price to pay, after all.

***

It's almost dark by the time they get to the Hall's back door. The usual cacophony of daytime emotions has thinned out, although Bastian can tell that the lecture must be well attended because there are plenty of people near the front of the building. They all seem to be clustered in that area, which means the rest of the Hall ought to be easier to navigate, just like Nunez suggested it would be.

They stay hidden in the shadow of an elm on the far side of the Hall parking lot. This gives them a decent view of the back door without them having to get too close.

"Eight fifteen," Henry says as he glances up at the ornate city clock they're standing near. "And Michaels is never late."

"The elm and the other trees around here say they haven't seen her," Laurel reports.

Henry frowns. "They're sure?"

Laurel opens her mouth, then closes it and raises her eyebrows. "Wow, okay. I'm not going to translate what they just said about you, but I'm going to give this elm a stern talking-to for being so rude. Yikes."

Bastian snorts, and Laurel adds, "Don't even get me started on what they're saying about *you*."

"I think someone's coming out," Chloe says.

She's right: Someone has appeared at the back door, but it isn't Michaels. This person is dressed in black and wearing the sort of headset used by Hall security. Even at this distance, Bastian recognizes the unruly red hair and slightly hunched shoulders, which are very much *not* standard issue for Hall security. He also recognizes the cloud of stressed-anxious-resigned looming over the person's head.

Henry squints. "Is that—?"

"Yeah." Bastian carefully feels for anyone else in the vicinity, but all he gets is Kent and a few security guards several hallways over. No one likely to need that door right now. Still . . . "Let me talk to him for a minute. Once I figure out what's going on, I'll call the rest of you over."

Rather than wait for the inevitable protests, Bastian trots across the parking lot, taking care to stay out of direct light and keep his senses alert for danger.

"No," Kent is saying when Bastian gets closer. "I don't see any—holy shit!"

"Hello, Kent," Bastian says, smirking in spite of himself. "I think you're in the wrong place."

"Tell me about it." Kent gives him a sour once-over, then says into his comm, "All right, Lucas just popped up. Your algorithm is as beautiful as you are, and I'm a fool for ever doubting you."

"Are you going to tell me what you're doing here?" Bastian prompts.

"Wait a sec; he's asking—"

Kent pulls off his headset and hands it to Bastian, waving it at him until he takes it and puts it on. "Uh. Hello?"

"Oh good." Sybil's voice sounds efficient and busy as always. "I told Kent we could find you if we just—"

"Why are you at the Hall?"

"Major's orders. She loaned us out to watch the Hall tonight."

Bastian frowns. "The compound doesn't loan out staff for routine city security. A hyran to overhear something and report back on it, maybe, but—"

"I know. We've got some theories, but it's weird. And it got weirder when Officer Michaels met us at the door and told us about your, uh, plans for tonight. She's gotten roped in to help Senator Nunez run interference, so we'll have to—"

"What are you doing here?" a voice demands.

A security guard has come around from the other side of the building and is glaring at Bastian and Kent. She ought to have been easy to detect in advance, especially since she's not making any effort to be stealthy, but Bastian was too distracted to notice her.

"We're extra security hired for the event," Kent says quickly. "Just testing the equipment before we get things started."

"Your buddy isn't in uniform," the guard says, her voice deeply disapproving.

Kent laughs shakily, then claps Bastian on the shoulder. "Oh, well, he's kind of a slob, honestly. But he still gets the work done."

"Let me see your IDs."

Bastian makes a face at Kent, who dutifully ignores him and takes several IDs out of his pocket. He hands them over, and Bastian tenses slightly, wondering if he'll need to plant some emotional suggestions for the guard. But she just sighs and hands the IDs back after a few seconds. "Stay out of trouble. It's my ass that gets chewed out if you freelancers disrupt the senators."

"Er. Yes, ma'am. We'll be on our best behavior."

The guard gives them both a stern look before turning on her heel and walking back toward the other side of the building.

"Where did you get those IDs?" Bastian asks.

"I'm *very* good at my job," Kent says with a sniff. "I've got IDs for everyone. Well, Sybil has them at the level 5 security desk. We can input whatever info we need in real time, so long as we're connected with the right headsets. Pretty neat, right? Of course, they won't hold up under close scrutiny, but Sybil and I are—"

"—in trouble. Maybe." There's a disturbing pause and crackle over the headset. "Tell Kent to get you up here right away. I just saw something you need to see."

Chapter 31

"SHOULDN'T CARTER AND Donnigan be attending the lecture?" Bastian asks. "What are they doing, taking a long bathroom break?"

"No. I don't think they ever went to the auditorium in the first place." Half of Sybil's face is washed out in the blue reflection of her separate laptop screen. Lines of code whiz by as her fingers fly over the keys, the light catching the silver rings on her fingers.

Henry frowns at the still images on the screens in front of them. Sybil has brought up several views from various cameras around the Hall. Some of them show the auditorium, swamped with senators, aides, and other community guests. Others show empty corridors elsewhere in the building. And one, pulled up in the center of the screen, shows Carter and Donnigan walking down an otherwise deserted hallway.

Henry can't help but make the connection to Michaels's security footage: It's definitely the same two people. Except that video was taken on level 1, and this doesn't look like the same hallway.

"I mean, obviously they're up to something sneaky because that's what they do," Laurel says. "But does it matter in terms of finding the vault?"

"It might," Sybil says grimly, "since they're heading toward a restricted area on level 3."

Not the vault entryway they saw, then. Does that mean it has multiple entrances? Or is this something else? "So we follow them," Henry says. "Find out what they're doing."

"We don't know for sure that it has to do with the vault, though," Bastian points out. "And we can't miss the opportunity to go look into the level 1 area Michaels showed us."

Chloe, who's been standing back a bit, clears her throat. "I think—I mean, I can maybe figure out the most-used paths. Narrow down our options on each level so we can do both at once without wasting too much time."

"That's perfect!" Kent says, eyes lighting up. "We can cross-reference with the security footage we have."

While Kent and Chloe consult, Bastian turns to Henry. "We'll have to split up."

Henry doesn't want to, really—but what he wants doesn't matter. "Splitting up makes sense. We can cover more ground."

"I'm redirecting the cameras around here, so don't worry about getting caught on the security system, at least for a little while," Sybil says, her eyes glued to her screen. She jerks her thumb toward a table behind the desk. "Let's play it safe, though. Those security uniforms will make it less obvious that you don't belong. Hurry up and get them on. Headsets, too, so we can communicate with you."

The headsets are adjustable, and the uniforms—cheap black pants, black jacket, white button-down shirt—are fairly easy to slip on. The accompanying black cap is a bit silly, but Henry is grateful for the extra help hiding their faces.

He glances over at Bastian, who is eyeing his hat dubiously. "Don't knock it," Henry tells him. "Could be a good look for you."

It absolutely isn't. It's much too big, and his ears stick out awkwardly. Henry snorts and tries to readjust it, with no success. But that might just be because he's trying so hard to hold back a laugh.

Bastian sighs and bats Henry's hand away, trying to keep things balanced by settling his headset over the hat. It's still a fashion atrocity, but this version seems less likely to result in his disguise falling off mid-mission.

"Okay," Kent says, calling them back to the screens. "We've got routes for both levels. Sybil and I can help with the security in those areas, but you'll need to be careful, obviously. Especially whoever goes to level 1—there'll be more activity there since it's a more central area."

"I can help with level 1," Chloe says. "It'll be easier to see the best route once we're closer, and finding the right one will be more important with the increased traffic. It's also . . . sort of weird around that one. The paths go dark in parts. Almost like a dead zone."

"Chloe and I can take it," Bastian says quickly. "Henry and Laurel can go after Carter and Donnigan on level 3. Let's meet back where we came in."

Sybil nods. "We'll do our best with the security, but this isn't our usual equipment, so I can't give you a guarantee. Just to be safe, I'm keeping the audio connections separate—Kent will take Bastian and Chloe, and I'll take Henry and Laurel. Best way for all of us to get out of this unscathed is for you to be quick and avoid other people as much as possible."

"Got it," Bastian says. "Let's go."

Something in his tone makes Henry reach out and touch his arm. "Bastian, wait."

Bastian sidesteps, but then he stops. "We don't have time to—"

"Give us a minute," Henry says to the others. He leads Bastian slightly away and says in a low voice, "What's going on?"

"What, you forgot the mission parameters already?" His voice is sharp, but when he sighs and pinches the bridge of his nose, Henry recognizes it as discomfort. "Sorry. I just . . . I think there's something weird about that level 1 access point. The possible dead zone complicates things."

Henry frowns. "Are you going to give me anything other than 'weird'?"

"No, not—" Bastian pauses, then amends, "Yeah, one other thing."

"What's that?"

Strictly speaking, Bastian grabbing him by the neck and kissing him doesn't do anything to provide more context, but Henry is suddenly much less interested in explanations than he is in keeping Bastian's mouth on his as long as possible. Except—

Someone coughs.

Mission. Right.

Henry pulls away reluctantly. Then he aims another kiss at Bastian's forehead but only manages to get his temple, thanks to the bulk of the headsets. "I'm only agreeing to split up if you agree to us having dinner afterward."

Bastian blinks, then lets out a short laugh. "We might be busy running for our lives, depending on how this all works out."

"You can pencil it in for after that, then."

Bastian's mouth twitches slightly upward, and Henry does his best not to think about how easy it would be to kiss him again.

"Deal," Bastian says, awkward and embarrassed and amused in a way that makes Henry's chest ache, knowing how rare that specific order, combined with that specific expression, can be. Knowing how desperately Henry missed it when he was locked away and thought he'd never see it again. He takes Bastian's hand and squeezes it, feeling the warmth through the material of his glove.

Another cough. Henry turns and sees Laurel giving them an impish look. "If you'd like, we could get some of *that* on a security feed and see if we can make General Carter blush."

Bastian rolls his eyes, which does nothing to hide the sudden redness of his face. "Laurel, go with Henry and figure out what those assholes are up to. Chloe and I will check out that level 1 access point and see where it actually goes."

Laurel salutes. "Understood. I'd say we can give you two another minute, but we really can't, so—"

"Let's go, Laurel," Henry says, mostly to keep Bastian from dying of embarrassment on the spot. But he makes sure not to let go of Bastian's hand until the absolute last moment.

***

Henry and Laurel take the stairs down to level 3 rather than tempting fate with the elevator. Via their headsets, Sybil directs them in a circuitous route that doesn't seem at all intuitive, especially since every aspect of every hall looks the same: doors made out of dark wood and adorned with shiny metal nameplates indicating which senator they belong to; black-and-white marbled floors that make their footsteps echo; warm lights poking out from chandeliers that seem to have been born in another era. It's enough to make Henry want to obsessively straighten his collar every few minutes.

They don't encounter anyone except for a lone aide who hurries past them without even looking up from her tablet.

"Around the corner," Sybil says in Henry's ear. "There's a door that needs a passcode, and then we're into the restricted part. Hang on."

Henry and Laurel stop just after the turn, where a sliding glass door blocks the rest of the hallway. It's not labeled, but Henry can see an ID reader on the left—the normal kind, not the one from the footage Michaels showed him or his memories of Level 49.

Henry glances over at Laurel. Her face is placid, but her shoulders are tense. "Are you okay?" he asks.

"Just thinking about strangling some jerks when we run into them." She turns and meets his gaze. "Oh, am I not supposed to talk about strangling people in the middle of the hallway? I didn't really have much time to prepare, so . . ."

"No, I just meant . . ." Henry isn't exactly sure *what* he meant. He's still thinking about the way her face looked this afternoon, carefully cheerful as she swept past what happened with James. Laurel always brushes off the difficult things like nothing can touch her for long, but to lose a friend she cares so much about—and for the second time . . .

"We're in," Sybil says. "I'm opening the door."

True to her word, the sliding door opens, revealing more hallway stretching out in front of them. The chandeliers are gone, replaced with the glowing blue lights Henry recognizes from the footage Michaels showed them.

Henry and Laurel nod to each other and step through.

"Okay," Sybil says. "Next is—"

There's a loud crackle, loud enough that Henry flinches and pulls the headset away from his ears.

And then the lights go out.

Chapter 32

THE POUNDING IN Bastian's head is slowly increasing, especially when he tries to focus on the odd emotional signature coming from level 1. He probably should have said something, especially after Henry asked, but it's not like he gathered much information about it in the short time they were getting ready. It's familiar, but also dim, somehow. Like there's something between him and the source, making it impossible to sense any more.

Chloe, on the other hand, is easy to read. Her fear and anxiety are mostly sublimated by the usual focus and determination that come with her tracking ability. She's swimming in her fake uniform, but she keeps moving, absently rolling her sleeves back up for the umpteenth time.

Between Chloe's tracking power and Kent's building blueprints, they've determined that the most suspicious area on level 1 is a gallery that also just happens to be a nexus for the odd dead zone both Chloe and Bastian felt on this level. It's unclear exactly how it connects to the footage Michaels found, but they ought to be able to determine if it's the same location once they get closer.

"It's coming up on your left," Kent says in Bastian's headset. "The gallery isn't open at the moment, but it's usually a tourist trap. Lots of traffic throughout the day. We're lucky to be going in there now, when things will be quiet enough for you to have a look around. Real security will be coming through in about fifteen minutes, so—"

"Just get us in, and we'll figure out the rest."

The odd fuzzy feeling gets more intense as they approach the gallery door. Chloe shakes her head like she's trying to dislodge an annoying fly. "Do you feel it?"

"Yeah." Bastian takes off his right glove and places his palm on the wall next to the door. Easy enough to feel *the passing curious-thoughtful-impressed of the tourists who come through on a regular basis, busloads of retirees from the suburbs and schoolkids who are just glad to be out of the classroom for the day; stressed-annoyed-agitated from the Hall workers hurrying by on errands and wondering if they've done enough negotiating and manipulating to get the outcome they're hoping for—*

Bastian pulls back, frowning. "It feels normal. I'm not sure why—"

"We're in," Kent says.

Shoving down his concern in favor of getting out of the hallway as soon as possible, Bastian quickly pulls his glove back on and opens the door. When no alarms or yelling ensue, he stands to the side and holds the door open for Chloe.

"You being gentlemanly, Lucas?" Kent says in his ear. "Or are you trying to make her cannon fodder?"

"If you've done your job, we don't have anything to worry about," Bastian says, trying to sound reassuring enough to settle Chloe's blip of alarmed-anxious-worried as she passes by. "Now shut up and help us figure out what's going on in this room."

The gallery is dark except for intermittent blue lights along the baseboards. Glass cases set apart at carefully placed intervals contain historical artifacts and facsimiles of important documents and photos. They're clearly displayed to feature in the best possible light, both literally and figuratively. Bastian doesn't bother to read any of the placards he passes because he can already guess what they say: The city would devolve into a haven for lawless heathens without the wise, guiding hands of the senators at the Hall, who tirelessly and selflessly govern for the advancement of all. Definitely not to benefit from backroom deals with shady organizations like the Compound Network.

"I double-checked, but there's nothing unusual in the building specs for this area," Kent says thoughtfully. "We're pretty sure Michaels's footage comes from somewhere nearby, though."

"A lot of paths converge here and then just . . . stop," Chloe says. She's frowning at the wall between two of the display cases. "And there's the fuzzy feeling, too. It's like a dead zone, but also not."

Bastian stands still in the middle of the room and tries to gently poke at the emotional residue around him. It's *there*, but in an oddly muted and dull way—fuzzy, like Chloe said. Like something has been applied locally to block asset powers, but whoever did it wasn't thorough enough with the paint job. The interested-*nothing*-bored-*nothing*-harried-*nothing* all bleeds into a mess that makes him feel queasy.

It takes a moment, but then he remembers where he's felt something like this before: the forest dead zone Quentin created to keep compound forces away from his sanctuary. And the crime scene here in the Hall, where they found Emily Tezuka's body.

And then there's the negation weapon Smith used when they were trying to escape the hotel.

Obviously, the Fail-Safe Protocol isn't just about negating assets. Like everything else the Compound Network does, it's an experiment, one conclusion built on another. Figured out how to create a synthetic negation serum? Great; now locate a natural negator, steal their blood, and make it stronger. Serum only dulls an asset's power rather than fully blocking it? Maybe a much stronger aerosol will work—test it out on unruly city assets to be sure. Want to get away with crimes and leave no evidence, including the kind someone in your own organization might be able to find? Modify that negation serum to prevent evidence from being left in the first place. Maybe also try it out on a particularly top secret entrance to a particularly top secret vault.

"Bastian?"

He realizes he's clenching his hands into fists, fingers tight and painful against his gloves. He forces himself to relax. "Sorry, what?"

Chloe flushes slightly. "I just—I know the path is here, but I can't figure out the exact location because of whatever's blocking us."

"Not much on my end, either," Kent says. "I can write up some code to crunch the possibilities and keep looking for a more accurate floor plan, but it'll go faster if you two find me some facts I can work with."

Bastian grimaces. "Never mind. I'll take care of it."

He hasn't tried really pushing himself since he and Henry did the strange energy exchange in the forest, but . . . well, the worst that can happen is that he passes out in the middle of a complicated, time-sensitive mission.

Bastian drags his fingers gently along the nearest wall, looking for patterns or significant emotional buildup, but it's mostly just the uneven cloud of vague emotions and nothingness. When it becomes clear that this isn't going to get him anywhere, he steels himself and lets down his shield just a bit.

There. It's not strong, but the shift is abrupt enough that he yanks his hand back from the wall and reflexively slams his shield back into place. This bit of wall doesn't look any different than the walls anywhere else in the room except that the blue lights by the floor flicker every few seconds.

Chloe hurries over to him and looks where he's looking, her forehead scrunched up. She takes a step back and considers the floor, then the wall again, like she sees something that he can't. "I *think* there's a path, but it's faint."

Bastian carefully touches the wall again. No powers this time, since he's looking for more tangible oddities. And there is one: a very thin seam in the wall that runs from above his head all the way to the floor. He can't get his fingers into it even when he takes off his gloves.

"There's something here, but I can't get it loose," he tells Chloe. "Let's see if we can find a panel somewhere to open it."

They examine the area around them, and then the exhibit cases nearby. They each do several cases before Chloe lets out a soft, "Oh!" and points to the side of an exhibit featuring the yellowing pages of some sort of ledger.

When Bastian gets closer, he sees that her finger is hovering over a button set into the side of the case. It's tiny, the same color as the wood and almost impossible to see. The panel surrounding it is innocuous; it looks like it's covering electrical wiring or something equally mundane.

"The path goes from here to there," Chloe says. "But . . ."

"Kent?" Bastian asks, moving so that Kent can see through the camera on Bastian's headset.

"Hmm. It's definitely connected to the Hall security system," Kent says. "Luckily for you, I am a professional genius, so—hey, Sybil, why are you laughing? Anyway, hang on a sec."

"Still fuzzy?" Bastian asks Chloe while they wait.

She shakes her head. "No. I mean, yes, but it sort of . . . fluctuates? My power works, but it's broken into pieces. Like the normal paths aren't completely there, and I have to make assumptions. Um. Does that make any sense?"

"Yes, actually. I think someone's done something here with negation serum to make powers harder to use. There's less emotional residue for me to feel than there ought to be. And less of what you use to track, sounds like."

"But why?"

"To protect something, probably. And what's more worth protecting than the compound's little vault of secrets?"

"It's okay to press it now," Kent says. "Probably. Almost certainly."

"That . . . doesn't sound good," Chloe says, her anxiety-fear-concern spiking. "Well—"

Bastian reaches over and presses the button.

A few feet away, the wall where he felt the seam begins to open silently.

"Secret passage," Bastian murmurs. He turns back to see Chloe giving him a questioning look, but he just shakes the memory away. "Let's go."

The area behind the wall is lit with the same bluish lights from the gallery, this time set into the ceiling. They're functional, but they flicker ominously as Bastian and Chloe pass under them.

They've only been walking for a minute or so when there's a loud crackle on the headsets. Bastian flinches, and out of the corner of his eye, he sees that Chloe does, too.

"Kent?" When Bastian doesn't get a reply, he tries again. "Kent?"

No answer.

He looks at Chloe, who shakes her head. Her eyes widen as he takes off his headset and tries fiddling with the buttons to reestablish the link. It's a waste of time, though; everything around him is fuzzy, indistinct energy, made worse by the fact that he knows the connection to Kent is dead. Something blocking the signal? Another layer of security here, maybe? Does that mean they're getting closer?

They stand there silently for a moment. Then Chloe starts walking again, and Bastian's mouth decides to say something without any input from his brain: "You should go back and see if—"

"The path keeps going," she says. "I'm pretty sure it ends at a door. And on the other side . . ."

She keeps walking, and Bastian makes a face, more at himself than her. If he were smarter, he'd figure out a way to get her to turn around and go back, to be safe. But he's not smarter, and anyhow, Laurel and Henry were right earlier when they said that all of them have good reasons to be here.

The hallway starts to slope downward, leading to a large metal door. It looks like something in one of the compound's stairwells, only bigger and heavier. Bastian doesn't see any place to use an ID, and there's no door handle. So, security is either tricky or non-existent, and without Kent, they can't confirm which one.

"It's through there," Chloe says firmly. "All of the paths converge, so this has to be it."

Bastian reaches for the door, then pauses and lets out a breath. "Okay. Just . . . let me check."

He pulls off his gloves again, sticks them in his pockets, and puts his hands on the center of the door before he can think better of it.

A flood of fear-wonder-concern-anxiety-smugness-calculating batters his brain with no consideration for his shield, which could be made out of paper, for all the good it's doing him. Bastian grits his teeth, closes his eyes, and keeps going, filtering through every emotion in this part of the building, trying to determine if anyone is close enough to cause a problem.

It's a good idea in theory (for a certain definition of "good"), but in practice, he isn't strong enough to hold on to any one person for long—not when there are this many—which makes his reads vague at best. Still, he comes away fairly certain that no one's waiting to attack them on the other side of this door.

But the fuzzy border of negation is still everywhere. And he gets the odd feeling that there's something familiar beyond the door, although he's not sure who or what it is. The more he tries to focus on it, the more quickly it fades away, until he almost thinks he might have imagined it to begin with.

"Let's go," he says to Chloe, trying to ignore the uneasiness in his voice. He pushes against the door, which is heavy but not resistant.

It swings slowly open.

The room inside is large and cavernous, a bit like a bank vault: wide, empty space in the middle surrounded by hundreds of rows of shelves near the walls. The baseboards feature the same blue lighting as the gallery, but it's brighter overall in here—enough that Bastian can see another door at the far end of the room. He realizes as they get closer that most of the shelves are stacked with computer servers, fans whirring and lights blinking.

"Let's take a look around," Bastian says, keeping his voice low. There's something about this place that inspires hushed tones.

They split up to go down opposite sides of the room. Bastian's side is mostly full of the humming, blinking servers, which probably house all sorts of unpleasant information the Compound Network would like to keep anyone from knowing about. Bastian is tempted to knock them all over, preferably with a sledgehammer (if he can find one), but he figures that's a bit premature. They need a bargaining chip they can take with them. Physical violence will have to wait.

Trouble is, he can't exactly fit a server in his pocket. And he has no way of knowing what information is being stored on any of them.

He nearly walks past one of the shelves, then does a double-take and turns back. Between two noisy servers, there's a small set of drawers, black with metal handles. It's similar to some of the drawers Bastian has seen in experimentation rooms in the compound. These look dented and discolored enough that they must be really old.

No, not old. Burned and broken.

Like they were in a fire.

Bastian narrows his eyes and reaches for one of the handles. It sticks for a moment, then drags open when he applies more pressure. Not a terribly secure way to keep important information, even if it's only a few paper files.

He touches the top folder, and *the excitement of a new project, the culmination of his previous work, the chance to join Major Valentine in creating something completely different, in shepherding in a new Compound Network with better access to assets, better control of them, no need to wait until they're born naturally when they can be created at any time and put down if they become unnecessarily tedious to work with—*

Bastian doesn't need to look at the author name on the file, but he does anyway: Dr. Wright. These must be some of the notes they never recovered from the compound after Valentine and Wright were removed from power. Nunez said Carter was still looking; he must have found some.

Bastian takes a shaky breath. A read—especially one he didn't intend to do and that can't be recorded right away—wouldn't do much good. But if there's something in these files that they can actually use . . .

Wright's notes read as though they're missing several pages, but his tone is familiar enough.

S-75423, E-67284, and FSP-7686265 are the three most important experiments currently running in the Compound Network. Work on these is generally si-loed to prevent security issues, but these brief notes serve as my personal accounting of the intersection of their goals.

S-75423 has been officially deemed a failure after the destruction of its original location. However, not all of the bodies were recovered, and the data we had time to collect indicated that at least one subject demonstrably obtained the power she was spliced with. Should she be recovered at some point, more testing will be required to determine the extent of the inheritance and its applicability to future experiments.

E-67284 is an ongoing, alternative approach to S-75423. Rather than splicing an empath's blood with an already-existing asset, E-67284 seeks to find a way to create an empath artificially. The hypotheses being tested involve creation using both adult and child subjects to see if and how abilities are inherited.

Bastian frowns. The splicing experiment is obviously referring to Laurel's compound, and the first subject in the empath experiment has to be John Doe, the artificial empath Valentine created. But a *child?*

Thus far, we've concluded that the adult subject of E-67284 did, in fact, inherit some empathic skills, though not anywhere near the level of a natural empath. The child, interestingly, appears to have benefitted from prenatal genetic modifications, though we may not see the full scale of her power until she's older. She will continue to be monitored, and I understand that her parents will be compensated throughout by the Compound Network so long as they cooperate.

It does skew the results a bit that she unexpectedly manifested as a memor, but the results will still be interesting.

Bastian stares at the folder in his hands, the lines of text blurring for a moment as his brain tries to comprehend the words. They experimented on the assets in Laurel's compound until most of them died, and then they covered it up and moved right on. They experimented on John Doe until he weakened and died, too. And they did some sort of genetic modification of a child—a very *young* child—to make her like Bastian. So they could use her, as well.

"Angelica," Bastian says under his breath.

A functioning, controllable empath is vital to the progression of FSP-7686265, which will ensure a fail-safe for the Compound Network, should any asset become unviable. We must be able to direct the actions of any and all assets, and FSP-7686265 will offer a set of negation options for that purpose. However, the Council will want multiple options for keeping assets in line, and empaths are potentially well-suited to this task. Their ability can be subtle and difficult to trace. That said, their self-destructive nature does make them potentially problematic. More research is needed into how we can adjust for that or, alternatively, keep producing more as the old ones wear out.

Wear out. Like assets are just easily replaceable parts in some big machine.

Which is probably how the Compound Network sees them.

At the bottom of the page, several lines have been added in handwriting Bastian doesn't recognize:

Oversight of these experiments has been transferred to General Carter as of xx-xx-xxxx. Partnership with liaison committee established to determine the future use of assets within the city. Route through him vs. Council (see A-2769 files 1-10).

Well. Sounds like Carter and Donnigan have been playing a game behind the Council's back. This is hardly enough proof to do them in, but—

Bastian hears a noise from the other side of the room, and then Chloe is scurrying toward him, face pale. "I think there's someone—"

The sound of a door slowly opening. There isn't anywhere to hide, so Bastian quickly stuffs the file in his jacket pocket. He starts to close the drawer, spots a few USB drives at the bottom, and grabs them as well.

The far door swings all the way open, and several figures step out.

One of them is very familiar.

"Ah," Quentin says, his voice carrying across the room. "I wasn't sure you'd make it in time."

"How did you get here?" Bastian asks, stepping away from the shelving and narrowing his eyes. "And in time for what?"

"In time for the rescue, of course."

"Rescue? What—?"

"It would be easier to show you. Come with us." Quentin turns and goes back through the door, his minions following him. He doesn't bother to wait and see if Bastian and Chloe are coming, too.

Bastian grits his teeth, but it's not like there's any other option. Particularly if he wants answers.

The room Quentin leads them into contains only one item: a body lying on a table in the center. At first, Bastian can't feel any emotions coming from it, which is . . . not good. But as he gets closer, he loses sight of everything else in the room and realizes two things: There *is* some emotional energy there, although it's very dim.

And it's familiar.

"Bastian, meet Moira," Quentin says.

Chapter 33

"WELL, THIS IS unexpected. What are you doing here?" asks a voice from somewhere down the hallway. It echoes in the dark—loud, but not overbearing. The mark of a professional orator.

Henry squints when the blue lights flare into existence again, bathing the area in a dim, eerie glow. A few doors away, standing in the middle of the hallway, is a small man with thinning hair that matches his thin smile. His hands are clasped behind his back like he's about to launch into a tiresome speech, just like he used to during liaison committee meetings at the compound.

"Senator Donnigan," Henry says.

"I'm fairly certain that no one has clearance to be back here at this time of night." Donnigan raises his eyebrows. "And if someone *did* have clearance, I doubt it would be two assets who are guilty of a variety of crimes. Were you that eager to add trespassing to the list?"

"Better than going to all this trouble to lure people into creepy restricted areas." Laurel glares at him. "Don't you have an event to be attending? Or did they lock you up here so that they wouldn't have to look at your slimy face?"

"Assets infiltrating restricted areas of the Hall could seriously threaten the relationship between the Compound Network and the city, you know," Donnigan continues, ignoring her.

"No, it couldn't," Henry says, his voice reasonable and even. "Neither of us are affiliated with the compounds anymore. And you and General Carter want that relationship to stay cozy, don't you? So I think the real question is, what is a senator doing in a restricted area while everyone else in the building is at a lecture?"

"Actually, the more important question is, how did you two get past security?

Perhaps you had some inside help? I warned my colleagues that trusting extra security sent over from the compound would be—"

"Shouldn't General Carter be here, too?" Laurel asks. "You're basically his lackey, right? Or is he leaving this to you so he can keep his hands clean?"

Donnigan's thin mouth gets thinner. "I think it's time I called some *real* security to—"

A loud noise pierces the quiet hallway: the repeating blast of a fire alarm. Henry, Laurel, and Donnigan clap their hands over their ears, and Henry looks around for the source.

(Heart beating wildly, already feeling the heat that isn't there, looking for unnatural flames like the ones that burned down the compound while he and so many others were trapped inside—)

The door they just came through starts to open again. It *could* be part of the automatic safety system, meant to allow people to get out of a burning building. Or it could be someone trying to get it open while running a distraction.

Henry catches Laurel's eye, and without a word, they bolt for the door. Donnigan is slow on the uptake, but he follows, a few critical seconds behind. Just enough so that Henry and Laurel can slip through and slam the door behind them.

Henry thinks he hears the lock engage, trapping Donnigan on the other side. He's not sticking around to check, though—putting distance between them is more important.

They're sprinting toward the stairs when Henry's headset crackles back to life, Sybil's voice almost drowned out by the noise on her end. "—ello? Are you there?"

"We're here, but we'd like not to be," Henry tells her. "What's going on?"

"Distraction, but it won't help if you get caught on the way out."

"Never mind!" Laurel yells as they skid to a stop in front of the stairwell. "I mean, mind *sometime*, but not now. We need to abort mission and get out of here. Unless you think it's okay to go back and smack Donnigan in the face."

"Probably better to get out of here." Henry yanks open the door to the stairs, and they race down toward the main floor. "Sybil, where are the others?"

"Kent is trying to find them—the restricted area they were in had interference, too. I think Carter and Donnigan wanted you all to get caught here, but you should be able to slip out with the people leaving the building, so—"

"What do you mean, Kent is 'trying to find them'?" Laurel demands. "Are they lost?"

"Well, not exactly. But . . ."

They've barely exited out onto level 1 when someone grabs Henry's arm so hard, he stumbles. The headset slips down to his neck, and his hat falls to the floor.

"Mortimer," says a rumbling voice. "I think you'd better come with me."

There's no time to do much other than get a quick glance: bushy eyebrows, stern face, four stars on the Compound Network uniform. Henry glances at Laurel, whose eyes have just started to widen. She's close enough to the main hallway that she could get lost in the crowd if she kept going.

"I suggest your friends stay put, too," Carter says. "We'd like to avoid a scene."

"I bet you would," Henry says, eyes still on Laurel. "It'd be a shame if the alarm stopped, and all the people on this floor could hear everything going on here."

Carter's steely eyes meet Henry's for a moment. Then he uses his free hand to rip off Henry's headset, drop it to the floor, and crush it with his heel. "Security in the Hall has gone downhill. I'll have to have a word with the liaison committee. Now—"

Henry jerks his head at Laurel, who narrows her eyes and looks like she's going to protest. But then she turns and runs toward the crowd leaving the Hall.

Carter frowns. "What was that? No loyalty in your group?"

"With all due respect, General, you don't know anything about my group. Like how big it is, where they're located, or what we were trying to do. Are you going to risk causing a scene now? Or would you rather negotiate?"

"You don't have anything to negotiate with."

"Oh? What about the vault?"

The alarm cuts out abruptly. Faint murmurs and chatter drift in from the atrium. Henry thinks he might hear an echo of Laurel yelling at Sybil over her comm, but that could just be wishful thinking.

He's flying by the seat of his pants here, but if Carter sneaks Henry out while everyone else is milling around, that's the end. Back to Council HQ and handcuffs and ultimatums that get people killed. Back to hating himself for not being able to figure out how to fix things.

Maybe there *isn't* a way to fix things. But Henry isn't about to go down without a fight. Not now.

"What do you know about the vault?" Carter demands.

"Enough," Henry says, hoping it sounds convincing. "Do you really want to talk about it here? Sir?"

Carter frowns. "You're lying."

"Maybe. Are you willing to risk it if I'm not?"

Carter looks at him silently for another few moments, hand tightening on Henry's arm. That's probably going to bruise.

There's the sound of footsteps and ragged breathing behind them. "Senator," Carter says with the briefest glance at Donnigan. "Make sure security sweeps the building for anything unusual, now that the alarm has been dealt with. And find us a good room for a chat."

Chapter 34

THE WOMAN ON the table has more gray hair than she did in her dream—it's almost entirely white, in fact, although her face still makes her look like she can't be older than fifty-something at most. She isn't hooked up to any machines, but her eyes are closed, and Bastian recognizes the pattern on her white hospital scrubs, even though he can only see the upper portion. Everything else is hidden underneath a scratchy-looking gray blanket that covers the lower half of her body. If he didn't know better, he'd say she just picked a weird location for a nap.

Bastian looks up at Quentin, who seems mildly curious about the proceedings (curious-thoughtful-interested) but not at all concerned. "How . . . ?"

"The Compound Network keeps all of its most important data here, including data in human form. Go on, read her. It will help explain things."

Some part of Bastian is screaming at him not to, but he tells that part of him to shut up and reaches out to gently touch her wrist.

(The pain is sharp and searing, more than he can bear, and he knows it's not his but it's sure as hell his now, *the stabbing in his gut, the pounding at his temples, and how can one person hurt so much, there isn't room in the human body for all of it, and maybe that's why they need him to hurt, too, and Dr. Wright is speaking—just a little bit more, they need the data—but Bastian's nose is bleeding and someone is screaming and he wishes he knew whose pain this is, and how are they not dead yet, how is* he *not dead yet—?)*

Bastian jerks his hand away and just barely manages to resist the urge to throw up. He's vaguely aware that Chloe has moved closer, a silent but steady presence.

He hasn't thought about that experiment in years—has actively *avoided* thinking about it. It was the last one, the one that provided Bastian with the sudden clarity that if he didn't escape the compound right then and there, he'd die.

They left him, stable but bloodied, thinking he was too broken to roll himself off the gurney and implement the plan he'd been working on with Kent. The one that got him out through the lower levels and onto the grounds and into the forest, where he finally ran out of steam and figured it was enough of a win that at least he'd die outside of the compound. But Laurel was there in the clearing, and . . .

He looks at Moira, trying to process what he just felt. *That's* why she was so familiar to him in the dream. He's felt her pain—so damned much of it, and for so long. They tortured her somewhere in the depths of the compound and connected him to it somehow, just to see how many people they could hurt at once. Because Wright and Valentine and the Compound Council were *curious.*

Was she asleep when they did it? Did they know she's a dreamseer? They must have, and maybe that was the point. What else are they going to make her feel while she's sleeping and can't stop them?

When he looks up, Quentin is smiling sadly at him. "You see why I wanted to free her, don't you? Locked up here in the vault, she's a commodity, a prize to be auctioned off to whichever compound most wants what she can do."

"But you didn't wake her up," Bastian says, hating the shakiness in his voice. "You just barged into her dream and—"

"I *would* have woken her up. I *will.* But the compound used a remarkably powerful soporific on her, and it will take time. And I'll need more energy. Of course, if I had help . . ."

Bastian stares at him, swallowing the dread before it can show on his face. Hopefully. "If you had help, you'd wake her up and let her go?"

"She would be free to choose. But she might be more inclined to offer *her* help—her energy—in the fight against the compounds if someone she trusted convinced her it was a good idea."

Bastian's anger flares before he can stop it. "What, you can't take 'no' for an answer? I think she was pretty clear about where she stands on that issue."

Quentin sighs. "Do you know what your problem is, Bastian?"

"I'm told I have a lot of them. Which one are you referring to?"

"You want to help people, but you go about it all wrong. Rather than focus on your own health and well-being, you try to self-destruct, and you end up making very little difference in the end."

"Spoken like an asshole who doesn't understand anything about actually helping people."

"Do *you*?" Quentin asks. "If you destroy yourself—if you don't make use of opportunities like the one Moira's energy offers—doesn't that just make things harder for the people you claim you care about?"

He walks around the table to stand in front of Bastian, a dull cloud of amused-thoughtful-smug moving with him like a localized storm giving off the smell of ozone and imminent destruction. Moira's choice for his manifestation in her dream suddenly makes a lot of sense. "But maybe this isn't really about helping people. Maybe it never was. You're a practical young man who's spent his entire life just trying to survive. No . . . I think this is about spite."

Bastian frowns. "What's that supposed to mean?"

"If you refuse to replenish your energy, if you choose to die instead, you destroy something the Compound Network wants. Something they've spent your entire life trying to steal from you. They can take your blood and study your brain, of course, but they'll never be able to completely recreate a living, functioning empath—they've proven time and time again that they can't. So if you die, you take that opportunity away from them. In a way, it would be like winning."

There ought to be a law against assholes being right, Bastian thinks sourly. He's never put it into words like that, but it's hard to dispute the fact that if he dies, he'll definitely be setting the compound back, even if it's only a little.

But . . . What if what he and Henry did in the forest could change things? What if his revenge on the compound didn't have to be about dying? What if it could be about living?

"We can't change who we are, Bastian. We can't change the fact that other people are always going to want to use us. But we can make choices. My choices led me here. Now it's *your* turn to make a choice." Quentin sounds like he's talking to a child who's taking too long with the menu. "Are we going to be allies, Bastian? Or am I going to have to kill you?"

Bastian opens his mouth, but his response is cut off by a sudden noise, oddly muted and repetitive in a way that makes his skull ache.

Quentin tips his head thoughtfully to one side, then sighs. "I suppose we'd better get going before whatever set off that alarm causes too much of a ruckus. Carter's leniency doesn't extend to support if we make off with data rather than just providing it to him."

"Wait, you and Carter—?"

One of the people with Quentin, a burly woman, reaches for Moira's body.

Desperately trying to keep up with what's happening, Bastian steps toward her. "Hey! What are you—?"

Years ago, Bastian stood in an alley and watched John Doe, an experimental empath created by Major Valentine, use his power to manipulate Henry. That confrontation had a happy ending, more or less, but Bastian has never forgotten what it was like to watch someone lose their ability to feel coherently and know there was nothing he could do to stop it.

Being on the manipulated side versus the spectator side is a whole new level of disgusting.

He doesn't *feel* disgust at the moment, though, because Quentin isn't letting him. A whole lifetime of work to build the strongest possible shield to protect himself, and Quentin brushes it aside like a mildly annoying gnat, replacing it with a haze of lethargy-docile-disinterested that has Bastian sinking to the ground in mild confusion. It's an empathic attack, but it also isn't; it's an invasion, but it's also gentle, a suggestion from someone older and wiser and kinder. Someone who knows best.

Bastian is vaguely aware that the woman is carefully lifting Moira from the table and carrying her away. That's probably a bad thing, but he can't remember why.

Quentin crouches down next to him and pats his shoulder. "Come find me when you're ready for my help," he says. "There isn't much time, but we'll be waiting. You might even get a chance to say hello to Moira and Angelica before we go back to the sanctuary."

Then he stands and follows the others out of a door on the far side of the room. When the door opens, the pulsing sound gets louder for a moment; when it closes, the sound dims, and Bastian's head suddenly clears.

He shoves his shield back into place, giving himself whiplash and an intense headache. He grits his teeth against it and turns to Chloe, who's sitting on the floor next to him, still looking dazed from Quentin's attack. He gently but firmly shakes her shoulder. "Hey!"

She blinks several times. Then she yelps and backs away.

"Sorry!" Bastian holds up his hands. "Are you okay?"

Breathing heavily, Chloe lets her eyes dart around the room. "I—um—yes, I think so. What . . . what was that?"

"Our cue to exit." Bastian grimaces and gets unsteadily to his feet. "I'm guessing it's still hard to use your power right now, but do you have any idea where the best route out of here is?"

Chloe's eyes start to fall closed, but they shoot open again almost immediately. "The paths are getting cut off—too many people. Something must have happened."

Back door, says a voice, small and frightened and oddly sleepy. *It's scary. Please come help.*

Bastian knows that voice. And he knows the one that follows it up with, *Don't be stupid, Junior. Do what the kid says, and find us after you get out.*

Did Quentin somehow addle his brain even more than Bastian realized? How can he be hearing both Angelica and Moira here, especially over the fuzzy partial negation in the vault?

"I can find us a way out," Chloe says, voice tinged with focus-determination-anger. "We need to meet up with Laurel and the others."

Where are you? asks a new, more panicked voice in Bastian's head. He curses and nearly falls over again. "Is my head a super highway now?"

Why is it so hard to hear you? Laurel demands. *Never mind; don't answer that. Get to the back door on level 1 where we came in. Something's happened.*

"Define 'something.'"

No time for definitions. Except for one: "Hurry." Intransitive verb. Means—

"Yeah, all right, I get it." Bastian turns to Chloe. "Best way out of here that gets us to the level 1 back entrance?"

Chloe takes a deep breath, then nods. "Follow me."

Chapter 35

TO HENRY'S SURPRISE, Carter dumps him off on a Hall security guard—a real one—who in turn deposits Henry in a small room that must be used as an aides' break room. It looks similar to the one he, Bastian, and Michaels were sent to while investigating the John Doe murders: It's all cramped space and uncomfortable furniture. This room, however, is mostly taken up with one long table situated on uneven, off-white tiles that are oddly sticky. The whole place smells of disinfectant trying to be citrusy but failing miserably. Like an artificial lemon expired in a bed of dust.

The play must be to make this look like a routine detainment, Henry thinks as he pulls out a chair and sits down. That means Carter will likely be back soon—as soon as he can make it look legitimate. This isn't his home turf, after all; he'll need to get Donnigan to make sure no one suspects the Compound Network is taking liberties.

The whole thing reeks of a trap: luring them into areas of the Hall where they shouldn't have been, then catching them in the act. But that would mean Carter knew they'd be here. Who could have tipped them off?

Henry realizes he's clenching his hands in his lap to keep them from shaking. The alarm has stopped, and the ringing silence is seeping into his skin, and he needs to *keep his shit together*. Giving himself up means he can occupy Carter and Donnigan for a while. He has to trust that Bastian and Laurel and the others can find their way out of the Hall amidst the chaos, hopefully with useful information from the vault. And even if they don't, Senator Nunez has the USB drive. It may not be enough, but at least it's something.

He has no idea how long he sits in that room, silent except for the hum of the lights, until the door opens again. He tenses at the noise but manages to stay still otherwise. No sense in getting up until he knows what he's dealing with.

A woman in a dark green Compound Network uniform holds open the door for the man behind her. He has a white cane attached to his wrist with a small loop, and his hand is on her elbow as she guides him into the room. Once they're both through, he steps aside, and the woman lets the door fall shut.

Their uniforms mark them both as majors, and they're both familiar. But the man is the one Henry puts a name to first. There's no mistaking the salt-and-pepper hair or the pleasant, deceptively innocuous smile.

"Hello, Henry," says Major Alexis.

Henry clenches his jaw and wonders what exactly he's supposed to say to the man who betrayed him and got him conscripted into seven months of hell.

"I suppose I deserve the silent treatment," Alexis says after a moment. He nods toward the woman. "You remember Felicity, of course."

Henry's eyes snap back to her, and the synapse finally fires. Warm brown eyes, brown hair with red accents (and gray now; that's new), sharp cheekbones, a slight smirk at the edges of her mouth that's always there, if you know how to find it.

"Holy shit," he says without meaning to.

Felicity Tremain laughs, completely at odds with her staid appearance, an echo of the snarky, clever daredevil he knew in training. "I think the words you're looking for are, 'Thanks for saving my life,' but I'll also take, 'You haven't changed a bit in twenty years.'"

Damn. Twenty years. "You saved me from Carter just for old time's sake?"

"Don't flatter yourself, Mortimer. You're a good guy, but not worth the time and effort it took to get Carter off our backs for a bit. Not on your own, anyway."

That stings more than it should. She said something similar when they were not-quite-dating teenagers, and she told him she'd put in a request to transfer to another compound after training. He didn't blame her at the time— high-level positions in the Compound Network are hard to come by, and Felicity always made it clear that she would do whatever it took to get one. And he doesn't blame her now; not really. Although he's curious about what *does* merit her efforts.

"Felicity has been in charge of your compound since the incident seven months ago," Alexis says. "She's—"

"Wait, you're working with Carter?" Henry can't stop his voice from rising, and he clenches his hands even tighter. "All the assets who've gone missing, all the raids in the city—you oversaw that? It's even worse than before, and you—"

"I won't ask how you know anything about it," Felicity interrupts, her voice going sharp as her good humor evaporates. "And I'll just point out that your friends have been making it much harder than it needs to be."

"My—?"

"Some of us have to work within the system. There's no other way to change things, as you proved during your time as an ineffective commanding officer. If you'd bothered to pay attention at all to what Major Alexis was telling you—"

"All right." Major Alexis holds up his hands. "You two can discuss your differences of opinion sometime when we aren't on a schedule."

Henry couldn't care less about a damned schedule, but the part of his brain that can still think critically reminds him that it must've taken some doing for Alexis and Felicity to get in here. Whatever their motives for doing it, Henry ought to at least hear them out.

"We don't have much time," Alexis continues, "so let's use what time we *do* have wisely. Have you and your people figured out how to get into the vault, Henry?"

"I don't know what you're talking about," Henry says immediately.

Alexis gives him a long-suffering smile. "We really don't have time for this. As I just said."

"I've got all the time in the world," Henry tells him.

"He means there isn't anything about whatever they're doing that depends on him right now." Felicity frowns and crosses her arms over her chest. "Does that make you the scapegoat? Because I guarantee that's not going to help your friends. Sure, they'll keep you locked up in here for a while, maybe send you back to Council HQ in the end. But that doesn't mean they won't also go after Lucas and the others. You've made yourselves a pain in the ass for the Network. You have no idea how far they'll go to stop you."

"Not as far as I'll go to stop them."

He knows as soon as he says it that it's an idiotic thing to say. Just because he doesn't see a security camera in here doesn't mean there isn't one. There are probably a lot of ways for both these two and Carter to use his words against him.

But . . . so what?

(Bastian's awkward, exhausted, determined voice in the crumbling school, the way his eyes looked when he tried to explain his inexplicable faith in Henry— *I'm* so fucking tired *of them winning*—and in the end, isn't Henry's "idealism" basically just that: fury and hurt and a refusal to believe that the world has to stay the way it is, not if people are willing to do even the smallest bit—?)

There's an awkward beat of silence while Henry and Felicity stare at each other. Henry is pretty sure he's supposed to feel intimidated and ready to cave, but he mostly just feels calm and unbothered by the whole thing. What can Alexis and Felicity do to him that someone hasn't already done?

The moment of silence goes on for a bit longer. Then Felicity's lips pull back into an almost feral grin. "All right, Mortimer. Thanks for reminding me why this is worth it."

"Why what is worth it?"

Felicity waves a hand. "This. You. I always figured you weren't the kind of guy who backs down under pressure, but I had my doubts, given how you handled this. Still, I think it's worth giving you a chance."

"Gee, thanks." Henry turns to Alexis. "Which of you is in charge here? And what are you in charge *of*?"

Alexis taps a finger on the table. "As I keep saying, we don't really have time to—"

"Let me stop you there. If you want me to do something, you're going to need to give me details. I'm done letting you withhold information I need. Equals, or nothing." Henry leans back in his chair. "I'm just fine sitting here until they come to cart me off to wherever."

Felicity laughs, not bothering to hide it behind a hand or the pretext of politeness. "Aw, come on, Major," she says to Alexis. "Wouldn't it be more fun if you just told him the truth?"

Alexis sighs. "Fine. The short version, then: Felicity and I are here to help you. I regret to say that our desire to help isn't entirely altruistic, but we do want you to survive this. Our benefactor is someone high up in the Compound Network who would very much like to have some information that can only be found in the vault. Our job is to get it for them. Unfortunately, Carter is very keen on keeping the location and contents of the vault a secret. We know it's here in the Hall, and we know someone—or multiple someones—are helping Carter hide it. But we don't know any more than that."

"And what does your benefactor want from the vault?"

"So you *do* know about it," Felicity says, leaning against the wall near the door. "Glad we got that out of the way."

"I didn't say—"

"You've got a tell. Mostly the fact that you suck at lying."

"Our benefactor wants the truth," Alexis says. "There are things in the vault that don't exist on any record outside of it. Things General Carter would like to keep hidden, likely because they show he's taken liberties outside of the Council's authority. We're hoping you'll help us make those things known."

"Why? So you can take over from Carter?"

Alexis smiles faintly. "I'm a teacher, Henry. I'd like to get back to that as soon as possible. With Carter in charge, though, it doesn't look like that's going to happen. Not if he keeps doing his best to stir up trouble."

"We're trying to change things using dirt from the vault," Felicity says. "It's not about personal gain; it's—"

"—about doing the right thing?" Henry smiles humorlessly. "All those years you both spent ridiculing me for that exact thing, and now that's your big plan? Just help people with no expectation of reward?"

"*I* expect a reward," Felicity says. "A promotion would be great, once this is all over. But I don't want Carter's job, and even if I did, that wouldn't be why I'm doing this. I don't have your idiotic devotion to heroism, Mortimer, but I do think your heart's in the right place. The way we've been approaching the asset situation isn't working, and no one's talking about why. This entire organization is obsessed with keeping power in the hands of a select few—and those few just use it to force assets to do whatever they're told. It's stupid and ineffective, and people need to stop pretending it isn't. The only way that happens is if we drag the secrets out into the light. So why not help us find the ammunition to do that?"

They don't know how close they are to the vault right now, Henry realizes. They're just going off hearsay and whatever documentation they have access to—which likely doesn't include Emily Tezuka's copies of the Fail-Safe Protocol files. Alexis must have recovered the ones she sent to the compound when he got rid of Henry, but those versions didn't have the extra code.

If they can definitively prove a connection between those files, the vault, and any actions Carter took outside of Council approval—killing a senator's aide, for example, or taking control of experiments for his own purposes without running it through the Council first—that might be the bargaining chip they need.

"Henry," Alexis says, leaning forward, "you understand how important this is, don't you? It's the reason you were chosen for the compound in the first place. You have a power that hasn't been seen in—well, never, officially. If you don't leverage it, someone else will find a way to use it to hurt everyone you care about. I *did* try to warn you. The only way to keep that from happening is to help us make a good enough case that Carter's plans can't continue."

"We've seen what happens when I bring people plenty of evidence: absolutely nothing." He hates the anger and hurt in his voice, but he's getting *very tired* of having to remind people of this. "Why would this time be any different?"

"Because you have more allies," Felicity says. "Half the staff in your compound are loyal to me. And that entire compound is littered with dead zones that make it possible for assets to plan escapes. All of which we're covering as best we can."

Henry stares at her. "Why would you—?"

"Officially, the dead zones are part of an experiment on different applications of the negation serum. Unofficially, we set them up to have minimal security and draw in assets who notice that their powers aren't working. If they're powerful enough to sense a dead zone, they've got a decent shot at escaping." Felicity frowns. "It would've been better if the plantspeaker hadn't been caught trying to sneak into restricted areas, but—"

"Wait, Laurel was doing *what*?"

"I had to lock her up for a bit, but it gave me an excuse to get her into the city after Carter and Donnigan called that stupid raid on the hotel. Which reminds me, you didn't let them take the information Kwan provided, did you?"

Henry considers evading the question, but it would be pretty pointless now. "No."

"Good. Still, I don't like that Carter has a source we don't know about, and I don't like that someone was trying to use the plantspeaker to get information at the compound. Not when I've spent months organizing the flow of intel in and out of that place."

"But . . . if you keep helping assets escape, someone will notice."

"Yeah, that was the point—someone did. Someone you're going to help us help, right?"

"Senator Nunez and Officer Michaels are good allies to have, too," Alexis says. "The connection with city officials could work in our favor. And we know you've been in touch with other assets in the city—Alex Barrett and his group, I think? All of those, along with Felicity's and my connections, could make for a formidable force, if we had the right leverage."

"At first, I was hoping that sending Turner and Tassos here to work event security might net us more information about the vault, and we could use that for leverage," Felicity says. "Obviously, that's not how it worked out. But we might have set a new precedent that allows a broader range of compound staff to work at the Hall more regularly—not just assets on duty. More avenues for connection and information-gathering. So it's not a total waste."

"You've thought about this," Henry says slowly.

"We've been planning it for years," Alexis agrees. "Felicity has been preparing to run a compound—specifically, to run yours—since she finished training. But the turnover from Valentine didn't go as expected."

"Carter chose you instead," Felicity says, and there's the slightest hint of annoyance in her voice.

"Only so he could get rid of me when that became more convenient for him," Henry points out.

"That wouldn't have been a problem for me."

"Wouldn't it?"

"*Anyway*," Alexis says, "I'm sure you understand that the timeline has accelerated. Carter has moved his projects forward and become too much of a threat to leave unattended. We need the evidence in the vault."

"And you think I can get it."

Alexis smiles. "I think you're resourceful and connected in ways Felicity and I can't be at the moment. And you have a well-developed sense of justice and a desire to protect others."

"Which you want to use."

"Only because it'll be mutually beneficial. Don't you think?"

Henry crosses his arms over his chest as he looks at them. Of course they want to use him. But that doesn't mean he can't get something out of them at the same time. That's how this game works, after all.

"I can help you find the vault," Henry says. "But before that, you're going to do a few things for me."

Felicity frowns. "You can tell us first, and then—"

"No. My way or nothing. Take your pick."

"The longer we wait, the more likely people will get hurt," Alexis says. "Surely you don't want that."

Henry says nothing. Eventually, Alexis sighs.

"All right," Felicity says. "What do you want?"

Chapter 36

OFFICER MICHAELS IS waiting for them under the elm in the back parking lot, Kent and Sybil pacing near her. Well, Kent is pacing; Sybil is leaning against the tree, hand to her ear, mouth drawn into a firm line.

Laurel has been purposefully (and ineffectively) trying to ignore Bastian's glare at her back as they hurry away from the Hall. Reaching the rest of their group only makes the situation worse because he immediately notices who's missing.

"Where's Henry?" he demands.

"Hello, Officer Michaels," Laurel says pointedly. "Hello, Kent and Sybil. I'm glad you all made it out safely. You can tell I'm glad because I'm expressing my concern and relief about that before I get into what I need, which is . . . actually pretty important, so I suppose we'd better just get to it."

She sighs and turns to Bastian. "Henry let General Carter catch him so the rest of us could escape."

Bastian takes this about as well as she thought he would: Without a word, he turns on his heel and starts to march back toward the Hall.

Laurel grabs his arm before he can get too far. "I know, I know! But he did it so that we could get *out*. Are you seriously going to ruin that by going back *in*?"

Bastian's face is hard and cold and angry. And if Laurel isn't mistaken, *scared*. "You could've told me while we were still inside. We could have—"

"There are too many blocked paths right now," Chloe murmurs. "Even if we found him, we wouldn't be able to get him out without someone noticing. That probably means *they* aren't trying to get him out right now, either. It would cause too much of a ruckus. Can you tell where he is?"

Bastian's eyes fall half closed, and Laurel is reminded of the way he and Chloe stood outside of the burning compound, trying to determine where they needed to go to save Henry. They're both quite good at what they do, and they probably *could* find him.

Laurel isn't at all against saving Henry; she is, in fact, quite pro-saving-Henry. But if Chloe is right about the blocked paths, and they go in and get caught . . .

Michaels clears her throat. "If Mr. Mortimer wanted you to escape, it would be best to avoid going back in. I can look into—"

"He's on the first floor," Bastian says, opening his eyes. "And we can't leave him. Quentin is in there."

Laurel stares at him. "What? Why would *he* be there?"

"He wanted something from the vault. Some*one*. Several someones, maybe. He was waiting when Chloe and I got there. I don't know how he got in, but it sounded like he's working with Carter—not that *that* makes any sense—"

"Wait." Sybil straightens up. "Go to channel 2 on your headsets and listen to the chatter."

Laurel nearly forgot the comms. She checks the channel, then turns up the volume. But it's hard to make out individual voices while everyone is talking at once.

"—group seen leaving through one of the side doors on level 1. We suspect they came from the restricted area—"

"—carrying what looks like several injured assets, possibly a woman and a child—"

"Destination unclear. Follow them, but do *not* engage."

"Officer Smith's team is closest—"

"Try to avoid alerting city security forces; this one should be handled by compound teams only. Do you copy?"

Sybil lowers her headset. "I tapped into the nearest compound frequency while we were waiting for everyone to get out. Sounds like there's someone else who got out and is headed into the city."

Bastian rips off his headset with a frustrated noise, like a vine protesting its removal from a wall. "There's—they have important people with them. But Henry is—"

"I can help with securing Mr. Mortimer," Michaels says. "If you think these other assets are worth following, you should go do that. Maybe Mr. Turner and Ms. Tassos can secure a line for us to stay in touch?"

"Done," Kent says, looking up from where he's sitting. "I can't confirm that it'll be *completely* secure—and don't think it's not giving me hives just thinking about it—but channel 4 should be safe for us. Safeish."

"I can find us the best path to catch up," Chloe says.

There's an awkward pause. Then Laurel gently pokes Bastian's shoulder. "You can tell it's them, right? I haven't known Quentin long, but sneaking away into the night sounds like something he'd do, especially if he's taking unconscious people with him."

(She *hates* the idea of leaving anyone behind, especially if they're in danger, but this isn't her compound, this isn't her running away, this is a *plan*, this is what Henry would want them to do, and he'll be fine, especially with Michaels's help, while whoever is with Quentin might—)

"Henry will understand," Laurel says quietly.

Bastian presses his lips together. Then he digs around in his jacket and pulls out a bent folder and several USB drives, which he drops into Kent's lap. "Figure out what's on these as soon as you can. Especially the one labeled A-2769—I think that's our proof that Carter's been overstepping his bounds. And guard that folder with your life."

Kent stares at his lap, then up at Bastian. "Are these from—?"

"The vault, yes. So someone is probably going to try to kill you over them. Don't let that happen."

Kent pales considerably, but it doesn't quite knock the excitement off of his face. He always did like a technological challenge, if not a threat on his life.

"Okay," Bastian says. "Let's go."

***

The streetlights create hazy yellow bubbles amidst the shadows clinging to the older city buildings. The farther they get from the Hall, the more Laurel feels like the dark is just one step away from swallowing them whole.

They zigzag across a few parking lots before Chloe takes them down a new street. Finally, Laurel breaks the tense silence. "This looks familiar."

"Oh," Chloe says, coming to a sudden stop on the sidewalk.

"Good 'oh' or bad 'oh'?" Laurel asks.

"I'm . . . not sure."

Laurel follows her gaze and immediately understands the sentiment.

They've stopped across the street from the park with the stone entryway arch and the finicky spruce. The one they stormed out of not too long ago.

"They're here," Bastian says, voice sharper than the toughest succulent's leaves. He pauses, then adds, "I don't think they meant to be, though. Something's wrong."

Chloe frowns. "And the paths—they seem really full even though there aren't many people around."

Bastian abruptly shoves them both back against the side of a building just as a large SUV drives by. It's gray and innocuous, but Bastian glares at it anyway.

"Compound forces," he says. "They must be trying to surround the area. Or they already have, which would explain Chloe's blocked paths."

Laurel squints at the front of the park. It's still not very well lit, but she thinks she can make out a few groups of people moving around. Laurel isn't sure if they're assets, but she's not sure they're *not*, either.

She stretches her neck and cracks her knuckles. "You know, parks have a lot of plants."

Bastian and Chloe both turn to look at her.

"A *lot*," Laurel continues. "And the thing I've noticed about city plants is, they all seem very stifled. Like they could use an excuse to stretch out a bit. Maybe let out some of that hidden aggression. Take back some of the space that used to be theirs before landscapers put stupid rules in place that made their lives harder."

"Uh, Laurel . . ." Bastian says.

"So I think—" She pauses, frowning, her eyes falling on what looks an awful lot like someone carrying a child deeper into the park. "So I think if we asked very nicely, the trees here would be happy to help us with a really good distraction while Bastian goes in there and finds Angelica—I'm pretty sure I just saw James carrying her someplace. And the plants might also be willing to have a few words with the compound officers hiding around here."

Bastian's frown shifts from the grumpy one to the concerned one. "That sounds . . . dangerous."

Something desperate and hot and unpleasant unfurls in Laurel's chest. "Before, when my friends were in trouble, there was nothing I could do," she says urgently. "I was *so angry*, and things went *so wrong*, and I had to live with that for so long without being able to *do* anything about it. But now . . . well, now I have you and Chloe and Henry and Kent and Sybil and Michaels and maybe even Kwan. Now I know what James is really like. And now I have a chance to do something that could change everything, in the end."

She waits until Bastian is looking right at her before adding, "You don't have to like it, but I'm going to do it. I'm going to help people the only way I know how. I think you should, too."

Bastian opens his mouth, then closes it. Then opens it again. "Thank you. And be *careful*."

Laurel grins. "You, too. Now get going."

Then she flicks her fingers, and the trees start listening.

Chapter 37

THE FIRST SHOUTS go up as Bastian barrels across the street, hopping the low stone wall to enter the park. The dim streetlights illuminate an odd scene: trees dropping pine cones and lifting their roots, forcing compound retrieval officers out of hiding to defend themselves. Their alarm-confusion-fear is easy to read, even without a direct line of sight.

Bastian doesn't recognize most of them, but one stands out: Captain Smith is stationed near a set of swings, giving orders to her retrieval team. Her voice is too low to hear, but Bastian is fine with staying far enough away to not change that.

Whether Laurel intended it or not, the plant attack is hitting some of the assets as well. There are more here than Bastian expected—Quentin's group of twenty or thirty from the Hall and others who must have come to meet them. Unlike the officers, they're mostly fleeing, but some of them offer up defensive attacks with electricity and water and fire, which the trees don't seem to like much.

The chaos makes it hard to pinpoint the emotional signatures he's looking for, but he eventually picks up a familiar strain of fear-agitation-annoyance coming from a circle of trees a ways off the main path. There's a fire burning in a trash can nearby, casting flickering light on a small group of people clustered around someone sitting on the ground, back hunched. Near them, two people are slumped against a tree: a woman in white scrubs and a child leaning against her.

Bastian narrows his eyes.

"We shouldn't have brought them with us," says a frustrated voice. Its owner is pacing back and forth, and Bastian isn't surprised to see James's wild hair and tensed shoulders. "They'll slow us down."

"We can't rely on Carter to keep his word," says the man on the ground. "He could decide at any moment that the information we pass on isn't enough, and send his people after us. We need these two for leverage."

The small crowd around him parts, and Bastian watches a woman offer an arm to help him stand.

"You mean *you* need them," James says.

The group goes very still.

"James," Quentin says after a moment. "All of this is pointless if we aren't strong enough to take on the compounds. Moira and Angelica are some of the rarest assets currently alive. They'll make us stronger—all of us."

"And the assets I've brought you? The ones from Barrett's group? The ones from the compound? What was the point of that if all you needed was these two sleeping beauties?"

"They aren't *all* I need," Quentin says mildly. He sounds like a very patient parent trying to calm a cranky kid. "Everything we've done serves a purpose. Every contribution helps."

The words might be placating if they weren't laced through with annoyance-exhaustion-contempt. It's subtle—Quentin is good at hiding his feelings—but it's there. What he did in the vault winded him, and maybe invading Moira's dream did, too. At this point, he's clearly not up to dealing with anything other than getting some rest.

Rest, or . . .

"Bring me the girl," Quentin says. "We'll start with her."

"And if it doesn't work?" James demands.

"Then we'll have to get everyone to a safer place and try again."

Several of the others go to the tree where Angelica and Moira are slumped. Bastian has a clear view of Quentin now, weariness standing out on his ashen face.

It makes no sense. He has all of these followers to drain, and he's quite possibly the most powerful asset Bastian has ever met. But here he is, apparently unaware of Bastian's presence, ready to take emotional energy from a little girl because . . . why? Does the energy he takes usually dissipate so quickly? Bastian didn't stick around the sanctuary long enough to get the full rundown on how much energy an empath needs to drain or how long it lasts. But if *he* lasted for months before the pain got bad again, how can Quentin be like this? Laurel said she saw him drain someone, so he ought to be full up. Unless maybe it stopped working?

Or . . . maybe Quentin's "cure" isn't really a cure at all, even for him. Maybe it stops working after a few centuries. Or maybe the way he's been using his power has made things worse, made him willing to use whoever he needs to in order to survive. Including getting chummy with Carter to keep the compounds off his back.

(And if there's no hope for Quentin, how can Bastian believe there's any hope for *him*, even if he wanted to hope, even if he thought there was a way to be with Henry and Laurel and the others, for his power not to kill him in the end, maybe it was stupid of him to ever think—)

Quentin doesn't move as his followers drop Angelica's body in front of him. She's wearing scrubs similar to Moira's, but much smaller. Her eyes are closed, and her hair, free of its usual braid, is littered with grass and leaves.

Something in Bastian's stomach clenches. Without thinking, he stands clear of the tree he was hiding behind and *pushes* toward Quentin.

It's a dangerous and idiotic move. An emotional attack could easily go wide and hurt Angelica or Moira, and he doesn't have the insurance of Henry's negation to protect them. On the other hand, he knows exactly who he wants to hurt and who he doesn't.

The assets next to Quentin, including James, stumble away from him. Quentin, however, just looks up and sighs.

"I thought you wanted me to find you," Bastian says without preamble. "Or wasn't that a real offer?"

"Of course it was a real offer. Now just isn't the best time." Quentin tips his head, listening to the muted sounds of the chaos around them. It seems to have moved further away from the circle of trees, but it's still audible at this distance. "Your plantspeaker friend is making good work of the compound forces. I appreciate the help, but we still shouldn't stay long."

"Maybe you should follow James's advice and get rid of your baggage, then. I can take them off your hands."

Quentin smiles faintly. "Playing hero today?"

"Not really. I just think they'd both kick my ass if I didn't get them away from you."

"Well, I'm afraid you'll have to prepare to have your ass kicked, then."

Bastian has maybe a second to shore up his shield, but it doesn't do him any good. Something cold and sharp stabs into his brain, spreading slowly to freeze the rest of him. If he thought he was launching an emotional attack before, he was delusional. *This* is weaponized emotion, beyond anything Bastian has done when he's lashed out unintentionally with his power. It's dismissive and agonizingly thoughtless, a powerful asset flicking a bug off of his shoulder and getting on with his day.

Bastian is used to the pain that comes with his power—soreness if he's tired, headaches and nosebleeds if he's too ambitious. Severe injuries that landed him in med bay, once. But this is different. This is a strangely pregnant pause, followed by a brutal gut punch of energy reminding him that, even weakened, Quentin is stronger than Bastian will ever be. There's no point pretending otherwise.

And even if that's just the force of the emotional attack talking, it doesn't matter because Bastian vaguely feels his knees hit dirt.

And then he feels nothing.

***

"Wake up, Junior. We've got company."

Bastian blinks his eyes several times before registering that he's lying on his back, staring up at an empty night sky. No stars, no trees, no storm. Just dark blue, almost black, against nothing.

He sits up very carefully, sick to his stomach and feeling oddly wavery. His eyes go to the pond he always connects with that voice, but the pond is gone, too. He's sitting on nothing, looking at nothing, hearing nothing but that voice in a sea of darkness.

He should probably be concerned about that, but instead, he feels . . . nothing.

"You remember when you wanted it to feel like this," says another voice. "The nothing sounded good. Then there wouldn't be any pain. Then there wouldn't be—"

"All right, kid, give the guy some space."

It's Moira's dream, and it isn't. He can tell she's there, and he knows he isn't awake, but everything feels very far away, like it's happening on the other side of a mirror. There's a haze hanging over it all, like something wants him to stay docile and blank. Except . . .

"There we go. He didn't knock you completely flat, did he? You ready to play now?"

"I don't think I ever got to play," says the other voice. "Not really. I was supposed to sit and get poked with needles whenever they came over to visit Mom and Dad. But then they wanted to take me away, and Mom and Dad said no, and then I ran away to the alley where you found me."

"Angelica," Bastian says, barely a breath across cracked lips.

"It's a two-for-one today," Moira says brightly.

He can't see either of them, but the dullness is fading as his skin warms up.

"That Quentin guy did a number on this space last time he was here," Moira continues. "I was just starting to be able to repair things. Then I felt another presence here and realized it was helping."

"I came before," Angelica says, and Bastian can practically see her pout in response to having to correct an adult, yet again. "I told Bastian, sometimes I dream with

you. Only I think it's because of him, or through him, or something. I dunno; it's only when we're connected."

"Hmm. Then maybe it works better now because all of our bodies are in the same place."

Bastian remembers Angelica holding his hand when they escaped the convoy and how it made his attacks stronger. Maybe there is something about physical proximity and the strength of their powers. Moira isn't an empath, but if Quentin is right, there's a natural connection between dreamseers and empaths. And of course Angelica has some empath powers.

"Anyway," Moira says. "Time to get ready for what's next."

"And what's that?"

"Kicking Quentin's ass, obviously. Or were you just going to let him push you around and walk off with our bodies? Maybe drain a few assets while he's at it and leave them for the compound to clean up?"

"No, but . . ." Bastian isn't sure what the hell he's going to do, honestly. What can he do? Quentin has knocked him on his ass twice now, and Bastian's attempts at defense were complete jokes. Fighting the bad guy and saving the day really isn't his thing.

"All right," Moira says. "Let me spell it out for you, then."

The pond is suddenly back, more shimmery and noncorporeal than he remembers. And next to it—next to him—Moira is sitting with her legs drawn up, just like always. Her eyes are warm and brown, and there are more lines on her face than there were before. She looks like she's caught somewhere between her original dream appearance and her real one.

(He remembers the pain so vividly, the way it shot through every part of his body, the way he felt her agony like it was his own; they must have done it because of him, at least in part, so how can she just sit here with him now, like—?)

She smiles a strange sort of smile at him: sad but angry but understanding. "It wasn't your fault."

"I didn't say it was," Bastian says sharply, but even he can hear the awkward, guilty edge to it.

"Good. So long as we're on the same page."

"You didn't—" He takes a breath. "Why now? Why are the dreams happening now instead of back then?"

She looks away from him and out over the shimmering pond. "I've been here for a long time. Longer than I realized, before Quentin mentioned it in the most assholeish way possible. I didn't know I could have visitors. I didn't know I drew 'em to me in the first place. So maybe I had to get stronger. Maybe you had to get stronger. Maybe our souls called to each other across a vast void of consciousness. We can write poetry about it later, Junior. Right now, I want you to tell me about the thing you and your man did together."

Bastian stares at her. "What?"

"You remember when you woke up, and it was scary," Angelica says. She's sitting on the other side of Moira as if she's been there this whole time. "You thought you hurt him, but you didn't. Then when you were hiding in the trees and couldn't get up, you thought you would hurt him again, but you didn't. Why do you always think you're going to hurt him?"

Her eyes are more curious than judgmental, but they make him uncomfortable anyway. "What does that have to do with anything?"

"We can do the psychoanalysis later," Moira says firmly. "Just tell us what happened when you did it. It wasn't the first time you took someone's energy, right? Why was it different?"

Bastian swallows. "It was . . . When I did it at the sanctuary the way Quentin said, it felt like I was taking something. With Henry it was more like . . . I was taking something, but I was also giving something back."

"Hmm." Moira scratches her chin. "When Quentin does it, he hollows them out, right? That's not what he says, of course, but that's what it sounded like from how he described it to me. And then they take time to refill. But you're doing something different."

"I'm not," Bastian says, and he can't keep the self-loathing out of his voice. "I know I'm not supposed to care because they offer, and they're fine afterward, but it doesn't feel *fine*."

"That's because you don't want them to just blindly offer; you want them to understand what they're getting into. You want to work together. Like we did on the shield. You take something, but you give something back, too. It's reciprocal."

Bastian grimaces. "I don't care about—"

"Yes, you do," Moira and Angelica say.

"So, why not think about it a different way?" Moira suggests before Bastian can protest. "Rather than assuming you're a controlling jerk like Quentin, consider that maybe you're actually trying to help. It's like . . . the way the tide works. It's part of an ecosystem. Takes stuff out, brings stuff in."

"But I'm not really giving anything back. I can just . . . not hurt them. Sometimes."

"Did you ask?"

Bastian blinks. "What?"

"Did you ask? How did he say it felt? You've been through enough compound experiments; you know how this goes. You ask clarifying questions and get all the data before you jump to a conclusion."

It's true that he and Henry didn't exactly have time to debrief on the energy exchange in the park. Henry did seem a little less exhausted afterward than Bastian would have expected, but they didn't really talk about it.

Moira gives him a knowing look. "Maybe you need to get clear on what's actually happening when you do it. How it affects the other person. Figure out what exactly *you're taking, and what exactly you're giving back. Like when we did the shield—we created something together, right? It wasn't just taking and receiving. It didn't exist before, and I never would've thought to try without you."*

She jerks her head at Angelica. "Or the way Miss Angelica here has been helping me rebuild the dream. Who knows what weird and interesting things we assets could do together to scare the shit out of the Compound Network and people like Quentin?"

Bastian raises his eyebrows. "So you're saying the answer is to play nice with others?"

"I'm saying the answer is to think of something they haven't thought of. And hurry it up; I'd like to get back to my body soon, and I'm guessing that's the opposite of what Quentin wants, since it'd make it harder for him to get his claws in."

"We'll help," Angelica says. "It's harder from in here, but we have energy, too."

Something in Bastian's chest tightens. "Even if I could, I'm not going to—"

"Ecosystem, Junior. Give and take. Let's create something together, all right?"

Bastian licks his lips, swallows his anxiety, and nods once. "Okay."

He wakes to the sound of screaming and the heat of nearby fire. The smoke gets into his throat, thick with the scent of burning pine. It might almost be pleasant, if not for the very real indication that a tree could fall on him at any moment.

"Bastian!" says a voice near his head. Arms tighten around him. He looks up, blinking watering eyes, and realizes Henry is holding him. They're sitting on the ground just outside of the ring of trees, which is now mostly on fire. If Bastian is not very much mistaken, their saving-each-other tally is uneven again.

Still dazed, Bastian reaches up and touches Henry's cheek. "Hi."

Henry laughs, a short sound filled with smoke and relieved-grateful-love. "Hi, yourself," he says, covering Bastian's hand with his.

"What's going on?" Bastain mumbles.

"The assets and the compound forces have ramped up their disagreement," Henry says grimly. "So far, that means a lot of shooting and setting things on fire. I don't think the trees are particularly excited about it."

Bastian blinks a few more times, then sits up with Henry's steadying arm around him. "We'd better—"

"Wait." Henry takes a deep breath. "I have an idea."

"Is it a stupid idea?"

"Probably." Henry gives him a small, lopsided smile. "Want to help?"

Chapter 38

BY THE TIME Henry makes it to the park, all hell is breaking loose.

When Felicity and Alexis said they could get him out of the Hall without alerting compound or city forces, he didn't realize that it would be easy only because said forces were busy here, escalating the situation rather than helping, as usual.

(Like when the compound was burning, assets and officers and black coats all at each other's throats, and nothing Henry did mattered, even going back in to try to save people, because no one was paying attention to anyone else, and everything was rotten at the core, and nothing he did could ever—)

From a parking lot across the street, Henry strains to hear or see anything familiar, but nothing stands out. At the very least, he can tell that the scattered bodies on the ground have been hit with tranqs—so it really is meant to be a retrieval rather than something worse. For now.

"Need some help, Boss?" says a voice just behind him.

Henry spins around, surprised to find himself reflexively reaching for a gun he no longer carries. Then he sees Kent sitting cross-legged, back against the nearest brick building, tablet balanced in his lap while he taps rapidly.

"I need a word with city security so I can tell them how much they suck," Kent says with a sigh. "This isn't even my system, and I can still do *this* in five minutes."

The streetlamps in the park flicker, then brighten, making it easier to see all over the grounds, instead of just in pockets of illumination. Nearby, the movement of assets and officers falters, just for a moment, then resumes.

Kent makes a face and finally looks up at Henry. "Okay, I guess they're still willing to attack even when they can see who they're attacking. But at least we can see *them* now, too. You want to know how I did it? I mean, you probably won't understand, but it's pretty brilliant—"

"I'll take your word for it. Can I ask you to do me another favor?"

"I am a magnanimous, godlike technical genius, at your service. What do you need?"

"I need to find Bastian," Henry says before he's thought it through. Yes, that. But also . . . "Tell me he and Chloe found the vault and brought you something we can use?"

A slow, wolfish grin spreads across Kent's face. "Oh, yeah. Plenty that will get Carter in trouble with the Council. Sybil is taking care of code translation and securing copies right now."

Henry's chest lights up with a small but powerful spark of relief. "Good. We're going to need to hand some of that information over to someone else, but they don't need to know what we're keeping for ourselves. Now, what can you tell me about Bastian?"

Kent's grin falters. "Uh, right, so. We were supposed to be keeping in touch via those headsets, but Bastian dropped off a few minutes ago. I tried to let Laurel know, but she was, er, busy with the trees. That said, these pathetic street security cameras should be easy enough to hack . . ."

Kent taps a few times in quick succession, then shoots to his feet and points across the street. "There!" he says, shoving the tablet under Henry's nose. "See it? Take the main path and look for a circle of trees off to the right."

The security footage on the tablet is grainy, but Henry can just make out several figures moving near a copse of trees. "You're sure it's him?"

"I'm sure it's the headset on the ground there. So he's probably close by."

"And Laurel?"

There's a shout and a low, cracking noise. Henry snaps his head up in time to see a playground slide just inside the park wall collapse, completely covered by roots and vines.

"Follow the plant-based carnage," Kent says, sounding a little disturbed.

Henry takes a deep breath, then nods. "Stay here."

"Not a problem."

***

He's nearly to the circle of trees when he runs into a standoff between two officers and a telekine. By the time they notice him, he's already picked up a discarded tranq gun and firmly suggested that they all stand down.

"Who the hell are you?" one of the officers asks, raising his weapon.

Henry does *not* have time for this. "You should get out of the park. Now."

"I'm not leaving until I teach these assholes a lesson," the telekine says. The trash can nearest to her rattles as she uses her power to lift it.

(This isn't how it's supposed to work, they're supposed to *talk*, to try to understand each other, but of course no one's going to do that now—)

The officers are clearly torn between shooting the asset and shooting him, but they don't have a chance to do either because something abruptly drops from the nearest tree with a yelp, knocking the officers to the ground. Before the asset can finish her trash can attack, Henry shoots her in the arm. The can falls with a loud *thunk*, and the asset crumples, eyes fluttering shut as the serum in the tranq knocks her out.

"Don't get up," Laurel says cheerfully from where she's landed near one of the officers, a few leaves and twigs in her hair. "This maple is very short-tempered. I have no idea what it'll do if you make any sudden movements."

The second officer blinks, then starts to raise her gun, but Henry grabs it from her and throws it away. "Take your partner and get out of here," he says sharply. "Do *not* fire on anyone, and do *not* take these or any other assets in. Is that understood?"

The officers nod dumbly at him, probably more out of confusion and adrenaline than anything else. He's doing his best retrieval captain voice, so it's possible that they believe he knows what he's talking about. For now, at least, they seem willing to comply, getting to their feet and hurrying off toward the park exit.

"Hello, Henry," Laurel says, sounding a little shaky despite her earlier bravado. "Are you enjoying the chaos?"

"Not so much." He offers her a hand up, which she takes. "Can you look after the—?"

There's a sudden scream, and then the trees ahead of them erupt into flames.

He and Laurel stumble back slightly. They're too far away to feel the heat, but there's the smell of burning wood and . . . something else Henry doesn't want to think about.

(He can't breathe, and people all around him are dying, and the heat and his burned hands and his heart in his throat choking him as it all spirals out of control—)

Henry shakes himself. "Bastian is—"

"Go," Laurel says. "I'll deal with things here."

He hands her the tranq gun, just in case. Then he sprints toward the fire.

The smoke makes it hard to be sure, but he thinks he sees other people leaving the area. All he really cares about right now, though, is finding—there. A gangly body with a mop of dark hair, collapsed on the ground.

Henry bites back the terror and tries to stay low as he rushes over. "Bastian!" he says, but he chokes on the last half, and Bastian doesn't respond.

Henry wants to shake him, yell at him, do anything to get him to open his eyes, but he forces himself to stick with the basics: a quick check for injuries and, finding none, a careful extraction out of the copse of trees to somewhere a little less on fire.

Most of the fighting has moved toward other parts of the park now, probably because no one wants to mess around with a full-blown fire. No one's done anything to put it out, either, Henry notes grimly.

Something moves in his arms, and Henry realizes, with overwhelming relief, that Bastian is slowly blinking his eyes open. "Bastian!" he says, carefully setting him down on the grass.

Bastian stares at him for a moment. Then he reaches up and touches Henry's cheek. "Hi."

Henry blinks and laughs, short and startled, then covers Bastian's hand with his. "Hi, yourself."

"What's going on?"

"The assets and the compound forces have ramped up their disagreement," Henry says. "So far, that means a lot of shooting and setting things on fire. I don't think the trees are particularly excited about it."

Some part of Henry's brain is coming to a conclusion as they sit there. He's looking at Bastian, but he's hearing the far-away cacophony around them, and the part of him that isn't straining against the memories of the last time things went to shit like this is remembering how he managed to stop it that time. Sort of.

Bastian sits up awkwardly, and Henry keeps his arms around him. "We'd better—"

"Wait." Henry takes a deep breath, an impossible thought forming in his mind. "I have an idea."

The suspicious look on Bastian's face almost makes Henry laugh. "Is it a stupid idea?"

"Probably. Want to help?"

Bastian narrows his eyes, but the corners of his mouth are sneaking upward into a smirk. "Probably. What are you going to do?"

"*We* are going to stop this before it gets any worse."

Henry helps Bastian to his feet, and while Bastian seems like he's strong enough to stand on his own at this point, Henry notices that he doesn't even try. Behind them, the trees keep burning, and to either side, assets and officers are still scuffling.

Bastian snorts. "How are we going to stop them? Ask really nicely?"

"No." Henry takes another breath, but it doesn't do anything to calm the violent flutter of anxiety in his chest. "I'm going to negate all of them."

Bastian shoots him an alarmed glance. "You're going to—?"

"Not permanently. Just enough to get them to stop trying to kill each other for a minute."

"That might work on the assets, but not the officers."

"Right. That's where you come in. Think you can . . . convince them?"

Bastian's eyes are unreadable, like they can't decide on one expression and are trying to show all of them all at once. "Yes," he says at last. "But are you sure you want to—?"

"Yes. Only for a few minutes. Just until reinforcements arrive."

"Reinforcements?"

"I know someone who owes me. Or who's *going* to owe me. She got me out of the Hall, and she's gathering her people right now. When they get here, it should be enough of a distraction that the assets will be more interested in getting away, and the officers will be more interested in figuring out what's going on."

"And what does your friend get out of this?"

"Right now? Nothing. Maybe something later if she doesn't screw us over, and Kent and Sybil finish making copies first."

Bastian smiles slowly. "Are you saying you made a deal with the Compound Network that you're already planning to renege on?"

"I'm saying she might be able to help us take Carter down, if we pool our resources. But first, we have to get out of here in one piece, and I'm not going to sit around and wait for someone else to make that happen. You in?"

Bastian's eyes are broadcasting amusement now, and there's a smudge of dirt on his cheek that Henry is reaching over to brush off before he realizes it.

Then Bastian stiffens and turns sharply.

"I'd say I'm glad you survived, but we all know I'd be lying."

James is standing there, a burn slashing his left arm, his hair littered with pine needles. Henry's eyes go to the burn, not because it's deep but because, as a firestarter, James never would have gotten it if he still had his power.

If Henry hadn't taken it from him.

"Where's your boss?" Bastian demands. "No, scratch that. Where are Moira and Angelica?"

"They're safe. Quentin needs them, apparently. But he doesn't need you two. Not if you're not going to play nice."

"So, what? You're going to glare us to death? It's not like you can burn us anymore."

If they survive this, Henry reflects, they're going to need to teach Bastian how *not* to escalate dangerous conflicts.

"Turns out there's more than one way to kill an asset," James says, raising a gun that does *not* look like it carries tranqs.

"Let's not be hasty," says a mild voice.

Quentin steps out from the nearby shadows, disheveled but disapproving, like a dad who's caught his kids being naughty and is ready to dish out some consequences. Seems like he's had a bit of a night, but he isn't injured or tired, as far as Henry can tell. Which makes it hard to gauge just how dangerous he is right now.

Luckily, he clears that up right away.

"I think I've been patient," Quentin says. His voice is still mild, but his eyes are sharp. "I think I've offered help time and time again, but you seem committed to misunderstanding me. So I'll ask one last time, Bastian: Are we going to be allies, or am I going to have to kill you?"

"I don't think either one would work out well for you, honestly," Bastian says.

Quentin then lets out a long, quiet sigh.

Henry half expects him to give James the go-ahead to shoot them, but the attack is something else entirely. It's all Quentin, and it's unlike anything Henry has ever seen an asset do before: a sucking in of air, an invisible pull that hits somewhere around the solar plexus. Henry staggers, then reflexively strengthens his shield, weaving his negation barrier more tightly through it. As soon as he does, the feeling dissipates, but the echo makes his skin crawl.

A quick glance around shows that everyone else felt it, too: James, Bastian, the nearest assets and officers are all dropping to the ground. Some pass out immediately, while others just crouch there, stunned.

Bastian is on his knees, teeth clenched, and Henry's beside him in an instant. "Bastian, what—?"

"He's taking—but he can't do it to you because you're—"

Bastian must be fighting the energy transfer—or maybe Quentin is just trying to take more from him than from anyone else. Including James, Henry realizes, feeling sick. Quentin needs the power, and he's taking it from whoever he can. Including his supporters.

"We need . . . something different," Bastian mumbles. "We need to—"

"I know." Henry holds out his hand, palm up, the way Bastian did for him in the hotel room, giving them both an anchor when it felt like the world was out of control.

Bastian flinches against Quentin's attack, and his nose starts to bleed. Then he makes an irritated noise at the back of his throat, rips off his right glove with his teeth, and grabs Henry's hand.

Quentin is saying something, but Henry ignores it, along with everything else except Bastian's hand in his. He focuses on the negation first: slowly and carefully expanding the field, feeling the shift as the asset powers within it stop working. The fear almost makes him lash out with negation like he did at the hotel, but Bastian's grounding presence helps Henry keep his power contained and focused.

Then he starts to worry that deactivating powers will just give the compound forces an unfair advantage . . . except the officers' movements have stopped, too. Not because of Quentin's attack—at least, not entirely. Now, every non-asset Henry can see is sitting quietly, alert but not inclined to move. Watching. Waiting. Because they don't feel like doing anything else.

"Interesting," Quentin says. "But I don't think it will last. And clearly, it doesn't work on me. I wish you'd see that my solution is better for everyone. Are you really prepared to die just because you can't accept things as they are?"

It's obviously a dig at Bastian and his unwillingness to take energy the way Quentin does. But in that moment, Henry asks himself the same thing: Is he willing to die rather than admit things have to be a certain way?

Assets stuck in dangerous experiments they never agreed to.

Compound officers trained to throw their weight around in order to hide their fear.

Anyone who tries to change the system punished, bled dry of any hope until they fall in line.

Being resigned to the way things are isn't a badge of honor, he told Major Alexis once. *It's a choice you make to absolve yourself of guilt when things go wrong, and you do nothing to fix it.*

Henry doesn't know if he can fix this. But he does know that there's something he can do.

Quentin is still leeching energy from everyone around him, building up to some sort of attack that will probably flatten them all—and ruin Felicity's already-slim chances of calming things down once her forces arrive.

But Bastian is pushing back from the relative safety of Henry's negation barrier, stumbling to his feet to face Quentin, who looks mildly confused. He pauses, and the entire park falls unnaturally silent and still.

"You're using their power, too, aren't you?" Quentin says, an odd smile on his face. "Interesting. When *I* do it, it's unconscionable, but when *you* do it—"

"I'm not taking it," Bastian says, jaw tight around the words. "Moira and Angelica want to fight. Maybe it's time you asked yourself why so many people are so determined to fight against you."

Quentin pauses, then sighs and raises a hand. "I suppose that's it, then."

Without thinking, Henry steps in front of Bastian and *pushes*.

The negation barrier moves with him—stronger now, more solid, more like a bludgeon than the usual mesh of his shield. It's a weapon and a piece of armor all at once. The *push* isn't quite like anything he's tried to do before—a preliminary shove at the beginning of a bar fight. The promise of resistance in the face of someone who needs to *back off right now*.

Quentin looks surprised, but only briefly. He raises a hand again, and Henry knows he's screwed because whatever is coming will be too strong to—

Bastian yanks him backward and does something that slices through Henry's negation, hitting Quentin in the chest to send him stumbling back a few steps.

And with a sinking feeling, Henry knows what he has to do.

(Even though he can't, even though he feels sick just thinking about it, the way he hurt people like James and Mariah, the way he became a weapon in the Compound Network's war without meaning to, but that's no excuse because if he does it now, after everything, knowing what he's resorting to—)

"Together," Bastian says, clinging to Henry's hand. His voice sounds ragged and thick, and his nose is still bleeding.

If Henry does this, Quentin won't be able to hurt anyone ever again. Only it would mean doing what the Compound Network wants: depowering the assets they deem too risky. And who is Henry to decide who deserves that?

But in this moment, he'd be protecting both the assets and the non-assets from someone who wants to use them. Who doesn't see them as human beings except when it suits him.

It may not be the right thing to do, but it's a choice Henry can make and take responsibility for. A fix he can try.

"*Together*," Bastian says, nearly crushing Henry's hand. He sounds mildly annoyed, like Henry just said something inane—not like they're about to be attacked by what might be the strongest and oldest asset alive.

Quentin sighs. There's no audible snap, but the way he shakes his shoulders makes it clear that he's no longer being affected by their attacks. "If you're both *quite* finished—"

Together, then.

Henry gently squeezes Bastian's hand. Then he closes his eyes.

He can feel Quentin *push* something toward them, something that makes the wind pick up around them, but it bounces off of Henry's negation. No, not bounce; he catches it the way he caught Bastian's power just after they escaped the hotel, letting everything go soft and still around it, preventing it from moving. Quentin says something and tries again, but the only thing that happens this time is that the attack becomes sluggish, then stops altogether, dissolving as soon as it hits the negation barrier.

It makes no sense. The barrier can't possibly be strong enough to stop such a powerful empath. Henry opens his eyes to figure out what the hell is going on, and then he feels it: His negation barrier has grown an outer layer. Something a little wobbly and fluctuating between stiff and flexible, lending strength without taking away from the shape and texture of Henry's power. Just adding to it. Supporting it.

"What are you doing?" Henry yells over the steadily increasing wind.

"Thinking of something they haven't thought of!" Bastian says. "And I'm pretty sure I can't—ngh—keep thinking of it for much longer, so hurry up!"

"Enough!" Quentin sounds properly furious now, his hair wild around his face. He seems to be rapidly burning through whatever energy he just took, his skin going gray, expression pained. The wind and smoke and heat feel louder and closer as he raises his hand again, mouth set in a firm line.

Bastian and Henry glance at each other for a moment. Then Henry squeezes his eyes shut and *pushes*.

It feels different from all the other times he's permanently negated someone—and also the same. He can feel the moment when it happens because of the sharp pain across his lower back, the brief terror of not being able to breathe.

But there's also another layer to it—the spiky, awkward outer layer of his shield/negation combo that Bastian added. It's like a net of feelings: support and reassurance, relief and appreciation, the sense that Henry is doing something incredibly difficult, maybe something that's a huge mistake, but it's something he doesn't have to do on his own.

Because someone is holding his hand. In a death grip, but still.

Henry opens his eyes.

The wind slows, then stops.

Quentin staggers back, blinking rapidly, tipping his head like he's trying to hear something and is confused by the answering silence. His knees wobble, and then he suddenly drops to the ground as realization dawns. "What did you—? *How* did you—? How *dare* you—!"

"I know," Henry says, throat dry. "I'm sorry, but—"

Quentin sneers, a wounded animal, all sense of politeness stripped away. "Don't apologize. You've just proven that you're exactly what they made you. Do you have any idea what you've done? I can't help people like this!"

"Oh, you were helping them?" Bastian is breathing heavily and waving at Quentin's followers, lying unconscious around him. "All the people you just stole from—even people like James, who've spent years doing your dirty work for you—that was *helping*?"

"Not everyone wants to die like you," Quentin spits. "Some of us value survival. Some of us have made sacrifices—alliances we'd rather not make—in order to do the work we need to do."

"What alliances?" Bastian demands.

Quentin smiles thinly. "Carter will do anything to keep control of the Network's assets. That means always having more information than anyone else. When he got suspicious that someone was moving against him, he struck a deal with us: our survival in exchange for helping him gather and protect data from places like the vault, with no trail leading back to him. He's very keen on getting those Fail-Safe Protocol documents of yours, by the way."

"You're working with *Carter*?" Henry asks.

Quentin gives him a withering look. "He *thinks* I'm working with him, and I'm willing to let him keep thinking that for as long as it's beneficial. You see, some of us are prepared to—"

"It wasn't working anymore, was it?" Bastian interrupts. "The energy drains. You were just hunting for another cure."

"That's—"

"There were always better ways to survive," Bastian continues, much to Henry's surprise. "Maybe you should've looked into that from the start rather than just taking what you wanted from everyone around you."

Quentin opens his mouth, probably gearing up for another retort. But instead, he blinks slowly, expression going slack, and then slumps to the ground.

"Too easy," Bastian mumbles, sounding a little disturbed. He's still holding Henry's hand, but he doesn't seem to have taken energy from Henry in order to make Quentin feel like going to sleep. Either Bastian is stronger now, or Quentin is weaker. Or both.

Henry hears sirens coming closer, as well as the growing confusion of assets and officers coming back to themselves all over the park.

"Reinforcements," Henry says quietly to Bastian. "We should—"

"Bastian! Henry!"

Laurel is running toward them, Chloe at her heels. She has even more leaves in her hair than she did the last time Henry saw her, but she seems both relieved to see them and pleased with herself.

Laurel flicks her fingers as she hurries past Quentin with only the briefest glance. A thick collection of ivy from a nearby flower bed stretches out to pin both him and the nearest passed-out assets in place.

Laurel hesitates when she comes across James's prone body, but she quickly turns away. "Are you all right?" she asks Bastian. "Is everyone here all right? Is *anyone* here all right? I mean, I know that ivy is all right, but—"

"We're fine," Bastian says, although he doesn't exactly look it, especially with blood still dripping from his nose.

Laurel frowns, then rummages around in her pocket, pulls out a handkerchief, and shoves it at him. "Here. This won't work as well as the ones I soak in my herbs, but we don't have time for that. Did you know there are a *bunch* of compound forces coming this way?"

"That'll be Felicity," Henry says. "Major Tremain. She—"

"You know Major Tremain?"

"It's a long story."

"We need to find Moira and Angelica and get out of here," Bastian says, voice muffled by the handkerchief he's now holding to his nose.

"Did someone call for a rescue?"

Henry jumps and turns toward the nearest shadows, which resolve into a familiar woman wearing a familiar grin.

"Rescues are what I do," Tallis says. "In fact, I've already been pretty busy doing a few. We've got a van with a few sleepy assets in it on the other side of the park. One of them is Angelica, and another is a woman who wants to know when Lucas is going to get off his ass and thank her for her help."

Henry raises his eyebrows. "What's that all about?"

"Later," Bastian says.

Tallis grins. "I'm looking forward to hearing the whole story about how you all played hero. In the meantime, though, I'm pretty sure Barrett will kill us if we don't get to the van before the compound teams get here."

"I can find us a good path out of the park," Chloe says.

"Stop," someone interrupts.

Henry curses inwardly as a woman in compound-style fatigues advances on them, gun held high. It's a regulation tranq gun, but still. Getting knocked out right now wouldn't help their escape, and knowing Smith, she has a team lying in wait.

"Get them out," Henry says quietly to Bastian as they both stand up. "I'll stall."

"Don't be an idiot. You can't—"

"You saved some of my team back there," Smith says to Henry.

He isn't sure what she means at first, but then he remembers the standoff he and Laurel broke up before he found Bastian. "Are they all right?"

"Yes. Shaken, but not dead. Or even injured." She eyes Henry like she's in a staring contest with a dangerous wild animal. "You're one of those people now. You didn't have to help my officers."

Henry frowns. "What, I was just supposed to stand there while they hurt or killed each other? Maybe got some innocent bystanders caught in the cross fire, just for kicks? You know the rules, Smith: Minimize injury and casualties in the field. Contain conflicts as soon as possible. Basically, don't be an asshole, and keep your team safe."

Smith hesitates, then lowers her gun. Then she notices Quentin and the other assets on the ground. "Who are they?"

"Take them to Major Tremain when she gets here," Henry says. "If any of them wake up before then, just knock them out again. Especially if it's the guy in the ivy."

"I should take all of you, too," Smith says.

Henry sighs inwardly. "Yeah, I suppose you should."

"But you won't, will you?" Bastian's voice isn't combative, but it's firm. Knowing. Like he's just stating a fact.

Smith turns to him, and for a split second, Henry braces for an argument.

Then she goes over to Quentin, turns her back on the rest of them, and gets out her cuffs. "If you're gone by the time I turn around, I won't see where you escape to. So there won't be anything to report."

Henry pauses, then turns to Bastian. "Well, we wouldn't want to force Smith to write a report."

"I remember her reports," Bastian agrees. "Better to spare whoever has to read them these days."

Without facing them, Smith raises a very specific finger at Bastian, who grins.

"Chloe?" Henry asks.

Chloe nods, then leads them all away, into the night and away from the sirens.

Epilogue

One month later

THE FOG IN the city today is making things easier—and harder. Low visibility and dark clothing mean Bastian isn't as likely to be noticed by the people he's trying not to be noticed by. Downside: He's not likely to see the street he's trying to find, either.

"Next right," Kent says in Bastian's earpiece. His voice is a bit garbled—freelance equipment isn't as high tech as what they'd get at a compound, but it comes with the bonus of being customizable and untraceable, which is more important at the moment, what with all of them being officially on the Compound Network's most wanted list.

Having people like Michaels, Tremain, and Kwan on the inside, not to mention Nunez at the Hall, has made it a little easier to fly under the Network's radar so far. But Bastian knows he's pushing it by starting their off-the-books retrieval program so soon after the debacle at the park. They probably should have waited until they got word that their Council benefactor had used their intel to have Carter removed. According to Tremain, he's already under suspicion of misusing Network resources for personal gain and has had his activities curtailed while the Council decides how to proceed.

Working within the confines of a shady organization's directives is one thing; having a senator's aide killed, making under-the-table deals with politicians, and holding back experiment details from the Council is, apparently, a step too far.

It won't be long now. If they're lucky.

Of course, if they'd waited for all the red tape to work itself out, they would have missed important things—like what pinged their rudimentary tracking system earlier today.

Bastian still suspects that their benefactor has had something to do with the information getting to them. But he, for one, is happy to follow up on it without Compound Network interference. Now, and possibly for good, depending on how things go.

Nothing here, Laurel says in his head as he turns down another block. *But this forsythia bush has a good joke. Wanna hear it?*

"Not if it's another pun," Bastian mutters.

I'll take that as a, "Yes, Laurel, and thank you for encouraging fun and levity in my life!" But I suppose it can wait till we all get back to base.

"We're recalibrating," Sybil says, drowning out Kent's sudden cursing through the comm. "Hang on; we'll have a clearer location for you in a sec."

Bastian runs a gloved hand along the brick wall of the bank he's passing and lets his eyes fall half closed. In a perfect world, he'd be able to immediately locate anyone in the city via his power alone, but that would be a *lot* of emotions to sift through, and he's not sure his head could take it after the park. If he's not careful today, he'll have to ask Henry for another energy exchange, which is . . . inevitable, really. They still haven't quite figured out how to make them work long-term. Bastian doesn't mind, exactly, particularly since they seem to be good for Henry's health, too. But he feels awkward about bringing it up, especially when Henry is still recovering from the park showdown.

And speaking of Henry . . .

"You were supposed to stay with the others this time," Bastian says without turning around.

"And you were supposed to rely on the algorithm rather than using your power," Henry replies. He has his hands in his jacket pockets, and he matches Bastian's gait easily, like they're just going for a stroll. But he also has an earpiece in, and Bastian knows he's monitoring the area around them for security cameras as they walk.

Bastian makes a face. "If too many of us are in the same place at the same time—"

"We won't be. Is it a potential or an asset?"

Bastian sighs, then gently feels out again. "Asset. They've already manifested, but I'm pretty sure it was recently. I can't pinpoint the location, but Kent said he and Sybil could confirm with their supposedly amazing algorithm, which apparently needs to be tweaked yet again."

"The algorithm is beautiful, just like the beautiful brain of my girlfriend, who made it," Kent retorts. "Also, two blocks to your right and down the street. Not that you deserve that information."

Are you being rude again? Laurel asks. *I thought we talked about you being rude.*

"Yeah, okay. Don't you all have better things to do?"

Well, I've finished my sweep for assets in this part of the city, so I'll go meet up with Chloe and head back to base. We're working on a new secret handshake with Angelica, and Moira says you need to sign off on it before we can use it. I think she's kidding, though.

Bastian rolls his eyes. He should have known Moira was going to give him grief the moment he got back to Tallis's van after the situation at the park. He was worried she and Angelica would be drained—literally and figuratively—after the fight against Quentin, but they were just resting in the back of the van, tired but alert. The look on Moira's face when she first saw him, and her relieved-amused-grateful, nearly bowled him over.

"Hello, Junior," she said, her voice full of a genuine warmth he didn't know what to do with. "Took you long enough."

They haven't shared a dream since, but she's spent plenty of time gleefully ganging up on him, usually with Angelica and Laurel. And sometimes Henry.

In fact, when Bastian turns now, he finds Henry doing a bad job of concealing a smile. "Very professional mission management."

"Not you, too."

They walk for a while, the fog lifting slightly as the sun comes out from behind the clouds. "Maybe we should forget professional," Henry says. "There's a café down the street, and I know someone who said he'd buy me a coffee."

"And then we'd get arrested for being out in the open like idiots."

"You're right. A stale energy bar back at base would be much more romantic."

Bastian clears his throat. "Actually . . . I might have, uh, put together something back at base. You know. For later. I mean, assuming it's edible, and we have time for dinner."

Henry stares at him. "You made *dinner?*"

There's an agonized sound over the comm, and then Kent's voice says, "Now the algorithm—Look, just find someplace to stop for a minute while I get this sorted out."

It's honestly pretty ludicrous: They're walking briskly down the street, trying to reach an asset who may be in danger without realizing it, primarily relying on incredibly unreliable tech and knowing that they could be caught at any moment if they're not careful . . . and all Bastian can think of is the sun on Henry's hair and the slight quirk of his mouth and the way he so easily matches step with Bastian, ready to have his back no matter what they encounter.

Bastian ducks around the corner of a convenience store and feels the blip of Henry's surprise-confusion-concern. "Are you sure this is—?"

Bastian grabs him by the jacket and kisses him.

This is *not* an energy transfer (although wouldn't *that* be interesting to try?), but it's almost as good, maybe even better: Henry smiling against Bastian's mouth, cupping his cheek and crowding him into the wall. "Definitely not professional."

"Definitely don't care."

Henry pulls back slightly. "But you *do* care about the asset we're trying to find."

The fear-sadness-loneliness comes through, sudden and sharp, wrenching an annoyingly genuine sense of concern out of Bastian's chest. "Yeah," he admits. "I might care a little."

"Then I'll take a rain check on this, and we can go be heroes now. Or as soon as Kent and Sybil get that algorithm working."

"Never mind. I know where we need to go." He taps his earpiece. "Kent, you get that?"

"Yeah, yeah," Kent grumbles.

Bastian doesn't sense any immediate danger the rest of the way, but Henry keeps an eye out for cameras and helps them work their way around a few of the trickier ones. A few minutes later, they turn into an alley, stopping at the entrance.

"Bastian?" Henry asks quietly.

(It's not *his* alley, it doesn't even look the same, but he can feel the fear and wretchedness, the loss of hope, the asset's surety that something is *wrong* with them, that they'll never stop hurting—)

Bastian swallows. "Give me a second."

"More than a second," Henry says. "Whatever you need."

The alley is dark and dirty, filled with smelly dumpsters and a few broken boxes. Even the bit of sunlight that filters through the nearby roofs and telephone wires seems reluctant.

Bastian tries to breathe slowly, gently fortifying his shield so he won't overwhelm the asset with his emotions. He keeps his gait slow and steady, making just enough noise to announce his presence.

Behind one of the dumpsters, there's a young boy curled up into himself, holding his legs tightly and rocking back and forth. He's a little older than Bastian was—maybe seven or eight. His dark hair is limp and long around the ears, and his warm brown skin is covered in scratches. Like he was trying to scratch the feelings out.

The boy looks up at Bastian, a brief jolt of terror-alarm-dread stabbing Bastian in the chest as he scoots back against the wall, even though there's nowhere to go.

Bastian holds up his hands and crouches down without getting too close. "It's okay. I'm not going to hurt you."

The kid clearly doesn't believe him. Smart. "Who are you?"

"My name's Bastian. What's yours?"

The boy's deep eyes are wide, but the determined-defiant-curious sneaks around the fear. "Tomás."

"Good to meet you, Tomás," Bastian says, but he doesn't offer a hand to shake or get in the kid's face.

"What . . . what's going on?" Tomás asks in a small voice. "Everything is *loud*, and everyone is *feeling* things, and—Is something wrong with me?"

"No," Bastian says firmly. "Nothing's wrong with you."

Then he takes a breath and says what he always needed someone to say to him, but no one ever did: "You're an empath. And I'm here to help you."

Afterword

Here we are at the end of the Compound Series! I hope you'll indulge me in a few more (quick) thank-yous:

All my love to my Wednesday writing buddies, Sarah Mayes and Caitlin Woolley. Your creativity, generosity, and friendship have inspired me for years, and there's no way I'd be this far along in my writing journey without you. Let's do an in-person Wednesday meetup again sometime soon, okay?

Additional thanks to my fellow indie fantasy author Shayla Morgansen, who has been a tireless supporter of this series and might love these characters almost as much as I do. Thank you for your faith in this story—and in my ability to write it.

And thanks again to you, dear reader, for seeing Bastian, Henry, and Laurel through three books. I hope you had an absolute blast, and I can't wait to share what's coming next!

~ Katy

About the Author

Katy Morgan is an indie fantasy author and editor with an eye for detail and a heart for supporting the creative community. When she's not writing or editing, she can be found cross-stitching something sassy, daydreaming about hedgehogs, or drinking far too many mochas, usually all at once.

***

Thanks for reading *Hidden Bonds*!

If you enjoyed this book, please consider letting others know by leaving a review on Amazon, Goodreads, Storygraph, or another book review site. Reviews are one of the best ways to help new readers find indie work—and we can't do it without you!